BROTHER, CAN YOU RAISE A MILLION?

Money Flows
as Love Grows
in Jerusalem

A NOVEL by

RABBI SHLOMO WEXLER

GW00692180

DEVORA
PUBLISHING
JERUSALEM ◆ NEW YORK

Since this book deals with matters of a contemporary nature, there exists the possibility that some people may see themselves as subjects of this work. To them, and all others, we state that this book is a pure work of fiction. Any resemblance to persons living or dead is purely coincidental. Names of places or institutions which do exist, are published only in the spirit of the fiction and are not intended as a reflection on the quality or character of the place or institution mentioned.

BROTHER, CAN YOU RAISE A MILLION?
Money Flows as Love Grows in Jerusalem
Published by DEVORA PUBLISHING COMPANY
Text Copyright © 2003 by Shlomo Wexler

Cover and Book Design: S. Kim Glassman
Editor: Shalom Kaplan

Hard Cover ISBN: 1-930143-70-2
Soft Cover ISBN: 1-930143-78-8

Email: sales@devorapublishing.com
Web Site: www.devorapublishing.com

Printed in Israel

Author's Introduction

Some people read books to gain knowledge, while others read for fun. The author is reasonably sure that readers will find this book entertaining. He hopes that in a small measure it will also increase knowledge of and respect for those who devote their lives to supporting and maintaining religious institutions of higher learning.

There will be no lengthy listing of people who helped me put this book together. Unfortunately, I had to do it all by myself. The events described in the book have their source in my personal life experiences. For several years I was the Associate Director of the Ner Israel Yeshiva in Baltimore and the Registrar of the Neve Yerushalayim Seminary in Jerusalem. I did fundraising in both places, not always successfully, and I managed to gain a personal appreciation of the trials and tribulations of those who raise funds for educational institutions. The same holds true for the administrative work involved in running these institutions. To my knowledge, no one has written a work about these unsung heroes. I hope that this work will bring some public attention to the efforts of this group.

One cannot compare the fundraising for hospitals and major universities with that which is done in the yeshiva world. Particularly in Jerusalem, the situation is very difficult. Competition is brutal, and the number of wealthy people who are sympathetic to institutions of this nature is very limited. The fundraisers for yeshivot work for long hours and limited compensation and they are often subject to ridicule and abuse. The few occasions when a large donation is received are more than offset by many days where it hardly pays to open the mail or deposit the checks.

I wish to thank Mr. Yaacov Peterseil, Director of Devora Publishing, who found merit in this book. I am sure that his studies at Yeshiva University contributed to his understanding of the issues involved. My thanks also to my editor at Devora Publishing, Shalom Kaplan, and to other proofreaders and copyeditors at Devora for their guidance and assistance. My appreciation as well to Mrs. Zipporah Perlman, my secretary and editorial assistant.

In the later stages of publication, some people did make comments and suggestions about the book. In the final analysis, however, the book is my sole responsibility and no one else bears any blame for the mistakes and shortcomings that appear within. Readers who detect any errors or have anything good to say about the book are invited to express their opinions by sending an e-mail to my current e-mail address Wexler@trendline.co.il, or by writing to the publisher who will forward such material to me.

This book is dedicated
to the memory of

Rabbi, Doctor Samuel Belkin

הרב ד"ר שמואל בלקין זצ"ל

Rosh Yeshiva and Second President of Yeshiva University
1940–1976

His great scholarship and dedication were evident to all.

Less known was his courage to bear immense
communal and personal problems without losing
his warmth, humanity, and deep love for mankind

I will always cherish his concern for me during my ten years at
Yeshiva University, as will all the other students who attended
the Yeshiva during his administration

זרח בחשך אור לישרים, חנון ורחום וצדיק

His memory will live in our hearts forever

BROTHER,
CAN YOU RAISE A
MILLION?

Money Flows
as Love Grows
in Jerusalem

MELVIN

1

FOLKS. THIS IS MEL SEIDMAN, Melvin on my birth certificate. Just last week, I handed over two checks to a visitor from Israel, Rabbi Baruch Brill. The bigger one, dated September 15, reads $250,000 and no cents. The second one, good on the first of January next year, is only for 150 grand. The rabbi will have to wait four months before cashing the later check but, not to worry, you can be sure he won't lose it before then. For reasons which will become abundantly clear later on, my wife, Sandy, gave the rabbi an extra hundred dollars in cash.

The checks are from my foundation, which feeds off my business, Buffalo Auto Stores. With 21 branches in western New York and Pennsylvania, ours is a big business and, I might add, a very successful one. It grew out of a single store opened by my late father, Murray Seidman, in the mid-fifties. Today, the stores do a total of fifty to sixty million a year. Unfortunately, I am not the sole owner of the business, as my father saw fit to leave it in equal parts to my brother, my sister and me. All three of us work here in the main headquarters and my brother-in-law, Joe, manages a branch store. He earned his position by sheer talent, best illustrated by convincing my younger sister, Carol, to marry him.

Jack, who is three years older than me, is married to a sweet girl, Estelle, and has two daughters. Carol has one daughter so far and I, after enjoying freedom for the first 29 years of my life, just got married to Sandra Feldman, a girl from Syracuse. My job at work is to supervise the buying for the chain. It takes only a little skill to buy things cheaply but real brains to know what will sell well. For that I work closely with Carol, who is in charge of marketing. My brother, Jack, is president of the company and does everything that the two of us don't get around to doing. My beautiful wife of a few months wouldn't deign to work in the business, but she is nevertheless one of those who are authorized to sign the foundation checks. Of the required signatures on such checks, one must always be mine, since I was designated as the director of the charitable trust. That dubious honor was bestowed upon me because I was graduated from Yeshiva College before I got my MBA from Penn State. Finishing a yeshiva is supposed to indicate that I know all about Israel and the many Jewish institutions that are on the receiving end of the bulk of our charity funds.

I call my wife Sandy, her mother usually calls her Sandra and Rabbi Brill calls her Sarah. Everyone else calls her "princess." She really is a combination of Princess Di and Margaret Mead and she is worth a million dollars, literally and figuratively. Of the last item you can be certain, because Max Glaser checked over the financial records of the trust fund her father left her and the balance is still well over a million, despite her frenzied attempts to spend it all. Max, by the way, is the controller of Buffalo Auto and the financial guru of all the family members.

The Margaret Mead angle comes from the PhD Sandy has in History and Western Civilization. She was an assistant professor at Cortland State before we got married and now she is an associate professor at the State University in Buffalo. The looks?

Well I think she's gorgeous and her mother feels the same way. Rabbi Brill told her once to her face that she was a fair-looking woman and Rabbi Steiner, the dean of a yeshiva in Jerusalem, said it behind her back when she was only 14.

Sandy likes to give rabbis a hard time, particularly when they are collecting money for some cause. They are lucky if they can get her to part with as much as a hundred dollars. With Rabbi Brill, though, she was a real doll. Without batting an eyelash, she signed the two checks for $400,000, handed them to him with a smile and wished him 'mazel tov,' which means good luck.

Later, when the rabbi left with the money, she couldn't contain herself. "You're a great guy, Mel, and you did a wonderful thing," she said and kissed me with a lot of feeling. "You gave the man a new lease on life. I think he will succeed in his venture and will always be our good friend. In fact, I'm sure he'll visit us every year to report on his progress."

"At $25,000 a visit, I would just as soon forego his annual appearances."

"More like $40,000 a year considering he has to cover interest and capital payments," she corrected me quickly, "but who's counting? I, for one, look forward to his coming. At any rate, we'll be seeing him in Israel in June when he dedicates his school so at least next year he won't have to come to Buffalo."

"He'll be here. He wouldn't miss another chance of seeing you for anything in the world. You are his biggest and best supporter."

"Mel," she said not responding to my remark, "I have an idea. Remember how during our courtship you said you would like to write something?" I must have said a lot of silly things to her because I was desperate for her to marry me and she wasn't at all interested in what, to her, was a boring businessman.

"You never forget a thing, darling," I answered, "so I probably did mention such an ambitious idea in one of my weaker moments. In fact, years ago I once wrote something for the school paper."

"For your first creative project, Mel, why don't you write a book about us and Rabbi Brill?"

I didn't answer right away because I had to think of how to escape the undertaking. After a minute I said, "I have three good reasons not to. Firstly, I don't know all of the facts in the case. Secondly, I am not what you may call an author. Finally, and most important, the story will never be published."

"I can fill you in on all the facts, Mel. During my stay in Israel and during their visits to the u.s., Rabbi Brill and his wife, Rivka, confided everything in me down to the last detail. As far as writing ability is concerned, don't sell yourself short. I happen to remember that your term paper on Napoleon got an 'A'. Your writing has really improved since you went back to school. In any event, I can help you or we can get an editor." Here she paused to catch her breath and a minute later she continued. "In fact," she said, "I have an even better idea. Let's co-author the book and split the chapters between us. I will be glad to write some of them and you can do the rest. Publishing is the last thing you need to worry about. If it ever comes to that, I will take care of it. The important thing is that you will make me very happy if you tear yourself away from the tv on those nights when you are not in school, and exercise your mind."

Sandy never takes no for an answer, so I didn't even bother resisting. I simply set aside time at the word processor and got to work. At first it was hard but, after a while, the thoughts began to gel and the words began to flow. As far as Sandy was concerned, she knocked off her chapters without even working up a sweat. You should be able to tell her work from mine, but I've labelled the sections just in case. So, here's the story and, if you don't find it to your liking, blame the princess. It was really her idea.

2

EVERY STORY STARTS SOMEWHERE. A book about a rabbi could go back to Moses or even Abraham. But this novel is not a course in Jewish history, and I take it that everyone knows what a rabbi is. I feel it's best to keep the background parts of the tale to a minimum.

This story starts in pre-war Vienna, where my family lived for generations. Vienna had a big Jewish population, and the leading rabbi of the community was one Yakob Steiner, of blessed memory. Grand Rabbi Steiner served as a judge on the Rabbinical Court and as spiritual leader of one of the major congregations. He authored a large number of commentaries and responded to religious questions from all over Europe. My father attended both his synagogue and yeshiva and grew up together with the rabbi's son, Solomon. They were good friends and both escaped from Austria through the Youth Aliyah movement after the 1936 Anschluss with Germany. Youth Aliyah took young children away from their families and transported them to safety in what was then called Palestine. The sainted Rabbi Steiner, as well as most of the remaining members of our families, perished in the Holocaust.

Although he continued studying in an Israeli yeshiva for

a period of time, Dad couldn't see any future in Israel. Having grown up in an urban business family, he wasn't cut out for the pioneering life. Commercial opportunities in the larger cities were still quite limited after the war. So, as soon as he was ready, he headed for America. He was directed to Buffalo by the Immigrant Aid Society and never felt any need to go elsewhere. Here he married my mother and started his family and business.

Solomon Steiner, by contrast, was very happy in Israel and continued his family tradition of *Torah* (Biblical) scholarship. He was ordained after the war and, because of his family's reputation and his own outstanding scholarship, became a high-level instructor at a Jerusalem yeshiva. That position he held for 30 years and his fame spread far and wide. At the age of 57, however, he became restless. The leadership of his yeshiva passed into the hands of younger rabbis, whose ideas were quite extreme and not to his liking. The new heads of the school were quite rigid and sorely lacked the breadth and humanity of the Viennese scholars. Behind his back, students spoke disparagingly of Rabbi Steiner as the *Yekke* (Germanic) gentleman whose style differed markedly from Lithuanian traditions.

During all his years in Israel, the rabbi kept in close touch with my father and other survivors of the once glorious Viennese Jewish community. When he became convinced that his only course of action was to open a yeshiva of his own, he had a vast supporting network of friends to assist him.

That's why, 14 years ago, Rabbi Steiner arrived in the u.s. and contacted my father. Dad was walking on clouds when he heard that the son of the Grand Rabbi was coming all the way to Buffalo to see him personally over the course of a weekend. I was in my first month at the Yeshiva University High School, struggling to get settled in my studies, but that hardly mattered to my father. I was ordered to fly home for the weekend to be presented to Rabbi Steiner for a blessing. When I argued that I would lose time from my schoolwork, my father assured me that the inspiration of meeting a great rabbinical scholar would do more for my learning than remaining in class.

Rabbi Solomon Steiner was really impressive. His beard was long and almost all gray. He wore a black frock coat and had an angelic face. If you've ever seen pictures of great rabbis, you'll know how he looked in my eyes. He tried to put my parents at ease, but his presence threw them into a state of abject terror. My father didn't relax till after the Sabbath, when the visiting rabbi took him into the study for a long and cordial discussion.

That meeting had far-reaching consequences for both parties. Rabbi Steiner laid out his plans for the new yeshiva and enlisted my father's help. We were quite well-off by that time and my father was known in Buffalo for his charity. Even so, the sums involved seemed huge. Rabbi Steiner claimed he needed a million dollars to open the yeshiva and requested a quarter of that from the Seidman family. At that, he was doing us a favor. He could easily have asked for half a million and he would have gotten it, too. My father would have gladly put up the business as collateral if necessary to honor the memory of the Grand Rabbi of Vienna.

"I have a slight problem," my father said to him, "but I am ready to help the honored Rabbi."

"What is that?"

"I have already given a lot of charity this year and I am approaching the limit of charitable deductions on my tax report. I will have to speak to my accountant, Mr. Glaser, and see what can be done." Max Glaser, of course, is much better at holding on to money than giving it away. Nevertheless, he gave my father proper advice in this case.

"Give the rabbi two checks," he said. "One dated for December 1 of this year and the other for January 1 of next year. Make out the first one for $100,000 and the second one for $150,000. That way, you will be able to deduct the entire amount."

Rabbi Steiner didn't mind the extra bookkeeping at all. "I can wait with the second check because we are not closing on the building until mid-January," he explained.

Rather than erect a building from scratch, Rabbi Steiner had found a large apartment house under construction. The plans called for twelve spacious apartments, and the shell of the building was already up. The builder, Yossi Hurwitz, was under-capitalized and the banks were pressing him on his loans. Rather than face insolvency, he decided to sell what was already complete and pay off his debts. The resulting profit was less than he would have made by finishing the apartments and selling them one by one. He was afraid, however, that his resources would run out before the payments came in. He offered the land and the unfinished apartments to Rabbi Steiner for three-quarters of a million dollars and the rabbi, after studying the potential of the building, felt that the price was reasonable. He explained to my father that he would put the study hall, library and offices on one side of the first floor, and the kitchen and student dining room on the other side. Each of the larger areas would accommodate up to 100 students. The second floor would be reserved for classrooms and the remaining two floors would house the resident students. At maximum capacity, the dormitory would house 52 students and two counselors. Rabbi Steiner estimated that it would cost him an additional $250,000 to alter the building and provide furnishings for the yeshiva.

My father did not consider these plans grandiose. The rabbi was thinking in terms of a modest, private school that he could readily supervise by himself. What concerned Dad were the funds that the rabbi would need beyond the initial Seidman contribution.

"May I ask how the Rabbi will raise the balance of the money that is required?"

"Meir, I have a commitment for a mortgage on the land and building for $500,000. The rest of the money will be raised by more solicitation and subsidies from the government."

"And what will the Rabbi call the new yeshiva?"

Rabbi Steiner didn't hesitate for a minute. "The new yeshiva will be called 'Beit Meir,' the 'House of Meir.'"

"That is a wonderful name, although there already is a yeshiva in Tiberias named after that great sage." My father was thinking of Rabbi Meir, who lived some two thousand years ago at the time of the *Mishna* (early code of Jewish law).

The rabbi couldn't help smiling at my father's innocence. "The yeshiva is not being named after the Rabbi Meir of the Mishna or Rabbi Meir of Ruttenberg or even Rabbi Meir Berlin. It will be named after one Meir Seidman of Buffalo, New York."

My father turned pale when he heard that. "Rabbi Steiner," he pleaded, "I am not worthy of such an honor, not in my lifetime and not thereafter. I am a businessman and not a rabbi."

The rabbi's response was quick in coming and sounded like part of a well-prepared *Talmudic* (Jewish law) discourse. "One may not judge his own status in life, Meir," he stated, "because we are all commanded to practice humility. When a rabbi is observant and increases his scholarship, he is doing no more than what his position requires. When a busy layman is scrupulous in his observance and continues to study Torah, he is sanctifying the name of God and deserves great honor. Remember how our rabbis held the tribe of Zebulun in high esteem because it supported the Torah studies of the tribe of Issachar. You are a modern day Zebulun, because your charity will enable scores of men to study Torah. I and all the members of the faculty will be proud to teach at a yeshiva which bears your name."

Tears welled up in my father's eyes. He could not believe that a yeshiva in the Holy Land would be named for him. He thanked the rabbi and pledged that as long as the yeshiva stood, the Seidman family would sustain it. Before Rabbi Steiner left, my father asked for his help in two personal matters. One of them concerned the Sabbath problem at Buffalo Auto, while the other was related to me.

The Sabbath problem was complex. As long as my father had one store, he was able to keep it closed on Saturday. The store was open Sunday and the police didn't bother him because they respected his Sabbath observance. But the time of expansion was at hand, since one store alone could not sustain three children when they built families of their own. The new stores, especially those in smaller cities without Jewish communities, would have to be open on Saturday. My father's concern was not with Sabbath desecration; he would never work on the Sabbath nor would any of his children. The problem was with profits that the stores would generate from business conducted by gentile managers on the Sabbath. Enjoyment of such income by the actual owners of the store is prohibited under Jewish law. Over the years, there evolved a rabbinic procedure to circumvent the problem by assigning Sabbath profits to a non-Jewish partner in the enterprise. One of my father's managers, Pat Wilson, could be designated as a partner to meet the requirements of the Sabbath laws. The formal contracts for the ritual were so complex, however, that only rabbinic specialists could write them. The local rabbi, who was deficient even in some of the less exotic sections of religious law, was incapable of such work.

Once Rabbi Steiner received assurances that none of the

members of the Seidman family would ever go near the stores on the Sabbath, he volunteered to prepare a "Bill of Sale for Sabbath Profits" for my father. After a few months, the documents were executed and Pat Wilson was on his way to becoming a millionaire.

The second request was more personal. My father asked Rabbi Steiner to give me a blessing that I would grow up to be a Torah scholar, marry an observant woman, do good deeds and have children who would fear God and love the Torah. Rabbi Steiner bestowed the blessing upon me, and I hoped that in time it would be fulfilled.

SANDRA

3

ONE OF THE PREVAILING LITERARY pretensions of our time is the belief that every written work must contain some material of social significance. Insofar as this book is concerned, we make no such claim. Aside from the subsidiary benefit of curbing Melvin's penchant for wasting time, this novel is intended solely for the entertainment of our readers.

What? You won't read further if there are no momentous revelations? All right, then, we might find a few crumbs for you. Nothing heavy like a thesis, antithesis or hypothesis. What you might discover, if you look hard enough, is a little insight into the yeshiva world; not the students and what they learn, but the administrators and what they do to keep such institutions running.

A yeshiva is a high-level Torah school. Although some Jewish elementary schools call themselves *yeshivot* (the plural of yeshiva in Hebrew), we are not talking about them. In our usage, a yeshiva is for men, 18 years and up. Some yeshivot call themselves seminaries. That name was proper when men studied at such schools to be ordained as rabbis and teachers. Nowadays, only a handful of students actually seek religious certification. The rest study for the sake of knowledge that will enable them to live as very observant Jews. When a yeshiva puts out a catalogue, you don't have to bother reading it. In one form or another, all that is ever studied there is the Talmud and Codes of Law derived from the Talmud.

How long do the men study? As long as they can cope financially and intellectually. Even marriage doesn't stand in their way. It only means that such students leave the general classes and enter a department for married men, called the *kollel*. Except for a few well-to-do Americans, students pay little or no tuition at a yeshiva. The schools are supported in the main by contributions of charitable Jewish families and, for those yeshivot located in Israel, by some help from the government.

Mel and I are not part of the yeshiva world and our life style is vastly different from that which is practiced by true yeshiva families. We do, however, have a peripheral link to that environment. Both of our fathers studied in European yeshivot when they were young, and Mel attended Yeshiva University in New York. The deeper connection, though, is the financial one. Mel has already told you of some of the huge capital gifts that he made to one yeshiva and I will tell you of others. How we got caught up in this scene, and what effect it has had on our lives, is the essence of this book.

Mel is not strong on description, so I will relate a little more about the main protagonists. There's Mel himself, a tall, heavy-set man, not quite thirty but going on fifty. He takes life seriously and looks like an executive of a big company. Unfortunately, that's exactly what he is. Not only does he look the part, he actually plays it. He works in the business all day and attends public meetings at night whenever I can't keep him at home. His hair is still black and his eyes are brown. When he shakes your hand, you won't forget his strong powerful grip for a long time.

I am about five-seven and a natural blonde. My dressmaker

loves my figure, my hairdresser loves my hair, my dentist loves my teeth and my plastic surgeon just plain loves me. All of them have been handsomely rewarded for helping improve my physical appearance. They are proud of their handiwork, and most of the time I am too. My father, who owned Feldman's Department Store in downtown Syracuse, paid all of the above practitioners and never complained. He also paid the bills for my education and intellectual pursuits.

Mel and I are your ordinary run-of-the-mill millionaires. The central figure in the book, Rabbi Baruch Brill, doesn't have any money, but he has loads of personality. He's taller than Melvin but weighs much less; not an ounce of fat on his body and a lean look on his face. His black beard is neatly trimmed and he has a winning smile. If he weren't wearing a black hat and a long frock coat, he could easily pass for a doctor.

The rabbi grew up in New York and studied at an old line yeshiva in the metropolitan area. At night, he went to college and put together enough credits for a degree. He had a burning desire to study more Talmud, and that subject was all that really mattered to him. When he felt that he couldn't learn any more Talmud in the States, he made *aliyah* – immigrated, literally, ascended – to Israel and studied at the yeshivot there. He wasn't in Israel for more than a year when the dean of his school fixed him up with a wife, a girl by the name of Rivka Weiss. She was a native Israeli and fairly good-looking, but neither quality meant anything to the rabbi. What counted was her reputation for piety and fear of God. Baruch, as he now lets me call him, used up his five allowable dates and still didn't find out how truly religious she was. (More than five dates in the yeshiva world is considered a long, dragged out courtship and is frowned upon by the yeshiva faculty.) Only after marriage did he realize the full extent of her observance. She prayed three times every day and constantly recited Psalms. When she had any sort of problem she ran to her rabbinic mentor and followed his advice to the letter.

It was her faith that enabled her to get through the early years of marriage when Baruch was studying at a kollel. She withstood extreme poverty and the birth of three children before Baruch earned his first salary as a Talmud instructor at Yeshiva Beit Meir, the school endowed by my late father-in-law. Rivka made ends meet by using the kollel stipend, the government children's subsidies, gifts from Baruch's family in New York, loans from free loan societies and credit allowances in numerous food stores. Things improved only slightly when Baruch went to work because, while more money started to come in, three more children arrived to eat it up.

I first met Rabbi Brill a little over three years ago at my mother's home in Syracuse. What he was doing there is an interesting story that begins twelve years ago, when Rabbi Solomon Steiner established his yeshiva in a western suburb of the Holy City. Rabbi Brill told us that after receiving generous donations from Murray Seidman and others, Rabbi Steiner spent the next six months remodeling a building and recruiting students. He also engaged a cook, a secretary, a caretaker and one instructor, Rabbi Baruch Brill. Baruch worked very hard to succeed in his first position and played a vital role in the success of the yeshiva. Each year after the school opened, a new class was added and the faculty grew to four full-time instructors and more than fifty students. Even then the yeshiva continued to grow, as is evident from an event that occurred eight years ago. It is also an interesting story, which I've put together for you from a number of versions that I heard.

One spring day, the dean of the yeshiva sent word with a student that he wanted to talk with Rabbi Brill on a very urgent matter. Since most of the students had already left for the Passover holiday, Rabbi Brill had ample time to speak to Rabbi Steiner but was at a loss as to what the dean had in mind. Slowly he walked from the study hall to the dean's office on the first floor. Rabbi Steiner was sitting at his desk with an open volume of the Talmud before him. He was a man of medium height with a furrowed brow. Only a few streaks of black remained in his long untrimmed beard. The eyes were light blue but had a piercing quality about them.

"Sit down, Baruch," he said. "Would you like something to drink?" Rabbi Brill was a little taken aback by this display of cordiality. To members of the faculty, the dean had always been studiously aloof. The teachers rarely socialized with him and never sought meetings with him unless it was to request an increase in salary or a solution to a particularly severe problem with a student. It was never the dean's habit to meet with the faculty as a group. His pattern was to summon the instructors individually and communicate his plans to them.

Given this disposition, Rabbi Brill sensed that something of great importance was forthcoming and he politely declined the drink. Rabbi Steiner was in no hurry to get to the essence of the meeting, apparently needing some time to organize his presentation. He engaged Rabbi Brill in small talk without even listening to the answers. The obvious delay added to the rabbi's anxieties.

"From what I gather," the dean continued, "you've had an excellent year. Your students did extraordinarily well on my last examination." Despite his heavy schedule, Rabbi Steiner visited each class at least once a month and tested the students to check on their progress. In his first few years, Baruch was tense during the dean's classroom visits. After a while, the oral testing became routine, and caused him no great concern. He tried to reconstruct the last such session in his mind but could recall nothing unusual about the results.

"I'm grateful to the Dean for his evaluation," Rabbi Brill replied, addressing the dean in the traditional third person. "I have a select group of students and they all work very hard."

Rabbi Steiner did not let the humility pass by. Although he wasn't always lavish in his praises, it served his purpose now to make Rabbi Brill feel good about himself and his teaching skills.

"Don't be modest, Baruch," the dean said. "Your pupils are no more select than any of the others. Students are raw material and it requires skill and dedication to fashion them. If they make progress it is a reflection of the teacher's abilities."

Rabbi Brill did not bother replying or even disclaiming the praise. While what the dean was saying was reasonably accurate, Rabbi Brill realized it was more or less a formality. He waited patiently for the important part of the conversation.

"You know, Baruch, our yeshiva is four years old and has succeeded beyond all expectations. We now have about thirty American students studying here and twenty-five native Israelis. All of the students are single, however, and have no long-range commitment to the yeshiva. I would like to consider with you the possibility of starting a kollel at Beit Meir in the near future."

The word kollel had an enormous impact on Rabbi Brill. Kollel students were subsidized with something akin to college fellowships, and only the most gifted students were admitted to the program. Some kollels accepted single students, but the general rule was for the students to be married. The presence of a kollel would vastly enhance the status and reputation of Beit Meir.

"Is the Dean sure that we are capable of such a venture?"

Rabbi Brill asked. Aside from heavy expense, he knew that a kollel would present the yeshiva with difficult problems in the area of recruiting faculty and students. Running a marginal kollel would do the school more harm than good.

"One is never really ready for such a momentous step. If I had asked myself when I opened this yeshiva if I were ready for it, the answer would have been 'no.' In life we have to move ahead and face new challenges. We have to believe that the Almighty will bless the work of our hands and we can't afford the luxury of hesitation. The time is right for a kollel in this community and it is our manifest duty to proceed."

A sudden uneasiness overcame Rabbi Brill. It dawned on him that the dean had called him in connection with this new project, and he wasn't quite sure of where he would fit in. "A kollel is a wonderful idea and I wish the Dean good fortune with it. Am I somehow involved with this undertaking?"

"Very much so," the dean replied. "I have chosen you to carry major responsibilities at the kollel. Of course, it will mean a complete change of your status at the yeshiva, but one which I think you will welcome."

Again Rabbi Brill maintained his silence. Although he generally was not lacking in self-confidence, there were trepidations that he would be asked to do something beyond his ability. Still, even if in the end he couldn't accept the assignment, it was quite flattering to be offered the opportunity.

"What exactly does the Dean have in mind for me?" he asked.

The dean spoke in a casual way and did not proceed immediately with the answer. "You know, Baruch, the yeshiva is growing larger and I am getting older. It is becoming increasingly difficult for me to handle the administrative work, the teaching, the fund-raising and the personal counseling of the students. Before I can describe your role at the kollel, I must discuss another problem facing the school, namely the need to engage a *mashgiach*, a spiritual advisor and counselor to the students."

The larger yeshivot all employed *mashgichim*. In addition to the guidance they provided, they also kept tabs on the academic progress and moral behavior of the students.

"Although I can see that there is a real need for such a man, I hardly think that the yeshiva has reached the point where it can sustain a full-time mashgiach," Baruch interjected. "If the yeshiva had a hundred or more students, we could justify filling such a position. At this time, it would only place another heavy financial burden on the Dean."

Baruch could not but help admire the man behind the desk. Although the dean currently had his hands full with the school, he still had time to think of growth and expansion.

"You are quite right, Baruch. I certainly am not planning to engage a full-time mashgiach. What I do have in mind is a position where the man chosen would be a mashgiach for part of the time and work at the kollel for the balance. I will lecture at the kollel once a week, but I need a man to deliver two additional lectures each week and to closely supervise the students. It may be hard for you to realize it, but kollel scholars require almost as much attention as American students. Their problems are not academic, but they are often beset by personal and family matters which require sound advice and guidance."

"The Dean is talking about a very senior position and one that involves a mixture of qualities," Rabbi Brill protested. The man involved must not only be a first-rate scholar; he must possess that special ability to develop a close working relationship with the students. I have a feeling that it will be difficult to find the right person for such a position."

"It's not my intention, Baruch, to make an extensive search

for the man. I feel that I have such a person within our own yeshiva and I am looking at him right now."

Baruch stared at the dean in disbelief. "The Dean can surely not be serious in this matter. I am only 32 years old. I have never heard of a mashgiach under 50 and even an assistant director of a kollel should be an older person. Certainly the Dean realizes that some of the students are almost as old as I am!"

Rabbi Steiner paused once again to assemble his arguments. "I am not one who makes important decisions lightly. I have given this particular matter much thought, and I have the advantage of having worked with you for four years. I have never seen a teacher who establishes such good rapport with students as you do. It would be a serious error to choose a mashgiach who is of an older generation than the students and to whom the students cannot relate. I personally feel the age difference acutely when I speak to students who have grown up in a different world. Those schools that hire mashgichim who are too old for the students usually pay a heavy price for their poor judgment.

"Nor do I think for a moment that you will have much difficulty teaching at the kollel level. You yourself were a member of a kollel for five years before you came to this yeshiva, and you have already acquired a good reputation for Torah knowledge. I know that I cannot yet name you as the full director of the kollel, but I am sure that you will be carrying most of the burdens of this new department on your shoulders."

Baruch decided to himself that it would not be tactful for him to flatly reject such a flattering offer. He phrased his response with care. "I have too much respect for the Dean to reject the offer out of hand, so I will undertake to give the matter more thought before I present a formal reply. But may I ask the Dean what will happen to my present class if I become involved with the kollel?"

"I have a feeling that given sufficient time for reflection, you will be inclined to think more positively about the offer. In so far as your present class is concerned, we will play some musical chairs. It is not right to bring in a new man who would outrank the other three faculty members. Most likely we will promote each of the three present teachers by one year and engage a new instructor to teach the lowest class.

"I know that money will not be a major consideration in your decision, Baruch, but remember, you do have responsibility for a wife and six children. As the children grow older, you will need more income for them and for additional children who may come along. The new position will offer a far more attractive salary than what you are earning at the present time."

"As the Dean has indicated, money is not a critical factor with me. What concerns me most is my status and security. In my present position I feel very safe. My work has been blessed with good results and I enjoy more seniority than the other faculty members. I have become accustomed to my duties and I am free to study and undertake intellectual pursuits. I may very well fail as a mashgiach and, in that event, I will have nowhere to go. There is no room for a failed mashgiach in his own school. If I have to leave this yeshiva I may find it hard to find a comparable position elsewhere. It will mean starting at the bottom once again and, for a family man, it is just too big a risk to take."

The dean sensed an urgent need to reassure the reluctant Rabbi Brill. "I for one do not think that you will fail, Baruch. In the worst case, though, there will always be a position for you at this yeshiva. As long as I am here I can guarantee that, and I am sure that my ultimate successors will honor any such commitment. And I do know of cases where mashgichim gave up their positions and were able to resume their regular faculty rank."

"I thank the Dean for this vote of confidence," Baruch

replied. "I do need some time to think about it, and I will have to speak to my wife before I can make a decision. The Dean must realize that such a change in my status would impose additional burdens on her, and she has enough as it is." Baruch paused for a brief moment and then asked about something that had been on his mind for most of the conversation. "By the way, is there anything that the Dean has not told me about any other responsibilities entailed in this new position that might influence my decision?"

It was not that Rabbi Brill had any mistrust of Dean Steiner. His experience, however, taught him that even in the yeshiva world there were times when a full story was not told. Ultimately, the truth would emerge, but by then it would be after the fact.

"There is one item that I have not come to yet," the dean said. "In a way, it is an added benefit, but it will require some extra work on your part."

"May I ask what it is?"

"Yes, indeed. I know that you have been making at least one trip a year to the States to visit your family. Such a trip is surely quite costly and must put a considerable dent in your income. From now on, the yeshiva will cover the expense of your trip."

Baruch knew that the yeshiva was not in the gift-giving business and he could sense not merely strings but entire cables attached to the offer. "If I am not being presumptuous," he said, "there is an old expression in America to the effect that there is no such thing as a free lunch."

"Quite right, Baruch. This new venture of ours will cost the yeshiva an extra $65,000 a year. As you know, while the government subsidizes students studying at kollels, the stipends given are not sufficient for married students to live on. There are some schools that do not supplement the state subsidies but, in the end, they draw only the weakest students. To get higher quality students we have to augment the support of each member of the kollel by $2000 annually. That means that we are already talking of $30,000. To that we must add your salary increase, the cost of the new teacher and increased operating expenses."

"Can't the Dean request Mr. Seidman to help you with the kollel? He did help the yeshiva get started. Perhaps he might be willing to support a kollel as well."

"Things are not that simple," the dean replied. "Mr. Seidman did give us a quarter of a million dollars to build the yeshiva. What is not generally known is that each year since then he has contributed $25,000 to help pay the mortgage. Even if I were inclined to ask him to do more, I would not do so now because Mr. Seidman is in poor health and suffers from heart problems. I, myself, already make three fund-raising trips annually to the United States and my own health does not permit me to undertake any more."

Baruch knew what was coming, but he held his peace and waited for Rabbi Steiner to continue.

"There are some donors and some untapped resources that I could use to obtain part of the funds for the kollel, but at best I can see myself raising only about half of the extra money. We need someone to make a trip to America for at least a month and solicit from a list of donors in Jewish communities in the northeastern states."

"Why me?" Baruch asked. He knew that the dean would not discuss such a mission with him unless he was the collector the dean had in mind.

"To begin with, Baruch, you are the only man we have who can speak English in a manner that would not embarrass the school. You are, after all, a college graduate. I know it wasn't Harvard, but still, college is college. Secondly, you visit America each year anyway, and you know your way around. The important thing is that with me getting older we must develop new fund-raising talent."

Baruch was satisfied that he had garnered the full extent of the dean's plans and felt that it was the correct moment to conclude the meeting. "Well, I am glad that I have a more complete picture of the offer the Dean is making. I will give it my fullest consideration and arrive at a decision as soon as possible."

When Baruch left the yeshiva, his mind was in turmoil. He hardly noticed the beautiful vistas of the hills north and west of Jerusalem. The rolling landscapes were always a source of pleasure to him when he left school for home, but today his thoughts were far removed from the local geography as he walked slowly to his flat.

At home, Rivka was busy preparing the house for Passover. Now that the students were on vacation, Baruch was expected to help more than before in household affairs. He pitched in for a while in the Passover work, deciding to wait until later in the evening before discussing Rabbi Steiner's proposal with his wife.

He was somewhat grateful that the matter had come up before the holiday. As Pesach approached, his wife became increasingly tense by the minute and could not be depended on to make rational decisions. Otherwise, she was quite clear-headed and easy to talk to. When the children were asleep and she was resting on the couch, Baruch said that he had something important to discuss with her.

"I hope it's good news, because what I have to tell you is not too pleasant."

"I don't want to minimize your pre-Passover problems," Baruch said, "but I hear the same story every year and somehow we muddle through. I am sure that it will be the same this year."

"Thank God," she said, "we have been able to celebrate the

holiday properly every year since we've been married. With God's help, we will do so again. A husband, however, should help his wife at such a time, especially if he's not too busy at work."

"I've heard that before, Rivka, and I will do my share. The matter I wish to discuss, however, is not an ordinary one and certainly takes precedence over the daily complaints."

"I can't imagine anything more important than making a kosher Passover. It must be something extraordinary."

Baruch knew how single-minded his Rivka could be before a holiday, but he decided to proceed with the matter anyway.

"It's really a major event, Rivka," Baruch said. He then related to her verbatim the entire conversation that he had had with Rabbi Steiner.

"That's wonderful news," she said, "and I thank the Almighty for it. I am proud of you and I can hardly wait to tell my parents."

"Not so fast, Rivka. Did I ever tell you the story of the rabbi in a small community who was offered a very good position in a big city. One of the members of the congregation asked another member what the rabbi was doing about it. The other replied, 'Our rabbi has spent the last few days contemplating the challenge and praying for divine guidance in making such a momentous decision.' 'And what is his wife, the *Rebbitzen*, doing?' the member asked his friend. 'The Rebbitzen? Oh, she's busy packing.'"

"You can't possibly be suggesting that you might not accept the offer?" Rivka said in a very concerned way. "You are being given an opportunity to teach Torah on a higher level. That's something that can never be refused."

"Listen, Rivka, I am currently teaching a high enough class and I feel I am doing so quite successfully. There are others my age who are still studying and haven't even found a position.

What I am being asked to do may be far above my capabilities, and it may be quite unwise for me to make such a move."

Rivka was not one to permit a religious mandate to be avoided. She groped for an argument that would overcome her husband's hesitation.

"I am sure that Rabbi Steiner would not have asked you to accept such a position if he didn't feel that you have the ability to handle it. Of course, if you have any doubts on the matter, you may ask Rabbi Shayalevitch for advice. I always turn to him when I have a problem."

"I have occasionally consulted him in matters of law. If I am to take on such a major position, however, I must make my own decisions without depending on others. In the final analysis, I will be the one on the firing line, not Rabbi Shayalevitch. I don't want to be in the position of blaming others for any situation in which I may find myself."

Rivka was a little put off by Baruch's off-handed dismissal of her mentor, who was known to be a scholar of international repute. "My teachers taught me that we should always seek the guidance of wise men when we have problems. They have greater Torah knowledge than we do and that makes it possible for them to give us the best advice."

Baruch knew that it would be futile to try to reason with Rivka. The dogmas that she had learned at school were unshakable and nothing he could say would ever change them. "Have you considered the effect of such a change of position on your life? I will be at the yeshiva from early morning until late at night dealing with the problems of 70 young men, and we will be getting calls at all hours. The help I give you now in the house will be further diminished."

"God will give me strength to face these responsibilities," she answered. "The wives of all great scholars have stood by their husbands and never complained. I will make a special effort to help you carry your new burdens, because I feel you will be doing a great mitzvah."

Baruch tried to get through to his wife on a more personal level. He knew that Rivka was very much dependent on him and would not like to be left alone for an extended period.

"Do you realize that I will be away from home for a full month before the High Holidays?" he asked. Rivka lost no time in putting that argument aside.

"Rachel was separated from Rabbi Akiva much longer than that, but she was happy because she knew that he was on his way to greatness."

It dawned on Rabbi Brill that he was not going to get any help from his wife in seriously evaluating the new offer. It was a decision that he would have to make all by himself. He let the conversation drift on to other matters after warning Rivka not to tell a living soul about the offer. For the next two days, he sat in the study hall mulling things over, including the fund-raising aspects of the offer. He was decidedly not a fund-raiser. He had never solicited a donation in his adult life and was dreadfully afraid of doing so. During his visits to the United States he did not venture far from Forest Hills, a traditional Jewish neighborhood in New York City.

Even traveling to the suburbs caused him a degree of culture shock. Now he would be spending time in such places as Syracuse, Rochester and Pittsburgh. He would have to worry about kosher food and proper synagogues in which to pray. Worst of all was the fear that he could not convey to American businessmen the importance of having young people devote their time to the study of Torah instead of going out to work. He was fearful of the rejections that were inevitable when one solicits for Torah institutions.

Also, while he couldn't confide his personal needs to Rabbi Steiner, being separated from his wife for such a long time would be a very hard thing for him to bear. Regretfully, he was not on the level of Rabbi Akiva.

The fund-raising condition that Rabbi Steiner had attached to the offer was the biggest stumbling block in his way of accepting it. He was already counseling the students of his class and others who were seeking his guidance. The lectures that he prepared for his class were almost as complex as those he would have to deliver to the kollel scholars. Combining the two jobs, however, would put him under terrible stress. Losing his vacation time, which was urgently needed for rest and recovery, could very well be the final straw.

After a few days of self-pity, he felt that the time had arrived to decline the dean's offer. He rehearsed various explanations for his action and chose late afternoon for the meeting with Rabbi Steiner.

"I am really flattered with the offer that was made to me, Rabbi Steiner, and my wife would readily consent to my accepting the position. Perhaps if I were a few years older, I would be more amenable to it but, as matters stand now, I must regretfully decline."

Rabbi Steiner was a man whose reputation was not achieved by letting people say no to him. He was extremely persuasive, and his scholarship carried tremendous weight. For the next hour he lectured and cajoled and argued. He found the weak spots in Baruch's nature and played upon them in a masterful way. Nevertheless, he could not break down Baruch's lack of self-confidence, which was impeding his willingness to accept the challenge. He came to the realization that he would have to change the offer significantly if he wished to secure Baruch's consent.

"I'll tell you what, Baruch. I can see that taking on two new jobs plus fund-raising may be a little overwhelming. Perhaps we ought to proceed a step at a time. Let's say that in the summer you make the business trip to the States and, in the fall, you teach at the kollel. I am willing to wait a year for a mashgiach. We have been without a mashgiach for four years and we can hold off a while longer. I will continue to do as much as before, and I will ask all the faculty members to continue providing guidance for their own students."

Rabbi Steiner's compromise struck home and a heavy weight was lifted from Baruch's heart. It was uncomfortable for him to reject the dean's offer and it was the first time he had ever turned down a chance to advance. Now that the new position had achieved manageable proportions, he listened to the dean more attentively. After some further discussion centering on remuneration, he finally accepted the offer.

So it was that Rabbi Brill moved up in the yeshiva world. He succeeded at the kollel and, within a year, he gradually assumed the duties of mashgiach. He never made peace with the fund-raising trips, but he managed to perform the solicitations well and wasted no time complaining. He was on his eighth annual visit to the United States when I finally met him on a Tuesday night in August.

4

RABBI BRILL HAD LEFT ISRAEL on the Wednesday preceding our meeting. The sun was rising Thursday morning as his flight finally set down at Kennedy. Four hundred and forty afflicted passengers in varying states of discomfort heaved a collective sigh of relief as their long ordeal came to an end. Not really the end, because there were baggage and customs and ground transportation to worry about. These chores, however, were relatively painless compared to sitting in a tightly packed Boeing 747 for 13 hours. Airline efficiency experts had succeeded in converting otherwise sensible airplanes into cattle cars. Clogged toilets, screaming babies and indifferent service irritated the captive audience even further. Rabbi Brill was no less weary than the other passengers, but his mind was on other things. "BB," as he was sometimes called behind his back by his students, or "Reb Baruch," as he was addressed by his peers, was more concerned about his annual ordeal in America. The annoyances he endured on the flight were only a prelude to the acute unpleasantness that he would experience during his month-long visit.

When the plane came to a halt at the exit walkway, Rabbi Brill reached for his carry-on bag in the overhead compartment. To that he added a briefcase that he had kept under the seat and joined the line waiting to leave the plane. The bag contained his tallit and tefillin, items required on a daily basis that could not be entrusted to the vagaries of airline luggage handling. Some travelers had made a prayer *minyan* on the plane, but he chose not to join them. Praying on airplanes was problematic to begin with. On eastbound flights he did so because he would otherwise miss the prayers entirely. He didn't join the prayer groups on westbound flights because he felt uneasy about reciting prayers in close proximity to the lavatories and being disturbed by women, not always appropriately dressed, making their way to the restrooms. This morning he would say his prayers at his mother's home, assuming his sister would be there to meet his plane and deliver him to the family home in Forest Hills.

His mind turned to some other items in his briefcase. The black bag contained various lists of contributors and his itinerary. His scheduled route included the cities of Syracuse, Pittsburgh, Cleveland, Cincinnati and Detroit, among others. Buffalo was conspicuously absent because that city was home to Murray Seidman and was strictly in the dean's territory. Mr. Seidman would not only give Rabbi Steiner his annual donation, but he would also call upon a number of friends and relatives to support the yeshiva.

Rabbi Brill presented his American passport at customs. This was his primary reason for maintaining dual citizenship. Twenty minutes saved at the end of a long flight was quite meaningful. He thereupon proceeded to wait for his baggage, which was fairly light. Israelis as a rule leave the country with empty suitcases and come back with full ones. Each member of the family and a number of close friends and relatives expect the traveler to pick up items in America that are not readily available in Israel. In the main plaza, he met his sister, Rachel, and together they drove to his mother's house.

His mother was delighted to see him and had prepared a home-cooked meal featuring the traditional European foods that he didn't get too often in Jerusalem. His father had passed away a few years earlier, but his mother was able to maintain the family home. She inquired about her daughter-in-law and all the grandchildren and then mercifully let her son catch up on his sleep.

On Sunday, Rabbi Brill caught the early evening plane to Syracuse and used the flight to sort out his list for the city. The short size of the list reflected the fact that Syracuse had a small Jewish community and all of the donors could be seen in the space of two days. Over the years, Rabbi Brill had culled the Syracuse list to eliminate those who gave less than fifty dollars. The typical contribution was a hundred. The only time the rule was breached was when a new contributor was involved. The amount of a first time contribution was not significant, because by maintaining close contact with the new donor, the size of the contribution could be raised within a few years. It was necessary to add new names to the collection list to compensate for attrition. Some donors moved to Florida and others passed away.

The best that Syracuse had to offer was a Mr. Herman Feldman, my late father, who owned a department store on Onondoga Street. He never failed to contribute less than five hundred dollars. Since such a contribution required extra time and attention, Rabbi Brill preferred to see Dad at our home on DeWitt. My father never refused to grant him an appointment when he called.

At Hancock Field, Rabbi Brill took a bus to the Hotel Syracuse. The room was fairly expensive but, since the hotel was centrally located, it paid to spend the extra funds. The rabbi had an hour or so to study and review the route he would take the next day. He knew the city well enough to dispense with the street maps that he used during the early years of collecting.

Early Monday morning he entered Goldstein's Variety Store to speak to Mr. Henry Goldstein. Baruch preferred to start the day with a successful call, and Goldstein was very dependable in giving him his hundred dollars. It was during his brief conversation with Goldstein that he received a severe shock. Goldstein and my father were close friends who worshipped in the same synagogue and both were charitable men.

"Did you hear what happened to Mr. Feldman this Passover?" Goldstein asked him.

"No, I didn't," Rabbi Brill replied. "I hope it wasn't anything serious."

"Unfortunately, it was a terrible thing. He was driving home from a meeting at the shul when he was hit by another driver who was probably drunk. He only lasted a week after that, and died at University Hospital."

It was not the first time that Rabbi Brill had heard of sad events in donor families long after they occurred. There really was no reason for us to inform the yeshiva of my father's tragic passing. Dad was close to the rabbi of the community and the latter was quite capable of looking after ordinary matters such as the *kaddish* (the mourner's prayer) and *yahrzeit* (observance of the anniversary of the death).

Rabbi Brill proceeded with his rounds, but was very disturbed by what he had heard. My father was the type of Jew who could not easily be replaced, and his loss would affect many institutions that enjoyed his support. Even though Dad had come to America at a young age, he grew up in a traditional home. His own home was kosher and he attended the synagogue on a daily basis. He was a Sabbath observer who had a strong feeling for tradition. He never went to work or conducted any business matters on the day of rest. I have experienced the Sabbath in lots of homes but I can't recall one that had a warmer Sabbath spirit than my own. Whenever a man of this nature passes away, collectors worry whether his children will follow him in terms of charity.

Rabbi Brill was also wondering what sort of a reception he would get from my mother. Even if no money were involved, he felt duty-bound to pay a condolence call on the family. He picked up a phone and was able to speak to mother directly.

"I was shocked to hear of your terrible loss," Rabbi Brill told her. "He was one of the finest men I knew, and his heart was always in the right place. It was a pleasure to be received so warmly whenever I came to see him. If it's all right with you, I would like to visit and express my condolences personally. This is just a social call in the nature of our friendship. I am not thinking in terms of the yeshiva."

Rabbi Brill was surprised at her warm response. "There are certain matters that I wish to discuss with you, Rabbi, and certain questions I have with which Rabbi Stern can't help me." Rabbi Stern was the rabbi of the local synagogue and Rabbi Brill always called on him for his personal contribution and a grant from the synagogue charity funds disbursed at his discretion. The local rabbi was a sincere young man, but not too worldly. Syracuse was just a starting position for him.

"Would seven-thirty be a good time?" Rabbi Brill asked.

"Just about right," she answered. "I'm looking forward to seeing you."

Our home is situated on Dewitt Boulevard. It is an older colonial wood frame home with four bedrooms upstairs. Although we could have afforded a much more lavish home, Dad was comfortable in the family house and saw no reason to move. In this location he was still able to walk to the synagogue on the

Sabbath and holidays. The furnishings in the house reflected the wealth of our family and the good taste of my mother. She was a classic homemaker and had no outside interests. The wallpaper was of an older style as were the carpets and the curtains.

"Can I get you a drink, Rabbi?" she said, after he was seated in the living room.

Our home was strictly kosher and Rabbi Brill did not hesitate to eat there. Nevertheless, he felt uneasy about Mom entertaining him during her time of sorrow. Technically, a wife's mourning period for a husband is only thirty days, but emotionally it lasts much longer.

"No, thanks," said the rabbi, "maybe some other time. I understand that you and Herman were married for more than forty years."

"Last Chanukah we celebrated our forty-third anniversary. My husband was 68 when he died, but he was in good health and he went to the business everyday. We had a wonderful life together and we have three fine children."

Rabbi Brill had met my older brother at the store some years earlier. He knew that Daniel, the youngest, was still in school, but he knew absolutely nothing about me. The rabbi spoke with my mother for a while until she brought up the matter that she wished to discuss with him.

"As you know, the accident was very sudden, but I had the good fortune to be able to talk to my husband for more than a week at the hospital. He knew that he would not survive his injuries, but his mind was clear and he was able to instruct me in certain very important areas. One of the things he asked me to do was to maintain his charities including his donations to your yeshiva. I don't think he trusted our son in this matter. Michael is a good boy and he supports the shul, the Center, the Federation, and the United Fund. He doesn't know much about yeshivot, though, and I don't think he would be very helpful to you. That's why Herman asked me to mail donations to all the names on his list. He kept a special book of his favorite charities."

"That's the way it should be. In most cases when our older donors pass away the children tend to disassociate themselves from their parents' charities. I hope that you will be able to continue your husband's generosity for many more years."

"I certainly will be doing that," she said. "He had a particular liking for you and your school. Whenever you visited, he always enjoyed hearing about life in Israel, especially Jerusalem. We were in Israel a few times, but that was before your yeshiva was built.

"Now," she continued, "there is something more than my annual donation that I am thinking about. My husband was, thank God, a successful man and left me in a very comfortable position. I have more than enough to live on and I will leave my children a handsome inheritance in addition to the business. What I have in mind is some sort of memorial to honor my husband. I have already put up a plaque in his honor in the local synagogue but it doesn't have the same meaning as a memorial in Jerusalem, the Holy City."

Rabbi Brill sensed that a major donation was in the offing and he was well aware that such matters were over his head. Larger donations were handled only by Rabbi Steiner. He was just an ordinary collector and could hardly recall ever receiving a donation for more than a thousand dollars. He didn't even know the rates for the major dedications at the yeshiva, although he often studied the plaques that hung on the walls in various parts of the building.

"That would be a very noble gesture," he said to my mother. "It's not only a memorial in the Holy City, but a memorial in a yeshiva where the students study Torah day and night. Their learning would be dedicated to the soul of Mr. Feldman, of blessed memory, and I am sure that the students will pray for your continued health. You can also make arrangements to have kaddish recited at the appropriate times."

"I have already made arrangements for kaddish," she replied. "My son recites kaddish whenever he is at shul. Since he doesn't go all the time, Rabbi Stern arranged for kaddish to be said at a yeshiva in Baltimore. I would rather have something that is part of a permanent institution and would be of benefit to Torah scholars."

"There are many fine opportunities for dedications at the yeshiva," Rabbi Brill said. "It could be a room or a study hall or even a full apartment. There are also scholarships which may be established." He had enough fund-raising experience to flatter the donor by mentioning the costly items first although he did not imagine that my mother was ready to dedicate an apartment or even a study hall. That is why he also included scholarships, which he assumed would be in her reach.

"No scholarships, please" she said. "The money gets used up in a year or two and there is nothing left unless I keep repeating the contribution each time. This is a single gift and I want something that will last at least through my lifetime."

Rabbi Brill composed his response to mother's request very carefully. "Your husband's death was a complete surprise to me and I did not come prepared to negotiate a memorial with you. Of course you know that I hold only an academic position at the school. I am the senior faculty member, and I do make one collection trip a year, but I am not familiar with all the opportunities available at the school and what donors are expected to contribute when subscribing. When I get back to the hotel, I will make arrangements to call Israel and speak with Rabbi Steiner, the dean. He can always be reached at 6:30 in the morning, Israel time, because he is at home studying before the morning services.

I will discuss with him what arrangements can be made. Since I will be in town another day, I would like to visit with you again tomorrow night and offer you an opportunity to select a suitable memorial. I will also work out an inscription for the memorial plaque while I am here."

"That is very kind of you, Rabbi Brill. I really appreciate your personal interest. I know that the memorial is very important to you, but there is something else that I wish to discuss, something of a more personal nature. That is the matter of my daughter, Sandra. It caused Herman a lot of grief over the past years, and me as well. I am hoping that you will be able to find some solution for the problem that I have with her."

"Your daughter?" Rabbi Brill asked, "I would have imagined that she would be happily married."

"Well, she's not married anymore, and I'm not sure how happy she was when she was married."

"Did this happen recently?" the rabbi asked.

"She's been divorced for about a year. The case cost us a fortune of money, but it was well worth it to be rid of that awful fellow she was living with."

"Were there any children?"

"Thank God for that, there were no children," she replied. "Sandra met Steven at the university about five years ago and fell hopelessly in love with him. He was smart but not serious about life, quite content to live off Sandra's money and exploit her to the limit. Meanwhile, he wasn't getting anywhere with his studies or with his career."

Rabbi Brill pondered the situation for a minute. In his position he had enough experience not to accept a one-sided version of a marital failure at face value. He therefore decided to question my mother a little more deeply. "Sandra must have seen something in him to get so strongly attached."

My mother adopted a somewhat milder stance. "You have to understand my daughter. She is a brilliant girl, a real beauty, and I am not talking just like a mother. Everyone considers her something special. The problem is that she doesn't think of settling down and raising a family like other women. She lives to have fun and enjoy life. That is what attracted her to this fellow in the first place. He had absolutely no ambition other than having a good time."

"Did you and Mr. Feldman approve of the marriage?"

"We were dead set against it but my husband was an old-fashioned man. He didn't believe in young people living together without being formally married. Even though he didn't like this Steven at all, he pushed Sandra into making it legal."

"From a religious point of view I can understand your husband's feelings," Rabbi Brill commented.

"It's a good point of view for a man and a woman who are serious about life. I am not so sure, though, that it is wise to enter into a marriage that is not based on wholesome family values."

"That is why it is so important to investigate things thoroughly before the couple gets serious," the rabbi said.

My mother reacted strongly to the implied criticism. "It was hardly necessary to investigate in this case. We told Sandra that this man was no good and would never amount to anything. She was, however, too deeply involved to listen to reason."

"When did her feelings for him change?"

"I'm afraid that they never really did. Deep down, I think she still loves him. Of course, once she caught him with another woman, her pride wouldn't let her stay married, no matter how she felt about him."

"Has she recovered at all?"

"Not really. She has her own apartment and we only see her on the Sabbath or when she comes over for meals. I recently dropped a hint about her getting married again, but she wasn't at all receptive. Given her beauty and her PhD in history, she would have no trouble at all finding a man. The problem is that she is still looking for someone who is wild and carefree, a man in the image of her first husband. I can't impress upon her the importance of settling down and adopting a more traditional life."

"Does she depend upon you financially?" the rabbi asked.

"Not in the least. My husband loved her very much and established a trust fund in her behalf that she could use while he was still alive. Two years ago she claimed the fund, and the money was awarded to her. She also has a full-time appointment teaching history at Cortland State College. There, she is an assistant professor and earns a very fine salary."

"I really think that matters will straighten themselves out after a while. Smart, rich and beautiful girls don't remain single for very long."

"I am not worried that she will stay single. I worry more that she will take up again with a good-for-nothing man and fall into another miserable marriage."

Rabbi Brill reflected upon the situation for a few moments. He wasn't sure whether my mother was merely unburdening herself or whether she really had some thought in her mind as to how he could be of assistance. "I sense that you have a serious problem with your daughter but I am not aware of how I can be of real help to you."

"I think you are in a very good position to do just that. You travel in many cities that have a Jewish population, and you meet successful businessmen and professionals on your trips. Perhaps you might run across some single young men in the business world or even some professional gentlemen. I know that you are not likely to meet academic types, but they are the ones I am most trying to avoid. Money is not an issue in this case. If it is a man who needs to be set up in business, we can take him into our own company. After all, we do need someone to replace my husband. If he is a professional man, we can help him set up an office."

Rabbi Brill was somewhat skeptical about my mother's hopes. Most of his donors were middle aged or older and their children tended to be married. Still it was possible that such an event could occur, and he didn't want to discourage her. "And, if I run into such a person, what will I tell him? I have never even seen your daughter."

"Listen, you said you will be coming back tomorrow to discuss my memorial at your yeshiva. It so happens that Sandra will be coming over in the evening, and you can meet her then. I also want you to join us for dinner. The meal will certainly be a welcome change from the tuna fish and Tam Tams that you have been eating at the hotel. Sandra will arrive at seven. Try to be here at six so we can finish our discussion before she arrives."

Rabbi Brill had eaten with my parents in previous years and he accepted the gracious invitation. "I might be able to do something for your daughter in Israel as well as in America. Would Sandra possibly be willing to move to Israel?"

"Everything is possible. She would even live at the North Pole if a man excited her enough. I am not sure, though, that any Israeli could meet her expectations in terms of culture and high living."

"You can never tell in such cases. Stranger things have happened. You do have to tell me a few facts about your daughter, though, things which would be difficult for me to ask her directly."

"What would you like to know?"

"For one thing, I have to know how religious your daughter is and what sort of Jewish background she has." The rabbi sensed that I was not observant. What concerned him more was whether I had an anti-religious attitude, or whether I had just drifted away from religious practice. In the latter case, he felt, there would be some hope of salvaging my soul.

"Well, this is Syracuse and there isn't much of a religious environment for young people. All of our children finished the local day school and were members of the NCSY Youth Group. They did, however, go to the public high school. When she finished high school, Herman suggested to Sandra that she go to Stern College in New York but she would have no part of such a school. Her heart was set on going to Syracuse University and that is what she did. As far as observance, she kept a semblance of kosher when she was married and she does now in her new apartment. Of course, I doubt that you would be willing to eat there."

"How about the Sabbath?"

"Well, you know that Mr. Feldman himself was a strict Sabbath observer. She would often go to the synagogue with him. But I don't think that she keeps the Sabbath at home. She still fasts on Yom Kippur and she never misses joining us for the holidays."

"Her Jewish knowledge?" Rabbi Brill was not overly impressed by my day school attendance. He had much experience with male day school students whose basic Jewish knowledge was sorely deficient.

"This may come as a surprise to you," my mother replied. "Sandra did very well in day school and developed a love for Israel and Jewish history. Since she majored in history in both college and graduate school, she has a superior knowledge of Jewish history. I know that she has read the Bible many times and is very conversant with all the philosophical Jewish works. Rabbi Stern is amazed at how much she knows."

"I think I now have a fairly good idea of your daughter's religious outlook. As far as personality and temperament, I will be able to judge for myself tomorrow night. Whatever I can do to help, I surely will. By the way, most of our marriages in Israel are arranged by *shadchanim* (matchmakers). Have you ever thought of trying one?"

"A *shadchan?*" A look of horror passed across my mother's face. "Even Mr. Feldman wouldn't have any part of such a thing. We ourselves went out on dates like any American couple before we got married. Sandra would be humiliated if she thought that her marriage was being arranged by anyone other than herself."

Rabbi Brill regretted his question almost as soon as he asked it. He realized that after being away from the States for almost 20 years, he had forgotten about some basic American cultural conventions. Shadchanim are anathema in America, even though they are an accepted part of the Israeli scene. Bidding my mother farewell, he returned to the hotel and waited until 11:30 P.M., when he could place the call to Rabbi Steiner.

5

RABBI STEINER TOOK THE CALL personally in the morning, Israeli time, with some anxiety. Rabbi Brill never called him from America except to inform him when he was returning to Israel and had to be picked up at the airport.

"Is everything all right, Baruch?" he asked. "Did you run into any difficulties?"

"Thank God, everything is in order. The trip was uncomfortable as usual, but my mother and the other members of my family are fine."

"Did I hear correctly that you are calling me from the Hotel Syracuse?"

"Yes, indeed. I ran into a situation in Syracuse where I need help and advice."

"What happened?"

"Does the Dean remember a Mr. Feldman from Syracuse?"

The dean had an encyclopedic memory when it came to the names of supporters of the yeshiva. He knew the exact amount of each donor's most recent contribution. My father was certainly not in the major gifts category, but he did give Rabbi Brill a substantial donation each time he came, and sent in several hundred dollars more in response to various appeals and solicitations. "Of course. Why? Did anything happen to him?"

"Yes. I regret to advise the Dean that Mr. Feldman was in a car accident this past spring and did not survive his injuries."

"Blessed is the True Judge." Rabbi Steiner intoned the traditional expression that must be offered when someone hears very bad news. "He was a very fine, traditional man, and he supported many charities including our yeshiva. I met him once before you joined our staff, and he gave me a thousand dollars to help start our school. That was during a visit that Mr. and Mrs. Feldman and their children made to Israel. I showed them the building plans and told them of my future hopes. Were you able to comfort the widow?"

"I did see her last night and that is why I am calling. Mrs. Feldman received me very warmly and spoke about Mr. Feldman's interest in the yeshiva and other Israeli institutions. It is her intention to establish a memorial to her late husband at our yeshiva. Of course, the Dean is aware that I am a simple emissary, a man who visits people and collects small donations. I have never negotiated a major gift and I don't even have the information necessary to do so."

"You have arranged for scholarships. Are we talking of something larger than that?"

"Absolutely. She wouldn't hear of any scholarship gift."

"From afar, it is hard for me to judge the potential. I gather that she has the means to do something of a quite generous nature."

"There is no problem of money. Mr. Feldman left her with substantial funds and she is quite comfortable. I don't think that she is in Mr. Seidman's class but I would think that when a rich woman talks of a permanent memorial, she realizes that there are more than a few thousand dollars involved."

"You have seen her over the years, Baruch, and can judge her spiritual level. Is she the type of woman who would be interested in dedicating a room or an apartment or even a school kitchen?"

"Not in the least. She is a woman who shared her husband's love of Torah. It would have to be something more sacred in nature."

"I have no objection to having Mr. Feldman's name engraved in one of our sacred areas. He was a righteous man and lived a very pious life, filled with charity and good deeds. Maybe we should think in terms of a classroom, a rabbi's study or even the library."

"I would be happy to suggest these opportunities to her but I am not aware of the subscription rates."

"I am glad that you have so immersed yourself in Torah that you have little knowledge of worldly affairs. Firstly, let me tell you that we have a set of printed amounts for each of these facilities. Secondly, let me add that we never collect the published rates for anything. The donor must feel that he is getting some sort of bargain. When we list something for $50,000, we are quite happy to sell it for less. We don't really lose money on such reductions. Once a donor has his name on a facility in an institution he becomes a lifelong friend. He identifies with the school and is eager to support it in future years."

"Well, I've learned something new about the business end of the school. Can the Dean be more specific about how I should proceed?"

"Psychologically, it is best to start very high. Sometimes you are pleasantly surprised and the donor accepts your suggestion. Even if the first suggestion is rejected, the tone is set for a generous gift and the contributor finds it hard to make a small offering. Start out with the study hall, which is listed for $100,000, and go down to the library at $50,000. After that there are classrooms for $36,000 and, finally, the dean's study for $25,000. Although it isn't shown on the printed list, you might also offer your own office for $18,000. On each level, you are authorized to accept as little as two-thirds of the posted rates. I will send you a fax after the lunch break today which will include a full description of memorial opportunities and the subscription amounts."

Rabbi Brill was somewhat overwhelmed with the amounts cited. "What do I do if she is only ready to give $5000 or $10,000?"

"There isn't much that you can do. As a last resort you might suggest a window or an ark cover. If that is all she is ready to donate, don't show disappointment. Get an agreement on the general text of the plaque before you leave. You have pledge cards with you so, whatever she pledges, have her sign for it. If it is a major gift, invite her and her family to come to Israel for the dedication."

Brief as they were, the dean's explanations relieved some of Rabbi Brill's anxieties. "Rabbi Steiner, thank you for your guidance on the dedication. There is another problem, though, that I'm not sure the Dean can help with. The matter concerns a daughter for whom she is seeking a husband."

"I can't believe that you are talking about her daughter, Sarah! When the family visited me some 14 years ago, I had a chance to speak with the girl. She had finished day school and spoke to me with such brilliance that I was amazed. I'm not sup-posed to notice such things, but she was also a very pretty girl. It would be very hard to imagine that a girl like that could remain single until the age of 27."

"Sandra did not exactly remain single. She is single now, but that is after a short, unhappy marriage. Would the Dean happen to know of any suitable young men for a girl of this sort?"

"Probably not, but this is not a matter to consider over the phone. I have to go to *daven* (pray) in a few minutes. Call me again if you achieve any good results or have any important questions."

The next day passed uneventfully. Rabbi Brill completed his scheduled solicitations by noon. After lunch, he visited prospects who were recommended by the original givers. Here the pickings were slimmer but he did manage to make one or two contacts that could be developed in future years. Most of his thoughts were probably on the meeting to take place with my mother that evening.

Promptly at 6:00 P.M., he arrived at our home and took his seat in the living room. My mother sat in the easy chair facing the couch waiting for Rabbi Brill to open the conversation. "Rabbi Steiner was deeply upset to hear about your tragic loss, Mrs. Feldman, and he asked me to convey his personal condolences. He remembers the family quite well from the visit you had with him in Israel some years ago. He appreciates the help that Mr. Feldman gave to start the yeshiva, and his generous support thereafter."

"How is Rabbi Steiner?" Mom asked.

"He is doing quite well, but his wife is ailing. Sadly, she recently discovered a tumor in her breast and is scheduled for surgery. Rabbi Steiner is very concerned about it and his worry shows on his face."

"That's certainly sad news," Mom replied. "In the last few years, though, some treatments seem to work if the tumor is caught early enough. Did you have a chance to speak to the rabbi about my memorial?"

"I did, indeed. He would be proud to have even the holiest facilities at the yeshiva dedicated in memory of Mr. Feldman."

"Did he mention anything in particular?"

"He made a number of suggestions that would fit your objectives perfectly. He described to me the larger facilities such as the main study hall and library, both of which are available. There are also two classrooms, the dean's office and my office, which is called the mashgiach's Counseling Room."

"What is the cost of dedicating these facilities?"

"Before I give you the published prices, I want you to understand something. These memorials are living memorials, not something out in the cemetery. Let's say, for example, that you reserve the study hall. In all of the yeshiva's letters and publications the Feldman Study Hall will be mentioned. In future years, hundreds of young men will remember that they studied Torah in the Feldman Beit Midrash. It is hard to put a value on having one's name on such an area.

"The other point to remember is that the rates quoted are the listed ones. Rabbi Steiner has authorized me to make certain allowances because of your husband's long association with the yeshiva and the type of person he was.

"Now, in answer to your question, I can tell you that the study hall is listed at $100,000. The library would cost $50,000, and each of the classrooms will go for $36,000. You can dedicate Rabbi Steiner's office for $25,000 and my office for $18,000."

My mother did not seem upset with the rates that Rabbi Brill quoted. "At the outset," she said, "you can eliminate the top and bottom items. The study hall would be a very nice memorial to my husband, but even with any reductions you may offer, it will be beyond what I can spend for this purpose. On the low end, I hope you will not be offended if I do not consider your own office. My husband used to tell me about his yeshiva in Poland and about the mashgiach. The latter had his place in the Beit Midrash and that is where he spoke to students. I can't visualize a mashgiach in a private office."

The rabbi was amazed that my mother could recall such things. In light of changing times, he felt a need to update her views. "You do realize that sometimes students have very personal matters to discuss?"

"Even so. My husband told me that he discussed such matters with the mashgiach in the study hall. The other students kept their distance and did not listen in. A good mashgiach never leaves the Beit Midrash."

"Maybe we think more along American lines today, instead of Polish ones, but I am not offended that you do not choose to dedicate my office." He was beginning to realize that my mother was not one who readily gave up entrenched ideas.

"Well," Mom said, "that leaves the library, a classroom, and the dean's office. You can eliminate the classrooms because they are not visible enough and important people rarely enter them. So I am now left with the library and Rabbi Steiner's office."

"Which would you prefer?"

"Obviously, I would prefer the library, but I am not ready to spend $50,000 for it. I am prepared to donate $30,000 for the privilege of having the yeshiva library dedicated to my late husband."

Rabbi Brill was astute enough not to accept the first offer while not rejecting it too harshly. "You are thinking in very positive terms, Mrs. Feldman, but perhaps you should have a better picture of what what we are talking about. The library is directly off the main study hall and is quite a large room. It is as big as two individual classrooms. Not only does it house all of the reference works, but there are three study tables for students to read volumes that do not circulate. Part of the library wall that faces the study hall is enclosed by a folding door. On Sabbath and holidays, women sit in the library and worship behind the curtain. The area involved is, in truth, the very heart of the yeshiva. Our books have been acquired over the years and they form a very valuable collection. It simply would not be fair for the yeshiva to give away one of its most precious memorial opportunities for less than the cost of a classroom."

"You did say that you are authorized to give me some reduction."

"Yes, I did. Given the type of person Mr. Feldman was and the support he gave the yeshiva, I am sure that Rabbi Steiner would agree to let you have the library for $40,000."

"That is somewhat more reasonable, but still not within my reach. When I first thought of a memorial, I assumed it would be in the range of $25,000. When you brought up the subject of a whole library, I was ready to go higher and I did." Mother spent a minute or two in reflection, and Rabbi Brill did not interrupt her thoughts. "All right," she said, "I am prepared to make my final offer. You know that 36 is a lucky number, twice the numerical value of *chai*, the Hebrew word for 'life.' I am ready, with a few conditions, to offer $36,000 for the library. It could be in a single payment, because it will come from the estate of my late husband. He set aside a goodly sum in his will for charity to be awarded as I determine. I have already made a donation to the local synagogue from this unassigned bequest."

Speaking calmly and trying to hide his inner emotions, Rabbi Brill replied, "The yeshiva will not reject a major donation for a matter of a few thousand dollars. You may consider your offer accepted and, as an official of the yeshiva, I am authorized to speak in the name of the school. Let me say that your generosity will long be remembered at our institution. What conditions did you have in mind?"

"Nothing important. I just want to make sure that the plaque is correctly inscribed and put in the proper place. I also want to be certain that the library is physically in the best possible shape. If it needs a painting or a cleaning, I expect that it will be done before the dedication."

"Rabbi Steiner prides himself on the condition in which the yeshiva is kept. Despite our tight budget, he has never reduced the maintenance expense. Nevertheless, I will make sure that the room is in perfect condition before you arrive."

"I didn't say anything about being there," my mother objected.

"It is Rabbi Steiner's policy that major facilities can be dedicated only in the presence of the donor and his family. It is my pleasure to convey, on his behalf, an official invitation to you and your family to visit the yeshiva for the dedication ceremony."

"That is very gracious of you and I do look forward to visiting Israel, maybe as early as this winter. As far as the family is concerned, I'm not sure that they will be able to attend. Michael takes care of the business and he would find it hard to leave at that time. Sandra's teaching at Cortland and Daniel is studying at Syracuse University. Those two might be able to make a short visit."

Rabbi Brill, who was still familiar with American academic calendars, was able to make a helpful suggestion. "This year the Chanukah holiday is late and coincides with the winter holidays and the vacation period in most schools. The Festival of Lights is a very appropriate time to dedicate a library and it would be a good idea to schedule it for then. It will give us enough time to prepare the library and the plaque for the ceremony.

"What about the inscriptions?" my mother asked.

"We live in a wonderful age, Mrs. Feldman. Rabbi Steiner had all the information about your family filed away. He requires that every donor leave his Hebrew name and the names of all the children whenever he visits the yeshiva. This morning, he asked a student who is studying to be a scribe to draw up data for inscriptions and he faxed them to me at the Hotel Syracuse. I did not have a chance to paste them up on a big sheet but I can lay out the pages on the dining room table for you. By the way, I see that Sandra's name is Sarah."

"Yes, she was named after my husband's mother. All of his family perished in the Holocaust, and he named the children after his deceased relatives."

"Do your children know of your proposed charity?"

"They know that I will be distributing a large sum to various charities. I mentioned that I would be giving some of it to Israeli institutions."

"Do you think they would object to your generosity?" Rabbi Brill had heard of many cases where senior donors pledged large sums only to have the children cancel them out before they were redeemed.

"I really doubt it. They have been supportive of me in the past, and I told you that they are all good kids. In any event, it makes no difference what they think. The money is legally mine to distribute in keeping with my husband's wishes. They certainly have no cause to feel that their father deprived them in any way. He left half of the business to them and the other half to me. That means that ultimately each child will own a third of a big department store. In addition, he set aside $1,000,000 in trust for each child to have at the age of 25, or earlier if married to a Jewish partner. Michael already has his money and, as I told you, Sandra got hers two years ago. Whatever else I may have said about her husband, there was no question about his being Jewish. The lawyer gave her the money when she asked for it. I don't know whether she spent trust fund money supporting him, but I tend to doubt it. In all probability, little Sandra is still a millionairess."

I never discussed my finances with my mother, but she was smart enough to estimate my worth.

Rabbi Brill then arranged the fax sheets in order. The inscription read:

THE FELDMAN MEMORIAL LIBRARY
of Yeshiva Beit Meir
Dedicated in memory of
MR. HERMAN FELDMAN
By his loving wife, Rachel, and his children
Michael, Sandra and Daniel
"And now write for yourselves this Book"
May his memory be a blessing forever
Chanukah, 1993

My mother was pleased with the inscription and made no changes to it. "I want Sandra to look at the wording because she is very versed in such matters. She should be here any minute now."

It was, in fact, only a few minutes later that I arrived. Rabbi Brill said some time later that he could not remember seeing a better-looking woman in his life. Of course, he doesn't watch television, never goes to the movies and doesn't read any magazines. Still, a girl likes to hear such a compliment, even if it is not exactly the voice of experience speaking.

"For you, Sarah, I can only repeat the verse that Abraham said to his wife, who was also named Sarah: 'I now know that you are a fair looking woman,'" Rabbi Brill said.

"That you took from Genesis," I replied. "The Egyptians also had the same opinion of Sarah, even though she was 65 years old at the time." My mother glowed with pride as she heard me show off my religious knowledge.

"I see that you still remember your Torah lessons," Rabbi Brill praised me. "You must have been a good student at the day school."

"I was one of the better ones," I answered, "but this knowledge is not from day school. In the course of graduate studies, I read the Bible over many times, not only in English, but also in the original Hebrew.

"Rabbi Steiner did mention that you were advanced in your studies and I see that his judgment was correct."

While seated at dinner, he asked me if I knew that my mother was dedicating a library at the yeshiva.

"I knew that she was talking to you about some memorial, but I had no idea that you would sell her a whole library. You must be a very persuasive salesman."

"Not at all. I am only a collector for one month a year and, in the past, I never negotiated a major gift. Given your mother's intentions and her charitable nature, I think anyone could have established this memorial with her."

"You are being very modest, Rabbi Brill. What do you do at the yeshiva when you are not collecting?"

"I'm the mashgiach for the yeshiva and the assistant director of the kollel, that is an institution for...."

This was an opening that my evil impulses could not resist and I didn't wait for him to finish. "Oh, you don't have to tell me what a kollel is. That's where married fellows spend their time instead of going to work."

A look of pain passed over Rabbi Brill's face. "That's a somewhat jaundiced view," he complained. "For one who has spent many years in graduate school, you should appreciate higher education. Many of our kollel students become rabbis and teachers and fulfill their family obligations honorably. I myself spent five years in a kollel."

"I wasn't talking about the really serious students," I backtracked defensively. "Admissions to the kollel are often based on piety rather than scholarship. I'm sure that many kollels have students who are going absolutely nowhere at other people's expense."

"I can't speak for other yeshivot," he answered. "At Beit Meir all applicants are thoroughly tested by Rabbi Steiner and when he finds a truly qualified student he offers him a special bonus to enroll. Even after the men start they are tested at frequent intervals."

"Your school may be an exception to the rule. From all that I have heard, it appears that many kollels are superfluous."

"I'm sure that you could say the same about many graduate schools in this country and virtually all of them are supported by public funds."

"One wrong does not justify another," I said. "But this is not the occasion to debate such matters. I would rather discuss the inscription on the plaque."

The rabbi was glad to change the subject because he feared that a heated debate would antagonize us. "By the way," he said. "I am glad that you are taking pains with regard to the inscription, because it is very important. I remember that once I had the occasion to visit a yeshiva not far from New York. One of my friends there pointed out a plaque which read:

In Loving Memory of
Robert Alan Green
Killed in Action
By His Parents
Mr. and Mrs. Joseph Green

"Of course, the text here is only a draft and I am open to suggestions," he said to me.

I studied the drawings for a minute and then replied. "I would prefer a different quotation if possible. Please use the verse from Genesis, 'This is the book of the Chronicles of Man.' It was considered by some rabbis of the Talmud as one of the most important verses in the Torah and I feel that is more appropriate to the memorial."

"That is a very apt choice," Rabbi Brill said. "Sarah, I would be very happy if your observance would someday match your knowledge. Nevertheless, we will be happy to accept your suggestion. Is there anything else you wish to add?"

I wasn't going to let him get the last word on my observance. "Rabbi, you have the right to feel that behavior rather than scholarship is primary, but I do not share your view. I see these two qualities as separate and distinct areas. I enjoy studying and I will continue to do so. As for my practices, I have no rigid guidelines about them and I could, if properly motivated, do more. But there are some rather obvious limits to my potential for observance."

"From what I understand, you have not gone totally astray," he replied. "I have personally seen men and women completely removed from religion who have returned to full observance. But, before we get off the track, give me the rest of the changes that you want on the plaque."

"You should include the date of my father's passing, the yahrzeit, if you will. My mother and I will certainly not forget, but I'm not sure about my brothers."

Rabbi Brill realized that both he and Rabbi Steiner had overlooked the yahrzeit: he hadn't requested the exact date of the passing and the dean didn't want to leave a blank in the artwork. "You are quite right, Sarah. Such information usually appears on memorial plaques. Please give me the date."

"My father passed away on the 28th of Nisan. Let me make the changes on the drawing." I wrote the date in Hebrew on the paper and also replaced the Biblical quotation in both Hebrew and English. "How is that?" I asked an utterly awed Rabbi Brill.

"Excellent. I couldn't do better myself."

Dinner continued and Rabbi Brill enjoyed the meal immensely. It was the old-fashioned American Orthodox cooking to which he was accustomed at his mother's home. His wife, who was a native Israeli, went heavier on salads and appetizers than he would have preferred. He repeatedly complimented my mother on her cooking.

Before he bade us farewell, he renewed Rabbi Steiner's invitation to us to visit Israel. He explained that Rabbi Steiner always desired to have major donors present when the facilities they donated were dedicated. He told us that the Seidman family from Buffalo was on hand for the dedication of the yeshiva building to which they contributed heavily. I was favorably inclined to accept the rabbi's invitation. "It might be a welcome change from Paris," I said. "Of course, I will have to shop for a more modest wardrobe."

"I am sure that you don't have to be instructed in what the laws of modesty require for women in Jerusalem," the rabbi said. "Just add another five inches to your dress, raise the neckline and lengthen the sleeves and your present attire might just about pass. Your mother would also have to cover her hair."

"You are forgetting that I was also married and, technically, I should cover my hair, even though I did not do so when I was married."

"You are right in a technical sense, but I feel that a hat would be sufficient in your case. I take it you know that you are not allowed to marry a Cohen."

The Cohanim are a priestly class among the Jewish people who may not marry divorcees, harlots and women of dubious lineage. "I hope you are only referring to my being a divorcee."

Rabbi Brill turned a little red. "I have no reason to think otherwise."

"Thank you. I doubt very much, though, that I will have enough time to meet someone suitable in Israel."

"You can never tell. But I would like to discuss the time period with you. It would be very helpful to the yeshiva if the library were dedicated at the end of your stay rather than at the beginning."

"Pray tell me why," I requested.

Rabbi Brill was quite open with us. "Sarah, you and your mother are very high class people. You have every right to expect a proper and dignified ceremony. From what I have seen of public rituals at our yeshiva, you would not be pleased at all with our arrangements. I am asking you to devote some time in advance to help us plan and carry out the dedication in an appropriate manner."

"That is hard to believe," I mused aloud. "How did you handle the Seidman family when they donated the money to start the yeshiva."

"Maybe I shouldn't reveal it, but the truth is that Rabbi Steiner hired a public relations man for a few weeks before the event and everything went reasonably well."

"Why can't he do the same thing again?"

"Rabbi Steiner has a peculiar weakness."

"Which is what?"

"He puts more faith in me than is warranted because I am an American who went to college. He will tell me 'Baruch, you know how these things are done. Plan a real nice service for the Feldmans that will make them happy.' I have never done any public relations in my life and I would not know where to begin."

"You begin with a budget. You need money for flowers and dancing girls and a good rock band...."

"Sandra," my mother screamed, "cut that out. Don't tease Rabbi Brill anymore. He asked for your help in a nice way and I want you to give it to him."

"Ok, Mother, I'll be a good girl and do it."

"That's better. If you will be courteous to Rabbi Brill I will ask him to set you up some nice dates in Israel."

"If you start that, Mother, I will change my mind."

My mother felt the need to reassure Rabbi Brill. "Don't listen to her, Rabbi. She likes to fool around. Actually she planned some very nice events at Cortland State and I am sure she will do the same at the yeshiva."

Rabbi Brill was visibly relieved. "Thank you Mrs. Feldman. There is one other matter that has to be settled. It is customary, when a large gift is in the offing, that the donor signs a pledge card for the amount. The yeshiva will then be able to send you a letter confirming the arrangement."

"That won't be necessary, Rabbi. While you were bantering with Sandra, I wrote out the check. Here it is. Put it somewhere where you won't lose it and then deposit it in a tax deductible account as soon as you can."

The rabbi handled the check for thirty-six thousand dollars as if it were a priceless manuscript. He had never held a single piece of paper of such worth and it gave him an eerie feeling.

Rabbi Brill felt that it would be advisable to explain to us the situation with regard to tax exemption. "This check will be deposited in the account of the American Friends of Beit Meir. The yeshiva maintains an office in New York and the IRS tax exemption was granted to the American Friends. We are, in fact, in better shape in this area than similar organizations because we actually conduct educational programs in the United States for our alumni and friends. None of those who ever made donations to the yeshiva have had any problems with the IRS."

After a few more minutes, Rabbi Brill took leave of us and returned to the Hotel Syracuse. He had planned to fax the pledge card to Rabbi Steiner in Israel but no pledge card had been signed. He then decided that it would be all right if he were to simply fax a copy of the check. The fax machine was in Rabbi Steiner's office and no one else had access to it. He scotch-taped the check to a blank sheet of paper. On the bottom he wrote a note to the effect that we would be visiting Israel for the library dedication at Chanukah. He added a request to Rabbi Steiner to call Mrs. Brill and tell her that he was well.

At a much later time in our relationship, Rabbi Brill confided his feelings to me when he returned to the hotel after meeting our family. He said that he had great difficulty falling asleep. He was excited about his unusual success and was disturbed by our conversation. It bothered him that a woman like me might be lost to the Jewish people. I could easily get involved with a non-Jewish professor and, despite my background and training, could enter into an intermarriage. Even if I didn't go that far, I could repeat the error of my first marriage and find a man who was antagonistic or unsympathetic to Torah Judaism.

Of course, he didn't think that there was much that he could do about it. He couldn't recommend a woman like me to any of his students as long as my religious conduct was so minimal. Even if I were to strengthen my observance, there was an attitudinal problem. I showed no reverence at all for the traditional dogmas and standard values. There is always hope for an uneducated woman to modify flippant and critical attitudes, but with highly educated and opinionated people, it is much harder to alter their ideas. Women who study in traditional schools do develop deep respect for their teachers and their institutions, but such feelings were clearly missing in my case.

He could not help comparing me to his own wife. His Rivka was a paradigm of faith and virtue. She prayed daily and recited Psalms. She would not take any important action in life without first asking her rabbi. Appearance and dress were secondary to her. She must have been a very good student in her Beis Yaakov school, but her fundamental knowledge had not increased much since then.

Rabbi Brill finally let himself be overcome by sleep. Tomorrow he would be in Rochester to start his collections in that city. Rochester would be followed by other communities, until the entire route was covered. It was ironic that within the space of a few hours, he had raised as much money as he would in thirty days of collecting.

6

BY THE TIME RABBI BRILL returned to Jerusalem, word of his success had spread through the yeshiva and among the families connected to the school. Rabbi Steiner told Rivka about it and she, being under no constraints of silence, casually told one or two of her close friends. She asked them to keep the matter quiet but, given institutional mores, she was guilty of some wishful thinking.

When he returned to work for the fall semester, Rabbi Brill sensed an increase in respect and deference on the part of his students and other faculty members. It was not that he was ever lightly regarded at the school. Far from it. As the mashgiach and head of the kollel, he was in effect the manager of day to day studies at the school. When Rabbi Steiner was busy or traveling abroad, Rabbi Brill was the final authority on academic matters. Some of the instructors who had previously been calling him Baruch were now addressing him frequently in the third person. A teacher was now likely to ask, "Would the Mashgiach object if I undertook such and such a program?"

The only place where enthusiasm was lacking was in the dean's office. Rabbi Steiner had always been very warm to Baruch and treated him as a son. Now, some of the warmth seemed to have dissipated. Rabbi Brill was at a loss to explain the change and his wife had to explain matters to him.

"Baruch," she said, "the rabbis teach us that two kings cannot share the same throne. Until now, Rabbi Steiner had no competition in the administrative area. True, you went out to collect once a year, but collectors are not highly regarded in the yeshiva world. Once you start bringing in major donations, you change from being a collector to being a genuine fund-raiser. Fund-raisers carry a lot of weight in an institution because everybody is dependent upon them. Rabbi Steiner now views you as a threat to his monopoly."

"I can't see why that should be the case," Baruch argued. "We are all working for the same institution. I have been scrupulously loyal and respectful to the dean. With my minimal experience in administration and fund-raising, I hardly pose a threat to anyone."

"I'm sure that he is not afraid that you will attempt to push him aside. Things are more subtle than that. You remember the story of King Saul and David. Saul was a great warrior but David was even more successful. When the women of Israel started chanting that Saul conquered the thousands while David defeated the tens of thousands, King Saul became insanely jealous and took ill. It is not the money you brought in that is bothering Rabbi Steiner but the adulation that you are now receiving which, in the past, was reserved only for him."

When Rabbi Brill began to understand the nature of the situation, he was much less disturbed by it. He persisted in treating Rabbi Steiner with reverence and respect.

On numerous occasions his thoughts wandered back to me, and he felt the need to do something in my behalf. The possibility arose one evening when he got a call from Mrs. Lili Goldberg. Lili, the wife of Rabbi Eliezer Goldberg, was a professional matchmaker. I didn't discover it until much later but I can tell you about it now. She was an American who knew the Israeli scene well enough to run a very successful enterprise. It was not idealism that drove her, but the necessity to supplement her family income.

Rabbi Goldberg was a teacher in an elementary school affiliated with one of the religious movements. Teachers in such institutions are paid even less than those in the state schools and work under more difficult conditions. With Lili's additional income, the family managed to survive. The rabbi had held an important pulpit in America but he readily gave it up to make aliyah to Israel. He never achieved great success in the Holy Land but not once did he regret his decision to make the move.

On the phone, Lili asked to see Rabbi Brill personally. Such meetings were usually held in the rabbi's office before the night session began. The late session started at eight and Rabbi Brill had to be present. He arranged for Lili to come at seven, which would permit her at least a full hour to take care of her business.

To get to his office, Lili had to pass through the back part of the study hall. There were only a few boys present when she arrived and none of them took any real notice of her coming. She was a familiar figure at the yeshiva and her visits were followed in a few months by some notice of an engagement or wedding. Whenever they saw her, the boys wondered who would next be sacrificed on the altar of matrimony.

"I heard that you were extremely successful on your last visit to America," she said by way of opening the conversation.

"Where did you hear that?"

"It is my business to hear everything that goes on in the yeshiva world. Information is vital to my work."

"I won't deny that I did well, but nothing has changed.

You can still come in and talk to me whenever you have any merchandise to sell."

The term 'merchandise' may seem a little crass when referring to eligible young ladies. That, however, is a translation problem. Rabbi Brill used the Hebrew term 's'chora,' which has a far more complimentary connotation than mere goods.

"The merchandise that I have tonight doesn't have to be sold. This particular item will sell itself."

Rabbi Brill had heard the same line on previous occasions and was no longer as gullible. He proceeded very cautiously. "It so happens that we do have several students who have approached me about marriage. As a rule, I never bring up the subject with students who are under 23. I just let nature take its course and wait for them to come to me when they are ready. If they pass the age of 23, I pursue them actively because Rabbi Steiner feels that it is wrong for a man of that age to remain unmarried. But I want to make sure that any girls you recommend are of high quality. Some of those that you sent in the past discouraged the students so badly that they lost their faith in the institution of marriage." The rabbi really wasn't serious when he said it but Lili was very sensitive on that point.

"How can you say that, Rabbi Brill," she said with a pained look on her face. "I screen all my customers very carefully because I have to worry about my reputation. It may surprise you that one of the girls you complained about in the past has just given birth to her fifth child to a very fine gentleman."

"Taste in such matters varies with the individual. Tell me what you have to offer."

"Before I even tell you about her, I must advise you that unless the student you suggest is at the very top of the advanced class, it doesn't even pay to continue. This one requires a *Talmid chacham*, a Torah scholar, who is absolutely superior."

"Two of my students who are looking for girls do meet that criteria," the rabbi replied. "The other two are good students but not world beaters. What makes your client so special?"

"The girl, Chana – I can't reveal the family name yet because you would recognize it right away – is a superb student. She has finished Beis Yaakov at the top of her class and is quite serious about her studies. Her family is prominent and her father is a very distinguished scholar who serves on a Rabbinical Court. She's an attractive girl with a good sense of humor and a fine personality. I can guarantee you that for any boy who meets her it will be love at first sight."

Rabbi Brill sensed that he was dealing with class merchandise on this occasion and he freely described the two students of higher academic status. Lili preferred the student called Jacob, and she asked Rabbi Brill to talk to him.

"I will be glad to talk to the man if you give me the name of the family. If anything results, the yeshiva will guarantee your fee in case the groom's family can't afford it. There is, however, one condition that I wish to impose upon you before proceeding."

"I will be glad to meet the usual conditions."

"This is not the usual request. This time I need some help for a woman, not a man."

"That is quite unusual for you. Do any of the faculty have single female relatives, or do you want to reserve someone for your daughter eight years in advance?" Rabbi Brill had a daughter who had just celebrated her tenth birthday.

"No, this is not for a young girl and not for an Israeli. She is not a relative or related to any of the yeshiva families."

"You are not going into competition with me, I hope?"

"No. This is a one-time venture. If there is anything in this world that I would rather not be, it is a shadchan. In this case, I have given my word to the mother that I would try my best to help her solve her problem with her daughter."

This incident, by the way, I learned from Lili and Rivka Brill. The rabbi was afraid to tell me that he actually approached a shadchan in my behalf. Lili was still a little suspicious.

"You're some sort of good Samaritan all of a sudden?" she asked. "What makes you feel obligated to a mother who asks you to find a match for her daughter? Such women ask every person they meet to find a husband for their girl."

"It happens that I have an obligation to this mother. She has just dedicated the yeshiva library as a memorial to her late husband."

"You mean Mrs. Feldman? Well, that is entirely different. You should have said so in the first place. What's wrong with the girl?"

"Absolutely nothing. She is a very good-looking woman and the most brilliant one I ever listened to. It also doesn't hurt that she has $1,000,000 in the bank in her own name."

Lili was stunned. She couldn't believe what she was hearing and for a moment she feared that Rabbi Brill had taken leave of his senses.

"Somehow I think your fund-raising success has gone to your head, Rabbi Brill, and you are seeing everything through rose-colored glasses. If your young lady is everything you say she is, she doesn't need a shadchan but a division of the Israeli army to keep all the men away."

"This is not a situation that lends itself to simplification. The young lady is about 27 years old and has no trouble at all in finding suitors. In fact, she has already been married and divorced. The problem lies in her attitude. She seems to go for playboys and, despite her first failure, she would marry the same type of man again. Her mother wants me to find a settled businessman or professional who would like to build a family and be an acceptable member of the community. She couldn't stand the girl's first husband and can't stand any of the men she currently goes around with."

Once the situation became clear, Lili's verdict was not long in coming. "You really have a problem on your hands, Rabbi Brill. Normal single men of 30 are not easy to find either in Israel or in America. If by a miracle you found a man who would meet the standards of a good-looking millionairess, she would not think of marrying him because she would consider him a bore. Such girls don't give a shadchan the time of day. Even if the mother would promise me a $50,000 fee, I wouldn't touch the case with a ten foot pole."

Rabbi Brill described my religious background and observance to Lili. "If she could find a Modern Orthodox man, she would keep a kosher home and observe the Sabbath. If she doesn't find such a man, she could easily get involved with a non-believer or, God forbid, a non-Jew."

"That is not unusual in America," Lili said. "Girls from some of the finest homes wind up outside the faith and are lost to our people forever."

"I know you think that you can't help me now but in these matters one cannot foresee the future. If you do happen to run in to anyone that meets the requirements, please let me know at once. The yeshiva will underwrite your fee and I will throw in something else for you. If you are successful in finding her a shiduch, I will designate you as the official shadchan of our yeshiva for the next two years."

Lili was amazed at the largesse of Rabbi Brill. Currently Rabbi Brill was rotating the yeshiva's shiduchim among three shadchanim. Given an average of 10 marriages arranged during the year, Lili's take was three or four matches. Being the exclusive shadchan would bring her six to seven extra matches a year, or somewhere in the neighborhood of 13,000 shekels of added income that she could sorely use.

"I see that you are willing to pay a very high price for this girl. I will not make any promises, but I will keep my eyes open. Who knows? God may be good to both of us."

7

AS THE DATE OF THE library dedication drew nearer, Rabbi Brill became increasingly tense. This was his first public ceremony and the people involved would not make it easier for him. He could manage with my mother, because she had a traditional European upbringing and was a humble woman despite her wealth. It was me that he was worried about. Not only was I knowledgeable, but I was known for having a sharp tongue and being totally irrepressible. He was worried that I would say the wrong things, wear the wrong clothes and make demands that the yeshiva could not meet.

At the beginning of December, he confided his fears to Rabbi Steiner. "We will have to fix up the library for the dedication," he said. "I hope the Dean has set aside some of the money that I brought in."

Rabbi Steiner looked at him with some dismay. "The function of a library is to provide reference books for students. Thank God, our collection of books is sufficient for the purpose. So far the students have not required any books that were not available at the yeshiva. In fact, I would be very happy if they mastered even half of the books that we do have. It is not necessary for the library to be a show place. I know that in those institutions where the libraries are overly ornate, three or more librarians are employed just to remove the dust from the books. You will not find that condition in our library. Perhaps you worry too much about your princess in America. This is a yeshiva, not Buckingham Palace."

Rabbi Brill was enough of an American not to share the dean's philosophy. He was also offended by the implication that his judgments were being affected by the influences that I was exerting upon him. "I am taking a special interest in this case," Rabbi Brill replied, "because it was my solicitation and I personally promised the mother, not the daughter, that the library would be in top shape."

Rabbi Steiner sensed some of the umbrage and he hastened to placate Rabbi Brill. "Rest assured, Baruch, there is enough money left from the gift to paint the library. I can recommend the painter who paints the dormitory rooms to do the job."

Rabbi Brill winced noticeably. "That fellow is not qualified for such a job. He gets most of the paint on the windows and on the floors. I really need a higher class painter for this project."

"You can have a better painter if you can find one," Rabbi Steiner said unhappily, "but you can't close the library down."

"We do have to move the books around. How am I going to paint behind the bookshelves?" Rabbi Brill asked.

"Let's not overdo this thing. There's hardly any need to paint behind the books. Just paint around the bookcases."

Rabbi Brill felt a sharp pain in his stomach. "Perhaps the Dean has forgotten that there are only two wooden bookcases. The rest of the bookshelves are open metal bookcases that are screwed together. It would look terrible if someone painted around bookcases of that nature."

"I'm sorry, Baruch. What you are talking about will not only cost a lot of money but take several weeks. I'm not even sure that you can get the work done before your party arrives in Israel."

Not having any choice in the matter, Rabbi Brill asked his wife to call around and get the name of a good painter. "Most of the people I know," she said, "don't do much painting and, when they do, they hire yeshiva boys on vacation. These boys may or may not be good students, but painters they're not."

"Perhaps, you have some friends who are somewhat better off. Please try to find someone."

A day later, she came up with a name and Rabbi Brill asked the man to come and see him. When the painter arrived, Rabbi Brill sensed that he was looking at an accomplished tradesman. "I'd like you to paint the yeshiva library," he said to him, "and do a good job of it."

"What happened?" the painter asked incredulously. "Somebody died and left you a million dollars?"

"Not quite that much," Rabbi Brill answered, "but enough so that the library can be fixed up."

The painter followed him to the library and was satisfied that the job was big enough to warrant his attention. "There is plenty of work here and we will need a lot of help moving the books."

"The books have to be covered, but they stay where they are."

"You're kidding. It's winter. I need the work but not that badly. Listen, painters live on their reputation and I would ruin mine if I worked around those open shelves. The paint would never match the color behind the books. Why don't you hire some boys from the yeshiva. Give them a few shekels and tell them what to do. No painter worth the name would undertake the messy situation you have here."

A very discouraged Rabbi Brill realized that he was fighting a losing battle. Lacking a choice, he called the dorm painter and told him what had to be done. He begged him not to get too much paint on the floor or the bookcases, although he knew that his request was futile.

The rabbi had more success with the plaque maker. This man was a true artist and he was able to design and lay out a plaque that would meet with universal approval. He had made many plaques for the yeshiva and knew exactly what was required. He promised a proper installation and, most importantly, he assured Rabbi Brill that he would be ready with the work on time.

A couple of weeks later, the painter was still on the job when we arrived in Israel. The flight was a pleasant, ten-hour trip and traveling first class made it much better. We rented a car at the airport and drove at a leisurely speed to Jerusalem. I was surprised at the extent of new construction since my previous visit. It seems that the country was on a firm footing and quite confident of its future. After we checked in and had dinner, I placed a call to Rabbi Brill. It was early evening on Tuesday when I reached him.

"We're in the King David Hotel now," I said, "and I would like to meet with you tomorrow."

"How was your trip, and how are you all feeling?"

"We are all well, thank you, but a little jet-lagged. My younger brother came along to participate in the ceremony. What time will you be free tomorrow?"

Rabbi Brill thought quickly. He needed another day to clean up the painting mess and figured it would be best to schedule the meeting in the evening. "I would be delighted to see you at seven tomorrow night. We will have at least an hour before the night classes begin."

"I would rather not waste the whole day," I said, "as time

is short. We have to set the date and place of the ceremony, because we have many friends to invite. Even if you can't see us, I would like to visit the yeshiva and get an idea as to what has to be done."

The last thing that Rabbi Brill wanted was to have me wander around the Beit Midrash unattended, asking questions of the students. "All right then," he said in resignation, "you can come during our lunch hour, which runs from 12:00 to 1:45 P.M. At the end of the break we daven the afternoon prayers."

I asked him for the best route to the yeshiva and assured him that I would see him at noon. As soon as I got off the phone, Rabbi Brill ran to the library and told the painter to clean up as quickly as possible and get out. Even to his untrained eye, the library would not pass muster.

The next day, I arrived with my mother and brother and, since the students were still in class, the rabbi was able to usher our party into his office without attracting too much attention. He was pleasantly surprised by my appearance. I was wearing a long dress, well below my knees, with sleeves of proper length. My head was fully covered with a hat.

"I want you to know," I said, noticing his approving glance, "that I had to travel to Boro Park in Brooklyn to buy these clothes. I hope that everyone will be happy." Rabbi Brill's office was in back of the study hall, while the library was off the front part of the hall. He could have walked me through the study hall to the library, but he chose not to. He didn't want me to get used to the idea that I could walk through the hall while the students were studying. Instead, he led me through the corridor in the building to the rear library door. As soon as I entered the library, I shrieked in horror.

"What happened here?" I asked. "I know that you have to help the blind, but do you have to employ them as painters? And when is he going to finish behind the bookcases. At most, we only have ten days."

I could see that Baruch was very uncomfortable. He shrugged in resignation. "Sarah, I want you to know that I feel the same way that you do about the library. Unfortunately, Rabbi Steiner was not disposed to closing the library for an extended period to allow for proper painting."

I turned to my brother and said, "Daniel, I have to meet with Rabbi Steiner. While I am doing that, drive mother around and show her some of the sights in the city. Pick me up later in the afternoon."

"You won't be too hard on Rabbi Steiner, I hope," Rabbi Brill said anxiously. "He is a man who believes in functionality rather than aesthetics and, even in its present state, the library has served its purpose for twelve years."

I made an effort to remain calm and handle the situation in a more rational manner. "A library of holy books is a sacred place, would you not admit?"

"It most certainly is," Baruch responded.

"In that case you may apply the verse 'This is my God, and I will glorify him.' That means that our religious objects and places must be surrounded by beauty. I'm sure that Rabbi Steiner knows the verse, because he davens every day."

For a few months, Rabbi Brill had forgotten about my knowledge. It was going to be an interesting session between Rabbi Steiner and me. Rabbi Brill would have loved to be present, but discretion told him that it would be wisest for him to stay away. Since Rabbi Steiner was in his office, he led us back to the office area. Introductions were not necessary because we all remembered the rabbi from our previous visit. Rabbi Steiner, for his part, never forgot anyone.

"Sarah would like a few words with you, Rabbi Steiner, and

I told her that it would be all right." He escorted my mother and brother out of the office and walked with them to their car.

"I must tell you," Rabbi Steiner said to me, "that it was a wonderful gesture on the part of your family to dedicate the yeshiva library. It is a very appropriate memorial to your late father, may his soul rest in peace."

"My mother thought so too," I replied, "and my brother and I went along with her. There is, however, a matter that I wish to discuss with you. Rabbi Brill promised us, when we subscribed to the library, that the facility would be put into excellent condition."

"Of course, my daughter," Rabbi Steiner said. "I was well aware of the commitment that Rabbi Brill made, and I am sure that you will be happy to know that I authorized Rabbi Brill to have the room painted."

Instead of just complaining, I decided to approach the matter in a more scholarly manner. "Rabbi, let me ask you why Moses erected the Tabernacle in the desert and why Solomon built a Holy Temple in this very city."

Rabbi Steiner was shocked at my temerity. No student would have ever addressed him in that manner. Nevertheless, our family was now a patron of the yeshiva and had to be dealt with cautiously. He therefore decided to give me a straight answer.

"King Solomon, himself, explains that the Temple was built essentially for prayer. It is written that the King said, 'Behold I have built for Thee a House of worship.'"

"I take it that the Tabernacle in the desert was built for the same purpose, although the prayers were entirely sacrificial in nature rather than oral?"

"I guess it would be correct to say that." He was getting a little irritated and his blue eyes were glaring at me.

"Then I may conclude that the functional aspect of these facilities was worship?"

"Certainly."

"It is possible to worship in simple surroundings, is it not? In fact, our ancestors, Abraham, Isaac, and Jacob, all worshipped in the open fields."

Rabbi Steiner was catching on rather quickly as to the direction in which I was heading. "Yes," he answered cautiously.

"Do you know how much gold and silver and wool and seal skins and precious jewels were collected to build the Tabernacle and Temple and make them beautiful structures?"

"The Torah and the Book of Kings do list the material in detail."

"Do you remember that King David said, 'How can I live in a house of Cedars when the Holy Ark resides in a tent?'"

"What exactly are you driving at?" the dean demanded.

"I will put it to you simply. When you build a House of God, whether it is a synagogue or a yeshiva or a library of sacred books, the place has to be aesthetic, not just clean. Remember that we are told, 'They shall make for Me a Temple of worship, and I will dwell in their midst'. I would hate to think that when the spirit of God is in our library, it should be subjected to your idea of a paint job."

Rabbi Steiner realized that not only was I lacking in respect but that I also possessed a very sharp tongue. "You are unfortunately right, Sarah. Deep down, I would like to make the yeshiva a showplace. Remember, however, that our yeshiva supports a large number of families and numerous students who all require food to eat. Given your knowledge, you know that if there is no bread, there is no Torah. Certain things take priority, and we have very limited resources."

"Are you telling me that if you had the funds, you would improve the physical appearance of the library?"

"I am, indeed."

"In that case we have resolved the matter. I will assume full responsibility for putting the library in shape both financially and aesthetically. I will even take pains not to disrupt the students in their studies. We can move the critical books to back tables in the Beit Midrash. If anyone needs an exotic reference book from within the library, I will dig it out personally. All I need is your permission to go ahead."

"I don't see how I can refuse such an offer. But, promise me, Sarah, that you will stay within the bounds of propriety when you work on the project."

"Don't you see the length of my skirt and my sleeves? I made a special trip to Boro Park to buy them."

"I did notice that you were dressed modestly. But I cannot believe that you dress differently on other occasions."

"Why not?"

"It is so written in the Torah."

There I was at a loss. The only reference that I could think of was a verse in Exodus regulating the modesty of the priests when they ascended to the altar. I couldn't think of anything that governed the sleeve or skirt lengths of women.

"It escapes me at the moment where it is written," I said.

"I think you will find it in Deuteronomy. 'There shall not be seen in thee any unseemly thing.'"

"I thought that was only on battlefields."

"That's what results from learning the Torah literally and not studying the rabbinic commentaries. Of course we need God's help in battle, and unclean behavior will cause us to lose His support. But all of life is a battlefield, and we are in constant need of Divine protection. We cannot afford to fall into Divine disfavor at any time by indecorous behavior."

I decided not to contest the point and chose instead to reassure the dean. "I already promised Rabbi Brill that I will be on my best behavior while in Jerusalem. There are several other matters that we have to discuss, but they can wait. Can I get to work now?"

"You have my permission and blessing."

Rabbi Brill was waiting anxiously for me to emerge from my meeting with Rabbi Steiner. When I emerged with a cheerful look on my face, he was vastly relieved. "What did Rabbi Steiner tell you, Sarah?"

"He said I can do anything I want in the library, as long as I don't arouse any lustful thoughts, God protect us, in the minds of the students."

"That does not sound like an exact quote to me."

"I am paraphrasing a little. He actually used the term improprieties."

"That's much better. Let me take a break for Mincha and I'll meet you in the library afterwards."

8

AFTER THE SERVICES, RABBI BRILL posted one of the older students at the library door to make sure that we wouldn't be disturbed. A student could get a requested book from the shelves, but no one was to study in the library. "What is your plan, Sarah? We only have 10 days and very limited funds."

"The short time period is the problem. I already took care of the money end. In America, it wouldn't take me too long to get the job done, but this is the Middle East."

"Where do we start?"

"The library has to be closed as of tomorrow morning. Take out a couple of sets of the Talmud and commentaries such as the Rambams, the Turim and the Shulchan Aruchs. You can add some other codes of law and Responsa. Put all the books on the back tables tonight. The rest of the books will be available by special request only."

"How will they be available if they are covered?"

"Who said they will be covered?" I asked.

"How can you repaint if you don't cover the books, Sandra?"

"Who said anything about painting?" I replied.

"I thought you were unhappy with the paint job."

"I am, but no amount of paint can hide that awful plaster. The library is going to be paneled and the ceiling will get acoustic tiles and new lighting."

"That will cost a fortune," Rabbi Brill objected.

"You are only entitled to worry about my behavior, not my money. Do you know any contractors in this city?"

"I know the fellow who remodeled the building that now houses our yeshiva. He is very successful and is now building real luxury housing. We can hardly afford his services anymore, but we call him for advice now and then."

"Can you please call and ask him to come over right away?"

Rabbi Brill called and reached the contractor on his cellular phone. "Yossi," he said, "we need you at the yeshiva. Can you get here as soon as possible?"

"What happened?" the latter said with a touch of cynicism. "You know I didn't guarantee the building for 12 years. You have a broken window or a stopped-up pipe?"

"It's more serious than that. We need someone who is a first class builder," Rabbi Brill pleaded.

"I'm really too busy now to give free advice. Call me after Chanuka."

Rabbi Brill held his hand over the receiver and whispered to me, "He says he's too busy now to give free advice."

I asked for the phone and started speaking to the contractor in flawless Hebrew. Rabbi Brill had never heard me speak Hebrew and he could hardly believe his ears. My Hebrew had only the slightest trace of an American accent. "Yossi," I purred, "I heard you were an outstanding builder and a man with a good heart. I am not asking for anything for free. You will be doing a big mitzvah and make lots of money in cold cash. Come down to the yeshiva as fast as you can."

"Do you know that the yeshiva owes me money for the last job I did for them a year ago?"

"This is my money we are talking about now, not theirs. Humor me and come down here, and I'll talk to Rabbi Steiner about clearing up his outstanding bill." Yossi finally gave in and showed up at the yeshiva some twenty minutes later. I was more than he expected, and he was happy that he had let me talk him into coming. I requested that he gather a crew of carpenters and get the room fixed up in a week.

"Right now I can spare only one man and a helper. If we get some rainy weather, I might be able to spare a second carpenter. Within a month we should have it ready."

"Listen, Yossi. We can't wait a month. In ten days, we have to dedicate the library. Every important person in town will be there. I will personally get up and praise you for your superb cooperation. Think of what that will do for your business."

"It will get me ten more requests for donation of services. Sarah, can you really pay what this is going to cost? In America, you can get good panels for eight dollars a sheet. In Israel, the same panel may cost more than 100 shekels. Its hard to get a large number of matching panels and this room will need more than 40 of them. I may have to go to Tel Aviv to get them. Acoustic tiles are available locally, but they are also very expensive."

"The money will be in your hands before you finish, and I will give you an advance to buy material," I replied. "Have your men start putting in the furring strips tomorrow morning. As soon as they get started, you drive me to the lumberyard and let me pick out the panels and the tile. You don't have to schlep to Tel Aviv. I will select panels so that they have enough on hand to get them started. They can get the additional panels in one day. Take a few minutes to measure and give me an estimate for the job."

Yossi paced off the library in both directions and said, "In

Israel we estimate everything by meterage. A panel is about 3 square meters. Good paneling will run between 200 and 300 shekels installed. Corners and cutouts add to the cost. The panelling, then, can easily run you 15,000 shekels. Ceiling tile is cheaper because the labor doesn't have to be as skilled. We may, however, need scaffolding, and that will increase the cost."

"I'll meet your price, but you must promise me the work will get done even if you have to roll up your sleeves and pitch in. Do we have a deal?"

"We have a deal. Rabbi Brill, if you could get this young lady to manage your affairs, you wouldn't have any problems at all. She's a real *metzia*, a real find!"

"Why, thank you, Yossi, that's real kind of you to say so. Start getting things organized and I'll meet you here tomorrow morning."

After Yossi left, I asked Rabbi Brill for additional time. Since he didn't have to teach any more that day, he continued the discussion with me in his office. The conversation focused on the ceremony itself.

"I want you to understand, Rabbi Brill, that if I request an elaborate affair, I am not seeking my personal glory. I get more than enough honors all year. I am doing this primarily for my mother. She lived a very quiet existence in the shadow of my father and had nothing else in her life but him. If a lot of attention is focused on her, and she is made to feel important, her self-confidence will increase, and she will be able to face her grief in a better way. Of course, the yeshiva will also gain by the exposure."

"I understand your motivation, Sarah, and it appears to be wholesome. Rabbi Steiner, however, has done his utmost to keep the yeshiva out of the limelight and not attract undue attention to the institution."

"He's afraid of the evil eye?" I asked.

"It's not only that. He firmly believes that 'honor eludes those who chase after it.'"

"My experience has taught me differently, Rabbi Brill. I have often seen that those who avoid exposure are not practicing humility but are evading public scrutiny. I take it that this institution has no Board of Directors or overseers and that Rabbi Steiner can do whatever he pleases."

Rabbi Brill was not going to let my accusation pass without an attempt at rebuttal. "That is not entirely true. Leaving aside the fact that we believe that God is always looking over our shoulders and keeping tabs on us, there are limiting factors on earth as well. A yeshiva lives and dies on its reputation. If we produce knowledgeable and God-fearing students, the yeshiva will be well-regarded and flourish accordingly. No amount of publicity can cover up poor work. In the end, the truth always emerges."

"Don't count on it," was my response. "I have directed the winning campaigns of our congressman from Syracuse for the last two elections. He is a very good man and relatively honest as congressmen go. Nevertheless, without projecting a positive image for him in the media, no one would have voted for him. I am not saying that you should put an ad in the paper saying that your faculty is smarter than the rest or that a recent survey shows that your students are 11% more God-fearing than those in similar schools. Such things are done more subtly. You praise a student who gets a faculty appointment in a prestigious yeshiva or you relate how your students visit the sick or help the needy in the community.

"Dedicating a library," I continued, "is a sign of communal acceptance, a sign of growth and an indication of scholarship. One of the main criteria in academic evaluations is the quality of the school library. I think an event such as this should be shared with the community."

"How are you planning to do that? You wouldn't want me to send around a sound truck as synagogues do when they usher in a new Torah scroll."

"That won't be necessary."

"What then?"

"Let me tell you my general plan. I am thinking of an early ceremony that would be open to the students and the general public. That would be followed be a dinner for invited guests in the school dining room. Finally, the library would be dedicated and a short meeting would be held in it with my family and the faculty."

"You apparently do things on a very broad scale," Rabbi Brill said. "We are not exactly a State University. I have a feeling that Rabbi Steiner will go along with the dinner and would certainly approve of the library meeting, as long as the men and women sit separately at both functions. However, I don't think that he will agree to the public meeting, and we have no room for it in any event."

I realized that Rabbi Brill was in awe of Rabbi Steiner and would never muster the courage to argue an issue to the point where he could prevail. "You have been with Rabbi Steiner for twelve years, and you still haven't learned how to get your way with him. Let me handle that end of it. What we have to work out is only the place. I guess an outdoor event is not feasible at this time of year."

"Not at all. It is cold and wet in Jerusalem now and it gets dark very early. It wouldn't make sense to have it earlier in the day and split up the ceremonies, because that would make it harder for all concerned."

"Are there any public buildings around here?"

Rabbi Brill pondered the question and mused aloud. "The nearby synagogues are small and Rabbi Steiner would not consent to holding it in another yeshiva."

"What about a girls' school? That wouldn't represent any competition."

"Say. That's not a bad idea. There is a big Beis Yaakov school down the block. They have an auditorium that can seat several hundred people and since the room is often used for worship, they must have curtains to separate the sexes."

"I can accept the idea of separate seating, but are you saying that Rabbi Steiner would require the women to sit behind curtains when no worship is going to take place?"

"I am saying that Rabbi Steiner would require that women sit behind curtains when no worship is going to take place. It is the customary practice here to separate men and women even at social events."

"I'm willing to wager that Rabbi Steiner's father allowed public meetings in Vienna where the women weren't forced to sit behind curtains."

"You are probably right, but times have changed. Regardless of his personal convictions, Rabbi Steiner cannot allow the yeshiva to depart in the least from the most stringent religious practices prevailing in Jerusalem. The pressure to conform has never been greater. Deviating in any way would ruin the reputation of the yeshiva."

I wasn't going to make a stand on the separation issue, but I had to have a public meeting or else our family and friends would find the dinner unbearable.

"I guess that it's time for another talk with the worthy dean."

"Probably, but be careful, Sarah. Rabbi Steiner is not in the best of health and it would hardly be right to add to his many burdens."

Late in the afternoon I got in to see Rabbi Steiner again. My plan was to soft-pedal my approach – give in on a few points that were dispensable, but try to achieve my main objectives.

After outlining my program for the ceremonies, I waited for Rabbi Steiner's verdict.

"I can see the need for a dinner," he said, "because that would be a 'seudat mitzvah', a meal associated with religious observance. Obviously the library has to be dedicated. I do not know why you need a private meeting and why the faculty wives should be invited to attend. A public ceremony before the dinner, especially one that would disrupt our students from studying, is out of the question."

"Let's take one thing at a time," I said. "The purpose of the private meeting is for me and my mother to make some additional presentations to the yeshiva. I hardly think that you would allow me, a sharp-tongued female, to speak at a larger yeshiva gathering."

"We would be very happy to announce the additional gifts in your behalf at the main gathering."

"Sorry, Rabbi Steiner. If we're good enough to give the money we are good enough to present it. Your idea would be like taxation without representation, a policy that Americans cannot accept."

"I will certainly allow you to present the gifts. What I am afraid of is that you might choose the occasion to make a speech advising the faculty to remodel the yeshiva in your image."

I felt like saying that it wouldn't be a bad idea, but I remembered that Rabbi Brill had cautioned me about aggravating Rabbi Steiner. "We will not burst into song. Even Moses and King

Solomon listened to women talking, so from a religious point of view there is nothing objectionable to our speaking." I knew that religious men are not allowed to listen to women singing.

The dean chose not to argue further. "If you limit yourself to merely announcing your gift, we would allow it at the faculty meeting. Will your mother also be making a presentation?"

"My mother will make hers, I will make mine, and my brother will also speak for himself."

Rabbi Steiner accepted the inevitable. There would certainly be a few thousand dollars involved now, and even more in future years. Some of the faculty might be uncomfortable with me but this was not the issue upon which to take a stand.

"May I ask you again why you have to impose upon the wives?"

Here I decided not to hold back. "These women make it possible for their husbands to teach at the wages you pay them. They forego basic necessities, and they skimp and struggle to make ends meet. Why should they be denied the opportunity to participate in a social affair? It is customary at all institutions of learning for faculty spouses to attend school social gatherings.

The dean responded, "Is it not written in the Psalms, 'The glory of the King's daughter is to be found within?'"

The verse was familiar to me, but I had never heard it used for this purpose. "How can you possibly use that beautiful verse to subjugate women and confine them to home? A woman should certainly develop her inner qualities, but must she keep them hidden from public view? Even the classical Woman of Valor was trading with the Canaanites while her husband studied in the gates. Are you suggesting that women are in some way inferior to men?"

Rabbi Steiner certainly knew enough not to fall into such an obvious trap. "Not at all," he replied. "Men and women have different spheres of activity and were endowed with special gifts by the Creator to best meet their unique assignments. A woman's responsibility is to her husband, her home and her children. That is a very essential area of human life and should command a woman's full attention and resources. She is by her nature best suited for such tasks."

"You must subscribe to the German expression 'Children, kitchen and church are for women.'" My quotation was voiced in polished German, which Rabbi Steiner knew well. I can speak French and German and can translate from Greek and Latin when necessary.

"There have been some exceptions to the rule but, in general, a woman fulfills her manifest destiny best when she is at home." It wasn't long before the truth began to dawn on me. Rabbi Steiner wasn't really concerned about giving the faculty wives a night off from their drudgery; he was afraid that I, an enlightened career woman, would not present a proper role model for the wives.

"I gather that you take a dim view of women university professors."

"I will not demean intellectual endeavors, but I would not encourage my daughters or daughters-in-law to follow in such a path."

"Do you think the faculty wives might become tainted if they hear the dean praise a woman who holds her own in a man's world, and to whom marriage is not the only goal in life?"

Rabbi Steiner did not hide the truth. "There is some merit to your assessment."

"Then I have an appropriate verse for you," I said with a smile. "How about 'A golden ring in the nose of a swine; that is a beautiful woman without discretion.'"

"To that I can agree. But let's conclude the matter. Since you have your heart set upon appearing before the faculty and their wives, I will let you invite them. But I will not pressure the men to come or bring their spouses."

"That's fine with me. Now I would like to explain why I have come to the conclusion that we need a public affair in addition to the dinner. There are two reasons for it. The dinner will be held at the yeshiva and, even excluding the students, you cannot accommodate more than 100 people. Half of those would be our friends and relatives and the other half would be patrons of the yeshiva. The general public, the neighbors of the yeshiva and the students would be excluded. Furthermore the dinner would not be suitable for the words of Torah that should be expressed on such an occasion. Many of the guests would not understand what was being said. The public affair could accommodate the students and the distinguished rabbinic scholars who would attend."

"You wish to corrupt my students as well as my faculty and their wives? We have always tried to shelter our students from fund-raising activities."

"Fear not. I will not ask to speak at the public affair. I will maintain a low profile, and Rabbi Brill has made it abundantly clear that the women in my family will have to be hidden behind a curtain."

"Where will you hold the open affair? The study hall cannot accommodate the students and all the guests."

"Rabbi Brill is making arrangements to rent the auditorium in the nearby Beis Yaakov school."

"But that place can seat more than 300 people."

Once more, I sensed the need to embark on a learned discussion. "Rabbi, did you not previously address me as your daughter?"

"Yes, as a courtesy."

"Didn't you apply a verse to me which referred to the daughter of a king as a princess?"

"All Jewish women are so considered."

"Well, if am a princess then you, my father, are a king, and we may apply the Biblical verse, 'In large multitudes is to be found the glory of the king.'"

"You are more of a devil than a princess and the devils who quote Scriptures are the worse kind."

"It is so kind of you to say that," I replied without anger.

"I take it that you will gather up the multitudes?"

"Yes, I will, and I will request you to invite the scholars."

"And who else?"

"I would like one of the chief rabbis and Rabbi Stern.'"

"Who, may I ask, is Rabbi Stern?"

"Rabbi Stern is the rabbi of our local Orthodox synagogue where my father davened. He studied in Lakewood and was ordained at the Chaim Berlin Yeshiva. My mother insisted that he come because he was close to my father and can offer him a personal tribute in his memory. We paid for his tickets, and he and his rebbitzen will arrive next week."

"Whom do you have in mind to speak at the formal dinner?"

"Ministers, ambassadors, and other public figures. Leave that to me."

"You may have to pay some of them to appear. We paid good money for such men at the Seidman dedication and I'm not sure we got our money's worth."

"I guess there's nothing new under the sun."

"Who will conduct the various affairs?"

"I would be honored if you were to conduct the public affair. Rabbi Brill would make the presentation to my family on behalf of the yeshiva at the dinner."

"What would the woman who has everything choose for us to present to you?"

"What did you give the Seidmans?"

"We gave him a kiddish cup and her a set of candlesticks."

"For a quarter of a million dollars?" I said in amazement.

"It is not the monetary value that's important, it is the sentiment. Incidentally, it would be more proper for such gifts to be presented by the dean of the school himself."

I immediately sensed that I had struck a nerve by suggesting that Rabbi Brill make the official presentations, so I quickly backed off. "May Rabbi Brill at least address the audience? He did make the original solicitation, and he has visited with my family many times. He knew my father well."

"Certainly. Is there any special gift you would like?"

"For my mother, anything of a religious nature. For me, a husband in my own image."

"I don't know about the latter. We can give you an engraved copy of the 'Gates of Repentance.' If you abide by the teachings of the book you will have a better chance of securing your original choice of a gift. Who will conduct the dinner program?" the dean asked.

"I am open to suggestions. Perhaps a bilingual yeshiva patron with a good sense of humor or a retired American rabbi now living in Israel."

"Let me think about it and I'll be in touch with you."

The meeting over, I reported the results to Rabbi Brill. "I'll be here tomorrow morning to work with the carpenters. If you can get the books out of the library tonight, it would be helpful."

Back at the hotel, I spoke to my mother and advised her of what I was doing. My mother was quite shocked. "Don't get me wrong, Sandra. I'm happy that you are doing mitzvahs, but I didn't mean for you to spend a lot of your own money on my project."

"It's perfectly all right mother, I want you to be happy. If the library isn't in top shape and the ceremony isn't first class, you won't feel good about the whole affair."

"You're a wonderful daughter, Sandra, but you don't have to do this at your expense. By my estimate, you will be out $30,000 before you finish and I'm not even counting the extra presentations. To make matters worse, most of the money you spend will not be tax deductible. It's my library so, whatever it costs you to fix it up, I will pay for it. Whatever you spend on the dinner and the guest speakers will be your charity. Furthermore, wherever possible, try to get tax deductions. Give the money to the yeshiva as a donation and let them pay the bills."

I hadn't paid much attention to the tax angle. Material gifts to tax-exempt organizations are legitimate deductions, but you have to verify the costs. There might also be a problem when expenditures are made abroad. My mother is smart in these matters, so I followed her advice. Normally, I don't accept any financial assistance from Mom because I have enough money of my own. In this case, however, I was going overboard on the spending, so I didn't feel too bad about her bailing me out. "That's very sweet of you, mother, and I will accept your generosity." I believe in doing things right and I see where I learned it from.

9

I SHOWED UP AT THE yeshiva early Thursday morning and entered the library through the rear door. Yossi was waiting for me and there were already piles of lumber on the floor. "Yossi," I said, "I want you to know that these block walls are crooked. Before I let you put the panels on, I am going to use a level to check the furring strips vertically, and they'd better be straight. I am also going to check horizontally with a long board across eight or ten strips to see that every strip is in line. You may have to put in some shims to get it done right."

"You have nothing to fear, Sarah. I do everything just perfect."

"I hear that from every contractor and I've learned not to believe any of them."

"You are a fine lady and I'll make you happy."

This was my cue to solve another problem. "If you really want to make me happy, Yossi, get me three more carpenters right away."

"What for? You're going to panel the study hall, too? Even if you are, I can't spare my carpenters."

I pointed to the metal bookcases, none of which stood

straight, and said to Yossi: "No. I am going to replace this garbage with built-in bookcases."

"Oh, that's different," he said, with obvious relief. "For that you don't need carpenters. You need cabinetmakers, and they're easy to find because they charge so much they never have enough work to do. You going to use formica or a natural wood finish?"

"Which do you recommend?"

"Normally, I would suggest a natural finish, but if you are pressed for time you'd better use formica. With natural wood you need time to apply stain and then varnish or shellac. It will smell during the dedication and the shelves may not be dry enough for the books to be put on them."

I considered the alternatives and opted for expediency over beauty. "All right, formica it is. Get your men started and take me to the lumberyard. Do they sell formica there?"

"They have samples. You can pick your colors there, but let me order the formica elsewhere. It will be cheaper."

At the lumberyard, I was able to get a good match between the formica and the panels. I took Yossi aside and asked him what he paid for a sheet of formica. When he cited the price, I realized that it was not too far removed from the lumberyard cost. "If I can get them to meet your price will you let me buy it here?" I was afraid that Yossi would buy seconds at the small dealer.

"It makes no difference to me," he said.

"Listen," I told the manager of the yard. "We'll buy the panels at the quoted price if you will reduce the price on the formica to what Yossi gets it from his dealer."

He looked at me with disdain and said in a condescending voice, "I'm sorry, lady, we don't do business that way in Israel."

That got my dander up, and I told him how I felt about his attitude. "Yours is not the only lumberyard in this area. I checked the phone book and there are three more in town or nearby.

Come on, Yossi, tell him what he can do with his panels and let's get out of here." It didn't take the manager long to realize with whom he was dealing. I grew up in a very successful business family and wasn't anything like his regular passive customers. The markup on the panels was so generous that any rational dealer would quickly give me the discount on the formica. "Miss Feldman," he called after me, "I've reconsidered. You are buying the material for a good cause so we'll give you a better price."

Back at the yeshiva, I arranged to meet with Rabbi Brill again after Mincha. I then established my temporary office in the library and began to plan the ceremony. Fifteen minutes later a young student knocked on the door and said that Rabbi Steiner needed a 'Yoreh Deah,' a Code of Law, that had not been put on the back bench or was already in use.

"Which volume?" I asked, remembering that my father's set of this Code of Law came in three volumes.

The boy was somewhat embarrassed. "I'm not sure. I was going to look up the relevant section."

"What subject is the dean lecturing about?"

"He is teaching about immersion pools – *mikvas*."

"That's at the end of volume two," I said. "No one is allowed in the library now, so I'll get it for you." I had never formally studied the Codes of Law but once, out of curiosity, I looked up the laws relating to pre-marital immersion in a mikva. That was when my father insisted that I visit the mikva before marrying Steven. I remembered that the laws of immersion were in the second volume and they were immediately followed by the structural laws of immersion pools. I handed the book to the student and casually asked him if Rabbi Steiner was talking about a mikva that was presumed to be kosher but was found, upon measurement, to be short of the requisite 40 measures of water." The boy gasped in surprise. "How did you know that?"

"It is a subject that relates to the entire area of presumption based on the status quo. Pay attention because it will come up frequently in your Talmudic studies."

When the boy returned to class, Rabbi Steiner asked him whether the 'policewoman' had let him into the library.

"No," he answered, "she got the book for me herself."

"You told her which volume?"

"I wasn't sure myself. She asked me what the subject was and she said it was at the end of volume two."

Rabbi Steiner was stunned. He knew that I knew the Bible and philosophy but he didn't think I knew anything about the codes. The student then added, "She said that if I'm learning the laws about a mikva that was measured and found short, I should pay close attention because the law has important ramifications."

Rabbi Steiner didn't want the exchange to get out to the rest of the yeshiva, but too many students in the class had heard the boy's response. Asking the students to keep quiet about it would only hasten the spread of information. He shrugged his shoulders and said, "She happens to be right that this is a crucial case." He continued his lecture and made a mental note not to send any more students for library books.

Word spread quickly through the yeshiva and even reached the ears of Rabbi Brill. He gathered from the comments that not only did I have a lot of knowledge, but that Rabbi Steiner was not overly happy with my high-handed approach to the library.

When Baruch saw me next, he commented on my display of wisdom.

"I'm not sure that Rabbi Steiner enjoys the way you are doing things, but I am proud of your wide and varied knowledge."

"It really was nothing more than random chance and a lucky

guess. But I am dismayed at Rabbi Steiner's old-fashioned views on women. It is as if he never entered the twentieth century."

"He greatly respects women."

"Sure. As long as they know their place he holds them in the highest esteem. He apparently believes in the Talmudic expression that women are simple-minded."

Rabbi Brill took the time to explain the meaning of the rabbinic teaching to me. "The Talmud is not saying that women are stupid. Most people interpret that statement to mean that women are frivolous in their mental attitudes rather than dimwitted."

"If that is the interpretation, it is quite true. If women in the traditional society are barred from higher studies and relegated to dull, domestic chores, they will not readily develop into intellectual paragons. Do you, yourself, also believe that they should not study the Talmud?"

"They are not commanded to do so, as men are, and the Talmud discourages men from teaching them. There is nothing which prohibits women from studying Talmud on their own." He paused for a while before continuing. "This is a very interesting discussion, but I prefer not to digress from the main objective of our meeting, which is the planning of the dedication ceremony. We must go ahead with that."

I would have loved to probe the matter further but it was apparent that he wasn't too comfortable with the subject and wanted to avoid it. Reluctantly, I returned to the items that had to be dealt with.

"I think that Rabbi Steiner has agreed in principle to my plan for the ceremony. I will not be able to invite our friends and relatives to the public ceremony because it will be way over their heads. My mother, Rebbitzen Stern, and I will sit somewhere on the side behind a curtain. You will have to arrange for at least one curtain when you rent the hall from the Beis Yaakov."

Rabbi Brill could hardly believe that I was able to convince the dean to hold a large public meeting. "I don't how you do it, Sarah. You are the only one in this whole wide world who can get Rabbi Steiner to agree to do something that he really doesn't want to do. Did the dean say whom he plans to invite to the gathering?"

"I left that entirely up to him. I only insisted that one of the chief rabbis and Rabbi Stern, from Syracuse, be on the program."

"What sort of program do you have in mind for the dinner?"

"I requested that you say a few words and Rabbi Steiner will make the presentation to our family. The rest of the speakers will be prominent public figures."

"It wasn't necessary for you to go to bat for me."

"You are the second-in-command at the yeshiva and you did solicit the library donation from our family. You also knew my father personally. Why shouldn't you be on the program?"

"I recognize my importance to the school and to this ceremony. Nevertheless, Rabbi Steiner does not always view the instructors as established professionals. He would surely not want any of them to outshine him at a public ceremony."

"To be honest, I couldn't care less. You deserve to speak and, if he can't make peace with the idea, that's his problem. I also wanted you to make the presentations but, when he objected, I backed off. There he does have a valid claim that presentations should be made by the dean of the school."

"Which politicians do you have in mind?" Rabbi Brill asked.

"I'm hoping to get the American ambassador, the Minister of Religious Affairs and the Mayor of Jerusalem."

"How do you expect to swing all that?"

I had given the matter a lot of thought and was well prepared with the answer. "The key is the American Ambassador. Once I have him, I invite the Mayor and ask him to deliver greetings and introduce the Ambassador. The Mayor is new and would like to get closer to him. For the Minister of Religious Affairs, I may have to bestow a little bread on one of his pet institutions."

"Well, we're back at square one. How do we get the ambassador?"

"Apparently, you don't know all of my background. I believe I told you that I managed the recent campaigns of Congressman Harrison. He is one of the few Democrats ever elected from Syracuse, and he owes me a big one. He did invite me to run his office in Washington, but I didn't want to discontinue my studies. Congressman Harrison is now on the Foreign Relations Committee, and I will be speaking to him as soon as he gets to work, which is 9 A.M., American time."

"It is always good to have friends in high places. I hope that you will be successful. Who is going to be chairman of the dinner program?"

"As I said to Rabbi Steiner, I am open to suggestions. I need someone who speaks English well and who has some experience conducting public affairs. I do know a few people in Israel who could do it, but they know nothing about the yeshiva world, and Rabbi Steiner would find them even more objectionable than me."

"I will try to think of someone. What about the food?" the rabbi asked.

"Do you think the yeshiva cook can cater a decent affair?"

"Not at all. It is well beyond her capabilities."

"I'm sure that there are acceptable kosher caterers in Jerusalem. Maybe I should ask the chef at the King David to volunteer?"

"Don't you dare. I have enough trouble already. I will get in touch with the caterer who did my son's bar-mitzvah. She made a very nice affair and was easy to get along with."

Following my meeting with Rabbi Brill and additional work in the library, I took out my credit card and put in a call to the House Office Building for Congressman Harrison. I was put through right away.

"Hi, Sandra. You're calling from Israel?"

"Yes. My mother is dedicating a library in memory of my father at the Beit Meir Seminary. We would be very honored if the American Ambassador to Israel would personally convey a message to the assembled audience on that occasion."

"When is the ceremony taking place?"

"On Sunday night, December 28, in Jerusalem."

"It is of course the holiday season. If he is in the country, though, I will do my best to make sure that he comes. How come you didn't invite me to the dedication?"

I had not even imagined that Harrison would consider coming to Jerusalem, but I reacted very quickly. The congressman was a devout Christian, and I used that to my advantage.

"It was an oversight due, partially, to not wanting to impose upon you. On second thought, it would be a wonderful idea for you and your wife to spend Christmas visiting the shrines in Bethlehem and Jerusalem. It would help you with both your Jewish and Christian constituents back home and will give you something to talk about in your speeches. Let me now formally invite you to participate in our dedication ceremony together with the Ambassador. And I'll suggest to the Ambassador that he introduce you to several key figures in the Israeli government."

"It would be an excellent place to spend a week or so. We've already had twenty inches of snow in Syracuse and it's mighty cold. I'll drop over to the State Department and throw some weight around. Give me a number in Jerusalem where I can reach you this afternoon."

"Remember, there is a seven hour time difference. You can call me until 4:00 P.M., American time, at the King David Hotel in Jerusalem. After that it would be best to call me first thing in the morning, your time." I gave him the fax and phone numbers of both the King David and the yeshiva.

"Also," I added, "get in touch with the Israeli Embassy for guidebooks and other information. They will have the red carpet out for you when you arrive. If you can add another colleague or two to your mission, you are sure to get widespread press coverage."

I knew the congressman quite well. He wasn't too imaginative but, when given a good idea, he was persistent in following through. I had every reason to feel that I would be hearing from him before I went to sleep.

I scheduled meetings for Sunday morning with the caterer as well as with an electrician who was recommended to me. I wanted to install sunken fluorescent fixtures in the acoustic tile ceiling. That done, I took a cab over to the Ministry of Religious Affairs to convey an invitation to the minister to participate. The minister wasn't in but I was able to talk my way into seeing the director general of the Ministry and relate to him the nature of the invitation and the affair. The official couldn't commit the minister to attend.

"Can you at least schedule some time for me to invite him personally."

"That I can do," he said. "How about Sunday, early in the afternoon?"

"That's fine with me."

I left the office and returned to my hotel for dinner with the family. That evening, Rabbi Brill had a visitor in his office. It was none other than Lili herself.

"Rabbi Brill, I heard you really picked yourself a winner this time. I didn't trust you when you said she was good-looking but, from what reliable people told me, she's a knockout. What is more, I heard that she is turning the yeshiva upside down and Rabbi Steiner is having fits. I also heard that she is spending money hand over fist. Most important, I heard that she is very learned. You really have a hot property on your hands."

"I'm glad that you have come to tell me what I already knew three months ago. The question still remains: What can you do for me?"

"Rabbi Brill, I am not here to tell you of your good fortune. Now that I know that you weren't trying to mislead me, I am ready to do business with you."

"You have a man for her?"

"As a matter of fact, I do. He is 27 years old and a *baal teshuva*, a returnee to the faith. Before studying at a yeshiva in Israel, he was a practicing accountant. He has an MBA degree as well."

"What does he look like?"

"You know, Rabbi Brill, that I lie less than the other shadchanim. I saw the man, and he is really a good-looking fellow."

"How religious is he?"

"He has been studying in yeshiva for three years and by now he is fully observant. However, I am happy to say, he is not in the least fanatic."

"I don't know if Sandra will have time to see anyone during her visit. She is quite busy rebuilding the library and planning a big affair. Nevertheless, if she feels up to it I will certainly encourage her to meet him."

"Listen, Rabbi, I would like to talk to Sandra myself. I have never met her, and I make it a rule always to meet my clients before I set up arrangements for them."

"Over my dead body," he said. "If she gets wind that I spoke to a shadchan on her behalf, I'm through. I can introduce you to her casually if you promise not to reveal what you do for a living. As far as your candidate, however, I am afraid that he will feel that she is not religious enough."

Lili had matched enough odd couples not to be swayed by Rabbi Brill's hesitation. "I can tell him that she is educated and sympathetic to tradition. I feel that if she takes a liking to him, there is a fair chance that she will become fully observant."

Rabbi Brill still harbored strong doubts about Lili's optimistic approach. "I have no indication that that is indeed the case. You may be going out too far on a limb. Your customer may become angry for such a misrepresentation and may look for someone else to work for him."

"Customers get angry only when you send them ugly or dumb candidates. Religious issues may bar a marriage but they are not something for which a customer fires a shadchan. I am willing to take a chance."

"Tell me more about him, and I will try to arrange for him to take her to dinner," Rabbi Brill said.

"Dinner? Why can't they just sit in a hotel lobby like everyone else does and buy a drink?" Lili countered.

"I gather from your reluctance to set up a dinner date that your candidate lacks either money or table manners."

Lili defended herself.

"He comes from a fine family and has not lost his manners. He has, however, been in Israel for three years and has used up all his savings."

"The yeshiva will treat him to the dinner if the event can be set up."

"Thanks, Baruch, I knew I could depend on you. What time do you meet with her during the day?"

"I meet with her after Mincha. Your best bet is to come to the yeshiva tomorrow morning with a good explanation for your presence." Rabbi Brill spent a minute trying to develop a cover story for Lili and finally came up with a solid idea. "Wait a minute. Wasn't your husband a practicing American rabbi before he came to Israel?"

"He had a congregation for a few years."

"Did he run any congregational dinners?"

"As a matter of fact, he did. He is a good emcee and tells a lot of funny stories."

"In that case, I have a good cover story for you. Sandra is looking for someone to chair the presentation dinner. We'll tell Sandra that I suggested that you talk to her about having your husband emcee the dinner."

"That's a great idea and, if he does a good job, I hope you will suggest an appropriate gratuity. By the way, he gets along very well with Rabbi Steiner, so you won't have any problems with him on that score."

Once again, Rabbi Brill was being confronted with the suggestion that he and Rabbi Steiner were rivals. "I really don't understand why everyone thinks that I have a problem with Rabbi Steiner. He may begrudge my recent success to some degree, but the donations I've brought in to the school are minor when compared to his. I don't consider myself a threat to him. If people let their imaginations run wild, they will create a problem where none presently exists."

"Everyone knows that you are a learned scholar, Rabbi Brill, but a psychologist you are not. You are too innocent to know what's going on and you are too nice a guy to get involved in any infighting."

The next morning was Friday. I came to the library early, because the men were only going to work a half day. Rabbi Brill met me in the library. The school was quiet and the Beit Midrash was practically deserted.

"Did you hear anything from your congressman?" was the first thing he asked.

"Yes, indeed. I was told that he and two other congressmen have decided to visit Israel for the Christmas vacation. He definitely will be at the dedication. He also was at the State Department and got them to fax the Ambassador that I would be calling and that the congressman was requesting the Ambassador's cooperation, both with regard to the dedication ceremony and the visit of the congressional delegation."

"That was quick. What about the mayor and the minister of Religious Affairs?"

"I will see the Mayor when I get word from the ambassador. I am meeting with the minister on Sunday."

"You are doing very well. Listen, Sandra, there are two matters that I wish to take up with you, one business and one pleasure. Which would you like to consider first?"

10

"LET'S GET THE BUSINESS OUT of the way. Pleasure calls for leisurely indulgence."

"My wife and her good friend Lili Goldberg will be coming over to the yeshiva. My wife has heard a lot about you and wants to meet you. Lili might have the answer to your problem with an emcee. She is married to Rabbi Eliezer Goldberg, who teaches in one of the local elementary schools. He is American-born and held a pulpit in the States before he came on aliyah . He is a wonderful fellow with a good sense of humor and tells delightful stories. He might be the man you are looking for."

"Why doesn't he come around himself?"

"He is teaching today. Most of the lower schools are now on a six-day week. If his wife thinks it is feasible, she will set up an appointment. He doesn't do it professionally, but he has run a number of affairs. Of course a gratuity will be expected."

"Does anyone do anything for nothing in this country?" I asked.

"It does happen but, in this case it shouldn't be expected. The Goldbergs are poor and barely make ends meet. We are not talking of a fee, but a gratuity."

"What's the difference?"

"A fee is mandatory and fixed in advance. When a gratuity is given it reflects both an appreciation for the services and the generosity of the donor."

"I've just learned something new. I will be glad to meet Rivka and Lili. Now, what was the pleasure subject?"

"Sandra, it's really not fair for you to spend your entire vacation working in the library."

"I will be touring with the congressmen and their wives for a few days. With my background in history, I'm a very good guide."

"I have no doubt of that. But in the final analysis it's still work."

"What are you getting at?"

"I think you should take a night off for social purposes."

"There are some discos in Talpiot but I am not sure I should go there alone. I might meet a non-Jew and embarrass the yeshiva."

"I am not thinking of discos and I am not thinking of you going anywhere alone."

I was getting suspicious. "You're not setting up a date for me?"

"We can't call it that around here. Let's just say it's a social opportunity."

"This town is heaven for euphemisms. Educate me some more. How does one distinguish between a date and a social opportunity?"

"A date implies pure pleasure and, for a student of Torah, it can't be justified. A social opportunity may also be a pleasurable occasion, but there exists at least the possibility that a more permanent relationship might emerge from it."

"Rabbi Brill, I have this eerie feeling that you are engaging in a little matchmaking and, if I am correct, why are you doing it?"

"We are instructed to model our actions after the Almighty."

"The Almighty is a matchmaker?"

"Yes, indeed. The sages teach us that after having created the world the Almighty didn't have much left to do. So they say He decided to spend his time pairing off men and women."

"You mean the Almighty was responsible for my miserable marriage to one Steven Suswein?"

"You are too sophisticated to take the teaching literally, and you should sense the obvious conflict between free-will and predestination. If, in the end, the Almighty was going to push two people together, all parents and matchmakers would be superfluous. What the Almighty does is determine the ideal mate for each person. He imbues people with wisdom and understanding so that their actions lead them, if not to the ideal mate, then to some very close approximation of it. Those who follow the dictates of passion rather than following their intellect or the guidance of dispassionate others, may find themselves in a marriage with a partner who isn't, and doesn't even resemble, the Divinely preferred partner."

"Love is not intended to be an intellectual process," I protested. "It's an emotional one. You are making it into some sort of business decision."

"The concept of romantic love as the precursor of marriage is a relatively new development. It is the factor most responsible for the rising divorce rate in Western countries. Among the very Orthodox, the rule is now for arranged marriages. We have returned to a tradition that originated amongst our people thousands of years ago."

"I would normally not agree to any such procedure, but my mother has been harping on the idea of me going out in Israel, so I am willing to spend a night on it. Who is it that has been drafted to provide me with rest and relaxation?"

"He is a fine young man, a good-looking fellow. He has an MBA from Pace University and he is a CPA. He is a baal teshuva. Three years ago he came to a yeshiva in Israel to study and he has been there ever since. He is about your age and his name is Simon Grossman."

"He would be willing to go out with an American divorcee whose religious observance is marginal?"

"His observance was at one time worse than yours but he found his way back. He heard about you from some of his friends at our yeshiva and asked to meet you. He obviously thinks that you can be rehabilitated."

"What does he intend to do after he finishes studying?"

"He has a good profession to return to and I imagine that if he goes back to the States, he will resume his past career."

"My better judgment tells me to decline but since I don't follow my intellect in such matters, set it up for Monday night. What if he makes a pass at me?"

"He will not put a hand on you unless and until he is legally married to you."

"Too bad," I said, much to Rabbi Brill's dismay.

I went back to work and waited for the women who were coming to see me. They did come a half-hour later and were introduced by Rabbi Brill. Rivka had a pleasant face but was noticeably overweight. Her makeup was minimal and poorly applied. Her clothes had a ragged look and her wig was stringy. I wondered why Rabbi Brill, who was a handsome man, didn't tell her to clean up her act. Lili, on the other hand, looked neat and trim. For a woman who was supposed to be poor, she managed to project an air of success and accomplishment. I realized almost instinctively that Lili was not a homebody. I pegged her as a real estate agent or someone who ran a housewares store.

"I am pleased to meet you," said Lili. "You are as pretty as Rabbi Brill said you were."

Rivka almost bit her tongue. Her husband was a very pious man and it was not like him ever to say anything like that about any woman's looks. Even if he felt that way, he wouldn't express it in words. In any event, Rivka wasn't as taken by my looks as Lili was. Rivka was an Israeli woman who had lived in religious neighborhoods all her life. Her concept of beauty was not influenced by pictures of women in the American media and, like her husband, she never read secular newspapers or watched television. The papers she did read never ran pictures of women. When they had to show a woman in health or educational features, they ran a diagram of a cow and marked the required areas on the animal. "Thank you, Lili. You're quite attractive yourself. What sort of work do you do?"

"You might say I'm in something akin to sales."

"I thought so. What do you sell?"

"Household help," she said with a straight face. Rivka could hardly contain herself.

"Do you work, Rivka?

"Very hard. We have six children still at home and I am a housewife." Her English was as ragged as her outfit. She had learned the language in school and from working in the home of an English-speaking family before getting married.

"I understand that you were once a rebbetzin, Lili."

"I still am, although my husband no longer has a synagogue. He teaches in an elementary school."

"I am told that he is an experienced emcee."

"In America, he was very good at it. Here, speakers are introduced by name and title. More like 'Rabbi Simon, faculty advisor to wayward girls at the Beth Sarah Seminary, will now talk. Please keep quiet.'"

I smiled. "Do you think he would like to chair the library dedication dinner?"

"I'm pretty certain he would. Who exactly needs to be introduced?"

"The American ambassador, one or more congressmen, the Mayor of Jerusalem and the minister of Religious Affairs."

"I mean, like anyone important," Lili answered wryly.

I took a liking to her at once. Lili was a cynical, sophisticated American. "Rabbi Brill will be speaking and Rabbi Steiner will make presentations. I want your husband to give Rabbi Brill such an introduction that even Rivka won't recognize whom he is talking about."

"You had better curb your suicidal impulses, Sandra. Protocol is a Biblical imperative around here. Eliezer will have to meet with you to work out the order of speakers and get some background on the guests and your family. It will have to be late in the afternoon, because he teaches till four."

"Sunday afternoon will be fine," I replied.

The women took their leave and Lili walked Rivka home. "I think your Baruch has a good eye," Lili said to Rivka.

"I don't know what you mean."

"He brought in a real winner in that Sandra."

"He wasn't looking for anyone. It just happens that she is the daughter of one of his donors who happened to dedicate a library."

"I certainly hope that's all it is."

As soon as the women left, I put in a call to the American Embassy in Tel Aviv. I introduced myself as Dr. Sandra Feldman, former assistant to Congressman Harrison, and requested to speak to someone in charge. I was put right through to the charge d'affairs.

"Good morning, Dr. Feldman. Welcome to Israel. We did hear from the congressman, and the Ambassador asked me to speak to you and make preliminary arrangements. You mentioned when you called that you were an assistant to the congressman. Are you now employed by him?"

"No. I managed his last two campaigns from his Syracuse office. Between campaigns I am a professor of history at the State University at Cortland."

"What brings you to Israel?"

"Our family owns a large department store in Syracuse. My father, who founded the store, died a few months ago and the family has chosen to dedicate a library in his honor at the Beit Meir Seminary in Jerusalem."

"And you would like to have the Ambassador attend the dedication ceremony?"

"I deem this a very significant event. It will enable the Ambassador to increase friendship for America among members of the religious community in Israel, and will show our country's interest in the cultural life of this country."

"The Ambassador has already attended a number of ceremonies at museums and universities."

"I am sure that the Ambassador has created much good will in the secular and non-sectarian communities. But in the religious world, he is not sufficiently appreciated. They do form a sizable minority in the country."

"It so happens that the Ambassador has an evening function in Jerusalem on the 28th. If you can schedule him so that he can be out by 7:30 P.M., he will be able to attend."

"That's wonderful," I said.

"Do you know the country well, Dr. Feldman?"

"I would think so."

"In that case, let me request a favor of you. The Ambassador and many of the personnel would like to be free for the Christmas holiday. Since you worked for the congressman and know politics well, we would appreciate if you could share some of the responsibility for the touring and the meetings with government officials."

"I will be glad to take them around on the 24th and 25th. I speak Hebrew quite well and I will be able to guide them. You should meet them at Ben Gurion and drop word at the Foreign Ministry that they are coming, and that I am coordinating their tour. Also, please send me a profile on the Ambassador and I will send a summary of the dedication events and the important people involved." I left my address, fax and telephone numbers and secured the equivalent numbers from the embassy.

"Where are you going to spend the Sabbath?" Rabbi Brill asked me when I finished my calls.

"My mother finds Jerusalem almost as cold as Syracuse. We'll try to get a plane to Eilat. Don't worry, though, I'll be here Sunday morning."

"I'm not worried about Sunday, it's the Sabbath that bothers me."

"One may swim in a pool on the Sabbath. I know that people go to the mikva on Shabbat."

"In the mikva there is no question of laundering garments, a forbidden labor on the Sabbath."

"Then we have no problem at all. I'll tell my mother that you said it is preferable for me to swim without clothes."

"I said no such thing," Rabbi Brill said, his face red with

indignation. "Besides, didn't you say that you would observe the laws of modesty during your visit to Israel?"

"I was under the impression that my vows of modesty applied only to Jerusalem."

"Israel is one country and all of it is holy."

"Eilat is in the Biblical borders of Israel?"

"It was captured by King David and sanctified."

"It has to remain under Jewish control for that type of sanctification, does it not?"

"It is under Jewish rule."

"The Prime Minister is anointed?" Only kings anointed by prophets are deemed legitimate rulers under Jewish law.

"Cut the nonsense. Even if your present commitment to morality doesn't apply, your original one does."

"When did I make that one?"

"At Mount Sinai."

"You mean the one my soul undertook without asking me?"

"Yes. Your soul knew what would be best for you and acted accordingly."

I had had enough fun at Rabbi Brill's expense and did not bother to reply. I hadn't brought any minis or bikinis in any event, but I wasn't going to give Rabbi Brill the satisfaction of knowing that. I finished my work and drove back to the hotel. The weekend in Eilat gave me a chance to rest and spend more time with my family. I returned to the yeshiva on Sunday and set to work with renewed energy. After checking on the carpentry, I sat down with the caterer. The menu was standard, but I tried to impress upon the caterer that appearances were very important. I patiently went over the settings, the decorations and the food service. "It is only a yeshiva dinner," she complained, "not a royal wedding."

"As far as you are concerned, I want you to read the first

chapter of the Book of Esther and imagine that you are the caterer for King Achashverosh."

"Anything you say, but that type of service costs money."

"It might bring in some new business for you when people see you catering in style."

"It will probably scare away my regular customers."

The meeting with the electrician went more smoothly. He was a professional and knew what had to be done. Following a quick lunch, I took a cab over to the Ministry of Religious Affairs on Yafo Street. After a short wait, I was ushered into the office of Moshe Ben Zur, the minister. "I hear that you are quite a dynamic woman. How does someone like you fit into the yeshiva world?"

"I really don't; it's pretty alien to me," I replied. "I got into it because my mother was very depressed after the passing of my father. She wanted to set up a memorial for him and chose to do so in a yeshiva because my father always supported yeshivot in Israel. I'm here to see that the affair is run properly and that it leaves her with pleasant memories."

"How may I be of assistance to you?"

"My family would be very honored if you were to attend the ceremony and deliver greetings on behalf of the Israeli government."

The minister did not attempt to hide his surprise. "The very religious institutions in Israel do not share the philosophy of the secular governments," he explained. "Necessity brings them together at times, but these occasions are strictly of a business nature. In social affairs there is a wide gulf between them."

I was not fully aware of the situation when I undertook to invite the minister. "Did you clear this invitation with Rabbi Steiner?" he asked. "He may not exactly be thrilled with my presence at the dinner."

"I don't understand that. I was led to believe that the yeshiva was certified by the Ministry."

"We do certify the yeshiva and, to the limits of our ability, we support it. An allowance is given for every American Student and monthly payments are given for each kollel member. We also submit our approval of the yeshiva to other governmental agencies and, based on our certification, other funds and benefits may be forthcoming."

"So what is the problem?"

"The basic problem is that Rabbi Steiner is intimidated by right-wing elements who hate the government and the secular people who run it. They are essentially non-Zionist people whose views have come to dominate the traditional community. You see, Sandra, there are within the religious community two separate groups. One calls itself 'charedi' which roughly translates as God-fearing. The other calls itself 'dati', religious nationalist. The latter group is in decline, and they are being overwhelmed by the charedim."

"How does one tell the groups apart?"

"Superficially, it's very easy. The Religious Zionist yeshivot fully support the State of Israel and arrange for their young men to serve in the army. They have programs that integrate army service with learning. The charedim, on the other hand do not appreciate the political state and, with some exceptions, their children do not serve in the army at all."

"I had some inkling of that," I said. "Looking at the person himself, though, what makes the difference?"

"That is a somewhat gray area. In general terms, the Religious Zionist views religion as part of a life that has many facets. The charedi makes his religion the central aspect of his life and lets everything else revolve around it. This attitude affects his work, his education and his exposure to the society. He often seeks rabbinic sanction for even the most trivial aspects of life. As a result, he is frequently considered narrow-minded."

"Are you saying that Rabbi Steiner is a charedi?"

"It's hard to say, exactly, with the older generation. Rabbi Steiner grew up in Vienna in a cultured family in a cosmopolitan society. He is not charedi by inclination. In fact, he would adjust very well in a yeshiva that subscribed to the view of Rabbi Samson Raphael Hirsch, who preached Torah and worldliness. Unfortunately, his yeshiva finds itself in a charedi environment. Rabbi Steiner could not attract native Israelis if there were any such stigma attached to his school. The result is that in many areas he outdoes even the charedim, which explains why he might be reluctant to feature a government minister."

"I see. How about Rabbi Brill?"

"Rabbi Brill grew up in America. By the time he got to Lakewood he already had half of his college education and, eventually, he finished it. You will find in him a very compassionate soul. Of course he has not lost his awe of Rabbi Steiner and is completely under his sway. If he developed a little more self-confidence, he could chart a more flexible course."

"How about the yeshiva itself? How does it compare to the larger ones?"

"Scholastically, it is better than most of them and on a par with the very best. Whatever people may think of Rabbi Steiner's views, no one questions his absolute integrity. When our inspector comes in, the students whose names have been submitted to our Ministry are actually there. If a student leaves the yeshiva, he reports it immediately. He will never seek a penny that he is not entitled to. We do not examine the students directly, but we have never had a complaint from any parents and none of the teachers have ever filed a grievance."

"I take it that that is not always the case with other schools."

"I am not at liberty to make such statements."

"I understand. If it will put your mind at ease, I did tell Rabbi Steiner that I planned to invite government and public officials, and he voiced no objection."

"In that case, it will be my pleasure to attend."

I thanked the minister for his acceptance and for the time he devoted in clarifying the issues for me. I returned to the yeshiva and found Rabbi Goldberg waiting for me. Together we reviewed the list of speakers and drew up a tentative program. Rabbi Goldberg was quite articulate and had a light touch. I had the feeling that he would perform very well as host of the dinner.

Monday was also a busy and productive day for me. I completed the paperwork for the press releases and arranged for photography and video coverage. I made sure that American and Israeli flags were available and I called the police to arrange special protection for the affair. By mid-afternoon I left for the King David to prepare for my evening "social opportunity" with Simon Grossman.

11

SIMON CALLED MY SUITE FROM the lobby of the hotel shortly
after 6:00 P.M.

"How will I know that it's you?" I asked half seriously.

"I will be wearing a black hat on my head and a scared look
on my face."

For an unprepared answer I thought that was pretty good.
"Relax, Simon. I don't bite. I will be down in a minute." I was
dressed in one of my Boro Park specials. It managed to hide
most of my better attributes, as intended. I spotted Simon almost
instantly, a tall, good-looking fellow. He wasn't radiating great
joy, but he didn't look scared, either.

"Hi, there," I said cheerfully. "You must be Simon Grossman."

"And you're Sarah Feldman. I am very pleased to meet
you."

"What's that in your hand?"

"I brought you flowers."

"Yeshiva boys don't bring flowers on a first date. It's against
the Shulchan Aruch."

"Rabbi Brill makes his own Code of Law. He said flowers
and here they are."

"Thank you, Simon. I'll leave them at the desk and they will call my brother to pick them up. They are really very lovely."

"Would you like to take a walk before dinner?" he asked.

"Sure. Then you will be able to tell me why you are scared of me."

"You have already intimidated a number of people who are far greater than I am."

"And who may they be?"

"Rabbi Brill for one, and Rabbi and Mrs. Goldberg as well. I also heard that you even stood up to Rabbi Steiner."

"Word travels fast in this city. What makes them so reluctant to accept me in the first place?"

"Over the years, they have developed in their minds a prototype of a good Jewish woman, and you simply don't fit the image."

"What am I lacking, Simon?"

"Religious women have been trained to exhibit tremendous deference to men in general, and to Torah scholars in particular. There is a built-in docility that doesn't let them project their views and talents in the presence of men."

"Do you subscribe to that view?"

"I was afraid that you would ask me that and I am still not sure how to answer the question. I am of course an American by birth and schooling. I worked with educated women and attended classes with them, so I am not shocked when I meet accomplished members of the opposite sex. For the last three years, however, I have been exposed to very demeaning views about women from men whose learning I deeply respect. Some of it may have tainted my formerly egalitarian opinions."

It began to dawn on me that although Simon was part of the yeshiva world, he had not adopted the prevailing style of his new environment. His speech and bearing were Ivy League all the way, and if it weren't for his present circumstances, I could easily develop a strong interest in him. "You don't speak like any yeshiva man I've ever met," I said. "Apparently you haven't quite fallen into the mold. What did you major in before you went to graduate school?"

"I was deep into the humanities at Columbia University. Remember you are dealing with a baal teshuva. Some of us find religion in a flash of inspiration, a moment of mental exultation. Others, like me, find it by patient reading of the basic sources and long consultations with rabbis and scholars. With me, as with many other intellectual returnees, there is selectivity in what we are willing to accept, and we often reject baseless extremism."

"I heard that returnees tend to be stricter than those who were born religious."

"It happens among those who feel burdened by the guilt of all the liberties they enjoyed during the 'sinful years.' They feel that they have to prove they are more religious than the natives."

"You don't feel that way?"

"I don't and I never did."

"Yet you do feel that there is some justification in bestowing upon women a secondary status in society."

"The problem is not with the contemporary ideas I hear at the yeshiva. The trouble is that such views are inherent in many of the books in the library you are dedicating. A religious Jew cannot be selective about the holy books that determine his view of life."

I knew, from my studies in history, that many of the views derogating women entered Jewish thought at a later date than the original formulation of the faith. I thought I could make some headway with that idea so I said, "The Torah itself wasn't as prejudiced against women as the Talmud and the later works. You could go back to the source."

"I do not care to distinguish between the Torah and the Oral Law. I believe that they are both Divinely inspired and are only different in form. In effect, they are both binding on me."

After some more discussion, we headed back to the hotel. I was pleased that Simon's bigotry was clothed in some ambiguity, but it was obvious to me that a few more years in the yeshiva would obliterate all vestiges of his liberalism.

"How does your ambivalence translate into reality? Could you come to terms with a woman who is a college history professor?"

"Sarah, believe me, that is the least of your problems. Only the most illiterate yeshiva students would be put off by your education. Your trouble takes the form of tangible gaps in your observance which are not symptoms of ignorance. They may very well reflect weakness of belief."

"I thought Rabbi Brill said that you felt you could return me to the faith."

"There may have been some wishful thinking there. What I did say was that I would not hesitate to meet you despite your lack of observance, because we must never rule out the possibility of return. I did not indicate to him that I, personally, would undertake to be the agent of your religious rehabilitation?"

"Why not, pray tell?"

"There are certain soul-savers who use an emotional approach and they can influence anyone. Those who use an intellectual approach are far more limited. For them to be successful, the subject must be just average intellectually and well below average in self-confidence. The more mixed up they are, the more likely it is that they will follow a well-presented approach. In your case, it is obvious that your intellect is superior and your self-confidence is awesome. It would be foolhardy for me to spend the evening engaging in polemics with you."

"What would you like to do?"

"I would like to devote an evening to building fond memories of the precious hours that I spent with the most beautiful girl I ever saw, the smartest woman I ever spoke to, and the richest person I ever met."

"You make me feel wonderful, but what are you going to do when you finally marry your mousy drudge without a penny to her name? Won't your fond memories of me spoil things?"

"Not at all. My mouse will look up to me and say that she always wonders how a brilliant, handsome specimen like me could have taken an ordinary dimwit like her. That will flatter my ego no end."

"What do you think I would say?"

"Something along the lines of, 'Simon, you are the dumbest slob I ever met. I can't believe that I ever let myself get involved with a poor schnook like you.'"

"That's what I like," I said sarcastically, "a real positive self-image. Let's have a pleasant dinner. I will mark the occasion as my nearest approach to becoming a rebbetzin."

Once we reached a clear understanding, the dinner was quite successful. Good food, good conversation and a wonderful ambiance made for a fine social evening. We remained in the lobby for a while until Simon escorted me back to my suite and wished me good night.

Tuesday morning, I was back at the yeshiva working hard and tying up loose ends. I advised Rabbi Brill that I would have to leave early in the afternoon to join the group welcoming the congressional delegation at Ben Gurion.

"How was your social opportunity last night?" Rabbi Brill asked.

"Delightful," I answered. "I had a very pleasant evening, and your young man is both literate and articulate."

"May I take that as a favorable report?"

"For a one night stand, you certainly may. On a long range basis, there is nothing to consider."

"I'm sorry to hear that. Would you care to elaborate?"

"Very briefly. Despite the gentleman's overall qualifications, he would, even in the present state of his yeshiva development, be far too inhibiting for my style of life. A few more years in the yeshiva, and he would be entirely out of the question for any woman with a positive self-image."

"Does he feel the same way?"

"It took him a few minutes to write the meeting off as far as *tachlis* – serious possibilities – were concerned. He had the good grace to relax and spend a pleasant evening. If you get him married quickly, you might still find him some woman who is not a total loss."

After lunch, I took a bus to the airport to participate in the reception for the American guests. Congressman Harrison was delighted to see me and introduced me to his colleagues. The Ambassador greeted the congressmen and then ushered all of us into a tour bus provided by the embassy. The drive to Jerusalem was an exciting experience for the congressmen, who had never visited Israel, and I served as a guide from Ben Gurion all the way to the King David Hotel. I explained the significance of the historical sights that we passed, and focused on the relationship of the various landmarks to the War of Independence in 1948.

After dinner, I made arrangements for a half-day tour in Jerusalem, Wednesday morning. I included the Western Wall, Yad Vashem, the Holocaust memorial, and the Knesset building. I then gave the group a long rest period and arranged to pick them up for the trip to Bethlehem and the midnight Christmas

Mass at the Church of the Nativity. The group consisted of the congressmen, their wives, older children and some members of their office staffs. The embassy had taken great pains to ensure the safety of the delegation. In Bethlehem, the security was sufficient in any event.

It wasn't until Thursday afternoon that I returned to the yeshiva to handle all of the last minute matters arising in connection with the dedication ceremony. I supervised the mounting of the memorial plaque at the entrance of the library and covered it with a veil. I also had Rabbi Brill recruit a crew of students to return the books from the Beit Midrash tables to the new bookshelves. I heard many favorable comments from the students about the appearance of the library.

I told Rabbi Brill that I would like to set up loudspeakers outside the Beis Yaakov building in the event that the audience would be larger than the hall could accommodate.

"Are you sure that we'll draw such a crowd?"

"We have been attracting a lot of attention here. The publicity will hit the newspapers tomorrow and the heavy police presence will attract a lot of curiosity seekers. If there is any chance of an overflow, it would probably be wise for us to make arrangements for it. If we fail to do so, there may be some repercussions."

I made the necessary arrangements and continued working. I was at the yeshiva Friday morning and Sunday until early afternoon, when I returned to the King David to get ready for the big affair. For the ceremony, my mother wore a very attractive outfit. She had no trouble finding one because all of her clothing met the modesty requirements. I, myself, could not find anything appropriate during my Boro Park shopping spree. I finally visited my dress designer in Syracuse, about six weeks earlier, to explain the problem and to order two gowns. The designer was somewhat incredulous, but I was a good customer and she followed instructions. The dresses were regal in appearance and acceptable by even the most stringent religious standards.

When the public affair got under way on Sunday afternoon, the school auditorium was jammed and crowds were forming outside. My mother and I sat in a curtained area near the dais, accompanied by Rebbitzens Brill, Goldberg and Stern. I had advised friends and relatives not to come before 6:00 P.M. and to proceed directly to the dinner. My mother could not follow the Hebrew of the speeches, so I whispered interpretations to her as best I could.

In his remarks, Rabbi Steiner discussed the Halachic question of why a library requires a *mezuzah* – a scroll with verses from the Torah – on its door, despite the fact that all the written contents of the mezuzah can be found within the library books. After completing the learned discourse, he praised my late father for living his life in keeping with the commandments of the Torah and for strengthening the hands of the guardians of faith. He wished my family long life and good health and promised that the yeshiva would always treasure its beautiful new library.

The dean was followed to the rostrum by the chief rabbi and a host of other rabbinic scholars. All of them extolled the yeshiva and its new facility, and praised Rabbi Steiner and the school faculty for their scholarly achievements. Outside, the crowds grew quite large. They were drawn by the presence of limousines, official cars and a whole range of police and other vehicles that congregated on the block to provide security for the Ambassador, the congressmen and the public officials. After the evening service, the dinner got under way fairly close to schedule and the crowds drifted away, except for the few who wished to witness the arrival of the celebrities.

The catering was passable and there was a separation between the tables reserved for women and those reserved for men.

There was only one mixed table at the head of the women's section, where the gentile congressional delegation was seated.

I had only expected Congressman Harrison to attend, but all of the congressmen and their wives were on hand. They had become attached to me during the tour and wanted to participate in the ceremony.

Rabbi Goldberg was in top form as he welcomed the guests and introduced the speakers. The speeches started early in the course of the meal, with the more important speakers reserved for the interval between the entree and the main course. It was the strategy of the emcee to have the public officials speak early and save Rabbis Brill and Steiner for the family references at the end of the dinner.

The mayor of Jerusalem extended civic greetings and hailed the yeshiva as one of the great institutions of the city. The mayor, of course, was new and had never been at the school before. With scores of similar yeshivot to be found in Jerusalem, he probably had not heard of Beit Meir until the dinner. Politicians, though, are never at a loss for words on such occasions and he outdid himself. He was followed by the minister of Religious Affairs, who was far more familiar with the yeshiva. Minister Ben Zur praised the school as a citadel of learning and emphasized the government's recognition and financial support of the institution. Congressman Harrison chose to deliver a foreign policy address emphasizing the long-standing friendship that existed between Israel and the United States. The Ambassador gritted his teeth when he heard the congressman make commitments for the United States that were completely removed from political realities, but he had no choice other than to suffer in silence. In turn, when the Ambassador got to the microphone, he stressed the importance of Americans helping Israel on a person-to-person basis.

"While the u.s. government can only offer limited assistance to religious institutions because of constitutional restraints," he said, "American individuals are free to support the cultural and religious life of the country. In the long run, such philanthropy may be of greater value to Israel than military and political assistance." The television cameras, which were grinding away when the public figures were speaking, were turned off when they finished. The crews then gathered up their gear and left the dining hall.

Rabbi Brill spoke about my family, particularly my late father. He knew the man on a personal basis over an eight-year period and remembered many conversations that were unknown even to members of our own family. He recalled how my father made a policy of never refusing a request for charity. He also spoke of his devotion to the goal of education, both religious and secular, for all of his children. He mentioned the pride that my father had in the accomplishments of his children and the special pleasure he derived from my scholarly work. "The library is an appropriate memorial for him, because he loved and understood what is contained in these books, practiced their teachings and transmitted their wisdom to his children." He recalled that my father was a man who attended synagogue every day and, in fact, was returning from a congregational meeting when he was involved in the tragic accident that cost him his life.

Rabbi Steiner made the official presentations on behalf of the school. He presented a silver candelabrum to my mother and special Bibles to my two brothers. Daniel accepted the books for Michael and himself. I was presented with a set of the 'Daat Mikra,' which contains more than twenty-five volumes of commentary on the Bible. The dean also rewarded my remodeling efforts with a plaque containing a gold key. He said that the key was only symbolic because the library, fortunately, was never closed. When the dinner was concluded, the guests gathered in the study hall at the entrance to the library, where my mother and Daniel removed the veil from the inscribed plaque on the wall. The dedication service was conducted by Rabbi Goldberg, who recited the appropriate Psalms.

With that, the dinner guests left and a small group of the family and the faculty and their wives took seats in the library. Daniel presided at the meeting and started by introducing my mother. She thanked all those concerned for the many courtesies that they had shown her during her stay in Jerusalem. She specially thanked Rabbi Brill for his help in arranging the library memorial and for his long friendship with my father and the family. She wished Rabbi Steiner and the faculty success in their work and she said she would always enjoy fond memories of a wonderful evening. She was nervous during her speech, but she maintained control of her delivery, except for some tears when she spoke of my father. She claimed that he was with the family, watching over them from Heaven, and was very proud of what they were doing.

When I was called to the platform, I spoke with poise and confidence. As a veteran of many political speeches and hundreds of lectures, I have no problem with public speaking. When I was preparing my speech, I was especially cognizant of the nature of the audience and their strong feelings on religion and Jewish history. Even though my own lifestyle was not always consistent with these values, I felt that I should show respect for the cherished values of Jewish tradition. My parents and grandparents lived by these values, and I never turned my back upon them even though I had departed from the full religious life that they led.

I based my opening theme on verses in the books of Psalms:

'He raiseth up the destitute one from the dust
and lifteth up the needy out of the trash heap,
To place him among the princes,
the princely of his people.
He maketh the woman of the household
a happy mother of her children.'

I painted a dramatic picture of my father's destitution as a boy of 18, whose entire family had been immolated in the Holocaust. With God's help, he survived the Holocaust period and started life anew. The name of his father and mother, victims of man's inhumanity to man, he bestowed on my brother and me. The Almighty raised him to the level of a prince, a man of wealth and influence. Not a prince at large, but a prince among his own people, society and culture that he loved. I described how my father built his business, but never neglected the spiritual values of Torah study and prayer. "Without his financial and spiritual heritage, I would not be standing before the distinguished scholars of Jerusalem this very evening."

The final verse I applied to my mother in the form of a prayer. There are several interpretations of the verse, but all of them visualize a mother happy with her children. "She who is now bereft of her beloved husband will at least be able to rejoice someday with her devoted children."

I then announced contributions of five thousand dollars each from my brothers Michael and Daniel. Adding my own personal contribution of four thousand dollars, our total family contribution reached fifty thousand dollars. I was not including my visit to the bookstore, where I purchased several thousand dollars of basic books for religious study for the library. The selection included the Talmud and various codes of law.

In conclusion, I proceeded to paint my concept of a yeshiva student in graphic imagery that held the audience spellbound. I spoke of the conflict between western ideologies and the age-old Torah values, and how such ideologies draw people away from the Torah life that was at one time universal. I ended with the thought that if God helps us to repent and we do return, then the days of old will be restored.

My speech was loudly applauded and I felt that it was well received. A number of faculty members, in addition to Rabbis Brill and Goldberg, told me how much they appreciated my insight into the yeshiva world. My mother also liked it, but she appreciates all my speeches, good or otherwise.

I spent the next morning cleaning up details left over from the affair. I paid all the bills and made a list of people whose help I had to acknowledge by mail. Rivka and Lili came by to wish me farewell and congratulate me on my performance. I quietly handed Lili her husband's gratuity in a sealed envelope and warned her not to open it.

"Why can't I look at it?" she asked.

"In your current lifestyle, your husband rules the roost. It would be an act of insubordination to open his letters."

"You're all wet, kid," Lili said. "Please don't get me mixed up with all the wimpies around here. My husband is a nice guy, but he doesn't know the time of day till I tell him. But, to make you happy, I'll wait till I get home before I open it."

"More power to you. If you were allowed to wear pants, I could say that you wear the pants in the family."

Rivka was somewhat bewildered at the exchange, but she didn't interrupt. She simply thanked me and wished me a safe journey home. Since the library was already in use, I was working in the main office. Rabbi Steiner asked me to come in to his office so that he could thank me for my efforts.

"You were right in many of your judgments, Sarah, and I hope I didn't offend you in any way. If I did, I am sorry and I hope you won't hold the yeshiva responsible for any of my shortcomings."

"From your perspective, Rabbi Steiner, you run a very fine yeshiva," I replied. "If I take exception to things, it is to the yeshiva *weltanschauung* in general and not to any one yeshiva in particular. At any rate, I will be out of your hair now for the foreseeable future, so you will not have to contend with any more problems that *I* may cause you."

"I cannot even be sure of that, Sarah. Even if you don't show up in the flesh, you have left an imprint on the yeshiva that will remain after you are gone. All morning I have been receiving calls from people who were at the meeting or who saw the events on TV. Only one man wanted to congratulate me on my speech. The others wanted to know who my public relations person was and how they could get in touch with him. Some who saw you on TV wanted to know if you were interested in shiduchim."

"They showed me on TV?"

"I don't watch TV, but so I heard. It seems that when the congressman was talking about you they showed some good closeups. If you were to move to Israel, you would readily find both work and eligible men."

"I will keep that in mind. Good luck to you, and I pray that your wife will have a speedy recovery."

The leave-taking from Rabbi Brill was a little harder.

"My mother feels that you treat her like your own mother," I said. "She was overwhelmed by your concern and friendly words. She says that whenever you are in the States, you will be a welcome guest in our home. I also want to thank you for your cooperation and patience. I am still far from being a saint, but I have become far less negative about the yeshiva world and the values for which it stands."

"I am glad that we have had a positive influence on you, but you have done much more for us than we have done for you. By the way, your family has not only helped the yeshiva but has helped me, personally. I have gained enormous stature in this institution and the yeshiva world at large."

"Baruch, I know that I may call you that now, you deserve a lot of credit on your own and I appreciate your dedication and your tolerance. I might add that your students have a world of respect for you and genuine affection. Keep up the good work."

"We would like you to stay in touch with the yeshiva. I will write or call on occasion and I hope that you will answer me."

"I will do that and next August, if God be willing," (I learned that expression from his wife) "we shall see you in Syracuse."

With me safely on the way back to America, the yeshiva resumed a semblance of normality. Relations with the city and the Ministry of Religious Affairs improved markedly. The biggest surprise was in the area of student applications. The number of those seeking to enroll jumped dramatically. This caused Rabbi Steiner a lot of heartache, because he hated to reject qualified students. He had no choice, however, insofar as residential students were concerned. The dormitory was already at full capacity, and no one else could be squeezed in.

He discussed the problem with Rabbi Brill and revealed that had been thinking about the matter for some time. He casually mentioned that he had a plan that would solve the problem in a way that would allow the yeshiva to double its capacity.

"How can that be done?" asked Rabbi Brill, who had little experience in such matters.

"There is a small, empty structure on the property that backs up to the yeshiva. If we could buy that property, we could build on the lot together with the vacant land behind our own building."

"What would we build?"

"We could erect a dormitory that will hold 80 beds and a dining hall that will seat 250. In the present dining room we would put in a second study hall. The smaller study room could then house the kollel or the youngest class."

"That's a pretty grandiose scheme. How much would that cost?"

"Give or take $50,000, we are talking about a million dollars. The building would be somewhat smaller than our present facility, but construction costs have escalated and land is expensive. I don't want to waste any time thinking about it now, because the money is nowhere in sight and we need at least $500,000 in cash to start such an undertaking."

"Did you ever draw up any plans for such a project?"

"As a matter of fact, I once asked an architect to draw me a small plan and a sketch of what it would look like." Rabbi Steiner pulled out two worn sheets of paper from a folder in a desk drawer and handed them to Rabbi Brill.

"I would like to study these, but I don't want to keep the originals. Is it all right to copy them?"

"I see no reason why not."

Rabbi Brill did copy the two sheets and put the matter aside. He didn't give the plan much thought because it was truly far-fetched and totally unrealistic. He resumed his work, but on a number of occasions his thoughts reverted to me. He sent me a letter to that effect and was now awaiting my answer.

MELVIN

12

MY END OF THE STORY RESUMES in early January. Rabbi Steiner, who calls my father every month, told him about the wonderful library dedication. We all knew about the Feldmans in Syracuse, but none of us had ever met the family. It was hard to imagine that a widow of a Jew in Syracuse would donate $50,000 for a yeshiva library in Jerusalem, but stranger things have happened in this world. The rabbi didn't discuss Sandy in detail but, when my father asked him who conducted the ceremony, Rabbi Steiner answered that the Feldman children made all the arrangements.

The business was having a good Christmas season. Sound systems were selling well because they are luxury items and people wait for the holidays before indulging. Sales of winter items like snow chains, anti-freeze and battery chargers were way up. Despite the increased business, however, we were all feeling down and very unhappy. The cause of our depression was our father's health.

On the morning before Christmas, Dad gathered all the long-term employees in his office and bid them farewell. He told them he was leaving the business after 38 years and would no longer be coming in. He thanked them for their support over the years and asked them to remain loyal to his children. He then took the bonus envelopes and, one by one, he called out each employee's name. Many had tears in their eyes as they approached him to take their gifts. The men shook his hands warmly and some of the women kissed him. Everyone knew that this would not only be Murray Seidman's last day in the business, but also his last year on earth.

Dad always felt that the early experiences in Europe before the war had seriously damaged his health. We didn't sense it because he worked so hard and never showed anything but optimism and good cheer. He often wondered aloud why the Almighty had spared his life when so many worthy people were ruthlessly slaughtered. Rabbi Steiner couldn't answer him and I don't think anyone knows the answer. What the rabbi said was that, having been the recipient of Divine grace, Dad should return the favor by performing good deeds and giving charity.

Whatever the cause of my father's debility, the symptoms were very evident. His heart was giving out and the doctors were talking of a pacemaker. Dad told them not to bother and just let nature take its course. He could barely walk, and he sat around the house trying to organize his affairs before the end.

I was with my father most of the time, since I didn't have a family and I was the one he especially trusted because of my ob-servance and religious training. One night, at the end of January, he called me into the study for a private talk.

"Menachem," he said, "this may come as a surprise to you, but when I wrote my will, I named you and mother as executors. I know that Jack will be a little upset with it, but I wanted to be certain that my religious instructions would be followed. You have shown more love for Torah and mitzvahs than the others, although all my children have shown me great respect. You will best understand the importance of what I am telling you."

I didn't interrupt him, because I was anxious to hear what he was going to say. Dad continued in a weak, halting voice.

"Firstly, when my time comes, I don't want Rabbi Singer to be involved with any of the funeral arrangements." Rabbi David L. Singer was the spiritual leader of the local synagogue where my father was president and our family attended services. Dad was the largest contributor to the congregation, and he devoted a lot of time and attention to the shul. He acted respectfully to the rabbi because the religion demanded it but he held the man in very low esteem. To him, the primary requirement for a rabbi was scholarship. Even I could tell that our rabbi was far from being a scholar. To Dad, the rabbi's deficiencies in Torah knowledge were even more painful.

The rabbi held his position by pure social charm. He was popular with the women and had a winning personality. He was, however, noticeably remiss in pastoral duties, and dad himself often had to fill the gap. "As soon as I go, I want you to call Rabbi Steiner in Israel. Don't make any decisions with regard to the funeral until you have cleared them with him. If he can come in from Israel, delay the services until he gets here. If he does arrive, have him conduct the leviah, the funeral." I made a mental note to keep Rabbi Steiner's number handy.

"I want you to look after your mother because she is not too worldly and is very dependent on me. Make sure that you stay in close contact with her and call her every day."

"I will, Dad. You don't have to worry about it."

"Now, about my charities. I've made arrangements with Max Glaser to augment our charity foundation by $3,000,000 from my personal assets. These added funds should yield a quarter of a million dollars a year. Since the foundation already has about three and a half million, the total income should be over half a million dollars annually. The business itself makes direct charitable gifts of about $300,000 each year, and I would like to see that continued. Our usual annual donations are well under the total of the charity funds that will now be available. So, son, you have my permission to make a large capital gift at one time, if you see the need to do so, and keep less money for yearly distribution.

"I can't tell you how to spend all the money because you and and your brother and sister do not share my European background and may feel the need to be more responsive to American causes. But I do want you to continue the $25,000 a year I give to my yeshiva in Israel, as long as that institution exists. Of course, any more that you can spare for Torah institutions in Israel would be very praiseworthy. I also want you to continue supporting the shul and the Jewish charities in the community."

"I'm sure we will keep that up."

"Menachem, I have a personal request to make of you. My other children have blessed me with grandchildren. I love the little ones very much and I have provided for them in my will. Likewise, I have set up a trust for any children that you may bring into the world. I want you to look for a religious girl who will help you bring up your children in the spirit of the Torah."

This was a touchy affair between my father and me. Every time someone mentioned a single Jewish girl to him, he got on the phone and insisted that I take her out. I can't tell you how many dates I suffered through to keep my father happy.

"You'd better stick around, Dad, because if you go, I won't be able to get married for a year."

"You'd better review the laws again, Menachem. You may not attend wedding feasts for the year of mourning but you may get married after 30 days. A marriage is legal even if it doesn't cost $100,000 to make the wedding. Furthermore, members of the family may attend, even when they are in mourning, if they are given some assignment to do."

"Now that you have removed all the obstacles, maybe you can find me a girl as well."

"Only you can do that, Menachem, but the longer you wait, the harder it will be to select one."

That was the last intimate conversation that I had with my father. In mid-February, he was admitted to the hospital and, a week later, in the pre-dawn hours of a Thursday morning, he breathed his last.

His death came suddenly and caught us by surprise. The doctors had assured us, when he was admitted to the hospital, that he wasn't in any immediate danger. I'm a little skeptical when it comes to doctors, but my older brother tends to believe in them. After Dad entered the hospital, Jack waited a few days until the situation stabilized. He then decided not to cancel an urgent business trip to Hawaii. He was scheduled to come home Friday afternoon, the day after my father passed away. About 1:00 A.M. Thursday morning, the doctors called my mother to tell her that Dad had taken a turn for the worse and that she should get there quickly. She called me and we both arrived in time for Dad's final hours. From the hospital I called my sister, and she came in time to take care of my mother while I attended to the arrangements. My mother is a fairly strong woman and didn't need any special help.

My first call was to the undertaker. I asked him to get the body released from the hospital as soon as possible, as I didn't want to be subjected to any pressure to consent to an autopsy. I told him not to make any arrangements about the body until we could meet with him sometime in the evening. The family has dealt with the undertaker over the years, and we knew that, in general, he would respect our wishes.

I drove my mother and sister to my parents' home because I couldn't make the next call from the hospital. Since it was already after 2:00 P.M. in Jerusalem, I had no difficulty reaching Rabbi Steiner. The rabbi answered my call in his office and, from the sound of his voice, I knew that he took the news very badly. He had difficulty expressing himself, and I could sense the tears as he was trying to regain self-control.

"Blessed is the true Judge," he said. "I feel as if I have lost a member of my own family. Your father was a tzadik, Menachem, and his memory will live forever in this yeshiva. Please tell me if there is anything I can do for you."

"Would it be possible for you, Rabbi Steiner, to come to America to conduct the funeral? My father specifically requested me to invite you to preside at the services. Of course, our family will cover all of your expenses."

Rabbi Steiner did not answer at once. I knew that he wanted to come, but something was holding him back.

"Under ordinary circumstances, Menachem, I would be on the next plane out, even though my own health is not what it used to be. However, I cannot leave my wife alone now. She can no longer get around by herself and needs constant care of the type that I cannot delegate. Nevertheless, I will not permit the yeshiva to be unrepresented at the funeral. As soon as we finish this conversation, I am going to ask Rabbi Brill, the mashgiach of the yeshiva, to fly out at once to Buffalo. He will guide you in all religious matters that have to be decided. He is an American and you will have no trouble communicating with him."

I wasn't eager to prolong the conversation with Rabbi Steiner because he was obviously distraught. But I had no choice in the matter, as I needed his advice on certain questions that required immediate answers. "I'm terribly sorry to hear about your wife. I knew that she was ill but I didn't know how bad it was.

May I ask your help with a few problems that must be resolved before Rabbi Brill gets here?"

When he sensed that he could be of some service, Rabbi Steiner regained some of his composure. "I will do my very best to answer you."

"Rabbi, I know that we are instructed to perform burials without delay. Here in America it is a little after 7:00 A.M. There is a slight possibility that we could have the funeral today, although I tend to doubt it. We can do it tomorrow but, if at all possible, I would prefer to have it on Sunday."

"Are all the children present?"

"No. That is part of the problem. I will shortly attempt to reach Jack in Hawaii and tell him to return at once. He had to go there this week on very important business. He certainly can't make it today, and he may, in fact, not get here until tomorrow afternoon."

"In that case, Menachem, you really have no problem. It is always permissible to delay a funeral while awaiting the presence of the oldest son. Even if he were there, it is sometimes permissible to delay a funeral if it is urgent to do so for the honor of the deceased. In Israel, it is not frequently done but, in America, there is such a tendency. In the case of your father, who was prominent in his community, it would be wrong to deny his many friends and associates a chance to pay their last respects."

"Is Rabbi Brill able to conduct an American funeral?"

"It is well within his ability. He knows the laws thoroughly and he is an experienced speaker and lecturer."

Of the man's knowledge, I had no doubt. No one becomes a mashgiach at a yeshiva and the head of a kollel unless he is a first-rate scholar. I was more concerned about his presence in the pulpit, since he had never practiced as the rabbi of an American congregation. I decided that I would wait to meet the man and judge for myself if I could entrust the services to him. I had to bear in mind that more than half of the audience would not be Jewish and that even the Jews who attended would know very little about yeshivot.

"I thank you, Rabbi Steiner, for your time. Please send us a fax as soon as you know which flight Rabbi Brill is taking. There are several early morning flights leaving New York for Buffalo but he may have to transfer from Kennedy Airport to La Guardia."

"I will send you the fax as soon as I have the information. Please do not make any arrangements for the purification and preparation of the body until Rabbi Brill gets there. Also, I want you to arrange for the body to be watched by observant men until it is time for the funeral. Is your mother within reach of the phone? I wish to express my condolences."

I gave my mother the phone and she spoke to Rabbi Steiner for several minutes. He must have said the right things to her because she seemed to feel better after the conversation. What took place in Israel following my call to the rabbi was related to me by Rabbi Brill on the first Sabbath after his arrival. I'll tell you about it now even though I will be getting ahead of myself in the story.

Rabbi Steiner summoned Rabbi Brill from the Beit Midrash as soon as he hung up the phone. The student who called the rabbi told him that something terrible must have happened, because he had never seen Rabbi Steiner so disturbed and shaken. Rabbi Brill could only think that it must have been some bad news about Rebbitzen Steiner, so he dropped everything and ran to the dean's study. Even with the advance warning, he wasn't prepared for the scene that confronted him in the office. The dean was sobbing aloud and his face was pale.

"I have just had word from Menachem Seidman that his father passed away. I feel as though part of my life and my life's work have come to an end. We were like brothers when we fled from Europe. He made it possible for me to realize my long-standing goal of directing a yeshiva of my own. He encouraged me not only with money, but with words of support and good spirit. I don't know whether it would have even been possible to sustain the yeshiva without his help."

Rabbi Brill was quite shaken himself. He knew the role that Murray Seidman had played in starting the yeshiva and in maintaining it. As much as he was concerned about his own future, he was concerned about the impact on Rabbi Steiner. The man had had his hands full even before the news, and the bad tidings might be more than he could cope with. So Rabbi Brill's first task was to help Rabbi Steiner regain his self-control. "I know that both the Dean and the yeshiva have suffered a severe loss. As far as the yeshiva is concerned, I have faith that our institution will survive. It has a good name in the city and, after these many years, the Jewish community will not let it fail. God will help us in our distress. But I am concerned that the Dean may allow this loss to destroy his health. There comes a time for all of us to be called to the true world, some earlier, some later. In such matters, it is better to look back rather than ahead. Murray Seidman led a full and productive life. There aren't too many people in this world who have had the privilege of having a yeshiva named after them while they were still alive. His charity enabled hundreds of students to learn Torah. I'm sure that his own children inherited a good part of his outlook, and they will carry on with his work. The loss of close friends is something that all of us have to bear in the course of a lifetime."

Rabbi Steiner sat quietly for a minute and then replied.

"It is not so much for the loss of a friend that I mourn, but for the passing of an era. Meir was the only living link that I had to my youth in Vienna and the glories of my family in that community. The community produced men who honored God and served their fellow men. That is all now part of the past. Men like Meir Seidman are not replaceable."

"A generation comes and a generation goes. We can only do our duty while we are on earth."

"That is well put, Baruch. I thank you for your words of comfort, even though I called you in for another purpose."

Bells began to ring in Rabbi Brill's mind. He didn't know what Rabbi Steiner was going to ask him to do, but he imagined it would be something in connection with the passing of Mr. Seidman.

"How may I be of help?"

"Believe me, it grieves me to the very bottom of my heart that I should have to ask you to do something that is my responsibility. The Lord, however, is not letting me fulfill my duty in this case, and I have to depend on others. Meir Seidman spoke to his son before he died and asked him to invite me to conduct the final services for him when his time came. If it were at all possible for me to go, I would not hesitate for a moment. I would be willing to endanger my own health, but I cannot leave my wife in her present state. It would be unthinkable for a yeshiva that proudly bears the name of a donor not to be represented when the final honors are bestowed upon him."

Rabbi Brill began to gather the drift of the conversation, and he mentally reviewed the consequences of an unscheduled trip to America. It was just about three weeks to Purim, and Passover was in the offing. These were the best months for students studying at a yeshiva because, by late spring, there would be many distractions. He knew how hard it was on his wife when he left for his annual trip to America each summer. He also remembered his own loneliness and anxieties during the separation. The unqualified success of his last trip to America at least offered some compensation for the pain. But this trip could be only one of severe stress and sadness.

"I gather that the Dean is asking me to travel to America to convey the condolences of the yeshiva to the Seidman family, and I also imagine that I have little choice in the matter."

"The last half of your statement is quite true. The survival of the yeshiva is at stake, and all of us have to do as much as we can. With regard to the first half, you have not fully understood what I am asking you to do. The funeral will not be held until Sunday because one of the sons is out of town. Meir Seidman wanted me to conduct the entire funeral service and that is what I am asking you to do."

Rabbi Brill began to feel some very intense pressure. "I'm sure the Dean is well aware that I have never conducted a funeral, either in America or in Israel. I may know the laws of mourning on a theoretical basis, but one needs practice in such matters. Mr. Seidman was an influential man in Buffalo, and all of the community leaders will be present."

"In your own words, Baruch, one must have faith. If God is going to help the yeshiva, He will start by inspiring you with the wisdom to conduct yourself properly and discharge your duties well. I will, of course, brief you on issues that may arise, and provide you with information on the background of the Seidman family. But I will not do so now, because during the next few hours it is urgent for you to make arrangements to travel and to prepare for your journey. Once you settle the business matters, I will sit with you and instruct you in your responsibilities. Before you leave, let me give you some of the money you will need for the trip."

Rabbi Steiner walked over to a curtain in his office and raised it. Rabbi Brill had never seen what was behind the curtain, but he realized it was a safe. The dean took out an envelope and handed it to Rabbi Brill. "There is $2500 in cash in this envelope. You will need more than that and I will make arrangements for you to receive it. I have kept this money for many years for just such an emergency. It was originally a present from Mr. Seidman for my personal use. I could never accept such a gift for myself, but I couldn't offend him by rejecting his kindness. The money will now be used in his honor and I feel that it is proper to spend it for that purpose."

Rabbi Brill went to his office and called his travel agent on the phone. He explained the situation, saying he needed any available ticket on any flight leaving Ben Gurion for America later that evening. The agent was not optimistic. "You would think that in the off-season it shouldn't be so hard to get a reservation, but the airlines have cut back drastically on their flights, particularly those that leave before the Sabbath. Most people find that they do not have enough time to enjoy the weekend if they travel Thursday night. By the time they arrive and shake off the effects of the flight, the weekend is half gone. There is only one flight out tonight on El Al, and that one has been booked solid for weeks. I tried to get a customer on the plane tonight, but with all my connections, I was not able to do so."

"Isn't there such a thing as emergency flights or considerations of a compassionate nature?"

"Sometimes it is possible where there is a death in the immediate family or a very serious illness. In the present case, you are not even related to the deceased. I know how important it is for the yeshiva to be represented, but I am not sure how much weight that consideration will carry with El Al."

"What do you suggest that I do?"

"I could get you on a plane to Europe tomorrow morning. You would spend Shabbos in France or England and catch an outgoing plane to the States from there. Even that would be difficult, but there would be more of a selection to choose from."

"Rabbi Steiner wants me to be in Buffalo to make the funeral arrangements before the Sabbath. I must be on that El Al flight at all costs."

"Are you on good terms with the Prime Minister or somebody on that level? It would take more clout than I could even imagine to get you on the flight. Of course, you can always pay some single passenger $1000 to delay his trip."

"That's no joke and it may very well come to that. Put me on the waiting list and I'll see what I can do from this end."

Baruch then called Rivka to tell her the news and ask her to help with the packing. She was a veteran of eight annual trips in the past, so she knew what was required. A winter trip was a little harder than a summer one, but she took it in stride.

"I may have some problem getting on the plane," he told her. "They are booked solid and my travel agent doesn't have much hope of getting a ticket."

"I will be glad to call Rabbi Shayalevitch for advice."

"This may not be in his area of competence."

"You should have more faith in pious men, Baruch. He always gives me good guidance."

Rabbi Brill did not want to undermine Rivka's dependence on her advisor, so he rephrased the original question. "Do you know anyone else whom we may call for help?"

Rivka thought for a minute and then said, "Wait, I have an idea. Remember how your girlfriend made a powerful impression on the minister of Religious Affairs?"

In Hebrew, the word for a female friend, 'yedidah,' is not as strong as the English term 'girlfriend.' It does, of course, imply more than a casual acquaintanceship. Rivka had applied the term to Sandra Feldman because she was a little jealous of the tremendous amount of attention Sandra got from Rabbi Brill during the library dedication program. She had no doubts about her husband's loyalty; she said it only to tease him.

"Sure I do. She also sent him a check for his favorite charity."

"In that case, why don't you give him a call?"

"That is a good idea. El Al has a lot of problems with the Ministry of Religious Affairs and they may find it in their interest to be accommodating."

Rabbi Brill called the Ministry and, when he explained the gravity of the situation to the Director General, he was put through to the minister. Ben Zur sensed the desperation in Rabbi Brill's voice and resolved to help. Sandra had been very generous to his charity a couple of months earlier and now he had a chance to do a favor in return.

"I'll try my best, Rabbi Brill. Stay by the phone and I'll call you back."

It took less than 15 minutes for the minister to call back with the good news. "Send someone over to the El Al office with money and your passport. The ticket is waiting for you."

Rabbi Brill didn't know how such things were accomplished, but discretion told him that it would be wiser not to ask questions. He thanked the minister profusely and began to wonder how much Sandra had actually sent him after the library dedication.

He continued making arrangements at a furious pace for the trip and for his absence from the yeshiva. When it came time for his conference with Rabbi Steiner, he was already exhausted. Nevertheless, he was there at 7:00 P.M. hoping to complete the meeting in time to avoid a panic trip to the airport. Rabbi Brill waited for Rabbi Steiner to open the conversation.

"Baruch, we can't afford any mistakes in religious law in this matter, and most decisions will have to be made by you on the spot without time to look up the answers. I want you to take a Code of Law with you on the plane and review every law in the sections on burial and mourning. Secondly, forget every funeral you've ever attended in Jerusalem. Many of the local customs in this community are at complete variance not only with American Orthodox practice, but even with Israeli. One example is not letting women stand near the burial area. Another is to prohibit the son himself from standing by when the body is lowered into the grave. Another is walking in circles around the coffin. These Jerusalem practices are not appropriate in Buffalo."

"I did attend some funerals in America some 15 years ago."

"Things have changed in America during the past 15 years. Religious practices in dealing with death have been corrupted by undertakers, cemetery directors, cemetery workers and rabbis without courage. It will be necessary to guide the family very correctly in all the laws, with extreme care and tact."

"Why is that?"

"This funeral will be attended by many gentiles and by prominent non-Orthodox Jews. Orthodoxy will be on trial. If our practices look primitive or foolish there will be a desecration of the Divine name. The Seidman family may then find reason to abandon the religious practices of their father. If, on the other hand, the services are conducted with dignity, it will bring sanctification of the Divine name and strengthen the family's commitment to the Torah way."

"That is rather a delicate position to be in."

"It is. Let me give you a quick review of the laws and the pitfalls you may encounter. I cannot cover every contingency but you will surely encounter many of the situations I will discuss."

There followed a full survey of the laws regarding death and burial. Rabbi Steiner covered the laws relating to the purification of the body, the shrouds and the casket. He reviewed the practices to be followed by the mourners before, during and after the burial, and the various restrictions upon those in mourning. He indicated which customs had priority and which could be dispensed with in an emergency. Rabbi Steiner had answered hundreds of such inquiries during his service as dean of the yeshiva, and he remembered his sources perfectly.

Rabbi Brill thanked him for his help and then brought up one area that was troubling him. "What shall I do if Menachem brings up the subject of a memorial for his father?"

"I want you to avoid such discussions during the seven days of mourning. While in certain situations it may be permissible to discuss such matters during Shiva, it is always inappropriate. It will give the appearance that our presence in Buffalo is motivated by greed. Tell Menachem that after the Shiva he may discuss the matter directly with me."

Rabbi Brill questioned this approach in his heart. He felt that Rabbi Steiner was not acting in the long-range interests of the yeshiva, but rather to protect personal interests. The Seidmans were, in a sense, Rabbi Steiner's 'clients.' He did not want to relinquish his territory to anyone else. In all his trips to America, Rabbi Brill had never been permitted to visit Buffalo.

He would have understood the dean's attitude if there were a commission involved. Rabbi Brill, however, was on a straight salary, and it made no material difference how much money he brought in. Of course, it might cause a change in his stature. He then remembered that the dean had been cool to him during the Feldman proceedings, and it confirmed his fear that the dean was trying to limit any excessive growth in his importance to the school. Given these considerations, he decided not to commit himself to Rabbi Steiner.

"I will not discuss the situation with Menachem while he is sitting Shiva. If possible, I will avoid it thereafter."

Rabbi Steiner was not at all pleased with the answer, but he could not afford to push the matter. Baruch was the only one who could represent him in America and he had accepted the request to make the trip without any reservations or demands. One day Baruch would learn why Rabbi Steiner was protecting his territory at the yeshiva, but the latter chose not to tell him now. He simply gave Baruch his blessing for a safe and successful journey.

Rivka did not normally travel to the airport with her husband. They would say their goodbyes at home and Rabbi Brill would take the car service to Ben Gurion. This time she went with him because there hadn't been enough time to make all the arrangements for his absence. "I should be back on Monday before Purim. After the Shiva is over, I have to interview students in New York for next year's class, because Rabbi Steiner will not be making his spring trip this year."

"I will miss you very much when you are gone," Rivka said with sadness in her heart, but she understood that there was no way of avoiding the trip.

13

THE FLIGHT TO NEW YORK went by quickly because Rabbi Brill spent as much time as he could reviewing the laws and preparing the eulogy. He was expecting to be picked up at the airport since he had sent a fax to me as soon as he had the tickets in hand.

Returning to earlier events in Buffalo, when I finished speaking to Rabbi Steiner, I called the undertaker to tell him that the funeral would take place on Sunday and that Jack and I would meet with him on Friday afternoon. I spent the rest of the day on Thursday making some non-ritual preparations for the funeral.

My first job was to get in touch with my brother in Hawaii, but I decided to wait till at least 6:00 A.M. Hawaii time. When I broke the news to him, he was really shaken. Jack was always very close to Dad and they had worked in the business hand in hand. On religious matters, I was closer to my father, but in business matters the reverse was true.

"What should I do, Mel?" he asked. "I mean, do we have to have the funeral tomorrow?"

"No, Jack. I called Rabbi Steiner in Israel and he said we can wait until Sunday. He's sending his senior assistant, Rabbi Brill, to help us with arrangements, and he'll be here tomorrow.

Instead of spending the night in California, as you were planning to do, take a late flight from the coast and I will pick you up in the morning. We will all be spending Shabbos with Mom."

"How is she holding up?"

"As well as can be expected. She was psychologically prepared for the event for a long time and has a lot of faith."

We then spoke for a short while about when to close the business and we decided to keep all the branches shut Saturday and Sunday. We discussed the newspaper ads and all the family notifications.

"You will have to make some important decisions today, Mel, but you knew what Dad wanted more than anyone else and I'm sure you will do the right thing."

I got my younger sister to call all the family members who had to be notified. We told them the funeral would be on Sunday, and to check the time in the papers. I told her not to call Rabbi Singer yet, as I would take care of it myself. Then I called our public relations director and told him to come over to the house. I spent a few minutes thinking about my approach to the rabbi. Not to inform him would be gross misconduct. On the other hand, I did not want him to get involved with the arrangements until I had spoken to Rabbi Brill.

I dialed the local synagogue office and asked to speak to the rabbi. When I told him what had happened, he expressed genuine regret. He sounded sincere, and I was not inclined to doubt it. He then asked how he could be of service, and I answered as tactfully as I could.

"My father left very detailed instructions with me as to what should be done in the event of his death, and his instructions will be our guide. I have secured permission from Rabbi Steiner to delay the services until Sunday because my brother, the oldest son, is out of the country and won't be back until tomorrow. I don't want to make final arrangements without him. If it is all right with you, my brother and I would like to meet with you at 1:00 P.M. tomorrow. It would be easier for all of us if you could come over to the home at that time."

Rabbi Singer realized that he was not going to be the central figure in the services and I don't know whether he was miffed or relieved. He was always on edge when he dealt with our family; I suppose he sensed my father's low opinion of him. He did agree to see us as requested and once again offered his help if we needed it.

By the time I was off the phone, John Sinclair had arrived. Some 15 years earlier, when he had finished journalism school, my father hired him for advertising and public relations. When the store started branching out we had no choice but to secure a regular advertising agency. John served as liaison with the agency and both were obviously doing good work because sales were constantly increasing. John reported to Carol, as most of the advertising budget went for marketing campaigns. As far as public relations was concerned, John was an expert, and it was in this area that his writing skills came to the fore.

"John, I want you to contact the newspapers and provide them with background material on my father. You knew him as well as anyone in the company. Stress his religious and charitable work in the local community and abroad. I want his yeshiva mentioned because he was very proud of it. Include the fact that Rabbi Baruch Brill, director of advanced studies at the yeshiva, is on his way from Israel to participate in the services. Let everyone know that my father was scholarly, devout and very kind. Above all, tell of his tolerance to people of all faiths and of the policies of equal opportunity that were truly enforced in the business."

"What about the funeral arrangements?"

"Just say that the funeral will be on Sunday but that arrangements are not yet complete. Further announcements will appear in the papers, and perhaps you can set up a phone number where people may call to get the latest information. The family will sit in mourning at my parents' home, and visitors are welcome during hours which will be announced. Make sure that in lieu of flowers, contributions are sent to the Beit Meir Torah Seminary. If you need any further information ask me or Carol."

"Is the company putting in an obituary ad?"

"I'm glad you brought that up. Put in a quarter-page in all the local dailies. Put in a separate half page to announce that all the stores will be closed Saturday and Sunday. Get Marty Cohen, the sales manager, to notify all the stores of the closing, and fax copies of a closing notice to all the managers. You have an assistant and a secretary, so put them to work. Send the news release to the out-of-town store managers so they can notify the papers in their cities.

I remained at my parents' house most of the day. By the time I finished working, it was late afternoon. I hadn't slept the entire night before, so I lay down for a few hours of well-deserved rest. When I got up, I spoke to my mother for a while and then returned to my own home.

John Sinclair did his work well. In the morning, when I picked up the paper on the outside porch, I saw my father's picture on the front page in the middle of a long news story. The second and third pages carried the company ads and messages of condolence from several other firms and friends of the family. The newspaper even wrote an editorial mourning the loss of a very public-minded citizen who had built an impressive business centered in Buffalo.

I had forgotten to ask Rabbi Steiner whether I should recite my prayers in the morning as was my daily custom. I hadn't recited them on Thursday because, prior to turning the body over to the undertaker, I was exempted from doing so. I didn't know whether the preparations that I had to make today were of sufficient gravity to exempt me further. I decided not to put on the tefillin but simply to recite the Shema.

Promptly at eight, I drove out to the airport to meet Jack. He had a car parked there, so I wasn't worried about him getting home, but I thought it was a good idea and the right thing to do. Jack was very tired. He had left the coast at midnight and had to change in New York for the flight to Buffalo. When I asked him if he could make it home by himself, he assured me that he could.

"Get some rest," I told him, "and come over to see Mom at noon. I'll wait for Rabbi Brill here. He's due on the next plane in and it doesn't pay to go back home. Rabbi Singer is coming over at 1:00 P.M. and we'll meet him together."

"We spoke for a few minutes and I got Jack some coffee. After he left I sat down to wait for Rabbi Brill. When the plane came in, I had no trouble recognizing him. He was wearing a long frock coat and a big black hat. His black beard was rather short, and there were touches of gray at the temples and in the moustache. I had expected a much older man but when I saw Rabbi Brill, I wasn't even sure that he had reached forty.

I greeted him cautiously because I remembered that there were some restrictions on mourners about inquiring as to the well-being of others. I have since learned that such restrictions do not set in until after the funeral is over.

"Rabbi Brill?" I asked.

"Yes, and you are a member of the Seidman family?"

"I'm Melvin Seidman, the one who called Rabbi Steiner yesterday."

"He knows you only as Menachem. I trust it is all right to call you by your Hebrew name. 'Menachem' means consolation in Hebrew and it is very appropriate at this time. It was thoughtful of you to call the rabbi, because he was very close to your father. He asked me to convey his sincere condolences to you and your family. He deeply regrets that he could not personally make the trip because of his wife's illness."

"I understand. I am grateful to you for coming on short notice. You seem rather young to be head of a kollel and a mashgiach. In my yeshiva, the mashgiach was in his seventies."

"Rabbi Steiner felt that a mashgiach should be contemporary with the generation that he counsels. I was reluctant to accept the position eight years ago but, by now, I have gotten used to it."

Rabbi Brill spoke with a slight New York accent and he was quite articulate. Although his voice had a distinctive rabbinic timbre, he was different from the bearded collectors that show up in our offices. I was anxious to see if he would be firm and decisive in arranging the funeral.

After he picked up his luggage, I drove him to my parents' house, where my sister served him coffee. He paid his respects to my mother and then joined me in the study.

"I didn't put on my tefillin today, Rabbi, because I wasn't sure whether I was supposed to. I did bring them with me. Should I put them on now?"

"It has often surprised me that people with religious training instinctively do the right thing even though they are not familiar with the relevant laws. In this case you were correct in your judgment and you are not to put on the tefillin or the prayer shawl until after the funeral. Every practice of the Jewish people has its origins in rational thought. Persons who have to bury the dead are not permitted to engage in positive religious practices, because Judaism demands that they focus their full time, attention and energy in preparing the final services. To do anything less, would be a dishonor to the dead. Now there are some who argue that if the heir has turned over the body of the deceased to a burial society and is no longer burdened with any preparations, then he has to resume religious observances. In our case, your undertaker is a far cry from a holy burial society. He has to be watched and supervised constantly, and that is your primary responsibility."

I realized that Rabbi Brill was both a scholar and an excellent teacher. He was taking pains not only to rule on the laws, but also to explain the reasoning behind each decision.

"Thank you," I said to him. "We have some major problems with the funeral arrangements. I will explain them one by one and hope that you can resolve them."

"I will do my best, Menachem. Tell me of your concerns."

"The first problem relates to the location of the services. My father was a prominent businessman and a leader in the community. Our company has some 400 employees in the main office and branch stores, and most will be attending the services. So will the public officials, prominent businessmen and professionals who worked with us. At the same time, Dad was very active in the Jewish community. He was president of the shul and a director in more than ten communal institutions. He was a heavy contributor to both Jewish and non-Jewish groups. All told, we can anticipate well over 1000 people attending the services.

"Where were you planning to hold the services?"

"That is the question. We ruled out Conservative and Reform temples because my father avoided them in his lifetime, and it would be disrespectful to bring him there in death. We also eliminated public buildings such as high schools, because it would give an impression of the theatrical and would not have the proper solemnity.

"What is left?"

"There is the community funeral home – Sinai Chapel – and our synagogue, Beth Torah. The chapel only seats about 500. The shul is larger and has a balcony, and seats about 600. In either case, there will not be enough space. We would hate to deny friends and associates the chance to pay their last respects. Also, with regard to the shul, if we are required to separate the men from the women, we will have great embarrassment in the case of gentile employees. The family has left it up to me, and I don't know what to do."

Rabbi Steiner had warned Rabbi Brill that he would be confronted with difficult and totally unanticipated problems that would require bold solutions. Rabbi Brill thought for a minute and made a suggestion.

"Before you were born, Menachem, and before there were such things as funeral homes, there was a practice in America that when great men passed away, the eulogies were held in several different places. The cortege would start out at the home of the deceased, where the first prayers were offered. It would then proceed to the synagogue of the deceased, where additional prayers would be offered. Finally it would proceed to a yeshiva, where the last selections were chanted. At each stop along the way, different people had a chance to pay their respects.

"My suggestion is to conduct a traditional religious service at noon at the synagogue. That would be followed by a public memorial service at the funeral Chapel at 1:30 P.M. The synagogue service would include the Hebrew prayers and the audience would be seated separately."

"The public service would be mixed?"

"I see no reason why not, especially if most of the audience is gentile."

"Would you be willing to conduct the public service?" I asked.

"If you prefer, I would."

"How would we direct the different people to the different services?"

"Can you still put an ad in the papers?"

"Our public relations director is holding space in the papers, and we have a phone number for people to call in for information."

"Very good. Word it this way: 12:00 noon - Orthodox Jewish Religious services at Beth Torah for family, friends and synagogue members. 1:30 P.M.- Community Memorial Service at Sinai Chapel, for civic leaders, company employees and the general public."

"There may be some logistical problems, but it is an excellent idea. Let me call our public relations man and put him to work on it."

I called John Sinclair and asked him to submit the ads. Then I explained our second problem to Rabbi Brill.

"This concerns our local spiritual leader, Rabbi Singer. My father held him in low esteem and left specific word that the man should have nothing to do with his funeral arrangements. How shall we handle that?"

Here Rabbi Brill didn't hesitate for even a moment. "Let me ask you, Menachem; if your father instructed you to conduct the services on the Sabbath, would you listen to him?"

"My father would never ask for a thing like that!"

"I know it. I am just posing the question theoretically."

"I guess that we would not be bound by his will."

"You are correct. In his determination to have a proper burial service, your father may not have sensed that he might create a situation that would embarrass a rabbi publicly. In ethical terms, the public humiliation of any man is equated symbolically with murder. If the man is a rabbi, the situation is even worse. There are special laws that require that a rabbi be given respect.

"Let me explain this a little better. The respect that is required is not for the man but for the position. We are taught that we must respect a king whether he is a tyrant or he is benevolent. The same is true for a rabbi or judge. Our sages tell that Samuel the prophet was respected in his generation and Jephtach was respected in his. Now Samuel was close to the highest level a human can attain. He heard the word of God and he crowned the Kings of Israel. Jephtach, in contrast, was a social outcast and leader of a gang of hoodlums. Yet, once he was appointed as judge, Jewish law demanded that he be respected.

"Your rabbi has valid ordination and was chosen by a congregation to be its spiritual leader. At the time of ordination, he was sufficiently learned to be awarded the title. He may not have kept up with all his studies since then, but he still has a claim to respect. Embarrassing the rabbi would bring strife and division into the community, and that would not honor your father's memory.

"Most important, from what you tell me, your father did not rule out Rabbi Singer's participation in the services. He simply requested that Rabbi Singer not make the arrangements, because he might make errors. Since we are making all the arrangements with Rabbi Steiner's approval, we are conforming fully to your father's wishes."

I was impressed with Rabbi Brill's analysis and exposition. I could see why he had risen so fast at the yeshiva.

"So then, how should we arrange for Rabbi Singer's participation?"

Rabbi Brill thought for a while and then he said, "I don't feel that Rabbi Singer is actually eager to conduct the service. He simply wants to avoid public embarrassment. Here is what we can do. After I open the service, I will call upon Rabbi Singer as the rabbi of the synagogue and of the deceased to deliver his message. Thereafter, I will deliver the traditional eulogy based on Talmudic sources.

"I think he will find that acceptable."

"But that alone may not be sufficient. Rabbi Singer is well-known in the broader community and has high standing. I feel you should ask him to conduct the public service and, with a chance to appear before very important civic leaders, I think he will be quite satisfied."

I was pleased with the solution to our problem with Rabbi Singer, but I told Rabbi Brill I wanted him to participate in the community service as well. "Then ask Rabbi Singer to introduce me and call on me to convey a message from your father's friends in the State of Israel."

"That will be perfect. Is there anything else you would like me to do now?" I asked the rabbi.

"Yes, as a matter of fact."

"What do you have in mind?"

"I'm worried about the purification of the body of the deceased. The ritual is called 'tahara' and is quite complex."

"I am sure that the undertaker has a man who does such work."

"In this case, I am afraid it will not be sufficient. Rabbi Steiner instructed me to conduct the tahara personally. The local man may be well-intentioned, but we usually find that such men are not versed in the laws. They perform the act as they once may have seen it done in Europe and, over the course of time, their memory tends to fade. What makes it worse is the fact that they are usually older men who may not have the physical capacity to do it right. Inevitably they seek shortcuts and avoid the full process."

"Will you be able to do it yourself?"

"No. In Israel, we usually have three or more men performing tahara. What I would like you to do is find me two Sabbath observers who will help me Saturday night in performing the Tahara."

"Am I personally allowed to help?"

"Under normal circumstances, it is not considered proper for a son to share in this ritual. Only under the worst possible conditions would it be allowed."

"I don't think we will have trouble finding two men. My father learned with another man in the congregation every Tuesday night. That man is both learned and observant. We also have a man who serves as the sexton in the congregation, and he was very close to my father. Are there any other matters that concern you now?"

"There is just one other area where some caution may be necessary. It relates to the question of pallbearers. In many funerals in this country, the pall bearing is often relegated to non-observant cemetery workers who wheel the coffin to the grave. In the case of your father, I feel that the coffin should be carried by hand."

"I'm quite sure that will not present a problem. The undertaker knows the cemetery workers well enough, and he will instruct the foreman to tell his men to stay away from the coffin."

"That is the easy part of the problem. The more complex aspect is to arrange for the pallbearers to be pious men. A request will have to be made that only the assigned pallbearers should do the work. You will need at least six observant men to assist me in this, and sons are not expected to be pallbearers."

"That will be a little harder to achieve, but we can use some members of our family and recruit the rest."

I began to see that making the arrangements under the strict supervision of a rabbi from a yeshiva in Israel would not be easy. Nevertheless, I was determined to honor my father's wishes, as long as it was possible to do so.

14

AT NOON, JACK ARRIVED, STILL tired from his arduous trip. After he consoled my mother and Carol, I introduced him to Rabbi Brill. We then all sat down to a dairy lunch prepared by the housekeeper. Rabbi Brill cautioned us against reciting any blessings before or after partaking of the food. It was a little hard for me to adjust to it, because I was always accustomed to reciting such prayers before eating.

"You will be able to say these prayers on the Sabbath," Rabbi Brill told us. "The laws of mourning do not apply on the Sabbath and the exemptions from positive religious observances before the funeral also do not apply."

While eating, I told my brother of the rabbi's plan to conduct two memorial services successively.

"I am glad you have solved the problem in a reasonable way. I was thinking about it on the plane and I didn't see any solution until this suggestion was made. As far as having Rabbi Singer conduct the second service, I have no objection. He is a good speaker, even though his content may be somewhat shallow."

"It wasn't long after our discussion of the local rabbi's role that Rabbi Singer himself came in. He offered condolences to my mother and sister and then to us. He conveyed a sense of genuine sorrow, and we appreciated the apparent sincerity of it. The rabbi did not object to the arrangements. I sensed that he was relieved that he wasn't being excluded entirely from the services and that he would have an opportunity to address the civic leaders of the city.

At 1:30 P.M., Jack and the rabbi joined me in driving over to the funeral home. Mr. Samuel Roth, who owned the home, was pleased that we had finally arrived. He had been quite nervous about our delaying the arrangements since he needed the maximum time possible to prepare for what was his biggest funeral in a very long time. I introduced Rabbi Brill and asked that the religious matters be taken care of first so that the rabbi could get some rest after his long flight. The undertaker obliged us.

He said that he would make his chapel workrooms available for the purification on Saturday night, and then showed us a selection of shrouds. Some of them bore rabbinic endorsement and Rabbi Brill made the selection from among that group.

"I will bring Mr. Seidman's tallit when I come for the purification," the rabbi said. I didn't know at the time that one of the fringes of the four on the prayer shawl had to be cut off before it was put in the coffin of the deceased. All told, the session with the undertaker left me with many questions. There were customs that I had never heard about and others with which I was familiar, but did not know or understand their purpose. I resolved to ask Rabbi Brill to explain these practices to us during the Sabbath. Mr. Roth asked us if he should arrange for the rending of the garments. I glanced at Rabbi Brill and saw that he was shaking his head, so I told the undertaker that we would take care of it ourselves.

Of course I was worried about that ritual. I myself knew that the custom of wearing black ribbons pinned to the garment was not acceptable in Orthodoxy. To cut the ribbon was meaningless because the ribbons were external to the garment, and it was the garment itself that had to be rent. I had heard how at some Orthodox funerals in New York the children were not only required to cut the jackets but all garments underneath. I was worried how Mel and Carol would take to it. We were, after all, people who were very much in the public eye. I knew I would have to bring the matter up to Rabbi Brill and, in a sense, I was glad that Rabbi Steiner himself was not present. With Rabbi Steiner there was no chance of any compromise in such a matter. I had reason to hope that Rabbi Brill would be a little more accommodating on the question.

The undertaker then took us to the display room for the selection of a coffin. Here, Rabbi Brill was facing a real dilemma. In many funeral homes, itemized charges are avoided to lessen the strain on the bereaved. The single charge for the funeral is based on the coffin price. The impression given is that the client is only paying for the coffin and all other services are free. There is logic in this, because the level of services correlates to the price of a coffin. By tacking on a fixed percentage to the coffin price, the rich, who select elaborate caskets, would automatically be charged a higher amount for all services. Given my father's wealth, the coffin price could be very significant. Unfortunately for the undertaker, however, the really expensive coffins were not acceptable under strict Jewish law. Religious rules forbid the use of any caskets containing metal in them, even nails. This also applies to the handrails by which the coffin is carried.

"Do we have to order a plain pine box?" I asked Rabbi Brill. I could sense the undertaker wincing when I asked the question. It was then that I remembered hearing about an article in the undertaker's trade journal. It advised the undertaker to have an assistant take the clergyman out for coffee when the undertaker was selling the coffins. It seems that under the stress of death, and under the influence of guilt feelings, the family could be induced to overspend on the funeral. They were easy prey to high-pressured salesmanship and only the rabbi or minister could protect the family from such exploitation.

Rabbi Brill was able to ease my fears as well as those of Mr. Roth. "It will not be necessary to buy a plain wooden box. There are some fairly elaborate coffins here made of wood and glued together without nails. I also think Mr. Roth would be more satisfied if the price of the coffin were to be determined only by the cost of the coffin itself and not include any others charges. All other funeral costs may be itemized separately."

The undertaker made some quick calculations and, when he realized that the rabbi's suggestion was actually in his best interest, he consented to the arrangement. Once the coffin was chosen, the rabbi excused himself and Jack and I made the financial arrangements. We agreed to the extra charge for moving the body from the synagogue to the chapel for the second service, and for other charges that the undertaker made up on the spot. Dad had set aside enough money for the funeral so that we didn't have to quibble.

When we finished at the chapel, I drove Rabbi Brill home. My sister and brother left to prepare their families to stay over the Sabbath in our parents' house. They knew that they weren't going to be allowed to drive from the home to their own dwellings after dinner as long as Rabbi Brill was around. I have never driven on Shabbat but I can't say the same for them. As far as space was concerned, there was room for everyone. The house has eight bedrooms plus a room for the housekeeper.

I had anticipated that Rabbi Brill would try to take a nap before the Sabbath but I saw him reading from the books in the study. My father's library of religious works was as extensive as that of any practicing rabbi, and Rabbi Brill had no trouble finding what he needed.

The Sabbath meal passed quietly without the usual singing. Rabbi Brill recited the the prayer over the wine, but he did not encourage us to sing the Sabbath hymns. While mourning was forbidden on the Sabbath, singing melodies in the privacy of the family home might be inappropriate. Rabbi Brill held forth during the dinner and it was a pleasure to listen to him. That he was extremely knowledgeable in Jewish law was obvious from the start. The surprise was that he took pains to express himself in a very simple manner, regardless of the complexity of the subject. He made sure to present all matters in a way that even unlearned people could easily follow.

Among the interesting things that he explained was the origin of the shrouds. He told us that in ancient days rich people were buried in the most luxurious garments available. Since the poor could not afford such clothes, they were publicly humiliated in front of those who came to attend the services. Often they would not conduct the services properly to avoid the embarrassment. The rabbis then made a rule that all deceased persons, rich or poor, had to be buried in simple white cloth that was in reach of even the poorest family. The rule protected the poor from being put to shame at the time of the funeral.

He also explained the requirement of the wooden coffin. This was not to prevent the rich from being ostentatious. Rather, it was a technical aspect of the law relating to impurity. Metal was a carrier of impurity under Jewish law, whereas plain wood was not.

After dinner, I was able to speak with the rabbi privately about the question of rending the garments. He sensed my anxiety on the matter and was able to ease my mind to a degree.

"You have been accustomed," he told me, "to undertakers who cut the ribbons before the service in the chapel. If we cut the garments properly at that time it might cause you embarrassment in front of your employees and associates. One thing we can do is wait with the cutting of the garments until we arrive at the cemetery for the burial. Most American rabbis perform the ritual at the cemetery in any event. The people who attend the public ceremony will be able to see you properly dressed. Not many of them will attend the actual burial. The problem will be during the Shiva mourning period when people come to console you at the home."

"May we replace the torn garments when we get home?" I asked.

"Technically, you may change the garments, but it would serve no purpose at all. If you put on different garments during the seven days of mourning, the latter clothing has to be cut as well, and you are back where you started. Over the Sabbath, I will study the matter further and will try to make this ritual less obtrusive than it is when practiced in Israel."

I thanked Rabbi Brill for his concern. Prior to the dinner, we had all walked to the synagogue for services and we did so again on Saturday morning. Because of our situation, the usual honors that we received every Saturday morning were not bestowed upon us. Rabbi Brill, however, was given considerable recognition and was invited by Rabbi Singer to deliver the Sabbath sermon. For a man who wasn't a practicing rabbi, he did extraordinarily well. He clearly lacked pulpit experience and he had very little flare for the dramatic, but he spoke like the teacher he was, in a calm and measured manner, and the worshippers at the services were quite impressed.

In the afternoon, the rabbi brought up the subject of the rending of the garments. He said that insofar as Carol and my mother were concerned, the problem would be minimal since limits are placed on the rending of garments worn by women in deference to the laws of modesty. These same leniencies would apply in the secondary cutting of their replacement garments as well. As far as the sons were concerned, since he was responsible for conducting the services he would have no choice but to cut the garments properly at the cemetery. Thereafter, if the sons chose to change the garments, it was no longer his responsibility but theirs. At that time, they would have to cut the garments by themselves. If they didn't request his assistance, they were free to use their discretion.

I understood the drift of what he was saying, and I thanked him for it. What he meant, in simple terms, was that at the cemetery, where he was in charge, the family would have to conduct the ritual according to the books. Thereafter, he would not function as a policeman, but would leave the extent of our observance of the law up to our own conscience. While this was not the strictest possible approach, the compromise was only in the area of cutting the replacement garments. The original garments would be rent far more properly than most American rabbis would dare to do. In my case, I intended to cut the replacement jacket properly as well.

On Saturday night, Rabbi Brill went to the funeral home with two volunteers. We stayed at my parents' house and reminisced about Dad before turning in. It was cold in Buffalo on Sunday morning, but at least it wasn't snowing and the wind was not too sharp. I was surprised at the size of the turnout at the synagogue: Every seat was taken and it was standing room only in both the men's section and the women's section. Rabbi Brill allowed the coffin to be brought into the synagogue, but only after warning those who were of priestly descent that they had to leave the building. Cohanim, as these people are called, may not remain in a building when a dead body is within the same structure. My brother-in-law, Joe, was one of those who had to step out.

Rabbi Brill called upon Rabbi Singer, as the congregational rabbi, to read one of the Psalms and deliver a message. In his eulogy, Rabbi Singer spoke of the support my father gave to the synagogue as well as to all other worthwhile institutions in the community. He praised my father for his hard work and industriousness, which resulted in the building of a major company. He said nothing about my father's character or personality and I was able to understand the omission.

In the major eulogy, Rabbi Brill offered a long discourse on the moral and ethical teachings observed very carefully by my father. He cited the Sages of Israel, who taught that when a man dies he is not escorted to heaven by the gold and silver and other material assets that he accumulated during his lifetime. The only thing that accompanies the soul to heaven is the Torah that the man has studied and the good deeds that he has done during his lifetime.

"Meir Seidman," the rabbi said, "will be able to meet the Lord escorted by vast knowledge of Torah and a long record of good deeds."

The rabbi also mentioned that one way of honoring a deceased person was to establish a yeshiva as a memorial to him. Nevertheless, some of the greatest scholars were not privileged to have yeshivot named after them, even after being dead for many years. In my father's case, however, he had a yeshiva named after him while he was yet alive and that yeshiva, 'Beit Meir,' would continue to carry the name of Meir Seidman long after his death.

"Even if a man donates a great sum of money," the rabbi said, "a yeshiva will not be named after him unless he is worthy of the honor. When Rabbi Steiner founded the yeshiva, he did not hesitate to call it Beit Meir because he knew that Mr. Seidman was a Torah scholar who observed the commandments strictly."

Rabbi Brill then turned to the children and spoke of our duties to honor our father's memory. It was not critical to accomplish this by acts of charity or the establishment of impressive memorials; rather, he said, it was far more urgent to honor a father's memory by following in his footsteps. From his vantage in heaven, Mr. Seidman would be watching his children to see whether they were living in keeping with the teachings and moral values he had spent a whole lifetime trying to implant in their hearts.

When the synagogue service was over, the pallbearers were summoned to carry the coffin to the hearse. The hearse transported the body to the funeral chapel for the second part of the service. Members of the family traveled to the chapel in cars provided by the undertaker.

Here it was Rabbi Singer who opened the services, with a reading of Psalms in English. He then introduced a number of public officials from Buffalo. Included among them was the Mayor of the city, a congressman and the president of the Chamber of Commerce. All of them extolled my father as a man of vision and industry who played a major role in the commerce of Buffalo and its philanthropic organizations. After delivering his own sermon, Rabbi Singer called upon Rabbi Brill to bring a message from the State of Israel.

This was somewhat of an overstatement, because Rabbi Brill enjoyed no special status in Israel that would entitle him to speak on behalf of the State. Rabbi Brill made sure to correct the oversight, explaining that he was speaking from the point of view of the religious community in Israel, and only in an individual capacity. He explained that the soul of man is not limited by geographical borders. Attributes such as kindness and charity easily transcend national boundaries. While heavily supporting charitable institutions in Buffalo, my father had a warm place in his heart for the State of Israel. This was his first place of refuge after escaping from the destruction of Europe and he always had fond memories of his Torah studies in the Holy Land.

This love for Israel had led him to establish a seminary in the Holy Land that bore his name and provided religious instruction for hundreds of students. As the senior faculty member, Rabbi Brill said he was personally able to attest to the ongoing support and encouragement that the dean had received from Meir Seidman. "While the yeshiva sponsored by Mr. Seidman received the lion's share of his beneficence, he also supported hundreds of other institutions in the Holy Land. No representative of any institution in Israel who visited his office left empty-handed."

After a few more speakers, Rabbi Singer called on me to say a few words on behalf of the family. I had asked for the time because I wanted to thank the community for honoring my father, and I wanted to reassure all of the employees that the humane policies instituted by my father would be continued in his absence. "Our company may grow," I said, "but it will never become too big to listen to the voice of every single employee."

Rabbi Singer read a few more prayers in English and the cantor of the congregation chanted a memorial prayer. Following that, we undertook the drive to the cemetery. Once again, the undertaker followed the strict instructions of Rabbi Brill to the letter. He had requested that the family cars follow the hearse immediately to the grave, instead of holding back while the cemetery workers conducted the burial and allowed the family to sit in the warmth of their cars. Rabbi Brill required significant participation from the children, even though it was uncomfortably cold.

He gathered the pallbearers at the back end of the hearse and, although it was a heavy coffin, he made sure that it was hand carried rather than wheeled. He instructed the cemetery workers to remove the grass mats from the top of the grave and to permit him to operate the belts that lowered the coffin into the grave. This was something that Rabbi Steiner had cautioned him about. In many cemeteries, the workers covered the grave with mats and deposited the coffin temporarily alongside the grave while the services were conducted. The family then departed, leaving the actual interment to be carried out later by the workers. Safely out of sight of the family, the workers would lower the coffin quickly with a forklift and use a bulldozer to fill the grave. Sometimes the workers left the coffin out in the open overnight and didn't perform the burial until the next morning.

Rabbi Brill explained to me that under Jewish law, the period of mourning cannot start officially until after the coffin has been lowered into the ground and fully covered with earth up to ground level. After the body was lowered, Rabbi Brill began to cover the coffin with dirt from the mound alongside the grave. He worked for several minutes and then put the shovel down where somebody else picked it up and continued the work. I found out later that it is the custom not to pass the shovel from hand to hand, but I never could find out the basis for the practice. When the grave was entirely filled to Rabbi Brill's satisfaction, he began to chant the memorial prayers. He then gathered the family together. He had us all recite the Blessing of the True Judge and then, starting with Jack, he performed the ritual of rending the garments. Jewish law requires that on the passing of a parent, the garments must not only be cut but also further torn by hand. After such a procedure, the garments may not be repaired, even if a way can be found to do so. Overcoats are not cut, but all the other regular garments are rent.

When that was done, Rabbi Brill had us recite the mourners' kaddish. Here, I learned something new. Although I had recited kaddish at the synagogue hundreds of times while I was conducting prayers, the kaddish recited by the sons at the grave site has a different wording than the standard prayer. While I read Hebrew well, I still needed assistance from Rabbi Brill. Jack required even more help.

Following the kaddish, all those assembled at the cemetery formed two lines and the mourners were instructed to pass between the rows. As we did so, those in the audience recited the prayer, "May the Almighty comfort you among all the mourners of Zion and Jerusalem." We drove home from the cemetery where all the preparations had been made for sitting Shiva, the seven-day mourning period. Mirrors were covered and the mourners removed their shoes. The undertaker provided low stools for us to sit on. I am in good physical shape and was able to manage it. For my mother it was impossible. I asked Rabbi Brill what to do. He quickly removed a seat cushion from one of the easy chairs and let her sit on the lower part of the chair. It was not too uncomfortable for her there, but she required assistance in getting up.

The meal of consolation was served to us while we were seated on the low chairs and stools. Traditionally, the meal consists of eggs and bread, the egg being a symbol of sorrow. When we finished the meal, Rabbi Brill gave us additional instructions.

We had announced that the hours of visiting for the general public would be from two to four in the afternoon and from eight to ten in the evening. At the synagogue, we advised the worshippers that prayer services would be held at 7:30 each morning and 4:30 each afternoon for the combined afternoon and evening services. We limited the visiting hours not only for the convenience of the family but also so that we should be able to recite the prayers without being disturbed.

Rabbi Brill told us not to inquire about the welfare of the families of those who visited. In general, during the first three days of mourning, the visitor is not permitted to open the conversation so Rabbi Brill suggested that, wherever possible, we should speak first. After three days it was not necessary to worry about such customs. While it was important for us not to engage in any levity, it was equally important for us not to embarrass our visitors by attempting to limit the nature of their conversation while they were trying to comfort us.

During the services, it was understood that I would be the one who did all the chanting. This normally would not have presented a problem to me because, at the synagogue, I did so all the time. However, the rules for prayers offered in a mourner's house are considerably different from those which govern prayers recited at a synagogue, and certain key prayers are omitted. Again here, Rabbi Brill showed great expertise as he reviewed these changes with me and I performed creditably well. Every day after I completed the afternoon prayers, Rabbi Brill addressed the worshippers. At first I thought that he was just trying to use the opportunity to teach. I realized after a while that he was also speaking in order to delay the start of the evening service.

It is a constant rabbinic problem that when the afternoon and evening prayers are combined, the evening worship is started before a sufficient period of time has elapsed following sundown. Since none of the audience would have the temerity to interrupt Rabbi Brill while he was lecturing, we never ran into the problem of reciting the evening prayers too early. During the teaching, the rabbi was quite relaxed. The audience was made up of regular shul members who are accustomed to hearing words of Torah.

Following the discussion, a special kaddish, called the Rabbinical Kaddish, had to be recited. Here too, the experience was new to me, but at least I had heard the words offered many times in the synagogue and I was able to do it.

During the week of mourning, we never had problems gathering a minyan. The regular shul-goers would come as long as they were sure they were not endangering the minyan at the synagogue. In the afternoon, many of the company employees who were Jewish left work a little early to attend the prayers.

Because of the services and the visitors, I didn't have much time to talk to Rabbi Brill alone. The only time we could really be together was in the morning. Although we did not study any formal texts because mourners are forbidden to study Torah, we did discuss various aspects of religious life. I feel that I learned more in one week with Rabbi Brill than in a whole year of my yeshiva studies.

It was at one such session that I brought up a matter that was on my mind. "I know that you said that the best memorial we could establish for our father would be our own ethical behavior, but I feel that in the present day and age that is not sufficient. There are conventional types of memorials and I would feel remiss if we didn't do something to perpetuate the memory of my father in a formal way."

"I take it that you are talking of something other than a cemetery memorial, such as a mausoleum."

"There I think that a regular monument will be sufficient and I am sure that we will do that in time. I was thinking more in terms of a living memorial."

"Menachem," the rabbi said, "the thought is a very proper one, but it is not appropriate for the week of mourning. Any discussion of a memorial would necessarily involve planning, calculations and many business and tax considerations. All of these are not the type of activity one should engage in during the first seven days of mourning."

"I do need to discuss the matter with you and I don't know whether you will remain with us until after the Shiva."

"The Shiva is over for you Saturday night and I wasn't planning to leave until Monday morning, if it is all right for me to stay here. I would be glad to meet with you first on Sunday morning and then with the other members of the family if necessary."

I was not really sure why Rabbi Brill was hesitating. I have heard of other rabbis approaching families for donations during the days of mourning. Somehow I felt that it wasn't only piety that was holding him back. Whatever it was, I decided that it could wait until Sunday, and I accepted the rabbi's suggestion.

"There is, however, another matter which I have to discuss with you, which shouldn't be put off. The family has already spent tens of thousands of dollars on funeral expenses, and I'm not even counting lost business. Everybody who was in any way involved in the proceedings has been handsomely rewarded. You played a key role in all the services and, I might add, you performed in an exemplary manner. You will not believe how many people spoke to me and told me how touched they were with your words. So far, we haven't yet given you anything and we haven't even considered your travel expenses from Israel."

Rabbi Brill thought for a moment and then answered. "As far as expenses are concerned, I did not use any of my own funds. The sorry truth is that even if I wanted to take a pleasure trip to America, I could not afford to do so. All of my expenses were covered by the yeshiva at the discretion of Rabbi Steiner. In his opinion, your father did so much for the yeshiva that expenditures in his honor are justified and it was he who authorized my trip.

"As for personal services, I am proud to say that I have never accepted any compensation or fees for performing religious rites since I was ordained. I have conducted or participated in scores of weddings for students at the yeshiva. When the parents wish to contribute something for the service, I tell them that it is not necessary. If they still insist, I ask them to make an offering in honor of the occasion to the yeshiva itself. In your case, Menachem, I have the feeling that no matter what I may do for your family, it will be infinitely less than what your family has done for me. Without your father's help, the yeshiva could not have existed and I would not have been able to be an instructor of Torah. If you nevertheless feel that you want to compensate somebody for services rendered, I will be glad to talk to you about that, as well, on Sunday."

I dropped the subject, but I am too much of a businessman not to realize that even in the yeshiva world there is no such thing as a free lunch. Rabbi Brill was putting off the discussion but I was sure that the matter would come up on Sunday and cost my family and me a pretty penny. I knew as well that, considering the level of Rabbi Brill's dedication, it would be hard for me to turn down any request that would be forthcoming.

Since we started our Shiva on Sunday after the burial but before sundown, Sunday counted as one full day of the mourning period. Saturday, then, was the seventh day. There is no mourning on the Sabbath, of course, but there is general agreement that the Sabbath counts as one of the seven days. Some authorities require that the mourners sit another hour on Saturday night in such a case, but Rabbi Brill did not insist upon it. On the final Sabbath we did discuss some of the laws of mourning that apply after the first seven days. The one that most concerned me was the one that dealt with shaving. I am always clean-shaven, but I knew that I would not be allowed to shave for a while. Rabbi Brill said 30 days and I felt that I could live with that.

The rabbi was more concerned with the daily recitation of

the kaddish for eleven months. I told him that I am normally a weekend worshipper but that I would attend services daily during the year of mourning as long as I was in town. I could not guarantee attendance at afternoon or evening services because of business responsibilities and I could say nothing at all as far as Jack was concerned.

"Say kaddish as often as you can," Rabbi Brill said. "It is most preferable for the son himself to say kaddish because that is the ultimate honor a son can accord his father. Before I left, Rabbi Steiner indicated that he would also be reciting the kaddish for your father and he, of course, attends all services. Try to have Jack cover for you in case you are out of town. I want to make sure that a son says the kaddish at least once a day for the entire eleven months."

15

ON SUNDAY MORNING, I MET with Rabbi Brill after services at the synagogue and breakfast at home. Carol and Jack and their families returned to their own homes on Saturday night and the house was put back into shape. The mirrors and pictures were uncovered and the stools were returned to the undertaker.

Sitting in the library, Rabbi Brill opened the discussion with an unusual disclaimer. "I am acting in this matter on my own authority. I want you to know that Rabbi Steiner asked me not to engage in any discussion with the family about memorials during the course of my visit."

"I can understand that for the seven-day mourning period," I said, "but why not thereafter?"

"As you understood, discussion of these matters would have been inappropriate during the seven days of mourning from a point of view of Jewish practice. After the Shiva, it becomes a subject that relates both to aesthetics and to personalities."

The dialogue was getting a little complex so I asked him to explain in a straightforward way.

"I know that I can be open with you, Menachem, because you are a mature and worldly man for your age. Yeshivot always look after the well-being of their supporters just as you would be concerned with the well-being of your customers and employees. If one of them were to take ill you would send a card or visit him in the hospital. By the same token, the yeshiva makes sure that it offers spiritual and personal assistance when any of its patrons are in need.

"The relationship between Rabbi Steiner and your father was not a mere business relationship. It went back almost 70 years and was truly a profound friendship long before the yeshiva was established. Rabbi Steiner would have certainly come to Buffalo if he could have, not in the interests of the school but as a gesture of personal friendship. Any solicitation of funds during the time the spiritual services were being offered would have compromised the nature of the assistance. People would instinctively feel that the help was extended primarily in hopes of gaining rewards."

"What about after the Shiva?"

"As long as it is part of the original visit, the thought might still persist even after the primary mourning period is concluded."

I knew that I wasn't getting the whole story, so I asked the rabbi to explain the personal aspects of the case.

"Rabbi Steiner said that if you inquired about memorials after the Shiva, I should request that you to speak directly to him."

I was really shocked to hear what he was saying.

"That is incomprehensible," I said. "He trusted you to deal with the most important supporters of the yeshiva at a time of great stress and emotion, when one difficult decision after the other had to be made. Why would he not trust you to negotiate a routine financial matter?" A sudden thought crossed my mind and I blurted it out before I could control myself. "You don't work on a commission, do you?"

"No Menachem, I do not. I have been making one collection

trip to the United States each year for the last eight years and I have never received anything other than my regular salary. Last year I secured over $50,000 for the Feldman library, above my regular fund-raising, and I earned no special reward."

"Why then doesn't he trust you?"

"It has nothing to do with trust. As you pointed out, he entrusted me with a service during which a single mistake could have caused irreparable damage to a relationship that has flourished for more than half a century. To tell the truth, Menachem, I don't fully understand Rabbi Steiner's hesitancy. It may be one of several things. A major gift, which would result in the expansion of the yeshiva, may place more burdens on his shoulders than already exist. He is in poor health, his wife is critically ill, and he simply may not be able to cope with new responsibilities. Another possibility is that he was reluctant to over-exploit his personal friendship with your father to benefit the school. I remember that when he started the kollel I wanted to know why he didn't ask your father to finance it. He replied that your father was in poor health and that he was already doing enough. I think he was embarrassed to show your father that he was so dependent on him."

The explanations were quite tactfully presented but once again I sensed that truth was being glossed over. "Would Rabbi Steiner perhaps begrudge you credit for raising a large sum of money?"

"It would be in very poor taste for me to ever indicate such a thing."

That was the old 'you said it, I didn't' ploy and, being a businessman of long-standing, I know it when I hear it.

"Let me ask you this, Rabbi Brill. When you solicited the Feldman donation was Rabbi Steiner genuinely pleased?"

Rabbi Brill reflected for a moment and decided he had to

tell the truth. "Not really. I didn't know why, but my wife and others explained it to me."

I had my answer and did not have to probe further. I didn't want Rabbi Brill to get into trouble by breaking any promises that he may have made to Rabbi Steiner, so I asked him if he had committed himself to the dean not to talk about a memorial with me.

"I took special pains not to commit myself to that because I realized it was not in the best interests of the yeshiva. Remember that I have invested 12 years in the school, all of my working life. I could see that Rabbi Steiner was displeased by my failure to agree to his request but my conscience did not allow me to do so."

"Listen, my father would have probably spoken only to Rabbi Steiner. I used to say hello to him when he came to visit but I was never able to get close to him. You are an American fellow and I have come to know you well. I would rather talk to you about this matter."

"You are free to do so. No matter what his personal feelings are, I cannot believe that Rabbi Steiner will overrule any commitments that I make on behalf of the yeshiva."

Once I had such an assurance, I felt no need to hesitate in dealing with the rabbi on the subject of a memorial. I painted a clear picture for him. "Let me go back to the time that my father spoke to me before he died. He had just put $3,000,000 into our family charity foundation from his own funds. Dad was a clever man. He made all the children multi-millionaires but he knew human nature. He knew that no matter how rich we were we would never have enough, so he locked the money away where it could only be used for charity. He also requested that we continue our annual grant to his yeshiva until the mortgage was paid up so that Rabbi Steiner wouldn't have to worry about the building.

"Then he said something strange. He said that we could use some of the money that he left for capital grants but didn't explain what he meant. Last week I began to understand his intention. My father was a very humble man. He couldn't come straight out and ask that we build a memorial for him like the pyramids the old Egyptian kings used to erect when they were still alive. That, however, was what he had in mind. He wanted to make sure that he would be remembered after he was gone."

"I think that a rational person could read that intention into his words," Rabbi Brill agreed.

"Unfortunately, he didn't specify the memorial he had in mind or the amount that he was thinking of. The only limiting factor that exists is his specific request that we maintain the annual donations that our foundation allocates. That means that the bulk of the extra money he left must still remain in the foundation to generate enough revenue for annual giving. Remember that between the United Jewish Appeal, the United Way and the Federation, we are talking of over $500,000."

"I can certainly answer your question about the nature of the memorial. Your father was a learned and God-fearing Jew, a respecter of Torah and Torah scholarship. It would not be in keeping with his memory to dedicate a skating rink or even a concert hall. A true memorial for a man such as your father would have to be religious in nature and related to Torah."

"Essentially that leaves only synagogues and yeshivot."

"That is not an insignificant remainder. Let me ask you, Menachem, what act of charity did your father do that gave him the most satisfaction in his life?"

Rabbi Brill was clever. He was working hard for his yeshiva in Israel and I could not fault him for that. I answered the question truthfully.

"He was prouder of his yeshiva than anything else. It meant

more to him than his shul and the local day school where we studied."

"Let me tell you why, if I may. All of these institutions are necessary and worthwhile. They all serve the cause of Torah. But in all of these places there is a human component. Your father's great satisfaction with the yeshiva was derived from knowing that this institution was run by a true scholar and a true friend. He was secure in the knowledge that Judaism would never be compromised at the yeshiva. I don't think that he felt as secure with the shul or the day school."

"You are most certainly right in that respect. The yeshiva, however, already bears my father's name and we support it heavily as is. I was thinking more in terms of a new memorial. Besides, the security factor is not unquestionable. Rabbi Steiner is in poor health and we cannot be sure what will happen with the yeshiva after he leaves the scene."

"That is precisely why I welcome this opportunity to talk to you. The way things stand, Menachem, not only would any new memorial donation you make be insecure but even the original gift that your father gave to establish the yeshiva may be imperiled."

"Why is that?"

"For that you have to know something about the yeshiva scene and, together with your knowledge of business, you will be able to understand the full picture. There are many fine, small yeshivot in Israel and Beit Meir is one of them. They flourish as long as the founder is alive and can maintain his following. In a very few cases, where the founder has groomed a successor carefully while yet alive, there is a successful transition of authority and the school survives. In most cases, however, the small yeshiva dies with the passing of the founder. Yes, there is a often a futile attempt to carry on the yeshiva by heirs or others but, in the end, the yeshiva crumbles."

"What happens to the property? The Beit Meir building is probably worth a million dollars."

"The real assets, one way or another, go to the founder and his heirs. It is often difficult, though, to pass down privately what looks like a public property and was built with tax-free public contributions. In America, it can't even be done legally. What sometimes happens in the case of a defunct synagogue is that the surviving directors turn it over to some small non-profit organization in return for kickbacks or similar considerations. In Israel, it is not quite necessary to go that far. The founder sells the yeshiva enterprise, including the property, to another rabbi who feels that he can maintain a school. The other man may already have a small nucleus of students or some wealthy backer and may actually succeed in running the yeshiva."

"What about the proceeds? Are they ever returned to the donors?"

"Never. The original gifts were freely given and written off for tax deduction. You must remember that the founder invested his life and often his life's savings in the yeshiva and, in most of his stewardship, he drew no salary above the bare minimum sufficient for existence. There is no pension established for him by the yeshiva and nothing to provide for his old age or retirement. His children, during those years, receive virtually no support from their father. There is therefore some measure of justice in bestowing material gains upon the founder's heirs. By the way, there are any number of privately owned synagogues in America that abide by the same rules."

"Speaking of children, doesn't Rabbi Steiner have children who could inherit his position?"

"He has two sons who have sufficient knowledge to teach in the yeshiva. They are, in fact, now teaching in other institutions. But running a yeshiva requires more than learning. It requires character, personality, vision and administrative ability. Neither of his two sons could run the yeshiva well for more than a year. By the end of the spring semester, the students would be heading for the exits."

"What about you, Rabbi Brill. From a layman's point of view I judge that you have all of the requisite abilities."

"I would be lying to you if I said the thought has not crossed my mind during the lonely nights on my American fund-raising trips. In all humility, I think I have the ability to run a yeshiva, but I have dismissed such thoughts because I would not want to run Beit Meir as a small private school. I do not have any personal resources and I barely make it through the month just trying to feed my family. I have no rich backers either, and undertaking such a venture would seriously jeopardize the security of my family and the welfare of my children."

"You must have some solution to the problem. I'm sure my father originally intended to do more than bestow personal wealth on Rabbi Steiner. He was terribly proud of the fact that boys were sitting and learning Torah in the school."

"A solution exists, Menachem, and I am going to present it to you. There's a certain threshold where a yeshiva ceases to be a small private enterprise and becomes a public institution in the truest sense. To achieve such a designation a yeshiva must have a substantial number of students and a large faculty. At that point, the yeshiva becomes Beit Meir in the public mind and not Rabbi Steiner's Yeshiva, as many people call it now. The larger yeshivot always survive the passing of the original founders. From your own experience, you would surely admit that an institution such as Yeshiva University could survive the passing of any dean or president."

"YU has thousands of students and scores of buildings. What is the threshold number of students in the yeshiva world?"

"When we talk of yeshivot we are not including elementary schools that are sometimes attached to a yeshiva. We are talking only of the number of post-high school students. The biggest yeshivot in the world may draw more than 1000 students. But the number of students in many of the larger schools that have been around for generations is under 500. Many well-established schools have less than 200 students. I would say, Menachem, that any yeshiva with more than 120 students is a secure, permanent institution."

"You are saying that Bet Meir would have to double its size to reach the threshold?"

"That is correct."

"Could you find that many students?"

"We could recruit even more than that without difficulty. The fact is that Beit Meir has become one of the toughest institutions in Israel at which to be accepted. We annually turn down hundreds of applicants and often we are under tremendous pressure to accept certain students. The reason for this is that Beit Meir is known as a serious institution. No one goes there unless he actually wants to learn and has achieved an excellent record before applying. Rabbi Steiner gives an extremely rigorous examination to all applicants and closely supervises them once they are at the school."

"In that case, why hasn't the yeshiva grown over the years?"

"The limiting factor is the lack of dormitory space. Virtually all unmarried students in the school are in residence. When your father helped Rabbi Steiner buy the apartment house, it only could house 42 students, three to a room. We have been putting four students into most of the rooms so that we now sleep 53 students.

"We have a plan to solve the problem. There is a lot with an unoccupied building backing up to the yeshiva but facing on another street. We would like to build a dormitory with a dining room and a kitchen on that land and connect it to the present building. Then we could use the present dining room for a new Beit Midrash. If we need additional classrooms, we could combine some of the dorm rooms in the old building and make classrooms out of them."

"About how many students would you be able to accommodate in the new dorm?"

"We were thinking of a dorm for 80 students and a dining room that could seat 250.Including the kollel, the yeshiva would then have a total enrollment of over 150 students."

"You must be talking of a lot of money."

"About a million dollars, including the land and furnishings."

The price did not seem outrageous to me. In fact, I was quite interested in seeing what could be done in Israel for that kind of money.

"Do you have any plans or sketches?" I asked.

"We didn't make any real building plans but I do have a floor plan and an elevation." Rabbi Brill handed me the two sheets that he had brought with him and I studied them. I am the building expert in the family and I go over all construction projects. Sometimes we build free-standing stores and sometimes we rent space in shopping centers. By now, I have come to understand construction pretty well. I went over the sketches with Rabbi Brill and found him to be pretty knowledgeable about the project. Finally I asked him the key question.

"How would you finance the new building?"

"As matters now stand, we have no way of doing it. If we had half a million dollars to start, we would undertake it. We could then get some government funds, enlarge our present mortgage and do some fund-raising. Without a major initial donation, it is simply out of the question."

"I take it that you would be happy if our family chose this as our memorial project."

"I would indeed. In fact I can suggest a name for the project that would eternalize your father's memory. I was thinking of calling it the 'Zichron Meir Residence Hall.'"

I knew that 'Zichron' meant in memory of. What I didn't know was whether Rabbi Brill would let us have the name for less than half a million and, if not, whether my brother and sister would agree to such a large donation.

"Could the family get the name for a large donation that is not quite a half million? When I was thinking about a memorial I was thinking in the range of $100,000."

Rabbi Brill has a lot of courage, I must admit. He didn't waffle and didn't hesitate. "The yeshiva would accept any help that your family can give towards the million dollars we need. We could set aside a number of rooms or even an entire floor in your father's memory, but the name of the building can only be given in return for a donation that will enable us to start the project."

"Are you staying overnight, Rabbi Brill?"

"Yes."

"In that case, I will discuss the matter with my brother and sister this afternoon. We will be able to meet tonight and give you an answer one way or another."

At 7:30 in the evening, the family gathered to meet with Rabbi Brill. By that time, we had reached general agreement amongst ourselves that only a yeshiva of some sort would serve as a fitting memorial for Dad. The local day school was out of the question because it was an elementary school and didn't provide Torah studies on Dad's level. The only American yeshiva that stood a good chance was Yeshiva University. The trouble there was that even if we gave $500,000 to the institution it wouldn't buy a permanent memorial such as a building. Maybe a professorial chair or several scholarships, but nothing really distinctive. Furthermore, as an alumnus, I was already supporting the school quite heavily and the business was also giving its share.

I argued that Dad had shown which institution was most dear to him by endowing and supporting Rabbi Steiner's yeshiva above all others. If we really wanted to honor him, we should do what was necessary to preserve the Beit Meir Yeshiva. We then asked Rabbi Brill to come in and, when the discussion got underway, I acted as the spokesman. "Rabbi Brill, I am sure you will pleased to hear that our family has agreed to dedicate the new dormitory of Beit Meir in memory of our father. We will donate the amount you asked for but we want to be sure that certain conditions are met."

The rabbi did his utmost to control his emotions and not reveal the inner turmoil that beset him. His feelings were a mixture of joy and dread as he grasped the enormity of what he had done. In a voice that revealed only a slight tremor he said, "I can assure you that the school will meet any reasonable terms."

"Firstly," I continued, "we require that the dormitory be called 'Zichron Meir.' We realize that you are entitled to sell individual rooms in the building to other donors, but we are reserving the façade of the structure, the lobby and the name itself, exclusively."

"That is understood."

"Secondly, you must sign a contract with a builder within the next four months for at least fifty per cent more than the amount we are donating. We will sign the pledge card only if it has that condition, and no money will be forthcoming until you send us a copy of the contract." That was Jack's condition. I trusted Rabbi Brill but Jack was afraid that the yeshiva would take the money and delay building or build a much smaller building.

"That is a fair condition as well."

"Next, there must be a public memorial service at the yeshiva in memory of our father when you break ground for the new building."

"I am glad you brought that up. All of you were present with your father when ground was broken for our first building. We will certainly have an appropriate ceremony when we start work on the new dormitory. We probably will begin to build in June so that we can move students in by September of the following year. Of course, it is understood that you will all be present for the ceremony."

My mother had been listening quietly to the discussion although she normally did not participate in family councils. She had tremendous respect for my father and let him dominate any such proceedings. She did, however, have strong opinions of her own and, in a subtle way, she quietly exerted a positive influence over us.

"You did say an appropriate ceremony, Rabbi Brill?" she asked.

"Of course, wasn't the first one satisfactory?"

"The nicest thing I can say about it was that it left a lot to be desired. It was, in fact, pretty chaotic, and my husband was a little upset by it."

"I wasn't there at the time, so I can't say. I think that the yeshiva has learned something in the past twelve years and I assure you that I will personally do my best to have a dignified ceremony."

"There is one last condition that we must impose which may not be entirely to your liking."

"I remain certain that you will not make any unreasonable requests."

"This one concerns you, so don't be so sure."

"You realize that I am only a senior instructor at Beit Meir, not the dean?"

"We are aware of that. But there is a matter of principle here. The Seidman family, as you can see, is not a particularly poor one and we are not inclined to accept charity or even gifts from a yeshiva that is struggling to survive, or from a rabbi who barely supports his family."

"I don't know what you are driving at."

"Rabbi, the yeshiva paid for your trip and you yourself provided us with ten days of religious services. Rabbi Steiner has committed himself to recite kaddish for an entire year. You and the yeshiva, however, are the only ones who have received no compensation for services rendered. Such expenses are deductible from estate taxes and you need not worry about our ability to pay for them."

"I believe I told you that the yeshiva provided such assistance solely out of esteem and friendship for your late father."

"I didn't accept the idea when you told it to me the first time and the rest of the family doesn't buy it now. To make a long story short, we are giving you two envelopes. One is for the yeshiva and one is for you, personally. We don't care what the yeshiva does with its money but we are restricting you from turning the money over to the school either directly or indirectly."

A look of dismay crossed Rabbi Brill's face. "I have a statement to make and then I wish to ask two questions."

"Go ahead."

"As far as the yeshiva, is concerned, I have no right to refuse a donation. I will accept the offering on the condition that everyone understands that the yeshiva was not motivated by any thought of gain when it undertook to be of service to the family."

"We definitely do."

"My two questions are, what do you mean by 'indirectly,' and what happens if I decline to accept my fee?"

Jack was ready with the answer. "Indirect means that you might decide to keep the check but waive an equal amount of your salary at the yeshiva. If you decline to keep the money for your own use, our family will decline to make its donation."

Rabbi Brill began to realize that although the Seidmans seemed to be gentle souls, they could be quite tough when they had to.

"Listen, I will not reject a half-million-dollar donation to ease my conscience. Here, too, I want everyone to understand that I was not looking for personal reward when I undertook my assignment."

"That's understood. Why don't you prepare a pledge card while we serve some drinks to confirm the deal."

"You may skip the drinks," the rabbi said, "because they are not in keeping with the spirit of the mourning period. As for the pledge card, it would probably be best if you filled it out yourself."

I took the card he gave me, wrote out our conditions on the back and signed the card on behalf of the family. I returned the signed pledge together with the two envelopes that I had prepared for Rabbi Brill. He didn't open the envelopes but he did thank the family warmly and praised us for the mitzvah that we were doing.

SANDRA

16

MONDAY MORNING, I WAS BUSY preparing for an 11:00 A.M. lecture when my mother called me at my apartment. She's not supposed to call then because I'm trying to concentrate on my work, so I figured she had something important to tell me.

"I hate to bother you before class, Sandra, but I just got a call from Rabbi Brill."

"What happened? He needs some more books for the library?"

"Don't be funny with me. He's not even in Israel."

"Where is he?"

"He's in Buffalo and he's on his way here. I invited him for dinner."

"Why did you do that?

"He said he had to see you and he knew that you now have dinner with me on Monday nights."

I chose Mondays because in the spring semester I had no lectures to give on Tuesdays. "Is anything wrong? He wasn't supposed to be coming until August."

"Something is wrong but I don't want to take your time now. Just make sure you don't wear pants tonight."

"No pants?"

"A long skirt and sleeves. I'll see you at seven."

I put the matter out of my mind because teaching a two-hour class plus a senior seminar requires all of my attention.

It was only when I was driving home from Cortland that I began to wonder what could bring Rabbi Brill to Syracuse in the dead of winter. It had to be important because he was missing his classes before Purim. At my apartment I changed to a Boro Park dress and put on a hat before driving over to my mother's place. Rabbi Brill had arrived and was talking to my mother in the living room. He was apparently happy to see me because he greeted me very warmly. As soon as I was seated, my mother left us to prepare the dinner. "You can take care of your business now, Rabbi," she said, before she left. "Dinner will be served in half an hour."

"You are looking very well, Sarah. How is your work coming along?"

I wanted to show off a little, so I said 'Baruch Hashem,' which means 'blessed be God.' No matter what question you ask a religious person in Israel about his condition, he will always give you that same non-committal answer.

"And how is your mother feeling?"

"Baruch Hashem."

The rabbi looked a little annoyed with me so I stopped fooling around and answered the question. "Actually, my mother is extremely well. She was in a terrible depression before we left for Israel and didn't even want to go on living. The trip did her a world of good and she's like a new person. She resumed her activities and she now socializes with her old friends."

"I am glad to hear that. It is written that just being in the Land of Israel makes people wise. It seems to make them healthier as well."

"It certainly did that for her. And do you know what really

clinched it? When the minister of Religious Affairs got up and said all those nice things about her at the dinner; she was in seventh heaven. It restored her self-confidence and made her feel good about herself."

"Speaking about the minister, he really went out of his way to help in this emergency. You see, we got word on Thursday morning about ten days ago, that Mr. Meir Seidman of Buffalo had passed away. Rabbi Steiner couldn't go because of his wife's illness so he asked me to come and represent the yeshiva. That is what brought me to America."

"That's the Seidman who gave the money to start the yeshiva?"

"Yes, it is. Well, I had to leave on short notice and there was only one plane going out on Thursday night. The plane was booked solid and my travel agent couldn't get me on it. My wife, Rivka, suggested that I call the minister. I did, and within fifteen minutes I got my ticket."

Rabbi Brill reflected a minute before the truth dawned on him. "Tell me, Sarah, when you sent him a thank you letter after the dinner, did you add anything unduly generous?"

I thought it best to tell the truth. "You know that the minister is barred from accepting fees for what can be considered official duties. The Ministry, however, may accept gifts and donations. I donated an amount to be spent for worthy causes at the discretion of the minister."

"How much?"

"A thousand dollars."

Baruch let out a sound akin to a whistle. "Not bad for a ten-minute speech. I have to teach three weeks to earn that."

"Maybe I shouldn't tell you the rest of it."

"You mean it gets worse?"

"I'm afraid so. My mother was with me when I was writing

the letters and she saw the check. She asked, 'Is that for the nice man who said those wonderful things about me? The fellow who kissed my hand when we were introduced, and called me Madame Feldman?'"

"'That's the one', I told her."

"'He's a very nice man and I want to send him a check too.' She wrote out a check and put it in the same envelope."

"How much?" Rabbi Brill asked.

"Two thousand dollars."

"I begin to understand why he put himself out to help me with the tickets."

"My father taught me the expression *Az min schmeert furt min,* which translated from the Yiddish means, 'If you grease the wheels the wagon moves.'"

Rabbi Brill was amazed at my Yiddish. Of course, I grew up in a Yiddish-speaking home. My father didn't switch to English until 20 years after coming to the States.

"I understand Yiddish but I can't speak it like that," he said. "Anyway, let me fill you in on my trip."

Before he could start, Mom called us in for dinner. At the table, Rabbi Brill told us about everything that had taken place in Buffalo. He described the eulogies that were delivered at both services and the Shiva and all that went with it. When he finished, I had a question for him. "I'm sure you didn't leave Buffalo empty-handed. What did the family do in the way of a memorial for their late father?"

"Life isn't that easy, Sarah. Rabbi Steiner specifically forbade me to discuss any donations during the Shiva."

"I can understand that, but you were there Sunday after the Shiva ended. You must have tried then."

"Again, life isn't simple. Rabbi Steiner instructed me to tell the family that if they wanted to establish a memorial they should speak to him directly."

I found it hard to believe what I was hearing. Memorial donations are easier to obtain when the family is under the emotional impact of the death. Any delay could have been costly to the yeshiva.

"I hope you were man enough to disregard any such instructions."

"It was not a matter of courage. It was a matter of principle and conscience. I felt that I could not accept an instruction that was not in the best interests of the yeshiva, and I acted accordingly."

"In keeping with the Talmudic principle that one cannot perform an improper act at the behest of another person?" I ventured.

"Precisely. Do you know the source of that teaching?"

"As a matter of fact, I do. I read it in a paper that one of my students wrote on the subject of soldiers who were ordered to commit war crimes and atrocities. I advised him to ask his rabbi for the Jewish point of view on this issue. He did, and he explained that the master is God and that the one who issued the order to do the wrongful act is at best a disciple of the master. When the master says to act in an ethical way and the disciple says to act otherwise, we must obey the master. So if the Torah, which is the word of the Master, instructs us in one way, we must disregard any instructions to the contrary."

Rabbi Brill was impressed and he told my mother how smart I was. She always thought so but was glowing with pride when the rabbi confirmed it.

"It wasn't easy to do it, and I am still very much afraid to face Rabbi Steiner. I have never disobeyed his instructions before."

"With $50,000 in hand, or thereabouts, it shouldn't be hard to face up to him. There is nothing like success to make a hero out of cowards. I hope that you didn't take less from the Seidmans than you did from us."

"Of course not. But despite the fact that I have a signed pledge card for $500,000 in my pocket, I am still fearful."

It was my turn to whistle. "That's what I call a big haul. Rabbi Steiner cannot in any form or manner turn that down. You have nothing to worry about, Baruch. By the way, do you know why Rabbi Steiner didn't want you to solicit from the Seidman family?"

"No," he replied. "I have no idea."

I guess I couldn't hide my surprise too well.

"You do?" he asked.

"I do, Baruch, but it is not for me to tell you. It was told to me in the strictest confidence and, even if I wanted to break the trust, I feel that you are better off not knowing. What are the Seidmans getting for their money?"

"They are making it possible for the yeshiva to start building a new million-dollar dormitory which will be named 'Zichron Meir' in memory of their father."

"Why, that's a wonderful gesture," my mother said, "and I think I know why you have made this special trip to see us."

This time my mother was faster than I was because I figured he wanted us to keep up with the Joneses and dedicate the other half of the building. I expressed this thought aloud.

"No, Sandra," my mother replied. "Rabbi Brill knows that we're not in a position to do that. I venture to say that he wants you to come to Israel to organize the dedication ceremony for the new building."

"Is that it, Rabbi Brill?"

"Yes, it is. Your mother is even more perceptive than you.

I am asking you to run the dedication and, since your mother enjoyed her recent trip to Israel so much, I am inviting her to come with you."

"I was planning to go to Europe with Mom this June."

"I would rather go to Israel," my mother said. "You might meet a nice Jewish man there."

"You have a one-track mind, Mother, I must say."

To Rabbi Brill I said, "I have some reservations about undertaking the project."

"It's a rather sudden request, so I imagine that you do. If you tell me what they are, I may overcome them."

"To begin with, Rabbi Steiner would have a fit if I come back."

"Why is that?"

"He hates me. He thinks I am an *oisvurf*" I used the Yiddish expression because there is no satisfactory English equivalent. Ill-behaved and disrespectful might approach the meaning, but not quite.

"Nonsense. He is not accustomed to independent women with minds of their own, so he was somewhat taken aback when you first appeared on the scene. By now I think he is far more reconciled to you."

Rabbi Brill didn't sound convinced of what he was saying but I let the matter slide. "My main reservation is that I shouldn't be doing the work that you are supposed to be doing."

"I am an academic person and I have no special talent for public relations."

"Not so. Any man who walks out of a home with a half-million dollar pledge is no inept bungler. You saw what has to be done at our dedication and there is no reason why you can't do the same thing at the next ceremony."

"Sarah, if it were anything but a half million dollar donation,

I would undertake it myself. But the Seidmans were upset by the ceremony we held for them twelve years ago, and for that we engaged a public relations professional. Rabbi Steiner won't hire anyone when I am around because he thinks an American can do everything. I personally assured the Seidmans that this time the ceremony will be dignified and I don't see how I can fulfill my promise. Rabbi Steiner will be looking over my shoulder and will not give me a free hand. When you dealt with him, he gave in on almost everything."

"Of course. I had to pay for most of what I got by myself."

"I'm certain that you will be able to convince the Seidmans to pay for what is required for a first-class affair. They specifically told me that under no circumstances will the Seidman family accept gifts or charity from anyone."

"What about my expenses?"

"I myself will underwrite all of your expenses."

"With what? You can't even pay your grocery bills."

"The Seidmans made me accept a fee for my services or else they wouldn't sign the pledge."

"How much?"

"Five thousand dollars."

"And you were complaining about what we gave the minister? They must have said that the money was for your personal use and not to finance a yeshiva ceremony."

"The matter is somewhat delicate but I feel that if I engage a public relations expert to do my work it is a personal expenditure. Let us say that you will be working for me rather than the yeshiva."

"A likely story. It won't hold up in any court on earth and certainly not in a heavenly one."

"You do admit that I can use the money to pay my debts,

don't you? Once they are redeemed, I can borrow enough money to finance your work."

Here my mother interrupted. "Sandra is just having some fun at your expense, Rabbi Brill. We are just as proud as the Seidmans. If they won't accept any gifts from the yeshiva, neither will we. If Sandra does it, and I hope she will, I will cover the expenses."

"Okay," I said to the rabbi. "Let's assume, for the sake of argument, that I am willing to accept your invitation. I will require a thorough briefing on the Seidman family, the late Mr. Seidman, and the plans for the new dormitory. Do you have the time to spend tonight?"

"I am staying at the Hotel Syracuse overnight so I can spend all the time necessary."

"Good. Let me get a notebook and we'll go into the study to talk it over." I made a half-hearted attempt to help Mom with the dishes but she shooed me away.

"You haven't washed a dish in years. Go talk to Rabbi Brill and please be nice to him."

"Tell me about the Seidman family," I said when we were seated in the study.

Rabbi Brill organized his thoughts and spoke in his deep voice.

"There are three Seidman children, Jack, Melvin and Carol. Jack has two daughters and Carol one."

"What about Melvin?"

"Melvin can't have children."

"Why not?"

"He's not married yet and observant Jews do not have children out of wedlock."

"How old is he?" I asked.

"He is just about 28."

"Is he normal?"

"He is a healthy, good-looking fellow, and bright, too. Has a BA from YU and an MBA from Penn State University. He does all the buying for Buffalo Auto."

"Is he heterosexual?"

"He certainly looks it. I know that he dates women quite frequently. Before Mr. Seidman passed away, he asked his son to make an effort to get married."

"I would gather that he is well fixed," I said.

"I most certainly think so."

"How much would you estimate?"

"I don't know for sure. He earns about half-a-million a year in salary and bonuses. Before Mr Seidman died, he divided the business among his three children."

By now my mother had left the kitchen and joined us in the study. She quickly gathered the gist of the conversation and was all ears.

"How much is the company worth?"

"Well, from what I understand, Buffalo Auto is not a franchise type of business. The company owns all the branch stores and a share of many shopping centers. The annual gross is between 50 and 60 million so the asking price for the business is well over 200 million. I would say that each of the children is worth about 75 million."

"I guess a girl could get by on that. Tell me, Rabbi Brill, didn't you say tonight that I was smart?"

"I did."

"And didn't you say I was pretty on your first visit?"

"I'm not sure. I vaguely remember saying something like that."

"Don't give me a hard time. You said it and a girl doesn't forget compliments like that."

"All right, then, I did say it and I still feel it is true."

"Then why didn't you let Melvin Seidman know that the girl of his dreams is only a few hundred miles away and would like to meet him?"

"The thought briefly crossed my mind but I didn't feel that you and Melvin would make a good match, so I didn't mention it.

"What's wrong with me?"

"Nothing at all. The problem is with Melvin."

"What's wrong with him?"

"To begin with, he regularly goes to shul three times every Shabbos and again on Sunday morning. Of course, now that he is reciting kaddish, he goes every day."

"That is a problem but not a fatal one."

"He also dons those quaint little animal skins on his head and hand every morning."

"So what? I wear animal skins, too. My mink I even wear on Shabbat."

"His skins come from kosher animals."

My mother had had enough. "Cut it out, Sandra. Your father wore tefillin every day and they are still here in the house."

"All right, what else does he do wrong?"

"He is a strictly observant of the Sabbath and he eats only kosher food."

"Listen, Rabbi, you may think of me as being very rigid but for 75 million dollars, I might make some minor concessions."

"It's not only the religion, Sarah. There are personality and character differences. Melvin is a very settled man with heavy responsibilities and he works very hard at them. You are a free spirit, wild and adventurous."

"What does this Melvin do for fun?"

"He attends meetings of the Chamber of Commerce, the Federation Junior Association, the UJA Young Leadership Group and the synagogue."

"Oh my God. What does he do for intellectual stimulation?"

"He reads *Fortune, Forbes, Business Week,* the *Automobile Parts Journal* and, sometimes, he studies sections of the Talmud."

"Well, that's it. For a minute, I thought I was on to something. Is there any hope of breathing the spirit of life into his nostrils?"

"Look, he is a modern fellow and, certainly not a kollel man. He is observant, though, and looks upon life in a serious way. I really wouldn't want anyone to spoil him."

Having finished the subject of Melvin Seidman, we went on to other things. I knew my mother was going to give me a piece of her mind for being so blunt but I'm not ready to give up my lifestyle for any man. To divert her attention away from her favorite subject, I committed myself to Rabbi Brill to undertake the dedication ceremony and he was relieved to hear it.

Just before he left, my mother asked Rabbi Brill if he would be in the States over the weekend. I knew what she had in mind as soon as I remembered that on Sunday we would have the unveiling of my father's tombstone.

"I have to spend the next three days interviewing students who applied too late to be tested by Rabbi Steiner in the fall. He asked me to do it because he won't be in America this spring. I will spend Shabbos with my mother in New York, and I was planning to leave for Israel on Sunday night."

"In that case, Rabbi Brill, I would like to invite you to participate in my husband's unveiling on Sunday morning."

"I would be honored to do so but I would have to fly both ways, to get here in the morning and to catch the plane to Israel at night."

"Just buy the tickets, Rabbi. We want you to come and I will cover your expenses."

The rabbi accepted the invitation and took a cab back to his hotel. On Sunday morning, he returned to Syracuse and joined the family at the unveiling. The Jewish cemetery is a separate area within a larger interdenominational cemetery and the graves are well maintained. My mother had ordered a double headstone with the name "Feldman" on it. Rabbi Stern had said that she could do so but I am not sure that Rabbi Brill would have approved. At the beginning, my mother visited the cemetery frequently, although we told her that she should not do it during the first year. She wasn't going to listen to us anyway so we made no attempt to stop her. Now she isn't going as often and we take that as a sign that she is recovering from her depression.

At the service, Rabbi Brill spoke not only of the loss to the family but also of the impact on the community. The type of person that my father was made him irreplaceable. Syracuse Jewry would have a deficit in its spiritual life due to his absence.

Following dinner, I drove Rabbi Brill to Hancock Airfield and he took the plane to New York. His sister was to meet him at La Guardia and drive him over to Kennedy for the flight back to Israel.

I know what happened when Rabbi Brill came home late Monday afternoon to be with his wife after a long absence. Rivka herself told me about that evening, but that part of the story can wait until a later time. I will, however, relate what happened between Rabbi Brill and Rabbi Steiner on Tuesday because that is very relevant .

Rabbi Brill reported to the yeshiva on Tuesday morning. He saw Rabbi Steiner at services and arranged to meet with him at 10:00 A.M. Rabbi Steiner was scheduled to give his weekly lecture at the kollel at 11:00 A.M. It had been established from the very beginning that Rabbi Brill lectured at the kollel every Sunday and Thursday morning while Rabbi Steiner did so on Tuesdays.

After entering the dean's office, Rabbi Brill started telling him of the events that had taken place in the Seidman home in Buffalo. He related them in chronological order. On occasion, Rabbi Steiner interrupted with brief questions but, in general, he was pleased with the way Rabbi Brill had conducted himself and with the religious decisions he had made.

As he continued telling the story, Rabbi Brill reached the point where Melvin Seidman had requested advice about establishing a memorial in honor of his father. A look of alarm came over Rabbi Steiner's face.

"What did you tell him, Baruch?" Rabbi Steiner asked.

"I followed your directions and told him that you had instructed me not to discuss any memorials during Shiva. He understood the reason and did not raise the matter again until after the Shiva was over."

"He brought the subject up again?"

"Yes, he did. On Sunday morning he spoke to me about it."

"Did you follow my instructions at that time?"

Baruch was overcome by anxiety. This was the moment he had dreaded and he was concerned about the outcome.

"Menachem Seidman insisted upon discussing the matter with me. I couldn't..."

Rabbi Steiner cut him short in the middle of the sentence.

In an angry voice he shouted at Rabbi Brill, "You did not listen to me, Baruch?"

"No."

"Baruch I don't want to hear anymore." Tears were forming in Rabbi Steiner's eyes. "I don't want to hear whether you were successful or not. The fact remains that you disobeyed me and did not ask Mr. Seidman to speak to me directly about the memorial. The yeshiva has been very good to you, Baruch. Twelve years ago I chose you to teach at the yeshiva and you grew to be head of the kollel and the mashgiach. You have repaid goodness with evil."

Baruch remained silent and speechless while Rabbi Steiner continued. "It doesn't matter what offerings you have in hand. When King Saul disobeyed the prophet, Samuel, and allowed people to take forbidden spoils to offer sacrifices to the Lord, Samuel said to Saul, 'Is not obedience better than offerings?'"

Rabbi Steiner by now had completely lost his composure and was openly crying. Baruch sensed that this was not the right time to tell Rabbi Steiner about the outcome of his actions. "If I cannot report to the dean now, I will wait until the proper moment or will submit my report through an intermediary."

"I am in no mood to listen now and you can tell the students that I will not be teaching them today." He gathered up his coat and strode out of the room.

Baruch was left sitting in a state of shock. Slowly, he pulled himself together and advised some of the kollel students that Rabbi Steiner would not deliver the lecture at the scheduled hour. Under normal conditions, when Rabbi Steiner couldn't make a class, Rabbi Brill would substitute for him. In this case he felt that it would be unwise to do so. He himself was tired from the trip and wasn't well prepared. More to the point was his concern that Rabbi Steiner, in his present frame of mind, might interpret any of his actions in a negative way.

He remained in his office for an hour and then left for home before his scheduled lunch hour. When he arrived, his wife was not there but he attached no importance to it. When she came in later carrying some groceries, he assumed that she had been out shopping. She took one look at him and immediately sensed that something was wrong.

17

"WHAT HAPPENED, BARUCH, ARE WE in trouble?"

"I'm very much afraid so. Rabbi Steiner did not take well to the fact that I spoke to the Seidmans about a memorial donation. He was so upset that he didn't even let me tell him the results."

"Be calm, Baruch, and don't worry about it. I spoke to Rabbi Shayalevitch this morning about the problem and he gave me good advice as usual."

"I don't object to your seeing your advisor for every little problem, but some of my dealings with Rabbi Steiner must remain confidential."

"Rabbi Shayalevitch is very discreet," Rivka answered. "He hears a lot of things, some of them very intimate, and he keeps his silence. I certainly would not tell him that you had a fight with Rabbi Steiner. I just spoke to him about the fact that your conscience would not let you decline talking to a family that was ready to make a big donation to the yeshiva. In fact, you will feel better to know that I didn't even mention the amount."

"In that case, no harm was done. In the future, though, try to confine your consultations with him to your personal problems and not to anything connected with the yeshiva. In addition to him being everyone's personal psychologist, he is an important figure in the yeshiva world and there are things that he shouldn't know. Out of curiosity, what did he tell you in this case?"

"He asked me if you had succeeded in your solicitation. He warned me not to mention the amount but just to tell him whether you felt that you were successful. When I said, 'yes,' he went into deep thought. After a while he said to me, 'I think I know why Rabbi Steiner is not eager to let your husband do any heavy fund-raising but it is not for me to elaborate further.' I didn't press him on that aspect but I just asked him what would likely happen now. He said to me, 'If Rabbi Steiner can still think rationally, he will not turn down the donation simply because Baruch disobeyed him. He will be angry and disillusioned but I don't think he will go so far as to reject the funds. Firing Baruch from the yeshiva would result in the loss of the donation because the Seidmans would not understand such an action and would withdraw the gift. They could probably do so legally on the grounds that Baruch was apparently not authorized to negotiate the pledge. Since the contribution will probably not be refused, I feel that Baruch is safe in his job.'"

"Did he say what would happen if Rabbi Steiner lets his emotions run wild and actually fires me?"

"He did say that even if you were discharged, you would have some time before the firing went into effect. After twelve years of work, you are qualified for job loss compensation and unemployment insurance. That should carry you through the end of the school year. He did say that he feels you now have sufficient reputation, experience and qualifications to find a new position rather easily."

"Did he add anything to that?"

"Yes, he did. He said that sustenance is from God, who is the provider for all mankind. He gave me a special prayer to read for God's help and blessing when you next face Rabbi Steiner."

"I can't find fault with the advice he gave you. So far it is quite sound. Did he offer any suggestions as to what I should do specifically."

"Yes. He said that at all costs you should tell the truth because the Almighty does not help those who aren't truthful. If you really felt that you could not in good conscience obey Rabbi Steiner, you should tell him exactly that. There is no point in putting the blame on the Seidmans and no point in trying to evade responsibility for your actions. No one forced you to disobey Rabbi Steiner except your own moral convictions."

"That is a very good point. What else?"

"He said that you should make it clear to Rabbi Steiner that, although you are his employee, you are not his student. You did not violate the rule that a student has to obey his rabbi. The rabbis who taught you Torah did so before you ever took the position at the yeshiva."

"I did, however, violate an order given by an employer to his employee."

"Rabbi Shayalevitch didn't mention anything about that because I think the answer is obvious. Regardless of any personal considerations, Rabbi Steiner has no business preventing anyone from soliciting or accepting gifts for the yeshiva. He may own the property on which the school stands but the yeshiva itself is a sacred institution belonging to the Jewish people. The welfare of a yeshiva transcends personal interests."

"It is easy to say that when you are not facing the man. In his presence, I am still nervous and afraid to talk defiantly. I am also worried about his health and well-being and I do not want to upset him any further when he already has so many problems."

"There isn't much choice in the matter. You go back to the yeshiva after lunch and wait until he is ready to call you in. I will read *Tehillim*, the Book of Psalms, and the prayer for *parnasa*, livelihood, and God will help us."

Baruch at least had the encouragement of his wife and, indirectly, the very competent advice of a scholar who had been on the yeshiva scene for many years. Rabbi Steiner was not so fortunate. In earlier years, he would have discussed the matter with his wife. Now, however, she was bedridden and he did not want to upset her with any personal problems. There were no rabbis with whom he could discuss the situation without compromising his image. In the yeshiva world he was at the top, a man in charge of his own school. It is lonely at the top and one does not talk about personal problems to those of lower rank.

In the end, he could only draw upon his inner resources. While age and troubles with his wife's health and his own had sapped many of them, he felt that he could still muster the strength to cope with the problem he had at hand. He retired to his study and reflected upon the circumstances. It dawned on him fairly quickly that his emotional and spontaneous reaction to Rabbi Brill's report was not called for. Rabbi Brill had specifically not committed himself to refrain from talking to the Seidmans after the Shiva period. He could not fault Rabbi Brill for acting in the best interest of the yeshiva, even though they were contrary to the personal interests of the dean of the yeshiva. He realized that in Rabbi Brill's earlier years, the man would have undoubtedly obeyed him. Now that he had scored a major success with the Feldman Library, his status had risen to the point where he felt a little more independent. He assumed that Rabbi Brill was successful to a degree with the Seidmans because he didn't look like a man who had come back empty-handed. After such reflection, he resolved that he would listen to Rabbi Brill's full report and try to control his emotions. If the amount reported by Rabbi Brill was not overly substantial, he would then weigh the question of whether to forfeit the donation and discharge Rabbi Brill for insubordination.

Late in the afternoon, Rabbi Steiner returned to the yeshiva and sent word to Rabbi Brill to report to his office. "I'm sorry that I lost control of myself earlier, Baruch, and didn't let you finish what you had to say. I was upset by your action and you well know how many problems I already have at this time. I have resolved to hear you out in full and let you know afterwards how I feel about it."

"I'm not angry at the Dean for losing his temper and his patience. Perhaps, if I were in his circumstances, I would react the same way. I am ready to complete my report but I wish to make a statement first."

"Go ahead, Baruch."

"I am not going to blame anyone for what I did. I did it not on the spur of the moment but after much thought, which led me to the conviction that what I was doing was right even if it meant disobeying my employer and paying the price for my disobedience. People must abide by their conscience, regardless of the cost. I was thoroughly convinced that what I was doing was in the best interest of the yeshiva. That, in turn, means that it was in my best interest as well, for I have the responsibility of supporting a wife and six children. I could not bring myself to endanger either the yeshiva or my family to abide by an instruction which I did not understand and which, on the surface, is both unreasonable and improper."

"I understand you point of view quite well. You may proceed with the report." Rabbi Steiner was now impatient to hear the results.

Baruch told Rabbi Steiner that before Meir Seidman passed away he had implied to his son that a significant memorial should be dedicated in his memory. He was too modest to spell out what he wanted and too humble to impose demands on his children. "My task" Rabbi Brill said, "was to convince Menachem Seidman that the only appropriate place for such a memorial was in the yeshiva that Mr. Seidman cherished throughout his lifetime. Thank God I was successful in making him understand that."

"How did you find a way for him to memorialize his father at the yeshiva in light of the fact that the yeshiva as a whole already carries his father's name, and any internal facilities would be redundant?"

"I was concerned about that problem but then the answer came to me. The memorial would have to be external. I remembered the Dean showing me the plans of a new dormitory building and, fortunately, I had copies of the plans with me. After much persuasion, I convinced the Seidmans that the new dormitory would be the most appropriate memorial and it would bear the name 'Zichron Meir Residence Hall.' I spent more than an hour going over the plans with Menachem, who is an expert in construction, and I promised that we would incorporate as many of his suggestions as possible."

"How did you determine a price for the memorial?"

"Well, I knew that Meir Seidman donated $250,000 for this building, an amount equal to one quarter of the actual cost of its construction, and for that he was awarded the name of the school. I decided to follow the Dean's example and try to get $250,000 for the privilege of naming the dormitory. I also remembered that the Dean said we would need at least $500,000 to start the project so I made my original request for that amount. The Dean himself was the one who taught me to ask for a higher amount than I expected to get."

Rabbi Steiner gasped audibly. He was in shock when he heard the size of the request and grasped the scope of Rabbi Brill's audacity.

"Did you realize that you could have lost a chance of getting any gift at all by asking for such a preposterous sum? Was Menachem offended by your request?"

"I don't think so. He did ask if we could give him the name for somewhat less and I said we could not. We could, of course, accept less than the full sum and give him some rooms or a floor, but the name required the full half a million dollars."

"There is an expression in English to the effect that some people have more nerve than brains. It is a very apt description for your actions. What did the family finally give you?"

Rabbi Brill delivered the answer slowly. "The family considered the matter during the the afternoon. In the evening, they called me in and pledged the entire sum."

"Five hundred thousand dollars?" Rabbi Steiner said in amazement and sheer disbelief. "You are not having fun at my expense?"

Rabbi Brill handed Rabbi Steiner a photocopy of the Seidman pledge card. He had photocopied the original because he did not want to carry such a valuable document around with him.

"I find it hard to believe that you were able to achieve such success. You must have made a superb impression on the family."

After studying the card, Rabbi Steiner realized that the report was in fact true and he began to weigh the consequences of the gift. He realized at once that he could neither reject the offer nor dismiss Rabbi Brill. Either action would have spelled the end of his relationship with the Seidmans and the dissolution of the yeshiva after his retirement.

"I will withhold my judgment until you finish your story, Baruch. You might have some more surprises for me up that sleeve of yours. Did the Seidmans say anything about the annual support that their father had been giving for the mortgage?"

"Meir Seidman instructed his son to continue to pay the mortgage after he died, until it was all paid up. When I suggested that we were planning to increase the mortgage to raise additional money to build the new dormitory, the Seidmans voiced no objection."

"That certainly is good news." Rabbi Steiner then slowly recited the blessing 'Blessed art thou, Oh Lord our God, king of the Universe, who is all good and bestows His goodness upon us.' The dean was offering the traditional blessing that Jews make when they hear joyful tidings. Rabbi Brill was wise enough not to ask him why he pronounced the blessing on the promise of the mortgage payments but not on the dormitory gift itself. "Is there still more to report?" Rabbi Steiner asked.

"There is, and not all of it will please the Dean."

"Go ahead."

"There were some conditions attached to the original gift and they are written out on the back side of the pledge card." Rabbi Brill pulled out a second photocopy for Rabbi Steiner to read. "As you can see, I had to accept a personal fee for my services and agree to the stipulation that I would use the money only for myself without directly, or indirectly, turning it over to the yeshiva."

"You agreed to the condition?"

"The Seidmans said that they would cancel the entire memorial if I did not accept a fee. It would have been sheer idiocy not to agree."

"But Baruch, you were working as a messenger of the yeshiva, traveling at our expense and using time from your work at the school."

"The Seidmans gave me an additional check to reimburse the yeshiva quite amply for my lost time and all the expenses involved. It is true that I was sent by the yeshiva and that I have never kept any fees that I earned while performing services for the yeshiva at any time in the past. If the Dean can find a way around my pledge not to reimburse the yeshiva directly or indirectly, I will listen."

"How much did they give you for the yeshiva?"

Rabbi Brill took the $5000 check from his wallet and handed it to Rabbi Steiner.

"I see," the dean said. "May I ask how much they gave you?"

"I would rather not say."

"You don't have to. Just tell me if it was more than the check made out to the yeshiva for the expenses."

"It was not greater."

"Is there still more to your story?"

"There is one more item. The Talmud teaches us that the last is always the best. It may, however, not be true in this case. I'm sure the Dean noticed that one of the conditions on the back of the pledge card calls for a dignified service to commemorate the establishment of the memorial."

"We have always had such services. Why did they feel it necessary to include the word 'dignified?'"

"Mrs. Seidman has a long memory. It seems that when the original yeshiva building was dedicated, the ceremony was somewhat chaotic."

"It wasn't the most organized service in the world, but I did engage a man with public relations experience to run it for me."

"In Israel, public relations is a euphemism for soliciting funds. The skills of the practitioners rarely include expertise in conducting public ceremonies. The Seidmans regularly attend UJA dinners and university affairs. They know what a function should be like. Meir Seidman told his wife that things were done this way in Israel, but she claims that he, too, was upset."

"What did you tell her?"

"I told her that this time I would assume personal responsibility for the dignity of the ceremony."

"I thought you said before the Feldman affair that you had no experience in running public functions?"

"I still don't and I never said I would actually run it. I simply promised that I would see to it that it was done properly."

The dean cast his eyes upward as if engaged in conversation with the Deity. "Who will find me an American PR person who speaks Hebrew and can reach the VIPs in Israel? Only an American will do it right...."

Even as he was saying it, a horrible thought occurred to Rabbi Steiner.

"Baruch," he said, with a look of stark terror on his face. "You didn't do what I am afraid you did?"

"I did, and she agreed to come in June to take care of it."

"I need another Roman circus like a hole in the head. She is the one woman in the world who stands between me and observing the commandment, 'Love thy neighbor as thyself.'"

"She is a fine woman and I cannot understand why the Dean dislikes her so intensely."

"It is because she does not fear God or practice humility. Now if an ignorant girl were haughty, I would say that she was unlearned and didn't know better. Here is a girl who grew up in a very traditional home, went through a day school and is extremely knowledgeable. For her not to know her place is inexcusable."

"She is a rich girl with many fine attributes and accomplishments. It is hard for her to act like a Beis Yaakov student." The Beis Yaakov schools produce the type of woman Rabbi Steiner liked – obedient, humble and God-fearing.

"You spoke to her on the phone?"

"No. I went to see her in Syracuse last Monday. She was

quite respectful, or reasonably so, and she volunteered to help us."

"At our expense?"

"No. Her mother will pay for everything. She thinks that Sarah has a better chance to find a husband here than in Europe, where they were planning to go for vacation."

"What else took place in Syracuse?" I think Rabbi Steiner was expecting Baruch to present him with a donation from our family. Maybe we should have sent along some money to make life easier for Rabbi Brill, but I figured that the June trip would cost us a bundle so I didn't donate anything further.

Rabbi Brill told Rabbi Steiner about our meeting and also about the unveiling.

"You earned yourself another fee?"

"I have no qualms there. I wasn't working for the yeshiva on Sunday. It was from the time I was supposed to spend with my parents." Baruch then reported about the students he interviewed in New York and waited tensely for Rabbi Steiner to deliver his official verdict.

The dean organized his thoughts and, speaking slowly in a low voice, he said, "Do you remember the story of Jonathan, the son of Saul? In the heat of battle, Saul made a vow that anyone pausing to eat before the enemy was vanquished would be put to death. Jonathan unknowingly violated the order because he didn't hear the oath when it was made and, as he pointed out, the honey that he ate was quite beneficial to him. A great victory was won and Jonathan was ready to pay the price for his action. Because of his great success, however, the people let no harm befall him.

"Your great success, Baruch, will spare you from punishment for your disobedience. I want you to realize, however, that what you did will exact a great price from both of us and that, in your zeal to obtain more security for yourself and the yeshiva, you overlooked some very obvious consequences of your actions. You clearly ignored the Talmudic dictum, 'Who is a wise man? He who foresees what will be forthcoming from his actions.'"

"I do not grasp the dire consequences even now."

"I will explain them to you. In one intemperate moment, Baruch, you doubled the size of the yeshiva and increased our annual budget from $250,000 to $450,000, starting a year from this September. As things stand now, I lose sleep trying to raise your salary and that of three other instructors. I also have to worry about the cook, the caretaker, the secretary and their children. Add to that the cost of food and gas and electricity and phone and taxes and you see why my hair is so gray. Now you will be adding to my burdens three new rabbis, another cook and caretaker, plus all the extra maintenance expense.

"It is true that I drew plans for a new building, but that was six years ago. I was younger then and it is possible that at that time I could have managed to cope with it. Now I am old, my health is failing and I see no way for me to handle the project. But for problems, we don't have to wait until after the building is up. What are we going to do until then? Who is going to arrange the financing for the new building? Who is going to deal with the architect, the builder and all the city bureaucrats? Who is going to supervise the construction and the furnishings? Who is going to recruit and interview 65 new students? I know what goes into a new building and I still have a bitter taste in my mouth from the first one we put up. Believe me, I am doing more now than I can physically and mentally handle. If I try to do any more, I will break down entirely."

Rabbi Brill waited for Rabbi Steiner to finish and began to understand some of the reasons why the dean was cool to the project. "I understand what you are saying, but we have been taught in the Talmud, 'It is not incumbent upon you to finish the sacred work but neither are you free to desist from it.' If you once undertook to establish a yeshiva, you must continue with it as long as you are able to do so. If you can no longer do it by yourself, others stand ready to assist you. The important thing is that we must have faith that God will help us and bless the work of our hands."

"And what makes you so sure that we are still worthy of God's blessing?"

"Well, for one thing, my wife saw Rabbi Shayalevitch today and he gave her a whole new set of prayers to say for our success."

Even Rabbi Steiner could not hold back a smile. "Baruch, you know full well that we are not allowed to depend on miracles. One does not go to sea in a leaky boat and assume that God will save him from drowning."

"I have given the matter a lot of thought and, if the Dean will hear me out, I will tell him how I think we may handle the situation."

"At this point, I have no choice but to listen."

"Let us put off the question of what will happen in September of next year and concentrate on the first 18 months. I accepted the dormitory donation and committed the yeshiva to it at a time when I was fully aware of the Dean's state of health. I understood that the burden of the project would fall squarely on my shoulders and I stand ready to accept my responsibilities."

"What about your present work? You already direct the kollel, serve as mashgiach and do fund-raising. Where will you find time for the extra tasks?"

"It is obvious that I will have to give up some of my present duties for at least the next 18 months and use the time I gain to take care of the new building. No one will volunteer to do my work. It will cost about $20,000 a year to pay replacements for the work I relinquish. We don't have to raise it in a lump sum, but we do have to raise our monthly budget by about $2,500 a month and prepare a plan to meet the extra expenses."

"Be a little more specific, Baruch."

"My plan is to give up one of my two weekly lectures at the kollel as well as five mornings and three evenings of supervision in the Beit Midrash. I will be able to work each afternoon as in the past."

"Who will fill in for you?"

"Rabbi Gross, who teaches the highest class, can deliver the kollel lecture that I miss. He is certainly qualified and he desperately needs the extra money that he will be paid for it".

"Finding a lecturer is not that hard. Where will you find a mashgiach? The man has to be fluent in both English and Hebrew and has to be able to establish good rapport with the students."

"I have just the man for the position."

"Who is he, may I ask?"

"Rabbi Eliezer Goldberg. He now teaches in an elementary school and is very unhappy. He would love to work on a yeshiva level. I know that he has kept up with his learning and I feel that he is qualified from a point of view of Talmudic knowledge. The important thing is that he was an American rabbi with a lot of experience in youth work. He is very poised and you saw how well he conducted the Feldman dinner."

"I thought he enjoys teaching. Would he be content to do only guidance and counseling?"

"He will be able to do some tutoring or review work when I am occupied. We would, of course, have to guarantee him that after the dormitory is up and I resume my normal schedule, he will be given a regular class."

"You feel that he could handle a class?"

"Certainly an entering class of American students."

"Would we have to offer him a yeshiva salary scale?"

"I should think so."

"In that case, you have already used up your $2500 dollar budget increase and you haven't figured on an extra cost."

"What is that?"

"It would not be proper for me to expect you to do more fund-raising and administrative work for the salary you are now getting."

"That's how it goes in the world. The poor are always willing to take and I certainly could use the extra money. The problem is getting the rich to give. That holds true here, even though the yeshiva is not exactly rich and I, myself, will have to raise the funds to cover my salary increase. I am willing to do that as long as I know that the others will get their checks first."

"You are very noble, Baruch. But there is one thing I must tell you in all frankness so that there will be no misunderstandings later. If you undertake this project, I can guarantee you that you will always have a secure job at the yeshiva at least at the level of instructor. There is no promise, express or implied, that you will rise to a higher position at the yeshiva than the one you have now attained."

18

THE WORDS HAD A POWERFUL IMPACT on Baruch. There was only one higher position at the yeshiva, the deanship itself. While succession could be five or more years away, Baruch always harbored secret hopes that one day he would run the yeshiva. He knew that it was a little far-fetched for an American, and a young one at that, to be named as head of an academy in Israel, but Rabbi Steiner had broken precedent before when he appointed him as head of the kollel and as mashgiach. What Rabbi Steiner had in mind, he could not tell. He speculated that the dean was considering some internationally recognized scholar for the position or maybe he was thinking of transferring the title to some other party for monetary considerations.

"I committed myself to this project of my own free will," Baruch replied, "regardless of any future advancement. It would be fair for you to tell me, however, whether such an opportunity is totally ruled out or is in the realm of possibility."

"Nothing in life is ruled out and, at this point, I have not made a final decision on the matter. I simply want to make sure that you fully understand that building the new dormitory and expanding the school does not automatically guarantee your advancement."

"I understand."

"We can work out a plan how to raise the extra funds when we meet tomorrow. If we are successful, your salary will be increased by 20%. I would like to continue now with my judgments on other aspects of your report."

"Please do."

"As far as the fee you got for conducting the Seidman services, the money is really due to the yeshiva as you did the work on assignment for the school. Of course, you had no choice but to accept the fee. Legally, though, the money belongs to us and is sort of a debt. You can't pay the money back without breaking your word and you will endanger the donation if you do. We can solve the problem as follows. By rights, the yeshiva should have paid you extra for your special work in America. You were sent to America on short notice and had to work intensively for ten days. We may assume that what we owe you is roughly what your services were worth. The amount of your fee was set by level-headed businessmen so it accurately reflects the value of your efforts. Since what you owe the yeshiva is equivalent to what we owe you for the extra work, we can exchange the debts and cancel them out."

"That arrangement is fine with me," Rabbi Brill said. "What about the Feldman fee?"

"There you were serving one of your own clients and I am sure that the yeshiva will benefit from your work. In the past, when you performed services at the specific request of the school, you voluntarily refunded the fees. Here you were acting on your own and you may not feel the need to return the income. I can see the difference and will not object to your retaining the money.

"All that is left to consider is your invitation to your *ptzatza*, your bombshell. The yeshiva gained friends and money from her activities and, to say the least, they were highly imaginative.

They did, however, lack in dignity. This yeshiva, as you know, is a low-key institution and I prefer it that way. I will put up with her because I have no one else who can do the job and her services are free. But please, Baruch, tell her to exercise some restraint."

"That I will do. If it will make the dean feel better, I can tell him that she doesn't show any great respect for me either. The only one who can keep her in line is her mother. When Mrs. Feldman tells her to cut out the nonsense she sometimes listens."

"Good. Talk to her mother and tell her that 'the words of wise men are best offered quietly.' I will meet with you tomorrow afternoon. Meanwhile, get to work on what we have discussed."

When Rabbi Brill went home for dinner, Rivka was still reading her Psalms. She finished the chapter she was chanting and asked him what had happened.

"That's a dynamite set of Psalms Rabbi Shayalevitch chose for you, because things worked out fairly well. I'm still employed at the yeshiva and I'm getting a raise."

"If you had read the Psalms yourself, you would have gotten more, but I thank God for whatever He gave us."

Rabbi Brill told her about his new responsibilities and how Rabbi Goldberg would join the faculty. Lili Goldberg was extremely close to her, and Rivka was delighted with the news.

"You've done a big mitzvah, Baruch. Eliezer was very unhappy at the elementary school and he always wanted to teach at a yeshiva. Will your own studies suffer if you devote so much time to the new building?"

"Yes, to some extent, but it is only for a year and a half. I will still be delivering one advanced lecture a week and serve as mashgiach each day at the afternoon sessions. It is not perfect, but I could not decline the responsibility."

Rabbi Brill asked Rabbi Goldberg to come over that night and talk to him about the position. Rabbi Goldberg, as expected, was thrilled with the offer and he readily accepted. He told Rabbi Brill that he could start the week after Purim. Rabbi Gross was a little more hesitant than Rabbi Goldberg, because he knew that his work would be compared with that of both Rabbi Steiner and Rabbi Brill, who lectured to the same group. He certainly was not on the level of Rabbi Steiner and he even had a way to go to be on a par with Rabbi Brill. On the other hand, he urgently needed the money for his family and he was willing to make the extra effort demanded of him.

A week later, Rabbi Steiner asked his students to remain in the Beit Midrash after the morning services. He did this often when he had to make special announcements or deliver a short discourse prior to a holiday or an important occasion. He chose this method of introducing Rabbi Goldberg to the students.

"We are extremely fortunate," he said, "to have secured the services of an outstanding scholar to assist Rabbi Brill in his work as mashgiach. Rabbi Eliezer Goldberg will be in the Beit Midrash every morning and two evenings a week. In the afternoons, he will teach a review class that is open to any student who feels the need for it. Students who have any questions about their studies or personal matters are free to seek Rabbi Goldberg's advice. As a former rabbi in America, Rabbi Goldberg is familiar with the American Jewish scene and students from that country will find him very helpful." He then asked Rabbi Goldberg to rise so that the students could later identify him.

Rabbi Steiner then went on to announce that Rabbi Gross would be given an opportunity to lecture once a week at the kollel. "Rabbi Brill will continue to act as mashgiach every afternoon and three evenings a week. If any of you are wondering what Rabbi Brill will be doing with all the extra time he has been given, I am pleased to announce some very good news. With God's help, the yeshiva is going to build a new dormitory connected to the back of our present building. That will allow us to accept some 65 additional students. Rabbi Brill is in charge of the new project. If any of the students have rich parents or relatives who might be interested in helping the yeshiva in this work, let them please speak to Rabbi Brill."

Rabbi Steiner was not really serious when he made the last part of the statement but, as it turned out, there were a few students who were able to point to rich families in their community and some whose own parents were in a position to make contributions. Rabbi Brill carefully noted all the details when such students came to speak with him.

Rabbi Goldberg was successful in his new position and the students felt that it was easy to talk to him. His review class was well attended not only by beginners in need of remedial work but also by some students on the intermediate levels who found the class helpful. Rabbi Gross got off to a somewhat shakier start due primarily to anxiety. After a while, though, he settled down and regained his usual confidence. The students took to him and followed his lectures attentively.

Rabbi Brill himself began to move ahead on the new building project. He had a long conference with Yossi, the builder, and together they met with the architect, who drew the plans for remodeling the first yeshiva building. The architect was somewhat reluctant to get involved.

"I'm twelve years older than when I redesigned the first building and it took me six years to get paid for my work. If I have to wait six years this time, I will be past retirement age and too old to enjoy the money."

"I wouldn't worry about it," Yossi said. "Your children will be happy to get the money. Actually, however, I remodeled the library for the yeshiva last December and got paid in advance. I guess that was because they had this cute, rich woman paying for everything."

Rabbi Brill couldn't pass up the opportunity to tease the builder. "Yossi, I never saw you work as hard as you did when that woman was standing on top of you and watching every nail your carpenters put in. I want you to work just as well on the new building even if she will not be around to supervise. As far as money is concerned, most of it is already secure and I believe that this time we will not be late with any payments."

Much to his surprise, Rabbi Brill discovered that Rabbi Steiner had an option to buy the property in back of the yeshiva at a fixed price and that the option was still in effect. This was a source of great relief to him, as he realized that he would not have to haggle over the price of the land. He had been afraid that the owner would raise the price when he heard that the yeshiva had acquired enough funds to build.

The owner was quite happy to hear from Rabbi Brill because the property had become a burden to him. It contained a ramshackle building that was unsuitable for residential use and was not attractive to renters of storage space. It was sitting empty while the owner was paying heavy property taxes on the lot. While the yeshiva was situated in a good residential area, nobody wanted to build a home on a property that backed up to a dormitory and study hall. This was a yeshiva where students tended to study at all hours of the night and make a lot of noise.

Rabbi Brill arranged a meeting with the owner and his lawyer and asked them to take the necessary actions to transfer the property. The yeshiva lawyer was notified and he quickly concluded the purchase. The architect had several meetings with Rabbi Brill to finalize the plans. The main floor of the new dormitory structure would contain a large dining room and kitchen. The dining hall would be large enough to seat more than two hundred students comfortably. At times other than meal periods, the room would serve as an assembly hall. The three upper floors would each contain six large bedrooms, one middle-sized room and one very small room. The large bedrooms would sleep four students. The middle-sized room would house two students, and the small room would be used by a counselor. Unmarried kollel men often served as dorm counselors in order to supplement their income.

The plan of action was to secure permits as quickly as possible for the excavation of the land and preliminary work on the foundations. Depending on the progress made, Rabbi Brill could possibly be able to offer the Seidmans an opportunity to dedicate the building corner stone. If the foundations were not ready in time, the ceremony would have to involve breaking ground only.

The big question was the fund-raising. When Rabbi Brill met with Rabbi Steiner, he outlined his plans to finance the new building. "I will ask the bank to increase the present mortgage by $300,000 and I will also try to get $100,000 of government assistance. That will leave us $100,000 short of the million-dollar goal that we have set for ourselves. Since that money will be used for the final stages of construction and furnishing, we will have some breathing space before we need it. It is my feeling that when friends of the yeshiva see the building being erected, they will come through with funds. What I would like to do is sell the larger dormitory rooms for $18,000 each. If we can sell eight rooms, we will be able to finish the dormitory and also cover our increased budget for the current year. If the Dean will draw up a list of the ten families most likely to help us in America or Israel, I will take the time to travel and see them. Is the Dean planning to visit the States after the holidays as he usually does?"

"I do plan to go, but it all depends on my wife's state of

health. If I go, I will try to reach a number of the families that are most likely to be of assistance. Some of them contributed to the original building and will probably be quite responsive to an appeal for the new one."

Rabbi Brill next arranged to see the Minister of Religious Affairs at his office in the Ministry. "I want to thank you, Mr. Ben Zur, for the special assistance you gave me in getting emergency reservations on El Al."

"Think nothing of it," the minister responded. "It was my pleasure. Were you at least successful on your mission?"

"Very much so," Rabbi Brill replied, "and that is one of the reasons why I have come to see you. In the course of my visit, I was able to secure a donation of a half-million dollars towards the building of a new dormitory at the school. The work is already under way but we do need the Minister's help in securing government assistance for the project. Before I tell you what we need, I want you to know that I saw Miss Feldman in Syracuse and she too thanks you for your assistance to the yeshiva."

"How is Sandra doing?"

"Very well, I believe. We have asked her to come to Israel to arrange the dedication ceremony in June and she has consented to do so. I'm sure she will be in touch with you when she arrives."

"I will be very happy to see her. She ran a wonderful affair for the yeshiva and I am sure she will do so again. How can the government help you with the new dormitory?"

"At this point, we are short about $200,000 to reach our budget for the new construction. We need government help to overcome half of the deficit."

The minister looked a little sad. "You know that money is tight in Israel and economic conditions are not good at all. There are, of course, some funds that you are legally entitled to for help with the project. Beyond that, some of the ministries have discretionary funds to assist such undertakings. The Ministry of Religious Affairs can certainly give you some money for the cause. Your best bet is the Ministry of Housing and Development, which has a large fund at its disposal. There may also be some funds that you can get from the Ministry of Labor and Social Welfare if you can convince them that the new project will generate additional employment. I am sure that you will be increasing your staff to cope with the new students. I meet with the ministers of the other departments in the government and I will put in a good word for you."

Rabbi Brill was very pleased with the meeting and he thanked the minister. He continued to work rapidly on the project and, by the time my mother and I arrived at the King David at the beginning of June, the temporary structure on the lot had been removed and the yeshiva was awaiting its building permit.

We arrived on a Thursday night and got to the hotel on our own. I decided to meet with Rabbi Brill on Friday morning at the hotel rather than at the yeshiva, because I wanted to get additional information before starting to work. He joined us at breakfast Friday and gave me a complete picture of what had transpired with Rabbi Steiner upon his return. All that I have written up to now was based on the briefing that he gave me that morning. It lasted well beyond the breakfast so we sat in the lobby and continued the conversation.

"Are you sure that Rabbi Steiner will give me a free hand to work on this ceremony?" I asked him.

"Rabbi Steiner doesn't have much choice in the matter, but he did request me to ask you for a favor. It appears that you were a little too flamboyant for him during your last project. It seems that he likes women who are somewhat more reverent and timid."

"And submissive?" I asked.

"Obedient, perhaps. He thinks yeshiva activities should be low key."

"I will be more respectful to Rabbi Steiner this time around. If you arrange an appointment for me Sunday morning, I will mend fences and 'walk humbly with my God.' Of course, I don't know how low key you can keep a major public ceremony. The yeshiva did enjoy a relatively obscure existence before I came here last December. Are you sure Rabbi Steiner wants to fade back into obscurity at this point? And how can we please the Seidmans if we keep the ceremony under wraps?"

"I am sure that you are smart enough to draw a fine line between the extremes."

"On what day is the ceremony planned?"

"The Seidmans are arriving next Tuesday afternoon. I would like to keep them busy until the following Monday and hold the ceremony on that day. Thereafter, I would like you to escort them on a three-day tour of the Galilee and release them on Friday to spend the weekend in Tel Aviv where they have family. Do you think you have enough time to make all the arrangements by a week from Monday afternoon?"

"I wouldn't have much of a problem if I could go at it full-time. If I have to take days off to shepherd the Seidman family around Jerusalem before the affair, I will never make it."

"What would you suggest? They are only going to be in the country for two weeks."

"I obviously need an assistant to entertain the Seidmans Wednesday, Thursday, Friday morning, and Sunday. I can take them to the Great Synagogue on Shabbat."

"I heard that you only go to shul to catch the rabbi making mistakes. The Chief Rabbi doesn't regularly preach on the Sabbath but, if he does, you will not catch him making any mistakes."

"A few prayers won't kill me. We could get a professional guide to go around with the Seidmans, but I don't think that they will be helpful as far as the yeshiva is concerned. Do you think that Lili might undertake it? She was a rebbitzen in America."

"She can do it and she would do an excellent job. There are two problems, however. First of all, we would have to pay her for her time because, even with Rabbi Goldberg working at the yeshiva, the family is still quite poor. Secondly, when she sees a single fellow, she immediately starts working on him and recommends girls for him to marry. She happens to know every single girl in town."

"I will take care of Lili. Just see that she gets to the yeshiva Sunday morning where I will meet with her immediately after I see Rabbi Steiner. I will meet with the Seidmans at dinner on Tuesday night and make all the arrangements with the family before they go on tour. Call me at the hotel on Saturday night and let me know if you have set up the appointments."

Rabbi Brill returned to the yeshiva and arranged the meetings. After Shabbat, he called me at the hotel to tell me that everything was in order. Rabbi Steiner would see me at 10:00 A.M. and Lili would come an hour later.

On Sunday, after breakfast at the hotel, I took a cab to the school. Mother was waiting at the hotel for some relatives to pick her up and take her around for family visits. Before breakfast she had picked out a nice quiet dress for me to wear. "Save the designer stuff for dates," she said.

At the yeshiva, I resisted the temptation to visit the library and see what shape it was in. The Beit Midrash was full and I imagined that there would be students in the library as well. I went directly to the office area, where Rabbi Brill and Rabbi Steiner were waiting for me.

After a few pleasantries, I went into Rabbi Steiner's office. There was no overt hostility and the rabbi seemed relaxed.

"How is my princess doing?" he asked.

"Baruch Hashem." I surprised him with my answer.

"I see that you are in a cooperative mood this time. How are your mother and brothers?"

"Baruch Hashem, they are all well. My mother came with me on the trip to make sure that I behave properly and modestly."

"I am not sure the leopard can change her spots so easily."

"I really cannot. Ideologically we are still far apart. But, although I can't change the spots, I will pull in my claws. I will avoid displaying non-conformity as far as possible."

"That is a step in the right direction. I want you to know that while I did not approve of all your methods last time, the overall outcome of the library dedication was favorable to the yeshiva."

"That is good to know. Were there any tangible results?"

"Indeed there were. Rabbi Brill may have told you that we have improved our standing with the Ministry of Religious Affairs. We have also had an increase in the number of applications from Israel and America. Apparently our American students were impressed with you and they spread the word. We also have had some increased donations from our supporters."

"What about the library itself? Has it been maintained properly?"

"Some boys like the place so much that they want to study there all the time. We have to chase them out. We have also scheduled some meetings and seminars with visiting scholars in the library."

"In that case, we may go ahead with the current project. I would like to avoid any actions that might exceed the limits of what the Dean feels is acceptable."

"I will be glad to discuss the program with you, but first I have another favor to ask."

"Yes, Rabbi Steiner."

"Sarah, you know how myths are started. Some minor event happens and, after the story is retold many times, it tends to become exaggerated. It seems that you displayed a little extra knowledge last time and by now all the students think that you are an expert in Talmud and the Codes of Law. We are studying the Talmudic volume of Sanhedrin this year and the subject is quite complex. I don't want the boys to run and ask you questions. We employ two mashgichim to handle inquiries and they are quite scholarly. It will not be necessary to show off."

Sanhedrin is the volume that deals with the Jewish High Court and various basic commandments. Despite my promise of good behavior I couldn't resist a little fun. "Have you reached the section that covers the seven laws that apply to non-Jews, somewhere around page 56b?" I asked with a look of innocence on my face. I knew that source from a paper I had read on interethnic tolerance.

Rabbi Steiner got a little annoyed. "That is precisely what I was driving at. I don't want students to think that you know the Talmud. Incidentally, that is the area we are up to this week and if you do have any views on the subject, please don't discuss them with anyone."

"I will refer all inquiries I get to Rabbis Brill and Goldberg. By the way, I was happy to hear that you appointed Rabbi Goldberg to help Rabbi Brill. I never tested his Talmudic knowledge but I know that he is a fine person with an outstanding personality. He will relate well to the students."

"I am glad you approve. What sort of ceremony do you have in mind for the dormitory dedication?"

"Well there will certainly have to be a dinner and a dedication ritual. We are faced with the same situation as last time. If you let the great scholars speak to the family guests and friends, you will have a problem. These people will not be able to follow what is going on and will be bored. What they need are public figures and a chance to hear from the family. That they can do at the dinner."

"How will you handle the really important figures?"

He was, of course, referring to the Torah scholars and yeshiva deans, who were the only ones that mattered as far as he was concerned.

"I haven't worked it out as yet. The Seidmans were not too pleased with the last dedication. Apparently the audience attracted by the great scholars did not display the decorum necessary for the dedication ceremony to meet American standards of dignity." I felt that I stated the problem very tactfully. I gathered that at the last ceremony there was pushing and shoving and loud noise when the actual dedication took place but I did not want to cast any aspersions on Rabbi Steiner's friends.

Rabbi Steiner replied: "I guess our people do not admire contrived ceremony. I venture to say that you will find more decorum at their prayer services than in an American synagogue. We have to solve this problem. We just can't have a dedication without inviting the great Torah scholars."

"Must they be present at the dedication part? That part is outdoors, and crowd control is difficult."

"A cornerstone ceremony is of a religious nature and they would expect to be present," the dean said. "If you can't think of anything by tomorrow, I will schedule a meeting with Rabbis Brill and Goldberg and figure something out."

"Rabbi Brill is good at such things. He worked out a brilliant solution to separate the religious audience at the Seidman burial from the employees and politicians."

Rabbi Steiner then wished me luck and said that Rabbi Brill had agreed to let me use his office for the week. I hated to displace the rabbi but I couldn't work in the library and I needed a private office.

Lili was waiting when I got out of the dean's office and she greeted me warmly with a few tears and kisses. It was only after we retired to Rabbi Brill's office that I understood the warmth behind the greeting.

"I will never be able to repay you for what you have done for my husband and me," she said. "You gave him the necessary exposure at the dedication dinner, and Rabbi Steiner was able to see his full personality. When Rabbi Brill suggested my husband for an appointment at the yeshiva, the dean was willing to accept him. Of course, we all know that there are far more learned people available, but the position calls for more than book knowledge. It calls for compassion and sensitivity, qualities that my husband has. He is very happy at the yeshiva and he is like a new man."

"Listen Lili, you may not be able to repay me in full but you can make a start. I need a favor from you that may take you a couple of days."

"In America, I used to do favors all the time. In Israel, life is very hard and I've had to overcome the impulse to give things away for nothing, particularly my services. For you, however, I will make a special price."

"When you hear what I have in mind, you will pay me for the privilege."

"Don't bet on it."

"You heard that the Seidman family is coming for the dormitory dedication. There are six members of the group who have to be taken on tours of the area on Wednesday, Thursday and Friday morning of this week."

"I've guided tour groups before and, as I said, I will charge you less than the professional tour guides."

"Lili, your six tourists are worth more than $200,000,000 amongst them."

"So, big deal. Take off another 10% from my fee."

"Lili, one of the party is a young, good-looking bachelor worth about 75 million." I didn't know at that time that Lily was a professional shadchan, but Rabbi Brill had indicated that she liked to recommend women to single men.

"Why didn't you say so in the first place? I will be happy to take your party around and, out of the sheer goodness of my heart, I will not charge a cent."

We arranged that Lili should come to the airport with me to welcome the Seidmans on Tuesday night and that she would be provided with a minibus and driver to take the guests around. We spent a half-hour working over the itinerary before she left.

Rabbi Brill ordered lunch for two from the dining room and the food was reasonably wholesome. Institutional food always leaves a little to be desired; yeshiva cooks are not chefs and they have to be very cost-conscious.

The rabbi told me that he had spoken to Rabbi Steiner while I was talking to Lili. "How did you make out with her?"

"She volunteered to tour with the Seidmans and not to charge for it."

"I find it hard to believe because Lili is not really in a position to donate her services. Sarah, I don't want you to absorb any expenses for this dedication. What the Seidmans don't pay, the yeshiva will."

"I will swear on my bat-mitzvah copy of 'What Every Jewish Girl Should Know' that Lili offered to work for nothing."

"Now I can believe you. Did you at least read the book?"

"Of course, I did. I read everything."

"Including the Talmud?"

"Oh, that. I was just having some fun."

"Rabbi Steiner actually felt that you were showing signs of good behavior, or at least he did until you started quoting Talmud. What are you doing with the seven commandments of the Noahites?"

"I studied them in connection with a paper on how a society creates a dual legal standard, one for citizens and one for ethnic minorities, within the same national borders."

Rabbi Brill considered this. "I feel that the commands were in fact very enlightened. We didn't think that it was right to impose such Torah laws such as the Sabbath on non-Jews. We did, if they were under our authority, require basic civilized and moral behavior."

"I can accept laws prohibiting the gentiles from killing or stealing. But how can you justify prohibiting idolatry for gentiles? There should be some freedom of religion."

Rabbi Steiner would have thrown me out of his office for saying that but Rabbi Brill was patient. "I believe," he said, "that in virtually all cases we legislated for the good of the minority. A society must insist that all members obey rules and we were sufficiently tolerant to let the minorities design their own set of rules autonomously. In the case of idolatry, though, we had to act to protect the majority. The non-Jewish minorities propagate their idol worship intensively, and some Jews would be drawn to it. You certainly recall that the Torah says we would lose the Land of Israel if we practiced the same idolatry as the gentiles."

"I now have a somewhat better understanding of these laws and I am glad you took the time to explain them to me. Did Rabbi Steiner discuss the problem of the different audiences with which we will be confronted at the dedication?"

"He mentioned it and he said I should work something out with you."

"Do you have any ideas?" I asked the rabbi.

"I am working on one but it would create logistical problems that may not be easy to resolve."

"For money you can solve almost all technical problems. Let me hear your plan."

"It involves two separate groundbreaking or cornerstone services depending on which type we are ready to conduct," the rabbi replied.

"It beats two funeral services anytime."

"We can have afternoon services at three in the afternoon for the yeshiva world for thirty minutes. From three-thirty to five, we would have the public meeting for that group at the Beis Yaakov building. At six, we could have a ceremony for the family and dignitaries, followed by the dinner."

"It is not a bad idea in theory but I can see the difficult problems that you anticipate. The main obstacle is obviously the dinner site."

"Right. Would it be possible to have the dinner in the yeshiva dining room?" the rabbi asked.

"It isn't big enough. The Seidmans will have many more members of their family and friends present than we had. The yeshiva should invite more friends and supporters than last time, and the students expect to attend the dinner. You are talking of close to two hundred people. We have to use the Beis Yaakov hall for the dinner."

Rabbi Brill shook his head. "I don't believe that you can do it if you are going to hold the public meeting in the very same hall. There is no way that you can set up and decorate the hall in time, even assuming that the public meeting doesn't run overtime."

"Can the public meeting be held out of doors if we rent chairs?"

"It's very hot in Jerusalem now and most of the academy heads are quite elderly. Rabbi Steiner will not agree to it."

"Then we have to set up the hall in 90 minutes."

"Not with the caterer we had at the last dinner. When she uses the yeshiva dining room for one of her dinners she starts at 2:00 P.M."

"What if we got her a big crew of volunteers to carry in the tables and chairs?"

"Where will you get 15 to 20 volunteers?"

"I could think of 65 right off the top of my head."

"Oh, no. Rabbi Steiner won't permit yeshiva men to act as waiters. They are 'Avreichim,' which means princes of Torah."

"I know what the word means. It's odd that Jewish women are called princesses and yet they are allowed to scrub floors and wash walls while the men are not disposed to lift a finger. I can't say it to him because I am on good behavior but please remind Rabbi Steiner for me that, 'If there is no bread there is no Torah.'"

19

"I KNOW THAT YOU CAN'T tell him that but I can't either. If we go by my plan, I will undertake to organize a crew of 20 boys to do the work and face the criticism after the fact."

"Baruch, you have to assert yourself a little more. There is nothing wrong with students helping their yeshiva, but if you prefer doing it your way, it's your privilege. There are some additional problems."

"Like what?"

"Some of the Seidmans have to be present at the earlier ceremony."

"Menachem can attend. He is a yeshiva graduate and he knows Yiddish pretty well."

"Jack has to attend also."

"Why?"

"Because the ceremony starts with Mincha and both men have to recite kaddish. In fact, I will request Rabbi Steiner to include a memorial prayer for the late Meir Seidman before Mincha."

"Jack won't have a problem with that part. If he has trouble with the learned discourses, he can be excused."

"I have saved the hardest question for last. Do you have a building permit already?"

"We have a permit for excavations and foundations. We may even get the full permit by the end of this week.

"I would like the Seidmans actually to put in the cornerstone rather than dig up a pail of dirt. The cornerstone will have the Seidman name on it and the ceremony will be far more meaningful."

"If I didn't know you better, I would say it's impossible. Then again, you have performed some miraculous things here in the past. You would need an engraved stone in one week, when it usually takes two to three weeks, and you wouldn't even have family approval of the text until Tuesday night. Secondly, Yossi would have to excavate a corner, put down footings and build a wall to carry the stone, all in eight days. Thirdly, unlike a groundbreaking, which can be performed many times, a cornerstone ceremony can be performed only once. Once it has been set in place it can't be cemented in again."

"There are problems," I agreed, "but they can be resolved. I will get after Yossi and, if you give me the name of a monument company, I will have the stone here on time. You are right about not dedicating the cornerstone twice. I would have the Torah sages at the early ceremony simply conduct a groundbreaking on the other end of the lot."

"It wouldn't look right to have groundbreaking after a wall is already up," the rabbi objected.

"Not if Yossi doesn't excavate all the trenches and if he backfills any open areas near the corner."

"He would just love doing extra work."

"If necessary, we'll pay him for it. I think, though, that I can persuade him to do it as a favor. One way or another, we have a plan of action and I can get to work. Don't forget that Lili and

I want to go with you to Ben Gurion on Tuesday to greet the Seidmans. I will rent a minibus that will leave here at 4:00 P.M. At seven we are treating them to dinner at the King David and you have to be on hand."

"Yes, Captain," he said with resignation, "I'll be there."

I got on the phone with Yossi as soon as possible and asked him to meet me at the yeshiva at 5:00 P.M. He was still in a state of euphoria at the thought of constructing a million-dollar building for which he would be paid on time, and he readily agreed to come over. I also had no difficulty in setting up an appointment with the Minister of Religious Affairs for Monday morning. I booked the caterer for that same afternoon at 4:00 P.M. Then I went back to Rabbi Brill's office and studied the building plans until Yossi got there.

"Hello my beautiful lady," he shouted, when he saw me. "I know that you want the building ready by tomorrow. I will try but I can't guarantee."

"Sit down, Yossi, and let me talk to you. You have twelve months to finish the building so you can crawl along as usual. For this week, I need a lot of work. Shall I talk feet with you or stick to meters?"

"Meters. I get mixed up with the feet."

"All right." I put the plans on the desk and pointed to the southwest wall of the building. "Yossi, I want you to come in with a backhoe tomorrow morning and dig a trench for the footings for five meters either way from the corner near the street."

"Why do I have to dig trenches? The whole lot has to be dug up to a depth of 2 and 1/2 meters. For that I use a bulldozer and dig until a meter behind the footings."

Patiently I explained to Yossi that he couldn't dig up the lot before the groundbreaking ceremony but that he did have to have the southwest corner of the wall built to a height of

85 centimeters and long enough to carry the cornerstone. Yossi looked at me as if I was crazy.

"Listen. If it were someone else sitting here I'd call him crazy. You are just plain nuts. I've built plenty of shuls and schools. People break ground one day and put the cornerstone in three months later. No one can do those two things in one day because they are at different stages of the construction."

"We don't always have to do things by the book. In life people have to be flexible." I did some more explaining until he got the point.

"Now, I know what you want to do. I'm not sure I can do it but, even if I could, it would cost a lot extra."

"Forget the money for a minute. Tell me what the problems are."

"Okay. You want me to build a wall on one corner of the lot to carry the cornerstone. Let's say I dig the trench out tomorrow. On Tuesday, I make the forms for the footings and on Wednesday I pour the concrete. I can't start putting in the block because I have to wait at least 3 days for the concrete to harden until I can start laying block. So I begin the wall on Sunday and you want it ready on Monday. Can't do it. It's deep in there and very narrow. There isn't room for more then a few men. It will take at least four days."

"Don't forget the Jerusalem stone façade," I reminded him.

"That makes it five days."

"I didn't ask you for block. Make the wall out of solid concrete that you can pour at one time, say Wednesday afternoon. Sunday, you put up the Jerusalem stone and Monday you backfill around the wall and cover it with a tarp."

"Solid concrete is very expensive and I don't know that my unskilled carpenters can put up the tall forms in a day and a half."

"Why don't you get the metal forms that you bolt together? Nobody uses wood forms any more."

"Your trouble is that you live in America. Here labor is cheaper. But I can get solid concrete and metal forms if someone will pay for it. Someone also has to pay for the backhoe."

"Without overhead and profit, how much extra will it cost to do it my way rather than the regular way?"

"I would say at least $1500."

"Yossi, how much did you donate to the yeshiva last year?"

"About 500 shekels."

"That's less than $200."

"I give to a lot of places."

"A rich builder like you gives only 500 shekels and expects to get a million-dollar contract?"

"My contract is only for $750,000. The rest goes for land and furnishings."

"That's still a lot of money. Anyway, I want to announce your pledge at the dedication ceremony. May I put you down for $5000?"

"Look, you are a nice lady but $5000, I can't give."

"How about $2500?"

"Never."

"Listen, Yossi. This is your last chance to look good in front of hundreds of people. I announce $2000 and you don't have to pay it. You simply do what I asked you to and we consider it worth $2000."

Yossi pondered my suggestion and then said with resignation, "In that case, announce $2500 because that is what I would charge if a stranger came up and asked me to build a wall like that in six days. Please announce it at the public meeting because the academy heads are the ones who may give me business some day."

"One or two more things, Yossi, if you have a another minute."

"For you I always have time, but no more donations please."

"I don't want you to try making up your donation by cutting corners on the dormitory construction."

"God forbid. You know me. Would I ever do a thing like that?"

"Would you like me to show you some walls in the present building?"

"I didn't build the present building. I only remodeled the interior. If the basic building isn't right, there isn't much that you can do later."

"All right, I trust you. I have no other choice, because I won't be around to watch you. However, you will be closely supervised."

"By who?" Yossi said in alarm.

"By the Almighty himself."

Yossi breathed a deep sigh of relief. "He's a lot easier to get along with than with you."

"He is certainly more merciful. If you ever put up a crooked wall for me, you would have to tear it down and build it over."

"I know, I know. The carpenters who worked in the library didn't talk to me for a month after you got through with them."

"Now they talk to you?"

"Yes."

"Good. I need a speakers platform about 4 1/2 meters long and 2 1/2 meters wide with steps and safety railings."

"You'll pay for it?" he asked cautiously.

"Sure. But we're not talking furniture, just plain lumber."

"That's no problem. Show me on the plan where you want it." I pointed to the eastern property line about halfway down.

"One last question. We have a cornerstone that will measure eight centimeters thick, 90 centimeters long and about 70 centimeters high. It will be on display on the platform and then has to be moved to the corner wall. How many men do you need to move it?"

"You're talking granite?"

"Granite or marble."

"There are some Arabs who can take that on their backs."

"No, thanks. Can two American businessmen manage it by themselves?"

"Never, you could be talking about 100 kilos or more."

"What about a crane?"

"Enough crazy ideas. You want to have some fun? I have an Arab with a donkey. The donors can put the stone on the donkey and walk it over."

"All right, but keep the donkey out of sight until we're ready." I figured a little comedy would lighten things up at the ceremony. When I finished with Yossi, I poked my head out of the office and sent a student to call Rabbi Goldberg. Within a minute, he was in my office and greeted me warmly.

"My wife told me you were in and hard at work. How have you been and how is your mother?"

"We're both fine and I will tell her you asked. I understand that you are enjoying your new position."

"Very much so. The hours are much longer but I deal with older students and it's more stimulating intellectually."

"Wonderful. I take it you know why I asked to see you?"

"Sure. You want something else for nothing." Rabbi Goldberg said.

"Very perceptive, I must say. It's really true. The rabbis have taught us that one who starts a mitzvah must also finish it."

"I've heard that one before. What can I can do to help?"

"You are still getting rave reviews from the last dinner you conducted for me. We have another dinner and a cornerstone-laying ceremony coming up and we need an emcee."

"Well, if Lili can be a tour guide for free, I can run a dinner for you. Do you have any VIPs coming?"

"I won't know for sure until tomorrow. I hope to have a few big fish."

"I wouldn't be surprised. Rabbi Brill really scored on this one."

"Listen, Eliezer, I have a little act for you to work out. The cornerstone will be on display at the speaker's platform and it has to be carried over to the corner where the Seidmans will set it in place."

"You expect me to carry a heavy monument?"

"No. Yossi is getting me an Arab with a donkey. Come up with a good line and I'll signal Yossi to send the donkey over."

"You're a real devil."

"Don't let anyone in on it."

"I won't even tell my wife."

"Good. I'll fill you in on the Seidman family during the week. They sell auto parts for a living. Don't forget to pay a lot of attention to the mother." When I was finished with Rabbi Goldberg, I took a cab back to the hotel. One meal a day at the Yeshiva is enough and there is no point in living dangerously. So I had dinner with my mother at the King David. The next morning I went straight to the Ministry of Religious Affairs to see Mr. Ben Zur. He was very happy to see me, even more than Rabbi Goldberg. He inquired about my mother and I told him that she thought he was a very nice man. "I want to thank you for the help you have given the yeshiva and Rabbi Brill. I understand that between the various ministries about $100,000 will be forthcoming."

"If not more. Rabbi Brill is very good at executive work and the other ministers told me that he made excellent presentations. When he was asked questions, he had the information at his fingertips and he didn't gild the lily at all. Our own allocations committee at this ministry was equally impressed."

"That is very encouraging. He is carrying a lot of responsibility."

"He can cope with it. Anyway, I gather you are here in connection with the dedication ceremony. When is it, and what are you planning to do?"

"It's one week from today and we hope to dedicate a cornerstone."

"You are having a dinner?"

"We are having an open air ceremony followed by a dinner."

"May I make a suggestion?"

"Sure."

"Have something like a reception before the dinner. Keep the yeshiva boys away until the dinner starts. This will give the family a chance to receive the guests as they enter. For the actual food service, you may separate the men from the women."

"I think we can work it out. The auditorium seats 300 and we have only 200 guests. We can set aside an area big enough for the purpose. Why do we need a reception before the dinner?"

"If the family formally receives everyone's warm greetings, they will feel good. If the guests have some drinks before dinner they will be in a better mood. If you are planning an appeal for funds, you will get a much stronger response."

"We haven't planned an appeal."

"Why not? Aren't you having the major supporters of the yeshiva present?"

"Yes, but the Seidmans may feel exploited."

"In that case, simply publish a little brochure on the new

dormitory listing the prices of rooms or floors. Even if you sell only one room during the evening, you will be able to pay for the dinner and the printing."

"Can I get a brochure ready in five days in Israel?"

"You probably can. I save the printed matter from the dinners that I attend and I would be happy to let you look at some samples."

"I don't think it would be right for me to take credit for your ideas."

"It's perfectly all right. I want to help those schools that cooperate with the Ministry. There are institutions that are perfectly willing to take our money but not willing to recognize us as legitimate. Beit Meir has been very cooperative in all respects."

"I need your help with the dedication as well."

"What can I do for you?"

"I would like you to speak at the dinner next Monday night."

"That will be my pleasure."

"I would also like to get another government figure to attend. This time around, I don't have any congressmen and I haven't yet approached the American Ambassador." I was building it up slowly. "We should also invite the Housing Minister because he will be helping the yeshiva."

"That can be arranged."

"I hope I'm not being presumptuous, but would the President or Prime Minister be available?"

"The President can be persuaded to attend and even the Prime Minister, although not both at the same affair. The question is why you need them?"

"I want to make the Seidmans feel important for one, and I want to generate some publicity for the yeshiva in the newspapers and on TV."

"In that case, don't bother with the President. He cuts ribbons all day and attends dinners every night. The papers don't even send cub reporters to follow him anymore."

"How about the Prime Minister?"

"That depends. If he uses the occasion to make some significant statement and you let the press know that it will happen, the event will be well-covered. If he has nothing to say, the coverage will be minimal."

"It makes sense to gamble and hope for a break. If you can order me a war for Monday, or even a government crisis, that would be just what I need."

"Don't even jest like that. That is what the rabbis call an invitation to the devil. The cabinet meets every Sunday and we decide on a number of things that are announced later. If something relating to education is passed by the cabinet, I might be able to persuade the Prime Minister to hold off on the release till Monday evening, but I won't know till Sunday afternoon."

"My luck has been running very well in Israel so maybe I will get another break."

"Before you get your hopes too high about the Prime Minister, I must tell you some of the facts of political life."

"You mean we have to pay for his appearance?"

"He doesn't take anything for himself. His party, however, is in deficit and that is how he helps out. He raises about a half million dollars a year by appearing at two functions a week, less when he is very busy, more when he is not. Also, there is always the danger that a major problem, God protect us from it, may cause him to cancel his appearance."

"I calculate that $5000 is what is involved for the Prime Minister."

"That is about right, and don't forget the $2500 for the Housing Minister."

"For another $5000 I could probably get the Pope."

"Don't fool yourself. There are some celebrities and even religious figures who get much more. Of course, speakers of that kind would not be welcome at the yeshiva."

"When and where should I schedule the Prime Minister?" I asked.

"Definitely at the outdoor ceremony. He has little patience for dinners and he has a reputation for campaign speeches. Put him on an outdoor platform and he is in his glory."

"All right, I'll buy the package. Let me know as soon as you have any commitment. I'll keep you informed and send you some material on the Seidman family to pass around." We said our goodbyes and I took a cab back to the yeshiva. Again Rabbi Brill treated me to lunch. The food was just this side of edible, but I was too hungry to mind. I had Rabbi Brill tell me everything that he knew about the Seidmans and I amassed enough material for my press releases. Part of the information came from articles in the Buffalo papers that Rabbi Brill had saved for me following Mr. Seidman's passing. The rabbi was enthusiastic about the brochure but not optimistic.

"Design one that can be used in America," he said. "We don't have clients in Israel who can pay $18,000 for a room."

"We can practice some of your enlightened dualism," I told him. "We use the same informational material in the brochure but print one price list for the American edition and a different one for the Israeli one. The American list will start with $18,000 and go higher, while the Israeli list will start lower and rise to $18,000."

"What can you sell in a dormitory for less than $18,000?"

"You can have patron plaques, donor plaques and founder plaques. Go into Shaarei Zedek Hospital and see how they do it. There is a board listing those who have donated beds at $1000 each or closets for $500.”

Rabbi Brill seemed satisfied so I continued.

“Did you get me the name of a monument maker?”

“I did. He said that he can cut and polish the stone as soon as he gets the order. If you fax the inscription to him by Wednesday morning, he can deliver the finished stone by Sunday.”

“Did he make any suggestion as to the type of stone?”

“He suggested white marble with engraved letters painted in black or gold. Maybe we ought to let the Seidmans decide.”

We worked for an hour on the cornerstone inscription. After we had three versions, I asked him to have the student scribe draw them up for review by the family. We then worked until 4:30 p.m. on the price list for donation opportunities in the new dorm.

“How late are you going to work tonight?” Rabbi Brill asked.

“At least until eight.”

“Would you like to have supper at the school?”

“The Torah tell us, ‘You should be very protective of your souls.’ I’ve already had one meal today at the yeshiva.”

“Our food isn’t as good as the King David’s?”

“Not quite.”

He reflected for a minute and then said, “Sit tight. I have an idea. I’ll be back in a few minutes.”

I figured that he was going to call a private family, because there were no restaurants near the yeshiva. When he came back, he told me that his wife had extended an invitation to me for dinner. The Brills lived only a block away from the yeshiva building. I assumed that he had done some arm-twisting so I gave him a chance to back out. “I wouldn’t want to trouble her. How many kids are home now?" I knew that his son was at a yeshiva but I didn't know whether his oldest daughter was home.

"Only five. It's just a dairy meal and, since my American trip, we are back in good standing at the grocery store." Like many religious families, the Brills bought at the local store and signed the credit book. When the rabbi got paid, he would reduce the grocery bill. He also had to pay installments on his debts to several free loan societies. When he got the fees for the Seidman funeral and our unveiling, plus the raise at the yeshiva, he was able to pay off all his bills and debts.

"That's very kind of you."

I imagined that the Brills lived poorly, but I had no idea how bad it was. The apartment was reasonably clean but small and dingy. It hadn't been painted for a long time and showed lots of wear and tear. In all, there were only three small bedrooms. I gathered that three girls slept in one room and three boys in the other. The master bedroom was tiny and there was only a bathroom and a half in the house. I don't think that there had been a maid in the apartment for years.

Rivka, however, was looking great. She had clearly lost a lot of weight and wasn't bursting out of her dress as in December. It was the same dress that she had worn when she called on me with Lili before the library dedication. It didn't look any better, but at least it fit.

When I told her how good she looked she smiled happily.

"You always look good," she said, "but now you are looking even better. How is your mother?"

"Thank you. She's fine. May I meet the kids?" None of the children spoke English, so she introduced them to me in Hebrew, one by one. The boys all had long side curls and wore white shirts. The girls had pressed blouses and long skirts. It was clear that they were wearing their Sabbath clothing and were under strict orders to behave under penalty of death.

Rivka was a good cook and a dedicated hostess. With the older girl serving, I enjoyed a fish schnitzel on a plate of fresh and frozen vegetables. With the desserts, the meal must have blown the weekly food budget. After a while, the initial tension faded and we enjoyed the dinner in a relaxed manner. I spoke to the children and asked them a few questions about what they were learning. They were good students and Rabbi Brill apparently kept them on their toes. When we were finished, I thanked the Brills for the hospitality and walked back to the yeshiva. There I worked for another hour and returned to the hotel.

Next morning I put on one of my designer outfits and went back to work. It was an elegant creation and not in the least understated. I figured that I wouldn't have time to get back to the hotel and change and I was right. I worked up to the last minute on the press releases and the brochure. I was still at it when Lili came in at about a quarter to four.

"You're going to a wedding?" she asked when she saw me.

"One can never tell," I answered.

"You are thinking perhaps of a rich bachelor who will be arriving shortly?"

"I always think of rich bachelors, but not this one."

"Why is that?"

"Rabbi Brill said we are incompatible. He is too observant and too settled for me."

"I thought you sowed your wild oats with your first husband?"

"I have a few more left," I said, wistfully.

We couldn't continue the conversation because Rabbi Brill

arrived and told us that we had to board the bus for the trip to Ben Gurion.

MELVIN

20

WE WERE ALL LOOKING FORWARD to the trip to Israel as none of us had been there during the last 13 years. Joe, Carol's husband, had never been to Israel and the same held true for Jack's wife, Estelle. Carol could understand Hebrew as she had finished day school and I could even speak in the classical idiom. My brother and sister had no problem leaving their children because they both had live-in housekeepers and they frequently traveled.

I decided that a non-stop to Israel would be too hard for my mother even though it would be first-class all the way. We left Buffalo at 7:00 A.M. Monday and caught a 9:00 A.M. flight to London. We arrived there at about 8:00 P.M., London time, and slept over in a good hotel. Next morning, we took a flight from Heathrow to Ben Gurion and arrived at 4:30 P.M. We traveled light so the customs and luggage didn't take too long. We decided not to travel heavy, even though there were a lot of people who expected gifts. Mother has a lot of relatives in Israel, including a sister with four married children. On my father's side, there were only a few cousins who made it through the Holocaust. In the end, we decided that money was the best thing to give and that didn't take up too much room.

Up until departure, we had been in close contact with Rabbi

Brill and we knew that he would be waiting for us at the airport. He had asked me to prepare a list of all the friends and relatives we wanted to attend the affair, and I had it with me. When we wheeled our carts out of the customs area, there were huge crowds on hand waiting to greet arriving passengers. Carol was the first to spot Rabbi Brill, although there were lot of people there with long, black frock coats. Standing with the rabbi were two women, one with a huge bouquet of flowers. Rabbi Brill was glad to see us and embraced Jack and me. He didn't touch any of the women.

When we were all standing there, he introduced the two women who were with him. "I'd like you to meet Lili Goldberg, the wife of Rabbi Goldberg, who is the Assistant Mashgiach at the yeshiva, and Sarah Feldman, our Director of Public Relations. Sarah presented the flowers to my mother who was very flattered. Lili was a woman in her forties who looked like Barbara Streisand without the nose. Sarah was a tall blonde with a perfect figure, about 25. She was clearly one of the most beautiful woman I had ever seen. She was dressed as if she were on her way to the opera. It didn't sound right that a woman who looked like that should be working in a yeshiva office, but I didn't suspect anything at the time.

Lili and Sarah went for the minibus and Rabbi Brill led us to a curb where the bus would pick us up. Carol, who is very outspoken and by far the most tactless person in the world, took me aside and whispered, "Melvin, did you get an eyeful of that blonde? She could be the answer to all those prayers you say."

"Never," I said, "the lady is married."

"No way, Melvin. Whatever gave you that idea?"

"She has her hair covered and single girls don't do that."

"That's the trouble with you men. The first thing a woman looks at is a lady's fingers and there are no rings on them. I hate to think of what you were looking at." Carol and I both figured it out at the same time. I knew that many religious married women continued to cover their hair even though they were widowed or divorced. Carol simply reasoned that no woman looking like Sandy could possibly remain single through her mid- twenties.

"For your sake Mel, I hope she doesn't have three kids. I'll find out for you." Carol never hesitates when she wants information. She goes right to the source. In this case, it was Rabbi Brill.

"Say, Rabbi, does that gorgeous PR girl you brought along have any kids?"

"To the best of my knowledge, she has never had children."

"Is she a widow or divorcee?"

"What difference does it make?" Rabbi Brill was being cautious.

"You forget my husband is a 'Cohen.' Under Jewish law he may marry a widow but not a divorcee."

"But your husband is already married." The rabbi was nonplussed.

"For a girl like that, he would drop me in a minute. Keep her as far away from him as you can."

"Relax, Carol," he said. "She is a divorcee and not interested in Cohanim."

"What about Melvin? He's still single."

"They would not be compatible in my judgment."

"I'm sorry to hear that," she said as the bus arrived. The driver loaded the luggage in the side compartment. Sandy took the front seat near the window and Lili occupied the seat next to her. Rabbi Brill sat alone across the aisle, behind the driver. When we passed Latrun, Sandy gave Lili a nudge and Lili rose to her feet. She was a little nervous but she got over it quickly.

"We are coming to Shaar Hagai," she announced, "the beginning of the ascent to Jerusalem. The Holy City is almost

3000 feet above sea level and some of the nearby cities are even higher. You will feel the pressure change in your ears as we climb the hills." Once Lili was warmed up she didn't stop. She told us about the Castel and all the battles. When we entered the city, she described all the city neighborhoods in painstaking detail. Our first stop was at the yeshiva where Rabbi Brill had arranged a minyan for Mincha prayers. I chanted the service quite well and Jack and I recited kaddish. The women waited in the office. Sandy didn't show anyone the library because she didn't want to reveal her true identity. After Mincha, she told the driver to take us down Ruppin Street so that Lili would be able to point out the Knesset, the Hebrew University and the major museums. When we got off at the King David, we thanked Lili for her information. Sandy sent her off in a cab and the family checked in at the hotel.

Rabbi Brill announced that the yeshiva was treating us to our first dinner in Israel and we should meet in one of the smaller dining rooms at 6:30 P.M. The King David is the best hotel in Jerusalem, we were often told. Their food tastes as good or better than anywhere else, and always looks more attractive. Their chefs think of themselves first as artists then as cooks.

We were seated at a square table set for eight. Rabbi Brill was at the head of the table and my mother was at his right. Opposite them, at the foot of the table, sat Carol and Joe. Clockwise from Rabbi Brill were Jack and Estelle. Sandy and I sat opposite them. Care was apparently taken not to seat Rabbi Brill between two women, although I am not sure that the law applies when the second woman is seated at right angles to the man. In any event, Sandy wasn't taking any chances.

Rabbi Brill ordered fish while everyone else chose meat. The food and the service were first class. I had a chance to tell Sandy about myself but she limited her conversation to the yeshiva and

Israel. Her vocabulary was quite impressive even though I later found out she was making a special effort to keep it simple.

About an hour into the meal, when we were finishing the main course, a waiter came into the dining room and announced in a loud voice "Telephone for Dr. Feldman, Dr. Sandra Feldman." If it were a loudspeaker page, Sandy would have probably ignored the call. With the waiter standing at the door, she had no choice but to get up and excuse herself. When she was out of sight I got the expected kick from my sister. "Strike Two," she whispered. "First strike is that she's too pretty and now she turns out to be too smart as well. One more strike and you are out of the picture."

Joe, who heard it all, made it worse. "In softball, you only get two strikes."

"You'd better play hard ball for this one," Carol said.

When Sandy returned, Jack was the first one to go after her.

"Doctor Feldman, do you have any cure for jet lag?"

"Take two aspirins and call a real doctor in the morning."

"You are not a real doctor?"

"I only use the title when it serves some purpose."

Jack didn't know what to make of it until Rabbi Brill intervened.

"A story is told about Dr. Robert Miliken, the theoretical physicist. When someone called his home and asked for medical advice, the maid answered that he was not the type of doctor that does anyone any good. Dr. Feldman is a professor of history and has a PhD degree in that subject."

Next it was Carol's turn. "I hope you don't mind my asking why a history professor with a PhD is doing public relations work for a yeshiva. Surely you are able to find a position more in keeping with your background."

"You will have to ask Rabbi Brill that question," Sandra replied.

"Sarah is employed as an assistant professor at a university in New York. When the Seidman family requested a very dignified dedication ceremony and I promised to provide it, I realized that the public relations people in Israel do not understand what Americans require. So I invited Dr. Feldman to plan and conduct the ceremony and she volunteered to do so gratis, as a favor to the yeshiva."

Carol had to find out more. "At what university do you teach, Sarah?"

"I teach at the State University of New York at Cortland."

"You don't live there, do you?"

"I live in Syracuse."

It took Carol another minute to make the connection. "You don't own Feldman's Department Store in that city, do you?"

"Not all of it."

"Part of it?" I tried to nudge Carol to indicate that she was prying, but Sandy didn't seem to mind. "My father left half the store to my mother and the remaining half to each of his three children. I only own one sixth of the store." Carol kicked me under the table and held up three fingers. I knew what she meant. I didn't know how much the store was worth but I knew that Sandy wouldn't be interested in me for my money. Now Jack had to get into the act. "Dr. Feldman, would you perhaps enjoy doing a little public relations work for Buffalo Auto Stores?"

Estelle, who was very straight, didn't realize that Jack was fooling around and she objected, "We already have a public relations man in John Sinclair and he is doing such a good job."

"John may be doing good work but Sarah is a lot easier to look at."

Estelle gave him a dirty look but she was not very upset. She was a nice looking woman herself and she and Jack get along very well. I was doing some heavy thinking myself and I remembered that the Feldmans had dedicated the library at the yeshiva. "This is not your first dedication ceremony at the yeshiva?" I asked.

Rabbi Brill answered for her. "She conducted the dedication of the Feldman library in an outstanding manner last December and I understand that she is the campaign manager for Congressman Harrison."

"He's a democrat from Syracuse, isn't he? Democrats usually don't win upstate," I said.

"Hardly ever," Sandy replied. "Now that I have been exposed, I can get to work. Who is going to represent the Seidmans in making the arrangements for the dedication services? There is no point in convening the entire family to settle all the little details. Is there anyone that all of you trust?"

Jack spoke for the family. "Melvin takes care of everything that has to do with charity or religion. He negotiated the original gift with Rabbi Brill."

"All right, I will discuss all matters with Melvin and whatever he says goes. Right?"

"Within reason." Carol offered. "Does anyone here realize that Buffalo Auto Parts deals with the Feldman's store?"

"No kidding?" Jack said.

"Absolutely. When Melvin buys too much of anything, and the *chacham* does quite often, we can't sell all of the item in our own stores. So we look for department stores that will take the item at cost. Feldman's has made quite a few buys from us. If the item sells well, they will often buy more of it later at a somewhat better price."

"Chacham" means wise man, but it is not always used in a complimentary sense. "Hey," I said in self-defense, "you have to buy in very large quantities to get the prices I get."

Sandra quickly entered the discussion. "I bought some of Melvin's stuff at the Buffalo Auto Store in Cortland and I found the prices quite reasonable."

That made me feel much better. I asked Rabbi Brill to lead the grace after meals. He had had the foresight to take along the little books for those who didn't know the prayer by heart. When we completed the recitation, Carol, who was not finished making trouble, said to Sandy, "If you end your meeting late, Melvin will be glad to escort you home."

Sandy smiled and led her right into the trap. "I really wouldn't want to take him that far out of his way."

"Why, how far away are you staying?"

"At least fifty feet. My mother and I have our suite down the hall from you."

That gave everyone a good laugh. I arranged to meet Sandy in ten minutes in the lobby. Rabbi Brill said goodbye to everyone and the families went up to their rooms.

In the lobby, Sandy outlined her plan for the services and explained why two separate programs were necessary. She told me that Jack and I would have to participate in both ceremonies because the sons of the donor were expected to be present. "What do we have to do at the first ceremony?"

"You have to chant the Mincha services for the worshippers and you and Jack have to recite kaddish at the appropriate places. You also have to hand gold-plated shovels to the distinguished rabbis so that they can dig up a little soil."

"Then what?"

"After that, the audience will go to the Beis Yaakov auditorium where at least you, if not Jack, will have to listen to learned Talmudic discourses for up to an hour and a half."

"That's not so bad. I attend a Talmud class at our synagogue once a week."

"Where is the class up to?" Sandy asked in seeming innocence.

Here I made another mistake. "I'm not sure you've heard of it, but we just started the Talmudic tractate 'Baba Metziah.'" I've learned since never to assume any lack of knowledge on Sandy's part.

"Oh, that's the one that starts with two people holding on to a tallit and both claiming that it's all theirs. Then they're given a strangely worded oath to take and, finally, they divide the tallit in half."

"That's the one," I said in surprise. Where did you learn that?"

"I first learned the Mishna in day school but I reread it at a later time."

"The oath is not strange at all. If each holder swore according to his claim, we would be forcing at least one of them to perjure himself because they both can't be telling the truth when they claim that it's all theirs. The courts don't want to force anyone into perjury."

"Why not? They do it everywhere else in the Talmud."

At this point I was glad that I had paid attention when our sexton was leading the class and discussed the question. "Normally, we don't worry about people lying in court. In this case, each one of the finders actually believes that he found the garment first and no one is intentionally lying."

"Say, that's very good," she said. "You were wide awake in the Talmud class. That's wonderful."

"I don't study all that much but I take it seriously. I also used to learn with my father, who was a real scholar."

"I'll have to test you further," she warned me, "but let's get on with business."

"What happens after the public gathering?"

"There is an intermission till about 6:15 P.M. Then we return to the building site for the cornerstone-laying ceremony."

"How can you break ground and lay the cornerstone in one day?"

"I'm a historian. I have mastered the ability of compressing eons of time into ephemeral periods."

"Tell me in English. I'm only an MBA."

"The corner of the lot where the cornerstone will be laid will be constructed and covered with a tarp. The spectators at the groundbreaking will think that all we have under the tarp are building materials. By my loose definitions, as long as we haven't dug up all the footing trenches, a groundbreaking is still kosher and, as long as we have a section of the wall erected, a cornerstone setting is within the bounds of legitimacy."

"I think necessity is causing you to split some of your beautiful blond hairs."

"I'm glad you appreciate both my sophistry and my hair, in that order. At the cornerstone-laying, you, Jack and Carol will use a gold-plated trowel to put down a little mortar and the cornerstone will be set in. Then we will hear a speech from a very distinguished speaker."

"What next?"

"We retire to the Beis Yaakov Hall where the family will receive the good wishes of their friends and family at a small reception. That will be followed by the main dinner."

"How about the dinner program?"

"We can't have entertainment because you are in mourning. We will have the pleasure of hearing a few very important speakers and then the yeshiva will present the members of the family with scrolls and gifts. The family spokesman, one Melvin Seidman, will then offer a very learned response to the presentations. Then it is all over."

"May I offer a caveat?"

"Go ahead."

"I am not a practicing rabbi and I may not be up to delivering learned discourses in the Holy City of Jerusalem."

"From what I've heard, you deliver great speeches at UJA dinners, the Boy Scouts and the Chamber of Commerce."

"May I let you in on a very dark, foreboding secret which you must promise not to tell a living soul?"

"I promise on my last copy of *Vogue*."

"Buffalo Auto employs a top notch public relations expert whose continued employment is contingent upon the applause I get for the speeches he meticulously crafts for me. Unfortunately, we forgot to take Sinclair along and, in any event, he has even less knowledge of Talmud than I do."

"In that case, I will throw in all the required speeches, at no extra cost, in the budget of the dedication ceremony that I wish to discuss with you."

The truth was slowly beginning to dawn on me. For one who has been involved in so many fund-raising activities, I should have been the first to realize that there is no such thing as a free lunch or, more precisely, a rather lavish dinner at the King David. I was going to be touched for a large sum of money by a fund-raiser who is at the top of the class. The yeshiva would not have involved someone of the calibre of a Sandra Feldman to raise trivial sums. "I gave at the office," I said, lamely. "You're not going to ask for more now, are you?"

"Rabbi Brill told me that the Seidman family has a position that it never accepts charity from others and certainly not from a yeshiva. It was in that spirit that you compensated both the yeshiva and Rabbi Brill for expenses that they ran up on your behalf."

"That was for services we received at the funeral. I never

heard of an organization charging the donors for fund-raising expenses."

"An unusual set of circumstances exists at the Beit Meir Yeshiva. The yeshiva has no regular budget to cover the cost of fund-raising. The rabbis who do it are not paid extra or given a commission. In the case of Rabbi Brill, the yeshiva does not cover anything beyond his travel expenses.

"When it came to dedicating the library in honor of my father, I felt that I could not allow our plaque to be placed at the entrance of a shabby library room. It required carpeting, paneling, lighting, bookshelves and new furniture. I also wanted a dedication program that would make my mother so happy that it would take her mind off her sorrow. Fixing the library and conducting the program cost more than $25,000. I started paying it myself but my mother wouldn't let me pay for the remodelling of the library and took care of that for me. On top of everything else, my brothers and I each donated an extra $5000 as our share of the library project. The final result was a beautiful library and a wonderful dedication service. The whole business didn't cost the yeshiva a penny and it gave the school a world of publicity that resulted in additional donations and student applications. What is most important, however, is that it made my mother feel great. If I had to do it all over again, I wouldn't think twice."

"What would happen if our family chose not to go beyond the original half-million dollars that we pledged?"

"For one, the ceremony and the dinner would be trimmed to the minimum that would be acceptable and I, poor Sandra Feldman, would pick up the tab personally for what was spent."

"Why would you do a thing like that?"

"Because I have earned the reputation of being the ultimate public relations person. Ultimate means that I conduct the best ceremonies possible at no cost to the sponsoring organization.

Preserving my reputation is worth the cost, especially when I am in a high tax bracket."

There was no way that I could say no to Sandra Feldman. Not only was I under her spell but deep down I knew that the yeshiva didn't have any extra money to treat us to lavish dinners and receptions. Split three ways in our tax bracket, it wouldn't amount to much and I didn't want to be in a position where I could cost myself a chance to make progress with Sandra. My best hope was to try to put a lid on the budget but I underestimated the lady. She does things in a big way. I don't think that money ever stood in the way of anything she ever wanted.

"OK, I surrender. The Seidmans will pick up the cost of the affair if you keep it reasonable."

"I will do my best, but you must realize that what may be cake to one party may be crumbs to the next."

"Look, Sandra, I'm a businessman. I like to talk in terms of the bottom line. Just tell me how much you are asking for and I'll let you know if we can do it."

"You are not buying inner tubes now, Melvin. The ceremony is a matter of taste and emotion. If you have to worry about cost, you will never get it done right. I can describe the type of ceremony that will make everyone happy and will tell you what it will cost. I can only hope that you will not try to cut corners."

"Break it to me gently."

"The budget includes the dinner and related expenses, the cornerstone and related expenses and smaller items such as rentals, advertising and incidentals. That part of the budget shouldn't amount to more than $8,000. The big part of the budget involves getting the speakers, and there we are talking about $10,000 or so."

"We certainly won't have any problem covering the routine expenses. Why do we have to pay ten grand for speeches?"

"Let me ask you something, Melvin. You are an officer in many charitable organizations. When they need a speaker at a major affair, such as a senator or a congressman, don't they pay a substantial fee?"

"They surely do, but there they may need a big name to draw the crowds who pledge money to the appeals. Here, we are not making any appeals."

"I have two reasons, or maybe three, why we need well-known public figures. For one, it enhances the reputation of the school if prominent men take the time to participate in its affairs. Secondly, it provides the only chance of getting adequate coverage in the media. Thirdly, it will make the affair memorable for your mother and the grandchildren. Imagine Carol showing her daughter a picture of herself shaking hands with the Prime Minister of Israel."

"If it is only for Carol to show off, you don't need the Prime Minister. She's the type who could brag about a third undersecretary in the Ministry of Agriculture who would be glad to show up for a measly $500."

"On that level, the politicians can't even speak English and your mother would never remember the name of the fellow. By the way, I don't want you to think that any of these public figures keep the money for themselves as do congressmen and senators. In all cases, the money goes either to the political party or some worthy cause supported by the Ministry. Ultimately, it filters down to the common people."

"Who showed up at your affair?"

"The American Ambassador, three congressmen on the Foreign Relations Committee, the Minister of Religious Affairs and the Mayor of Jerusalem. The affair was fully covered in the press and media."

"Whom do you have in mind for us?"

"I will get the same crew together without the congress-men, but I have to add the Prime Minister and the Minister of Housing and Development."

"Why the Minister of Housing?"

"The yeshiva is seeking a grant of $50,000 from the Ministry for your dormitory."

"You also expect something from the Ministry of Religious Affairs?"

"Not as much as from Housing, but I hope it will be significant."

"And how much from the Prime Minister?"

"Nothing specific, but the Bible tells us, 'Cast thy bread upon the waters for in the end of days it will be returned to thee.' Let us say that we are providing the yeshiva with a reservoir of goodwill that may be important at some time in the future."

"Are you sure that all of this is strictly kosher?"

"It isn't even remotely kosher. It's simply a matter of exploit-ing the greed in the hearts of men for the benefit of a higher cause."

"Isn't that equivalent to a mitzvah that is fulfilled using material derived from sinful acts?" I had learned that stolen ritual objects, for example, cannot be used in religious services.

"We are not saying a blessing on a stolen palm branch. The emotion that we are exploiting is not a tangible one. Religion has always exploited emotions such as fear, greed and a desire for fame, to serve its own end. I have not reinvented the wheel."

"Does the American Ambassador have to be paid off?"

"Not by us. I got him here last time by having my congress-man on the Foreign Relations Committee lean on the State Department. I was wondering whether Buffalo Auto has any congressmen on its payroll."

"We're not above supporting local officials who may be

helpful to us on a rainy day. National figures can't do much for us except in such obscure areas as reducing import tariffs on foreign auto parts. But, if we get a break, so do our competitors. In the final analysis, it really doesn't pay to bother."

"In that case, I will have to ask my own congressman to take care of it. The only danger in that is that he might decide to attend the Jerusalem ceremony in person. I will try to talk him out of it."

"All right, Sandra, put me down for $18,000. If I can't sell Carol on her share, I will have to cover it myself."

"I knew I could depend on you," Sandra said, "and I will write a terrific speech for you at no cost. There are a few other matters, though, for which we still need your approval."

"For no extra charges?"

"None."

"Go ahead."

"You know that the Seidman donation will cover only half of the cost of the new dormitory. The yeshiva will borrow on its mortgage and get some government money but it will still have to raise additional funds. We will certainly not make any appeals at your affair but we would like to place a descriptive brochure at each plate of non-family members, listing the donation opportunities available in the new building. You have no objections, I hope?"

"None at all. It seems perfectly legitimate. I don't even mind if you leave the brochures at every seat. Most of my family, though, are too poor to help."

"Speaking of your family, we need a copy of your guest list to send out the invitations. I believe you promised Rabbi Brill that you would prepare such a list."

I handed Sandy an envelope with all names and last known addresses. I also included a list of our friends who had made aliyah to Israel over the years. After she had the list, Sandy showed me three versions of possible inscriptions for the cornerstone. I asked her to indicate the one that she preferred and I agreed with her choice.

It read as follows:

THE ZICHRON MEIR
RESIDENCE HALL
Dedicated in memory of
MR. MEIR SEIDMAN
By his wife and children
10 Tammuz 5754   June 6, 1994

My father's name was written in Hebrew under the English. There was also an inscription above the top line giving the name of the Residence Hall in Hebrew. The texts that I rejected contained the names of all the children and I just didn't feel that so much information could be engraved on the stone without making it hard to read.

We finished our business and for a whole hour we had a chance to talk about ourselves. Sandy described what she was doing during the year and her plans for the future. She touched only briefly on her short marriage.

"Incidentally, Sandy, do you have a *get* (religious divorce) from your first husband?" It was too early to ask such a question but I reasoned that there would be no point in getting my hopes up about this girl if, in the end, I couldn't marry her. If a woman doesn't have a religious divorce from her previous husband, all children born into the new family are considered illegitimate according to Jewish law. No Orthodox rabbi would even perform such a wedding in the first place.

Sandy opened her purse and showed me a letter from the

Rabbinical Council of America attesting to her divorce. "Do you have any idea how much this little piece of paper cost me?" she asked.

"I heard that a bill of divorce can be arranged in Buffalo for under $1000."

"That's assuming the husband is willing to grant the get. It costs a lot more when he isn't. After I got the civil divorce, my father asked Steven to take care of the religious one. Steven, except in matters of fidelity, is an honest man. He told my father that he didn't believe in such things in principle and that he saw no reason why he should get involved with old-fashioned clergymen."

"What did your father say to that?"

"In a cleaned-up abridgement, he said, 'Steven, I know how much your principles are worth. You have three days to get yourself down to New York City and authorize a divorce at the Rabbinical Council. If you do, there will be a check of $25,000 waiting for you. That sum is about twenty times what you contributed to my daughter's support during the three years that you were married to her. If you don't make it in three days, you will never see another penny of Feldman money in your life.'"

"I take it that his principles weren't worth as much as $25,000?"

"You can say that again."

I caught the eye of a passing waiter and asked him to serve us some drinks. Over the drinks, Sandy asked me if her mother could join our tour in the morning. She said that her mother was tired of shopping or sitting in the hotel alone. I had a feeling that she wanted her mother to look me over and I took that as a positive sign. Mrs. Feldman would also provide my mother with some companionship so I readily agreed to it.

By then it was 10:00 P.M. and Rabbi Brill was back at the

hotel with eight of his students. We organized a minyan for the evening service. I noticed that Sandy was saying the evening prayers at some distance from the men. Her knowledge of Judaism was amazing, considering that she had no formal religious education beyond day school.

I didn't bother calling Jack to the minyan because I assumed he was sound asleep. I expected to have a problem getting him up in the morning and taking him to the Western Wall for the Shachrit services, but Jack woke up in time and we took a cab to that holy site.

At breakfast, Carol conducted her inquisition. "How did it go last night?" she asked me.

"Very well," I said. "Quite an interesting girl."

"How much did she take us for?"

"Whatever makes you think she was out for money?"

"The yeshiva doesn't import an operator like that from America to collect peanuts. I have no doubt that she put the bite on you."

"You are very analytical this morning."

"How much?"

"I thought I was delegated to act for the family in matters relating to this dedication."

"Within reason."

I wasn't going to let my sister bully me. "Dr. Feldman told me that what she was asking for was quite reasonable."

"You believed her, of course."

"She can be quite convincing."

"Especially if you are looking into those soft, blue eyes. Listen, Mel, you are OK when you represent us with men. The next time Sandra asks you for money, I want to be there."

"I wouldn't want to expose a sweet girl like that to your tongue. I would rather pay for it all by myself."

"If you went overboard last night, you may wind up doing just that."

"Don't let her bother you," Jack said. I'll pay my share and, if she doesn't pay hers, I'll cover half of the total amount."

"What about my share?" my mother asked."Don't I have to pay anything?"

I answered her firmly. "If you want to make any donations to the yeshiva on your own, you are free to do so. As far as what we have to pay now, Jack and I will take care of it."

Carol was stung by being left out. "I didn't say I wouldn't pay anything. I just don't want Mel to lose his head over a beautiful woman and get carried away."

"Don't worry," I said. "Your share won't cost more than a long weekend in Las Vegas. This money goes for a good cause and you can deduct your donation from your taxes."

At 9:15 P.M., Lili came in with Mrs. Feldman and introduced her to all of us. She seemed to be in good shape for her age, and dressed nicely. I didn't see much of a resemblance to Sandy but she looked fine on her own. I took her for a woman in her late sixties, a few years younger than Mom.

It wasn't too hot outside, so Lili decided to take us down the Dead Sea road to Masada. My mother was a little hesitant about going all the way to the top but, between Lili and Mrs. Feldman, she didn't have much of a choice. Lili gave us a running commentary but she wasn't too strong on her history. She had read the guidebooks the night before and was at least well prepared on the printed material.

My mother got along very well with Mrs. Feldman. In fact, for a good part of the trip they spoke in their native Yiddish, exchanging stories about Poland and Vienna. Mom insisted that Mrs. Feldman come along Wednesday and Thursday and the latter quickly agreed. I had a chance to talk to her on the tour and I did so several times. Each afternoon, the bus stopped at the yeshiva to allow Jack and me to chant Mincha and arrange for a minyan to be present at the evening services. On the first afternoon, I asked Sandy to show everyone the Feldman Library and she took us in. It was really a beautiful room and I realized that Sandy had spent more money to get it fixed up than she had let on to her mother.

On Thursday night, I ran into Sandy coming into the lobby after dinner and invited her to have a drink.

"How are things going with arrangements?" I asked her.

"Everything is on schedule. Did you have a chance to settle with Carol?"

"I finally told her the correct amount and she felt quite relieved. She was sure that I had pledged another hundred thousand dollars."

"Maybe I should have asked you for more?"

"That's a universal feeling. Whenever I make an offer and it is accepted, I always feel that I should have offered less. I learned to get over that pretty quickly. By the way, did you get any confirmations on the guest speakers?"

"I have a tentative acceptance from the Prime Minister and firm commitments from all the rest, including the Ambassador. I will be needing some of the extra money when you can spare it."

"Will you take a check?"

"No problem. Have you decided how you will transfer the $500,000?"

"Rabbi Brill said we should send it to the New York office to avoid any tax problems. I'll call Max Glaser tomorrow before the Sabbath and tell him to send it out. I signed the foundation checkbook before I left."

"That creates a small problem, which I think we can resolve creatively."

"What is that?"

"The program calls for you to hand over the check to Rabbi Steiner."

"I can give him a blank one."

"The check has to be photographed and used in our literature."

"If I give you a real check how do I know you won't cash it?"

"Why, Melvin," she said, feigning shock. "How could you possibly think that I would take you for another half million? You sound like Carol."

"I'm sorry. I really trust you."

"Just in case she bothers you, tell Max Glaser to keep his check till next Wednesday. If you don't get yours back by then he can hold up the one he has."

"That's fair." I took out a Buffalo Auto checkbook and wrote a check to the yeshiva for $18,000. Sandy thanked me warmly.

"About Sabbath services," she said, "there should be a Friday night minyan at the hotel. Saturday morning, I have been assigned to take you all to the Great Synagogue. They have a wonderful cantor and choir."

She kept her word and we enjoyed the experience. The synagogue was a lot bigger and architecturally superior to our shul in Buffalo. That was the last I saw of Sandy until we arrived at the yeshiva on Monday afternoon for the dedication.

SANDRA

21

ONLY DURING THE LAST DAYS of a congressional campaign did I work as hard as I did on Wednesday and Thursday. The cornerstone, the brochure, the programs, the rentals and the catering, everything had to be resolved. I watched Yossi pour the concrete on Wednesday morning and remove the forms on Friday. I had asked him to put a notch in the concrete so that the cornerstone could be set in on two sides and the bottom. The wall was about 40 centimeters thick up to ground level and then seven centimeters narrower from there. The setback was to carry the Jerusalem stone. To the height of the top of the cornerstone Yossi would have to run four courses of the decorative stone. I warned him that if he wasn't on the job with six masons on Sunday morning, I would have his head. He assured me that it would be ready. I told him that I would need two new shovels and three new trowels on Sunday in time for me to gild them and I promised to sell them back to him after the ceremony at a 25% discount.

"For 25% off, you can keep them," he said in a huff.

"Okay," I said. "Get everything done on time and they are yours for nothing."

"That's better."

"Better buy me four trowels," I said as an afterthought. "The Seidmans may want a souvenir."

On Monday morning, I took my dinner dress with me. I couldn't work in it so I realized I would have to take a few minutes between 5:00 and 6:00 P.M. to change over.

In rapid order, the cornerstone was delivered and set up, heavily draped, on the platform. A long tarp covered the built up wall and the rental people set up the chairs. The sound system was installed and tested. I paid to have a technician sitting all through the service and monitor it in case it started to whistle. I hate when that happens and everyone in the audience who has ever owned a stereo thinks he knows how the fix it.

Rabbis Brill and Goldberg couldn't believe how fast I was working. Israelis are accustomed to working at a leisurely pace and live by the dictum, "Never finish anything today that was due the day before yesterday." I worked them awfully hard and made Rabbi Brill call every donor who had ever made a substantial contribution to the school and extend to him a personal invitation to attend the ceremony. Rabbi Steiner called all the academy heads and noted rabbis and invited them to be present at the earlier public service.

Around noon on Sunday, I got a call from a spokesman at the Ministry of Religious Affairs that the Prime Minister had agreed to release information about a new subsidy to help parents with educational costs. He informed me that he had called all the media, bar none, to advise them that a big story would break at the dedication.

The religious papers had carried ads for the afternoon ceremony and, by a quarter to three, it was standing room only on the building site. Melvin led the afternoon service from the speaker's platform. He was a little nervous in the presence of all the rabbinic luminaries but he did well anyway.

Rabbi Steiner read the appropriate Psalms and Jack and Melvin handed out the shovels to a long procession of scholars who wanted to turn over some earth. The press was not there yet but my video recorded all the action. After the groundbreaking, Rabbi Steiner led the parade to the Beis Yaakov auditorium for a long succession of speeches. In between the scholarly speeches, Rabbi Steiner put in a good word for Yossi, the builder, and lauded his generous contribution of $2500. The dean had to do it then because Yossi wanted the yeshiva world to hear about his availability. I heard the announcement but I was too busy to listen to all the other discourses. Since they were all recorded I knew I would have the chance to hear them later on.

I went back to the building site to check on the corner wall. Yossi had removed the tarp and he had the Arab with the donkey waiting down the block. The donkey was in a truck eating his supper and looking very contented.

I was determined to start at 6:00 P.M. and I almost made it. The lot was crawling with secret service men and media people and every seat was taken. Rabbi Goldberg opened the services with a few stories to the effect that while wagon drivers were chronically portrayed as poor in Jewish literature, the merchants who sold them wagon parts did quite well. He said that the Seidmans kept Americans moving and thus generated a lot of jobs, especially for environmentalists who had to worry about air pollution. He always had a good sense of humor and he was in top form. The first speaker was the Minister of Housing, who spoke briefly. He quoted from the Ethics of the Fathers the description of a Torah student as one who eats a dry crust of bread dipped in salt. "Today's yeshiva man," he said, "no longer lives that way. He needs a bed and a closet and a desk. He needs a dining hall and nutritious meals and that is exactly what Beit Meir is providing." He then listed some statistics about schools and yeshivot that the Ministry had supported, and he indicated that the new dormitory would also be supported. He invited the Seidmans to invest some of their surplus capital in Israel and thanked them for their donation.

Rabbi Goldberg called upon Jack to unveil the cornerstone and then he read the inscription to the audience. He then asked the audience to rise for a special service to be led by a well-known cantor chanting a memorial prayer for the late Meir Seidman. I was sitting with the women of the family and Carol and her mother were crying loudly. I don't know why my mother started to cry but, when she did, I shed some tears as well.

After the prayer, Rabbi Goldberg read a Psalm and the sons recited kaddish. I slipped away from the family and took up a position near the corner wall. When the members of the audience took their seats, Rabbi Goldberg continued.

"Now comes the moment you have all been waiting for. This beautiful cornerstone will be put in place on the southwest wall of the building. You may remain in your places but just turn to the right and you will be able to watch the emplacement. We have to wait a minute for the crane to get here to move the heavy stone to the building corner. While we are waiting, I would like to advise the ladies and gentlemen of the press and TV that the Honorable Prime Minister of the State of Israel has arrived and he will address the audience as soon as the cornerstone is in place." The reporters and cameramen started getting their equipment ready. Rabbi Goldberg waited another thirty seconds.

"The crane is not here yet and I don't want to keep the Prime Minister waiting. Is there anyone in the audience who can carry the stone over?"

When no one responded, he continued. "In that case, I will pray to the Almighty to send us 'a poor man riding on a donkey' to help us in our moment of need." The latter expression was the rabbinic description of the forthcoming arrival of the Messiah and the audience didn't understand what Rabbi Goldberg was driving at. That is, they didn't catch on until he signalled to me and I signalled Yossi. Yossi had already mounted the animal and proudly rode up to the platform with the Arab following in his wake. When the audience saw them, they started to howl and cheer. The photographers and TV men starting recording the scene. Yossi and the Arab loaded the stone on the donkey and led him over to the corner. I went in and gathered up the family while the photographers were still shooting the smiling donkey. Yossi handed out the trowels with mortar and all members of the family had a chance to place the cement on the concrete. Yossi and the Arab smoothed out the mortar, lifted the stone off the donkey and placed it on the wall.

Rabbi Goldberg wished everyone *mazel tov* as I led the family back to their places. "Let's have a round of applause for the Seidman family," he shouted and everyone applauded loudly. "Now some applause for that great rider, Yossi, the builder, and the donkey owner, Muhammed Majah. Now, one final round of applause for Yisi the donkey." The cheering was loud and explosive. Behind the wall, Muhammed stuck a pail of oats under the donkey's mouth, which the audience couldn't see. When the donkey went for the oats, it looked as if he were taking a bow. Instinctively I knew that Yisi would make the front pages of every paper and would be featured on TV. Rabbi Steiner had a broad smile on his face during the stunt but I didn't know how he would feel about it later. The Prime Minister took the matter in good grace. He told the audience that he didn't mind being upstaged by a donkey as long as the donkey had four legs. When he was upstaged by two-legged donkeys, that's when he got upset. Those words he said in Hebrew. In his English remarks, he made his announcement about the new education grants that would benefit all poor families, both religious and secular. He then spoke about the yeshiva and the Seidmans.

Rabbi Goldberg followed by announcing the reception for the family at the Beis Yaakov auditorium and the dinner for invited guests. He asked the audience to wait while the Prime Minister left first, followed by other government officials and the Seidman family. To keep the audience in place he told a few jokes and made a few announcements. I walked with the family to the school and set them up in a receiving line outside the auditorium door so that they could receive the good wishes of the guests.

The Prime Minister greeted the Seidmans one by one as I introduced them. He shook hands with Joe, Jack and Melvin and he kissed Carol and Mrs. Seidman. I have a gut feeling that Carol was the one who made a move on the Prime Minister. I'm not sure but I'll be able to check the video because both of my photographers were grinding away. The Minister of Religious Affairs, an old hand-kisser, greeted the ladies next. Then came the Housing Minister and some other dignitaries. After that, the general audience arrived.

As soon as the dignitaries passed the family, I directed them into the hall and invited them to have a drink. Once they entered the hall, Lili directed the men to one area and the women to the other. Having the receiving line outside was my solution to the problem of how we could have both husbands and wives of the Seidman relatives greet the family together.

From the reception area, the guests entered the main hall and picked up their place cards. When the reception was over, the area was set up for the yeshiva students. All day we had been adding to the guest list as people called in at the last minute to tell us that they had decided to attend. By the time the dinner started, we had seated 230 guests in addition to 50 yeshiva students.

In the hall, we were able to set up hand-washing areas right on the main floor so guests wouldn't have to crowd the sinks. Jack Steiner said the prayer over the bread aloud and the dinner got underway. The speeches were fairly brief, starting with the mayor, the American ambassador and the Minister of Religious Affairs. The minister focused a lot of attention on Mrs. Seidman, while the mayor spoke of yet another important building in the holy city. The ambassador told how Jewish immigrants helped build the heartland of America and found the country to be a land of opportunity. It was due to their success in the u.s. that they were able to help establish cultural institutions in Israel.

After the main course was served, Rabbi Brill rose to start the presentation ceremonies. He traced the contributions of the Seidman family from the time the yeshiva started and he described how indebted the institution was to a single man, the late Meir Seidman. He was happy that the children were walking in the footsteps of their father and continuing his support of Torah. After a complete description of the building project, he called on Rabbi Steiner to present the gifts to the family. Jack got a tallit and a kiddish cup while Melvin got a deluxe set of the major work of Maimonides. For the women, I had a harder time deciding what to buy because I knew they had just about everything. In the end, we gave Carol a table set, which included a matching challah cover and tablecloth. Mrs. Seidman was presented with an oil painting by a well-known artist depicting a Jerusalem scene.

Usually, recipients of such gifts briefly thank the rabbis and sit down. Most philanthropists aren't polished speakers anyway. Jack followed the standard procedure but Melvin took the time to deliver the speech I had prepared for him. It traced the history of yeshivot from the legendary school in the days of Abraham to the current ones in every part of the world where Jews live. "These institutions helped the Jewish people survive in the diaspora," he said, "and, today, they are more important than ever. The highest level of Torah scholarship is to be found in the Israeli yeshivot in fulfillment of the verse, 'For from Zion shall go forth the law.' Our father helped all yeshivas but none were as dear to him as the one in Israel that will always bear his name." He cited several passages from the volume of Sanhedrin, which was being studied in the yeshiva, and indicated the supremacy of Torah scholars in Jewish life. He warmly praised the efforts of Rabbi Steiner to propagate Torah. He related that Rabbi Brill had spent ten full days with the family in their time of sorrow and gave the family courage and inspiration. At that juncture, he asked Rabbi Steiner and Rabbi Brill to join him.

"Honored Rabbis," he said, "it is with great pride and pleasure that I present this check for five hundred thousand dollars from the Seidman family to help build the Zichron Meir Dormitory of the Beit Meir Yeshiva, in memory of our husband, father and grandfather, the late Meir Seidman, may his soul rest in Gan Eden." As he handed the check to Rabbi Steiner, the crowd rose to its feet and gave him a long standing ovation. Melvin delivered the speech well and it was by far the most popular speech of the evening. When he concluded, he was embraced by Rabbi Steiner and congratulated by everyone else.

During his speech, Carol handed a note to Rabbi Goldberg. I didn't arrange for her to respond to her gift because I knew that Rabbi Steiner was not too happy with women speakers, particularly young ones. Having spent a few days with her, I knew she could be brutally frank and I was nervous about what she would say. Rabbi Goldberg caught my eye and signalled that Carol wanted to talk. I wasn't going to stop her because that would be the worst course of action to take, so I gave him a thumbs-up sign and he introduced her. Carol didn't need a script. She got up and told the audience, "I don't know the fine print like Melvin does and certainly not like my father did. But my father did manage to teach me to give charity, love my neighbor and consider the study of the Torah as being equal to the sum of all mitzvahs." She was able to quote the source in Hebrew. "Of course, I share in the family gift of the new dormitory but it is the men who get all the recognition and attention at a yeshiva ceremony. So I want to do something in my own name." Here she raised the brochure from the table. "I read in this pamphlet that I can have my name on a room for four students in the new dormitory, for $18,000. That honor is well worth it." She took out a check, presumably for $18,000, and gave it to Rabbi Steiner. Among religious people it is not customary for a woman to hand anything directly to a man, but Rabbi Steiner was in no mood to embarrass Carol and he accepted her check.

"Now that I have bought the Joe and Carol Cohen Dormitory Room, I want to say a word to all of you ladies and gentlemen. The Seidman family is paying for only half of the dormitory. The rest is up to you. I want every one here to pick up the brochure on your table and look at it. It tells you what you can do for the yeshiva. I know that not everybody here can afford to buy a big room, but everyone can buy a desk or a closet or a bed. In fact many of you can buy the wood furnishings for a room. That's six pieces, four closets and two desks, a $3000 value for only $2500. That's not just a bargain, it's a steal. The only place you can get a better buy than that is at Buffalo Auto. Now, don't anyone dare leave this place without buying something from the brochure and giving your order to Rabbi Brill on the way out."

Carol finally finished without doing any more damage to the decorum, and then I got another surprise. Rabbi Goldberg called on Mrs. Seidman. She told the audience that she had wonderful children who took care of everything and wouldn't let her share in the main dormitory gift. But Melvin had said to her that she could give her own donation if she felt that way. "I do feel that way and I want to give something that will be from me and bear my name. I am giving this check to Rabbi Steiner for the Frieda Steiner room in the new dormitory." Having accepted one check from a woman, Rabbi Steiner had no choice but to accept the next.

I learned later that Melvin wasn't happy about being outshone by Carol and was going to make a personal donation. Jack, however, put a restraining hand on him and told him not to spoil it for her.

Rabbi Goldberg was supposed to make the appeal himself but with Carol having done it there was no point in repeating it. He called on Melvin to recite the grace. After that, the dinner was concluded and the guests started to leave.

Rabbi Brill was standing at the exit collecting pledges in the brochures. He didn't have time to look at what was written in them but, when he was near the end, he handed me the batch and told me to make a quick count.

"How much do you think is in here?" I asked.

"I'm hoping that we're somewhere close to $20,000."

I took the filled-in brochures, sat down at a table and separated the major pledges from the smaller ones. I was astounded at what I read. Two more big rooms at $18,000 each were taken and all three of the $10,000 rooms were sold. Twelve families had subscribed to the room-furnishing package that Carol had pushed so hard. All told, the major gifts totalled $96,000. I estimated another $20,000 in the smaller gifts and I didn't know what Rabbi Brill was still holding in his hands. It was apparent, however, that including the two Seidman rooms, we had raised over $160,000 at the dinner.

"It's a good thing you didn't count the pledges, Rabbi Brill."

"Why is that?"

"The Sages say that if you count your money, it doesn't increase. If you don't count it, God sends His blessing and it increases substantially."

"You mean I underestimated?"

"You were way off. There was over $115,000 in the package you handed me. That doesn't include the Seidmans or what you have in your hand."

"Are you telling me the truth or are you just having fun?"

"Nothing but the truth, tonight. The way I figure it, you finished financing the building and you also covered the salary increases for you and Rabbi Gross and the full salary of Rabbi Goldberg."

"That's magnificent. I don't know how to thank you."

"I didn't make the appeal, it was Carol who did it."

"Nevertheless, it was your brochure that inspired her and made it all possible. When Rabbi Steiner hears what we have made tonight, he may even forgive you for that escapade with the donkey."

"He was mad about it?"

"He was livid. He feels that you exposed the yeshiva to ridicule."

"Do you know what to tell him?"

"I have no idea."

"Tell him the donkey's name was not originally Yisi. We gave him that name because it was short for Yissachar. You remember that Yissachar was the tribe most devoted to the study of Torah. The symbol for Yissachar was a donkey. The Torah was telling us that scholars have to be willing to carry their burdens like donkeys."

"I'm not sure he will appreciate your wisdom."

"I guess it's a good thing I will be going touring with the

Seidmans for the next three days while he cools off. I have this strange feeling that Yisi will be in every paper in the country and on TV tonight. I asked Lili to tape the nine o'clock news on her video." Lili, a die-hard American, kept her TV and video even though many of the families connected with the yeshiva wouldn't permit such devices in their homes.

"You will be back on Friday?"

"If it pleases God, I will be back." I knew that Rabbi Brill gets a kick when I use certain religious expressions.

My mother and I hitched a ride back to the King David with the Seidmans on the minibus. They were one happy bunch because they enjoyed the ceremonies and the dinner, including some indulgence at the reception.

"You were great, Carol," I said. "Your appeal has so far raised over $115,000 and that doesn't include your own contribution or your mother's. I think in time you might become a good fund-raiser. It's not too different from marketing. Here you are selling a noble institution as opposed to Taiwanese brake pads."

"Don't knock the pads, kid. They're one of our best sellers."

"I know, I bought a pair in the Cortland store and the brakes started squealing after three months."

"You must drive with your foot on the brake. What sort of a car do you have anyway, a heavy Cadillac?"

"As a matter of fact, I have a very light Honda sports car."

Jack, who was listening in, interrupted to tell me that he found the trick with the donkey really funny. "When the announcer said that the crane was late, I told Melvin that you finally blew one of the arrangements and that you weren't Superwoman, after all."

"What did Melvin say?"

"He said, 'Impossible. It's a set-up. Sandy doesn't miss

anything.' Sure enough, the donkey showed up and everybody had a good laugh."

Melvin asked, "Was that stunt in our budget?"

"You actually paid for it but, if you think it wasn't called for, I'll be glad to reimburse you."

"Don't worry about it. How much could it cost to hire a donkey?"

"I saw Yossi hand Muhammed 100 shekels."

"That's pretty reasonable."

The next morning, we left on a minibus for our tour of the North. Carol and Joe occupied one double seat in the back as did Jack and Estelle. My mother and Mrs. Seidman sat together, because by now they were good friends. Melvin was sitting alone and didn't have anyone to talk to.

"Do you mind if I sit with you during the trip?" I asked.

"Not at all. I don't bite."

On the first day, we toured Haifa and then we traveled eastward past Afula to spend the night at the guesthouse of Kibbutz Lavi. The next day was spent touring the Golan and Safed. We turned back to Tiberias and reserved two nights at the Kinar Hotel. On Thursday, we toured the city of Tiberias and the neighboring kibbutzim. One of the highlights was the boat trip across the Kinneret to Kibbutz Ein Gev.

MELVIN

22

ON THURSDAY, I REALIZED THAT I would be saying goodbye to Sandy Feldman and possibly never seeing her again. I wasn't ready to admit I was in love with her, but it was pretty close. The uncertainty came from the fact that I had never had any real love affairs before meeting Sandy and I couldn't fully understand my feelings. No woman had had an effect on me like she did, and none dominated my thoughts so completely. Sitting next to her on the tour bus was an experience I would always relish. Sharing the vistas of the Holy Land with her was something truly special.

I realized that if I wanted to be left with more than just pleasant memories, I would have to take some initiative and make a move. After painful hesitancy, I got up enough nerve to ask her to go for a walk with me and was quite relieved when she consented. We strolled on the promenade overlooking the Kinneret. The water was still and reflected the light of a full moon. The breeze that came over the lake was just enough to keep things cool after the heat of the day. After walking for a while, we sat down on a bench near the far side of the promenade where no one was around.

"Sandy," I whispered, "I have never had such a good time in

my life as in these ten days with you. I thought the trip would be a bore, but you livened it up."

"I had a very nice time, too," she said.

The way she said it caused me not only to feel pleased, but roused the physical urges that I had been experiencing since I'd first laid eyes on her. I finally lost the restraint that I had exercised for so long and let desire run ahead of good judgment. I knew I would get into trouble, but sitting around and doing nothing would also result in losing her, so I felt I could reasonably gamble on some action. I put my arm around her and pulled her close to me and planted a firm kiss on her lips. She didn't resist for a few seconds but then she gently pushed me away.

"What was that for?" she asked.

"Just to show my appreciation to a very sweet girl."

"It wasn't necessary, Melvin. You expressed yourself quite well verbally."

"Rabbi Brill did say I should get to know you."

"I'm sure he didn't mean in the Biblical sense." She thought for a while and came up with a course of action. She certainly didn't want to embarrass me or end my visit to Israel with her walking out on me in a huff. The ultimate public relations person would never antagonize a major client no matter how indiscreet he was. On the other hand, if she didn't make it clear to me that I was out of line, I might be encouraged to try it again or at least think that she didn't really object to my errant behavior. She chose a way that would transmit the message but not cause any real harm. "That little indiscretion of yours will cost you a fine of $1000 payable to the Beit Meir Yeshiva."

I wasn't going to let her get the last word. "In all the years that I've been buying for Buffalo Auto, I never got a better bargain than that. How much would I be allowed if I were willing to donate a whole new building?"

"Melvin Seidman," she said with a touch of anger that may have been real or feigned, "I am not for sale."

"Too bad." I said. "I will, of course, atone for my indiscretion. Shall I make out a check?"

"On second thought, I am not sure that the yeshiva could accept it, because the money is tainted."

I knew immediately what she had in mind, since that concept was plainly written in the Torah. "You are referring to the passage in Deuteronomy?" I asked. That was the one that said that donations of a harlot's fee or the proceeds from the sale of a dog were not of a type acceptable to the Temple. When she nodded her head, I decided to question the point.

"But that applies only to the ultimate recipient of the fee. He or she is not allowed to contribute it. If you actually received the thousand dollars you wouldn't be permitted to present it."

"You may be right but the Torah doesn't quite say it that way. It is entirely possible that once the fee is designated for an undignified purpose, even if the money has not reached the final recipient, it may be tainted. I'll have to ask Rabbi Brill for a definitive ruling on that."

I knew she was having fun at my expense. "You will do no such thing, Sandy. Rabbi Brill still thinks I'm a real *tzadik*, a righteous person."

"I think so too, Melvin. You are very honest and ethical, but in the final analysis, you are still a heterosexual man. I won't have to consult Rabbi Brill because I have just come up with a better idea of what to do with the thousand dollars. His wife, Rivka, is dressed in rags. The fees that Rabbi Brill got from us were used to pay up his loans and grocery bills. I think she was able to buy only one dress for Pesach, a leftover from the winter clearance sales. I'd like to take her shopping and buy her some decent clothes."

"With your taste, what can you get for a $1000 dollars?"

"Very little. But don't forget, I have some atoning to do as well."

"What for?"

"For walking alone with a man in the moonlight overlooking a beautiful lake, for not pushing him away immediately and for not getting up and walking home."

"That will add at least another $1000 to the kitty, even if you are not as big a tzadik as I am."

"It will end up costing even more, but she deserves it."

"Now that you've taken care of a needy woman, I'd like to talk to you about a needy man."

"You are probably the least needy man in the United States."

"Money isn't everything."

"You also have some other fine attributes."

"But I am not married and I do not have a helpmate. The Torah says that it is not good for man to be alone."

"It's not particularly good for a woman either, but it's better to be alone than marry someone with whom you are not compatible."

"I wasn't proposing to you, Sandy, but I like you very much and I want to continue our relationship after we get back to the States. Syracuse is not that far from Buffalo, and we do have a store in Cortland."

"Melvin, I don't think it would be the right thing to do. Look, I have a lot of casual friends and I go out on dates with many men, but not seriously. We dine and dance and I don't fine them if they try to kiss me. With you I couldn't maintain such a relationship. You are a religious man, if not quite the world's greatest tzadik. You need a wife, not a girlfriend, who will fill certain needs in your life. You might get serious over me and I would hate to hurt a nice guy like you. I would have to though, because there is no way that I could ever marry you."

I should have let it go at that point but I am a glutton for punishment. I asked her to explain herself and she took the time to do so.

"Look at it from my point of view. I am a divorcee, not a single woman. I have one failed marriage and I can't afford another. The next marriage has to last for the rest of my life and I have to be sure that the man I marry is one that I could live with for that long."

"What sort of man are you looking for?"

"Let me tell you something about my first marriage. If I hadn't caught Steven with another woman, I would never have left him. When I met him, he was in graduate school and didn't have a penny to his name. He was, however, concerned with many issues of the day and he felt that he could best advance his causes by working for Congressman Harrison's election. He involved me in the work and we became attracted to one another. I wouldn't have bothered getting married to him except that my father wouldn't let us live together otherwise.

"Steven was an English major and would have hung in there for many years without ever getting a degree. He was, however, highly literate, extremely witty and very articulate. It was exciting to talk to him about anything and everything. Since he didn't have any money, I had to support him. I paid for all the trips we took together to Europe and other countries. I didn't mind in the least because it was such fun. I enjoyed being with a man who didn't have a care in the world and wasn't at all concerned about his future."

Somehow, I didn't feel it was right for a girl like this to spend so much money on a worthless man who was exploiting her. I know how hard her father worked in building his department store and here she is frittering away all the money living a carefree and irresponsible life. "You think it was right for you to spend your father's hard earned money on a freeloader like that?"

She was quite upset with my comment. "I grant you that I was living it up on my father's money, but I was by no means an empty-headed heiress who never worked in her life. I earned my degree and, by the sweat of my brow, I make $50,000 a year. In addition to teaching, I have published articles in six different journals and I am secretary of the State Historical Society. My father left me a trust fund of a million dollars and I want you to know that the principal is still intact. By any standard that you may wish to use, I am a responsible, productive citizen."

"Don't tell me you supported a husband and lived like a jetsetter for $120,000 before taxes." I derived that figure by adding her salary to the interest on her trust fund at seven per cent.

"I neglected to say that our store nets about three million dollars a year, so that my share of the profits is $500,000."

"That's a little more like it. Do you ever think about settling down and raising a family?"

"I don't know if I will ever want to settle down but I probably wouldn't object to having a kid or two. If I may be so bold, I will tell you what sort of wife you need."

"Let's hear."

"What you need is a nice Jewish girl who, if she finished college, did so by the skin of her teeth. Her primary interest in life is finding a husband who will take care of her needs. She would look up to you and hang on to your every word as if you were some sort of demigod. She will attend the day school dinners with you, be an officer of the Sisterhood and sell used clothing at the synagogue bazaar. She won't crack a book but she will be up to date on all of the soap operas and latest fashions."

"You are painting the image in black and white. I do expect a wife to be interested in my work and religious activities. I look forward to having children and letting my wife run a nice Jewish household. Nevertheless, I still want a woman with some intellectual ability."

"You've hit the nail right on the head with your priorities. A man like you will work all day in the business and, on successive nights, you will attend UJA meetings, Chamber of Commerce dinners and day school affairs. It is only a matter of time before you are elected president of your synagogue, and spend your spare time fighting with the rabbi and the cantor. If you do get a Sunday off, you will be watching the Buffalo Bills. On Saturday, you will be in shul most of the day. That is certainly not a type of life to which I could adjust."

"Those are social and religious responsibilities that I have accepted. They are good for my soul and good for my business. I will never be a playboy, but I am sure that I could modify my lifestyle somewhat."

"With your family structure and heavy responsibilities, I don't think it's possible. What would your mother say if I left you with the kids for two weeks and went off to the Riviera? How would I be able to continue social activities that don't meet the standards of the family or the level of your religious observance? I would be miserable and it would be a constant cause of conflict."

"It may be that our lifestyles do not match at the moment but I think that with your family background and religious knowledge, you will, in the not too distant future, come closer to the role of the traditional Jewish woman."

"You think I will 'work at the spindle and look well to the ways of my household while my husband is known in the gates?'"

"Your mother and grandmother and my mother and grandmother did exactly that and were considered women of valor."

"Maybe if I were married to King Solomon" – who wrote 'Woman of Valor' in the Book of Proverbs – "I would be willing to live like that. Certainly not for Melvin Seidman."

I saw that the discussion wasn't getting me too far. Sandy was too young and privileged to think that she could ever be an ordinary housewife. I was too straightlaced about the role of women and I guess my preconceived notions were based on the women I knew. I wanted to salvage what I could so I got off the subject of marriage.

"Would it be all right to call you once in a while in the States?"

"Sure, as long as you limit it to that. No visits and no dates. I feel that it is my responsibility to warn you that I have no intention of entering into any serious relationship with you. You are not a young kid anymore so, if you ignore my warning and get hurt, you will have no one to blame but yourself."

We left the promenade and walked back to the hotel. I really felt bad about the conversation and the loss of any chance to make progress with this young woman. It's not that I didn't have any women to date. True, there were no single observant women remaining in Buffalo because they'd all left for New York and Israel, which offer greater social opportunities. Nevertheless, my mother and sister were always receiving calls from parents of eligible women suggesting that I go out with their daughters. Invariably, these girls were losers and leftovers. I don't care if a woman is poor but I am looking for someone with a little extra above the shoulders and none of them have it. A woman like Sandy comes along once in a lifetime and, even with all my money, she wasn't in the least bit interested in me.

SANDRA

23

THE MINIBUS TOOK US BACK to the King David, where the Seidmans checked out and went to Tel Aviv. My mother was very sad about parting with Mrs. Seidman, but I told her she could continue their friendship in the States. I said my goodbyes and headed back to the yeshiva with Melvin's check for $1000 in my pocketbook. There I met with Rabbi Brill and he was very glad to see me.

"Did you see all the papers on Tuesday, and the religious weeklies that came out today?" he asked me.

"I didn't get a chance. Did we get good coverage?"

"The very best. The left-wing papers said that not only were we behind the times in our religious ways but that we also reject modern technology and choose to build with donkeys rather than with cranes. The right-wing papers thought that we were very resourceful and didn't lose our equanimity in the face of a technological failure. There were some very nice editorials and articles after the original news story. The commentators had a ball with the events."

"Did we get any coverage on TV or in the Jerusalem Press?"

"We were the lead story on TV Monday night and we made

the Press as well. Speaking of the Press, their reporter wants to do a feature on you. I have the number to call on my desk."

"How about Rabbi Steiner?"

"I think he feels that we have sold our souls to the devil. I don't know where he heard the story of Faust, but that's with whom he identifies us."

"I take it that I am the devil?"

"I don't know whether he really feels that way or is just expressing his annoyance at becoming dependent on an American, and a female, at that."

"Would it help if I talked to him?"

"It very well may. Aside from the donkey, your behavior was modest and exemplary. He didn't get too much pleasure from Carol's appeal either, but he can't blame you for that."

"Before I talk to him, I have something personal to resolve. I have an amount in my pocket from Melvin Seidman that may only be spent on your wife. Both he and I feel that she bears the brunt of your work in the yeshiva and should not be required to make such sacrifices."

"Are you talking of household help?"

"No. I'm talking of the fact that she is dressed in rags and doesn't have the clothing that the wife of a mashgiach in a yeshiva should be wearing."

"My wife will not accept charity."

"This is not charity. It is a gift and I want you to prevail on her to let me take her shopping for a day and outfit her properly."

"Call it what you may. We cannot accept personal gifts from supporters of the yeshiva."

"Rabbi Brill, you are talking to a woman who knows the score. Your wife has been accepting hand-me-downs not only for the children, but for herself. She may be ashamed to tell you that, but from the way some of her clothing fits, it clearly was originally bought for others. If she can accept used clothing from people, she can accept new clothing as well. What difference does it make that we happen to be supporters of the yeshiva?"

"You remember the story of Elisha and Gehazi?"

That was a Biblical story where Naaman, the general of Assyria, came to Elisha to be cured from his leprosy. The prophet cured him and would accept no fee for his services. The prophet's servant, however, felt that a fee should be paid for the prophet's work. He ran after Naaman and solicited some money from him for some needy students. It made the impression on Naaman that Divine help could be bought for money and it put the prophet in a bad light. He cursed Gehazi for his act.

"Close," I said, "but no cigar. There was no service involved for which we might have been asked to pay, and this is money that Melvin feels would not be appropriate to donate to the yeshiva itself. Please ask your wife if I could take her shopping Monday afternoon."

"My wife never makes religious decisions by herself."

"Fine. If she asks you, tell her that I ruled that it was in order."

"I'm sure she will be delighted to hear that in addition to your other talents, you are now a rabbi too. In point of fact she will not even ask me such questions. If she doesn't know which shoe she should put on first, she will call Rabbi Shayalevitch for a ruling."

"Why don't you teach her the Abridged Code of Law? That particular weighty question is resolved in the early chapters."

"She firmly believes that women should not study rabbinic law."

"In that case, let her ask Rabbi Shayalevitch about my gift and let me know the answer on Sunday."

"I will do that. By the way, in light of your success, may I book for you for next June when the new dormitory will be dedicated?"

"You know very well that if you do a good deed three times in a row you become obligated to keep doing it thereafter."

"And what is wrong with that?"

"What is wrong is that if I keep running the affairs you will never learn how to run them yourself. You have to able to stand on your own feet."

"I find it much easier to stand on yours."

"I know. I know. But I gave up my European trip to be here this year because you said the Seidman donation was too big for you to handle by yourself. Next year, the building will be up and the fund-raising won't be so critical. Just plan a nice dinner and be finished with it."

"It won't be the same without you. I really want you to come."

"All right, please God, and, without a vow, I will make some effort to attend, but not to work."

"I am sure that if you are here you will advise and assist and I thank you for your commitment. Did you know that you are beginning to speak like a Beis Yaakov girl?"

"There is no harm in speaking as one if one doesn't start thinking like one."

Rabbi Brill wasn't too happy with my answer but he let it pass. He told me that he planned to say goodbye to the Seidmans at Ben Gurion before they returned home. He wished me a good Sabbath and suggested that I see Rabbi Steiner before I left.

I wasn't nervous when I went in to see the rabbi, because the affair was over and I didn't have to worry about impediments he could place in my way.

"I wanted to thank you," he said, "for the successful ceremony you ran for us on Monday. I have reservations about your methods but, in the short run, they seem quite fruitful."

"I tried to be a little more decorous this time around."

"It is not in the nature of the beast. The Jewish people have had great yeshivot in the past that didn't trumpet their wares in the street."

"I do believe that as a result of my efforts, the Dean and Rabbi Brill will be able to devote more attention to Torah studies at the yeshiva and less to fund-raising. In that sense, the publicity that helped raise the funds will enhance the scholarship and reputation of the yeshiva."

"I hope that your theory turns out to be correct. Remember that the new dormitory will double the size of the yeshiva and create administrative problems that we didn't have before."

"I think that in the long run you will also be better off. Let me talk economics for a minute because I come from a business family. We have seen failures of giant department stores with many branches, and failures of very small merchants. The small people who go under are understaffed and undercapitalized. The big ones that fail have become too big to manage. It is the medium size stores that do well. The same is true for yeshivot. The giant ones can't give their students the personal attention they need. The little ones do not attract enough financial support to survive. There is such a thing as an optimum size for a yeshiva and when you open your new dormitory you will reach it."

"You are correct in the general case but the theory may not hold in some particular cases. We have certain problems at Beit Meir which I cannot confide in you, which may cause your theory to fail."

"I am very much aware of the problem, Rabbi Steiner, and I can see the wisdom of not discussing it now. The rabbis taught us, 'It is sufficient to deal with troubles when they occur.' There is no need to indulge in them prematurely."

"That is correct and I wish you well in the future. We shall always be grateful for your help."

After a quiet Sabbath in Jerusalem, I returned to the yeshiva on Sunday and began to clean things up from the affair. Firstly, I paid the bills to the caterer, the florist, the newspapers and the rental company. I called Yossi to come and settle up. I then sat with Rabbi Brill and went over the pledges at the dinner. I wrote the text for a thank you letter that acknowledged the pledge and included a passage that Rabbi Brill would be calling on all donors to give them the proper recognition for their gifts. I was eating a yeshiva meal at my desk when Rabbi Goldberg came in and invited me to dinner at his house. I accepted readily because such a meal was less of a problem for Lili than for Rivka. The Goldbergs lived much better than the Brills. The apartment was larger and furnished in a more American style. I wondered how she could afford to do it when her husband was earning a very meager salary. I then remembered that Lili had said she was selling home improvement items or something like that. The meaning of that became clear when I was sitting in their living room watching the video of the Monday night newscasts and some of the video footage taken by our own photographers.

Lili was on the phone and I overheard snatches of conversation in Hebrew; Lili was telling someone that a girl was young and that he had to be patient. It was then that the awful truth dawned on me. When she got off the phone, I called her over, asked her to sit down, look me in the eye and confess.

"You are a matchmaker, a shadchan," I said in an accusing voice.

Lili turned bright red. "It's a more acceptable occupation in this country. Believe me Sarah, I didn't invite you over because you are rich and single and would make some man very happy."

"If I so much as hear one word from you about the glories of married life, I will walk right out. It's bad enough to have my mother on my back all the time."

"I won't say a word," Lili promised meekly. "Anyway, there is no one in this country that I know of who would be of interest to you."

Once that was settled, I enjoyed a pleasant evening at the Goldbergs and thanked the couple for their help during the dedication.

"What did you like best about the way I conducted the evening?" Rabbi Goldberg asked.

"The thing I liked best," I told him, "was that you did it for free."

"It's a novel experience for both of us," Lili admitted, "but money isn't everything."

On that note, I left them and headed back to the hotel.

On Monday, my mother came with me to the yeshiva because we had checked out of the hotel and would be spending the night in Tel Aviv. All I had to do at the school was write a few thank you letters to the guest speakers. I dropped a check of $5000 into the letter for the Prime Minister and $3000 for the Housing Ministry. That left me with only $2000 of Melvin's money for the Ministry of Religious Affairs and I knew that wasn't enough. My mother came to the rescue.

"Are you sending money to Ben Zur?" she asked, "the nice man who likes to kiss my hand?"

"The very same."

"He's French, isn't he?"

"I don't know, but he did work in the Israeli Embassy in Paris."

"Maybe he's originally from Hungary. He's a nice man. How much did I give him last time?"

"You added $2000 to my $1000."

"Just give him $500 of your own this time and I'll make out a check for $2500.

"I'm already sending him $2000 from the Seidmans."

"How much did they send to that creepy Housing Minister?"

"$3000."

"If that man gets $3000, then the nice Minister of Religious Affairs should get at least 4000." That was what he finally got.

When I finished, we said our goodbyes to the rabbis and took a cab to the Jerusalem Press for my interview with the editor of the women's section of the magazine.

After a few preliminaries, the reporter got down to essentials.

"What's a liberal American college professor doing in a charedi environment? I'm sure you know their attitude towards women."

I wasn't going to let her talk me into causing problems for Rabbi Brill. "I find them very protective of women. They give us special seating sections at dinners to protect us from evil-minded men and they make us wear extra long clothing to keep us warm."

"You don't find them living behind the times?"

"Not at all. They learn Torah, and Torah has all the latest information about everything."

She gave me a scornful look and didn't even understand that I was teasing her. "I heard that you have a more enlightened approach. I even heard that some people in the yeshiva world were upset with Rabbi Steiner for letting you run the dedication."

"Listen," I said. "Enlightenment means tolerance. I don't

have to share charedi views to work with them any more than an anthropologist has to believe in the views of the tribes he lives with. This is supposed to be a human interest story anyway, not a political attack."

She was more circumspect after that but I figured that she would not play up the story. It must have been the photographers who changed her mind. They snapped loads of pictures of me and apparently found me a good subject. I have never modeled professionally but I did some modeling of women's wear in my father's store and I knew how to pose. That must be the reason why I found myself on the cover of the Press Magazine when I stopped at a Tel Aviv newsstand on Friday, a few days later. My mother bought ten copies of the magazine to take home with her.

The last item of business in Jerusalem, before heading to Tel Aviv, concerned Rivka Brill. Rabbi Shayalevitch had ruled in my favor on the grounds of *Shalom Bayis*, domestic tranquility. Achieving domestic accord is one the highest priorities in Jewish Law. If a new wardrobe would enhance the status of a wife in the eyes of her husband, it would be permissible for her to overlook some of the teachings that encouraged people to shun gifts. Once the rabbi made his ruling, Rivka offered only token resistance. She had one of the older girls watch the kids and went down with me to the Mashbir Department Store. Department stores I know well, but I don't think that Rivka had ever bought any clothing in such a store. I had a talk with the sales clerk and worked out a plan that would not let Rivka discuss the prices. If an item fit, I would signal the clerk to put it aside for us. I was in the dressing room with Rivka and I realized that what was underneath the ragged dresses was just as bad as what was on the surface. After finishing with the dresses, I spent an hour in what is called the white-wear department in Israel but lingerie at Feldman's. Rivka was bewildered with my methods and couldn't believe that a person could spend more on clothing in three hours than she had spent in the twenty years of her marriage.

The trip home was uneventful and, on July 6, I started teaching my second summer semester class in Western Civilization. The class met each morning for six weeks. One afternoon after teaching, I dropped into the Cortland store of Buffalo Auto. The manager had called me the previous afternoon and told me that there was a package from Carol Seidman waiting for me. When I opened the package, I found a set of deluxe American brake pads wrapped in a red ribbon.

Early in August, Rabbi Brill came for his annual solicitation and had dinner with us. "I really shouldn't ask you for your yearly contribution after your outstanding services this year so, if you feel you did enough, you don't have to do any more."

"That was Sandy who did all the extra work," my mother said. "I just came along for the ride."

"Didn't you pledge to furnish a dormitory room?" he said, trying to catch himself too late.

"No one was supposed to know."

"I'm sorry, it slipped out."

"I didn't see your pledge, mother," I said.

"I asked Rabbi Brill not to show it to you because you would be mad at me. It's only the furnishings and not a room and Carol Seidman said it was a bargain. Anyway, Rabbi, what I gave was my own thing. You are here for the pledge my husband used to give you every year and I will continue that."

"Thank you, Shoshana. That's very nice of you."

"How is Rivka?" I asked.

"Rivka came to America with me this year. She is in New York visiting family and friends. She has some cousins in this country."

I didn't ask him how he could afford to take her. I simply assumed that he had saved enough from his higher salary to buy her a ticket. "That is very thoughtful of you. Is this her first trip?"

"Her very first. She will be going back before me because her school is starting soon, but I'm sure she will have a good time while she is here." I didn't know what school he was referring to. I simply figured that Rivka had undertaken to teach somewhere.

One Monday afternoon, a week later, I got an urgent call from my older brother at the store.

"Sandy, there is a lady here from Israel. She speaks English very poorly but she says she is Rivka Brill and wants to talk to you. She seems a little confused and frightened."

"Put her on the phone," I said, fearing that something terrible may have happened.

"Hello, Sarah," the woman said. I easily recognized the voice.

"Rivka, what happened? What are you doing in Syracuse?"

"I came to see you and I have for you an important message."

"Is everyone all right?" I asked her. "Did anything happen to Rabbi Brill?"

"He's fine, blessed be God, but that I come to see you he doesn't know." She didn't sound at all confused to me, just some inability to cope with English grammar. I asked her to put Michael back on the phone.

"Michael, send her in a cab to Mom's house. Tell her I'll be waiting for her when she arrives."

I ran down to the car and drove over to my mother's house. My mother was surprised to see me so early, as I usually arrive just at dinnertime.

"What brings you here this early?" my mother wanted to know.

"I got a call from the store that Mrs. Brill is on her way and wants to see me."

"The rabbi's wife?"

"That's who. I just spoke to her on the phone."

"Is anything wrong?"

"I hope not. But if it is a private matter, let me speak to her alone after dinner."

The cab pulled up and sure enough it was Rivka Brill. She was on the verge of exhaustion but otherwise looked great. She was wearing one of the better outfits that I had bought her, and she had lost another 10 to 15 pounds. My mother took one look at her and ran to get some orange juice. It was a hot summer day and my mother realized that Rivka was dehydrated.

We let her rest for a few minutes and, when she revived, I asked her how she had come from New York.

"I took the bus. I thought you live only an hour or two from the city but it was more like six hours."

"Did you get off at the rest stops?"

"I did, but I didn't buy anything because it wasn't kosher."

"How did you get to the store?"

"I got off the bus and asked people how to get to Feldman's. Almost an hour it took me to get there. When I came there I told your brother to call you."

"That took a lot of courage on your first trip to America. What would you have done if you couldn't find the store?"

"I would have gone to the police and asked them to find you."

I took her up to the guest room upstairs and asked her if she wanted to lie down for a while.

"No," she said. I'll be all right. Why did you take me to your mother's house?"

"Rabbi Brill won't eat in my own house so I figured you wouldn't eat there either. You have to eat something or you won't be able to deliver your message. If it's private, I can drive you to my place after dinner."

"I don't want to trouble you. I can talk to you here."

"First you have to eat. By the way, you look like a million dollars. You must have lost at least 10 more pounds. You look like a young woman."

"That's all part of the story."

Mom served dinner and Rivka brought us up to date on things in Israel that Rabbi Brill had not mentioned. After dinner, I took Rivka into the den where she sat down on the recliner.

"I can't believe how beautiful this home is," Rivka said. "The homes in New York don't compare at all."

"This is a fairly modest place," I said. "My father could have lived in a bigger house but this one is near the shul and he didn't want to ride on Shabbat."

We spoke for a few more minutes until I asked her to tell me what her message was.

"It's a long story but I feel that you will benefit from it. It started around Purim time when my husband came home from America. He had been away for a couple of weeks and we weren't together for a week before he left, so we had what to do before he told me about the results of his trip."

What she was saying in English was that she was menstrual the week before Rabbi Brill had to go to America. Religious couples don't have sex during that time. When he returned two weeks later there was some catching up to do in the bedroom before she got a chance to ask the rabbi what he had accomplished in the States.

Rather than record her story in her broken English and then translate it, I'm going to paraphrase it so that the reader will be able to follow. When Rivka can't find the right words in English she switches into Hebrew. In addition to those words, I have eliminated all the religious expressions such as "Thank God,"

Without including the words "With the help of God" or "If God be willing" that she utters in every sentence, this is in essence what she said:

"When the first wave of passion subsided, I got a chance to speak to Baruch. It often happens that when I come home from the mikva, I can discuss very personal feelings with him. I asked him what had happened in America and he told me that he had secured the Seidman pledge for the new dormitory and your promise to conduct the ceremony. I was very happy with the Seidman donation but I was troubled by your coming. I didn't quite understand why he needed you and I guess I was a little jealous. Of course I trust my husband. He is a God-fearing man and would never do anything sinful. But people had started calling you his girlfriend and Lili had said something about the way he looks at you, so I decided to talk to him about it.

"'Baruch,' I said, 'Tell me the truth. Do you think that Sarah is prettier than me?' And do you know what he said?"

"Of course, I do," I answered. Only an idiot would answer a question like that in a straight way, and Rabbi Brill is no idiot. "I'll bet he told you 'Beauty is vain and grace is deceitful; a woman who fears God is to be praised.'"

"How did you know that? He didn't tell you about this, did he?"

"Positively not. That is the only answer a sane man could have given you to such a question. What did you ask him next?"

"I asked him if he felt that you were smarter than me?"

"And I'm sure he answered, 'The essence of wisdom is the fear of God.'"

"Exactly. So I said, 'Baruch, no more quotations. Just answer yes or no. Do you love Sarah Feldman more than me?' Do you know what he said?"

"I know the quotation he used. 'I have made a covenant with God, why should I look a upon a young woman?'"

"You are uncanny, Sarah, a mind reader. That is the very verse he quoted, but I insisted on a straight answer."

"I'm sure he wouldn't say that he loved me more and I don't for a minute think that he ever felt that way."

"He said, 'You I love like a husband loves a wife. Sarah I love like a father loves a daughter. You can't compare the two.'"

"That's beautiful. He is a very wise man. So what happened afterwards?"

"I cried a little but mostly to myself. In the morning I ran to Rabbi Shayalevitch for advice."

"You always run to him for everything?"

"Certainly. One should always seek the advice of the wise."

"Why don't you try to think for yourself occasionally?"

"Because many times I might come up with the wrong answer. I've heard of rich people who ask their psychologist everything and famous people who don't lift a finger without asking their astrologer and the advice they get isn't even always right."

"The advice you get is always right?"

"Definitely. It is based on Torah as understood by a great scholar. The Torah is God's word and is absolutely true."

"Your husband is a Torah scholar. Why do you have to run to Rabbi Shayalevitch."

"My husband can advise others and he does so all the time. He can't advise me because he is not impartial. He might be more lenient with me because he loves me or more strict because he wants to show that he is not influenced by personal considerations."

"That seems right. What did Rabbi Shayalevitch have to say?"

Rivka started with the part about Rabbi Brill disobeying Rabbi Steiner on the Seidman solicitation. I've already written about that so it doesn't bear repeating. Here I will just record the personal advice.

"Rabbi Shayalevitch said, 'Rivka, I gave you prayers to say about your husband's parnasa because, in the end, God determines man's livelihood and it is well established that we may pray for our economic well-being. For your other problems, I have no prayers to suggest because they are your responsibility and not the Almighty's.' I was a little upset so I asked him what he meant."

"'How many kilos are you overweight?' he asked. I turned red and said about eight. 'Rivka,' he said angrily, 'I'm not your husband. Tell me the truth.' I admitted to fifteen kilos but he did not seem convinced. 'I want you to take off 18 kilos and not a gram less.' He was being harsh with me but in my heart I knew he was right."

"What else?" I asked.

"'I want you to stop going around in rags and without makeup.' I tried to argue that we didn't have enough money for such things but he wouldn't listen. 'When your husband married you, he promised in the wedding contract that he would clothe you as you were accustomed before marriage. That is his problem and you have to tell him of his responsibilities.'"

I couldn't help thinking that Steven should have read our *ketubah*. He didn't even feed me as required, let alone clothe me.

"'As far as makeup is concerned there are no excuses. The

rabbis have made many leniencies in allowing women to don makeup at questionable times so that they should not become distasteful to their husbands. Here you are not doing enough.'"

I was beginning to like this Rabbi Shayalevitch more and more. "What did he say about your mental abilities?"

"He was even harsher there. He asked me what have I learned in the last 15 years. I told him that I attend the weekly lectures in ethical behavior quite regularly. He got real angry. 'You have been hearing the same thing over and over for the last 15 years and you never even had a problem with your behavior in the first place. Your competitor, Sarah, never even went to Beis Yaakov and never attended an ethics class, yet her knowledge easily puts yours to shame. I'm not talking about her secular and worldly acumen. I am talking about the Torah, the Prophets, the Writings and even the Talmud and Shulchan Aruch. You have been reading Tehilim for 30 years and I am sure she even knows the Psalms better than you do.'

"I argued that women were not allowed to learn Talmud and he said, 'Men may not be allowed to teach them some parts of the Oral Law according to some theories, but there is no restriction on your learning by yourself as Sarah did. Nor is there any reason for you not to learn worldly wisdom and languages. Knowledge does not come by wishing for it. It comes by work. Rivka, this September, you are to enroll in college and learn English and other basic subjects. There are now college courses available in Jerusalem in institutions run by God-fearing men and women. If you gain this knowledge you will be able to help your husband and, more important, gain his respect.'"

"Did you obey Rabbi Shayalevitch?"

"You can see that I lost weight. I started doing exercises and I wear makeup every day. This September, I will be taking nine credits in English, History and Math."

"I'm really proud of you Rivka. How does Rabbi Brill feel about it?"

"He's not very verbal about such things but last week he brought me flowers for the first time in ten years and he pays more attention to me."

"Wonderful. But I'm sure that you didn't risk your life on a Greyhound bus to tell me about yourself. Did you talk to Rabbi Shayalevitch about me?"

"Yes I did. I told him I couldn't understand how you could turn away such a fine man as Melvin Seidman, who really loves you."

"How do you know that Melvin loves me? I don't even know that myself."

"When my husband said goodbye to Melvin at the airport, he asked him if there was anything he could do for him. 'Nothing, Rabbi,' Melvin said, 'except perhaps you can put in a good word with the Man upstairs to help me with Sarah Feldman.'"

I guess all's fair in love and war, even invoking the deities. "What did Rabbi Shayalevitch say?"

"He said that he couldn't understand it either, since Melvin was not only a nice man with charitable deeds but also a Torah scholar."

"How did he know that?"

"He heard Melvin speak at the dinner."

"He didn't know that I wrote the speech for Melvin?"

"You what?" Rivka's face registered shock and disbelief.

"I wrote his speech. Melvin delivers speeches well but all his speeches are written by public relations people."

"He did learn in a yeshiva, didn't he? And he told my husband that he attends a weekly Talmud class."

"That is correct. He does have a good knowledge of Torah.

Even though he can't be labelled a Torah scholar, he can be called a *ben Tora'* for sure."

"In that case Rabbi Shayalevitch's message for you is still in order and I hope you will listen to it. He gave me four arguments to support your going with Melvin."

"I'm listening, although I can hardly think of one."

He said that you are under the mistaken impression that getting married to someone less cultured or intellectual than you might stifle you, or that marriage itself might limit your thinking. He said that it was not the case and that even people in prisons can continue to use their minds."

"He has been reading Lovelace?"

"Is that the British poet who wrote about stone walls?"

"The very same."

"Rabbi Shayalevitch quoted him at length. The rabbi grew up in England."

"I see. What other arguments did he advance?"

"He said that you are under the impression that you have the right to squander your inheritance and live a very free life."

"He didn't argue with that, did he?"

"He made a very important distinction. He said that you could squander your material inheritance. Your father gave it to you without conditions and it's yours to do with it as you please. What he was talking about was your religious inheritance. He said that that heritage was accumulated over hundreds of centuries with blood, sweat and tears. You are not free to waste it. You have more Jewish knowledge than most women today and it is your duty to transmit it. You can only do it with children who grow up in a religious home with observant parents. If you don't get married, or marry someone not Jewish or not religious, your heritage will die with you."

"I could always lecture at the Sisterhood."

"They won't listen to you if you don't practice what you teach."

"That's two good arguments already. Let's hear the rest."

"He says that you should honor your mother and the memory of your father. You gave them enough grief with your first marriage. Now it's time to give your mother a little *nachas* (joy)."

"That's not new. My mother tells me that every day. What's the final argument?"

"He said that it's very important that Melvin loves you. People like me don't have to worry about such things because my husband is so God-fearing that he will not sin with other women. In your case, the only protection you have is the love of your husband, and you should consider it very important that Melvin loves you."

"Did he say anything else?"

"I don't know if he meant for me to tell it to you. He explained what it means when we say that beauty is vain. It is vain because it is not eternal. It fades away in time. What I think he was trying to say is that now when you are at the peak of perfection, you are free to be haughty and reject fine men. There may come a time when you will be fortunate to find a man such as Melvin."

"I probably could always buy a young man but I am aware of what he is saying and you are a good messenger. Now that you have unburdened yourself, would you like a drink?"

"A glass of tea."

"OK. I just thought of an excellent idea. I want you to stay overnight and tomorrow I will let you sit in on my history class. It will give you a feel for what you will face when you enter college."

"How far is Cortland?"

"About 60 kilometers."

"I would like that. What else do you do besides teaching? Are you going out with anyone?"

"Not at the moment. I am busy with the New York Historical Society, of which I am the secretary. We are planning our annual convention for the Thanksgiving weekend in Buffalo. There is a lot of work in connection with the convention and I will also be delivering a research paper."

The next morning I drove over to my mother's house and picked up Rivka. On the way, she asked me on what subject I was delivering the paper. I told her that all papers are limited to topics related to the history of New York State. I had chosen to study the cultural development of cities with a population of less than 20,000 in New York State.

"You do original research?"

"Of course."

I tried to explain what a hypothesis was and how you gather data to support or disprove a theory. She was getting some idea of what I was saying but didn't have a clear grasp of the overall concept. I have a lot of housewives and working teachers in my summer session class, many as old as Rivka, so she didn't feel out of place when she sat in. We were already into the middle of the 19th century in Western Civ, so it was fairly easy for her to follow. She told me that she caught the ideas but failed to understand certain phrases and expressions.

"How long will you be staying in New York?" I asked.

"I fly back next Sunday night."

"You are not afraid of traveling alone?"

"I won't be going alone. Lili Goldberg is visiting America and I am going home with her. She comes every few years to see her parents."

"I used to like Lili until she told me what business she's in."

"Didn't you say in your lecture today that if there is a demand for certain skills and services, society will meet the demand?"

I was pleased that she could repeat what she had heard and apply it. "I did say that."

"Well, given certain religious restrictions, a demand arises for matchmaking skills. Lili is doing nothing more than meeting a social demand. What is wrong with that?"

"I'll tell you what is wrong. There is a social need for real estate brokers. An honest real estate man cannot be successful nor can an honest shadchan make a go of it. Society tends to tolerate some fudging on property sales because only money is involved. When people lie on matters of life and death, such as marriage, it's a different story."

She insisted that Lili was a totally honest shadchan. I chose to believe otherwise. Back in Syracuse, Rivka enjoyed a good lunch at my mother's home and left for New York City on the afternoon bus. Over the next month I mulled over the message that she had brought with her from Jerusalem. Even today, I am not what you might call a fully Orthodox person. Still, my observance is a far cry from what it once was. If you wish to trace the first steps on my path back to the practices of my ancestors, you will find that they were taken during the weeks following Rivka's great American adventure.

MELVIN

24

THE TRIP BACK FROM ISRAEL was not particularly eventful but the family was in a good mood. They had enjoyed themselves in Israel and had a lot of fun. I was the only one who was not particularly cheerful because my mind was full of Sandy Feldman and I could think of no way of winning her over.

Carol put it best when she said, "I never believed that a girl in this world would turn down your money, your looks and your education. That was before Sandra Feldman. Maybe if she weren't so rich, you would have had a chance."

Joe wasn't more helpful. "Maybe if she weren't so pretty you would have had a chance."

"You weren't supposed to notice, Joe," Carol said.

"You can't help noticing," he said.

"You're both wrong," I said. "It's her head that's the problem. She thinks I'm a cultural wasteland and that's after all the money that Dad spent on my education."

"When we get back to the States," Carol said, "I'll buy you a subscription to the Book of the Month Club. Maybe you'll have something to talk about with her."

I did call Sandy once in July, just to see how her trip home was, but she wasn't too friendly so I tried to put her out of my mind. I even went out on a date with a woman from New York who was highly recommended, but that was a total waste of time.

Early in August, I believe it was the second Thursday of the month, I was at a meeting with some parts salesmen when I received a message at the hotel telling me to call in as soon as possible. On the first break, I dialed Carol and asked what had happened.

"Remember how wonderful you said it was that we had a tour guide in Jerusalem that wasn't costing us anything?"

"Lili? I offered her a tip but she said Sandy would kill her if she took a penny. What happened? She sent you a bill?"

"Much worse than that. She's at the office and urgently wants to see you."

"I can't get away for another couple of hours. Why don't you give her some money and send her off."

"I tried. She said it had absolutely nothing to do with money, past services or charity. She did indicate that it may be connected to Sandy."

"Why didn't you say so? Tell her to come to the hotel lobby and wait for me."

After I finished my meeting, I went down to the lobby and there she was. "Hi, Lili, what brings you to Buffalo?"

"I visit my parents in Cleveland every few years. I was there now and I decided to drop by and see you in Buffalo on my way to New York".

"That was nice," I said. "I understand that you have a message for me."

"I do, but I can't talk in a lobby. Where can we go for some privacy?"

"Buffalo Auto has a suite of offices in the hotel where we

conduct our sales meetings. It's on the third floor and I'm just coming from there."

"That'll be fine," Lili said. "Let's go."

I went up to the suite with her and offered her a drink from a well-stocked bar. We exchanged a few pleasantries before she came to the point.

"Melvin, I want to talk to you about Sandy, but I am not acting in my professional capacity and my advice won't cost you a penny."

"I knew you were not a real tour guide but I didn't realize that you were a shrink."

"Although I do happen to possess a graduate degree in psychology, I am neither of the two. You know my husband is a teacher at the yeshiva and he makes even less money than Rabbi Brill. Oh yes, before I forget, I want to tell you that what you and Sandy did for Mrs. Brill was the biggest mitzvah in the world. Anyway, being an American, I can't live on my husband's wages. So I took up a profession that is honorable in Israel but not here. I must confess that I am a professional shadchan. Since I've been in Israel I have helped more than 300 couples find wedded bliss. That means that I am one of the bigger ones in Jerusalem."

"A man like me hardly needs a shadchan. I get mothers from all over the country wanting me to meet their daughters."

"I know that and I am not seeking to have you as a client. I want to help you because of what the Seidmans and the Feldmans did for my husband. Because of your donations, my husband was able to get an appointment at a higher yeshiva, something very hard for an American rabbi to do. He is like a new man now since he doesn't have to worry about teaching unruly fifth graders."

"How can you help me with Sandy Feldman?"

"I can help you in a very basic way but first I must let you in on some of the mechanisms of the matchmaking business. When you get a case where both partners to a proposed match are against it, even the world's greatest shadchan can be of no service. Where both partners are in favor, there is no real need for a shadchan, except perhaps to arbitrate the negotiations. It's where one party is willing and the other party has reservations that a good shadchan can use her skill. I am working now under the assumption that you are interested in Sandy and she has some reservations."

"I would say that is correct, excluding certain religious questions for the moment, because I think those problems can be overcome."

"There is a common mistake in the business that separates the good matchmakers from the bad ones. When the latter face your situation, they choose to go after the girl and badger her until she is worn out from fighting and surrenders. She gets married but feels sorry about it for the rest of her life. I work the other way. I try to get the man to change the conditions that cause the girl to have reservations. Nothing can be done if the objections are based on physical limitations but, with behavioral or attitudinal problems, a lot can be accomplished."

"Tell me about it."

"Let me ask you something, Melvin, and I want an absolutely honest answer. What have you done to win the hand of Sandy Feldman since you met her, except sit and mope and feel sorry for yourself?"

"Nothing. What would you expect me to do? Send her a semi-trailer full of flowers, a 20-carat diamond ring?"

"Melvin, Sandy is a very rich girl and very mature. You are not going to buy her with trinkets or overwhelm her with sentiments. The problem is that the two of you are not culturally compatible and you are the one that has to do something about it."

I had to admit to myself that Lili was more positive in her approach than any members of my family, but I was still skeptical.

"I didn't hear Sandy talking to you," Lili continued, "but I can reconstruct the situation from my experiences. Sandy is a fun-loving girl. She doesn't enjoy community or social responsibilities except maybe in her area of scholarship. She wants to have a good time with sparkling intellectuals who are literate, articulate and up to date in the arts. She wants a man who quotes poetry, supports avant garde movements and is concerned with environmental causes. She wants a husband who will take her skiing in the Alps and swimming on the Riviera.

"You are pretty close."

"Now here you come in, a man of thirty going on fifty. You are very, very settled. You work all day in the business and attend Chamber of Commerce meetings at night. You go to shul meetings, day school meetings, Federation meetings and, probably, United Way and Boy Scout Governors meetings. On Sundays, you watch the Buffalo Bills. You don't read, you don't write, you don't play an instrument and you don't go on nature walks. For intellectual exercise you read business magazines and the Readers Digest. I could go on and on but I think you see the contrast. Sandy would be bored if she married you."

"Lili, I know the problem. I thought you had the answers."

"I do. You have to make some radical changes in both your value system and your life style."

"That's very easy to say. I am not a young boy just out of school and I carry an awful lot of business and community responsibilities. I can't become a different person overnight."

"Don't get me wrong. I am not asking you to undertake a complete transformation. I am only going to suggest that you take a few actions to show flexibility and willingness to change, enough to convince Sandy that you are not a hopeless clod. You have to overcome a built-in prejudice that academic types have for business people. If you don't get her in the end, you can always revert to your old habits. And you will not have wasted your time because some of the things I will ask you to do may be beneficial per se."

"Do you mind being more specific?"

"Not at all. The usual things, of course, will not hurt. You should call Sandy occasionally. Send Mrs. Feldman flowers for Rosh Hashana and send Sandy a small box of candy, but be casual and don't go heavy on it. Now I have solid information that Sandy will be in Buffalo for the Thanksgiving weekend for a convention of the New York State Historical Society, of which she is the secretary. She is delivering a paper on Wednesday afternoon before the holiday on the cultural life of smaller cities in New York State. The convention will be at this hotel. I want you to be present when she delivers the paper and I want a big bouquet of flowers from you at the rostrum."

"Such affairs are not open to the public," I objected.

"No, they are not. You have to be a history teacher or a graduate student in history to be eligible. You are not a teacher but you will be a history graduate student."

"Are you crazy or something?"

"Not at all. You have plenty of time to enroll in the History Department at the State University and you might even be able to matriculate on the strength of your MBA. You choose a course that meets twice a week and start writing a term paper. You invite Sandy to dinner and tell her you want to discuss your paper with her. Let me repeat that. You don't want her help in writing the paper. You want her to read the paper and express her views. This is a paper you have to do by yourself no matter how poorly you write. Don't let your PR man go anywhere near it. Give her time to evaluate it and set up a second date to discuss it."

"How do I get free two nights a week? I don't get off work early enough for afternoon courses."

"Your big mistake, Melvin, was to volunteer to do all the community work for the family. Carol has a big mouth and she will be happy shooting it off at all those meetings. She is also a day school graduate and can represent you there. You have to lay down the law. You are going to school and that's it. If nobody will attend the meetings that's just too bad. They only want you there for your money anyway, and you can always send them a check."

"That's a pretty elaborate scheme to win a girl."

"Not at all. Tuition is cheap at the State University and you can always apply for a scholarship. Just drop off two digits from your anticipated annual income. Membership in the Association probably doesn't cost more than $25.00 and you can even get a student rate. The course in history will actually do you a lot of good and so will writing a paper. Now, if Sandy asks you why you are in school, don't say that you are doing it to impress her. Say that your business education was too narrowly focused and that you want to broaden your horizons. Above all, don't tell her anything about it until Thanksgiving. If she doesn't believe your story, tell her you went to meet some nice coeds from New York who are at the school."

"You are ready to give me a money-back guarantee on this deal?"

"To show you how confident I am, I stand ready to donate 100 dollars of my own money to your favorite charity if it doesn't work."

"Is there any more to the plan?"

"There are a few minor details. Your professor will probably be at the convention and he probably knows Sandy. Make sure that he has the impression that you are a serious student. In addition to the main plan, there are a few supplementary activities that might be helpful."

"Such as?"

"Take out memberships at the Buffalo Museum and the Buffalo Symphony, if your company doesn't already have them. Read a book or two and subscribe to some literary magazines. Watch how students and professors dress and leave your hand-tailored business suits at home when you go to the convention."

"Is this the type of instruction you give to all your clients?"

"I have to remind some of the men to brush their teeth and some of the woman not to chew gum. In most of my matches it's all or nothing on the first date. There is no second chance."

"Listen, I appreciate your help, Lili, and I'll think about what you've said."

"Melvin, this is my address and phone in Israel. Keep me posted."

"I will, if you promise not to say a word to Rabbis Steiner and Brill. Rabbi Steiner thinks that Sandy is practically a gentile and even Rabbi Brill doesn't think she is religious enough for me."

"I think they are selling the girl short. She wouldn't have learned that much about Judaism if she didn't care for it, nor would she have done that much for the yeshiva. By the way, my husband says her religious knowledge is staggering and he is in a position to judge."

I drove Lili to the airport and spent the night thinking about what she had said. At lunch the next day, I had a talk with Carol and Jack in the executive dining room where we eat together and review business problems. Carol, as usual, did most of the talking. She wanted to know what Lili had said and I didn't tell her much. I just put it in general terms that Lili advised me that if I wanted to have a chance with Sandra or any other intellectual woman, I would have to change my lifestyle.

"What makes her an expert on matrimony?" she asked.

"This may come as a surprise to you, but Lili is one of the most successful professional matchmakers in Jerusalem."

"You're pulling my leg."

"No way. That's how she supports her family on Rabbi Goldberg's salary, which is not sufficient to live on."

"Wait a minute," she said in alarm. "You didn't hire a shadchan to corral Sandy? She hears something like that and you will never see your girlfriend again."

"That I know. Lili just wanted to give me some professional advice out of the goodness of her heart because of what we and the Feldmans did for her husband."

Carol picked up an imaginary violin and began to run the bow across the strings. That was her symbol for a sob story that was unbelievable. "Mel," she said, "I don't know if her advice will pan out but, if it does, you will pay through the nose."

"It's a long shot but, if it succeeds, I'm ready to pay."

"What did she tell you do? Send her a ton of jewelry?"

"You know that Sandy can't be bought."

"Diamonds aren't a girl's best friend anymore?"

"Not if she owns her own mine. Lili said I should return to school and complete my education."

"You already have more education than anyone in the family. An MBA from Penn State doesn't carry enough weight?"

"It's a nice degree and I worked hard for it but, in the end, it's only a business degree. What do I know of philosophy and history and literature?"

"There's no money in those subjects."

"That's the point. Culture and business are separate worlds. I may be a big tycoon and still be a boor."

"How about buying a liberal arts degree? There are a couple of places in California that sell them real cheap."

"Carol, that's enough. Come the first of September, I'm enrolling at the State University."

"You are doing nothing of the sort. You are the family representative on the day school board, the board of the synagogue, the UJA and the Federation, et cetera."

"My term in office expires on August 31 after four years of dedicated service to God, the community, and Buffalo Auto."

"Your resignation won't be accepted by the Board of Directors of Buffalo Auto."

"You only have one vote and I have one. Jack has the deciding vote. What do you say, Jack, about my going back to school?"

Jack pondered the matter for a minute and said, "Mel, do you really want to learn something or is this a hare-brained scheme to impress that dizzy dame of yours?"

"I'm serious about learning and, if I enroll, I will do my work conscientiously. If it helps me with Sandy, that's a plus. If it doesn't, I'll take up with some of the women in the class. I will finish the semester, however."

"I don't see how we can object to that. Carol will have to fill in for you at the community meetings. She likes to talk and those meetings will give her a captive audience."

Carol offered an obscenity I can't repeat here. "If you let him go to school, Jack, you take at least one night a week. I'll take the other. I've got a family, don't forget."

"And your Scrabble group and bridge group and other socially essential causes," Jack said.

"You don't play poker with the boys, my tzadik?" she countered.

I tried to cool things so I told them we could miss some meetings and cut out personal appearances at some of the minor organizations that were only after our donations.

"I'm going to check your report card, Melvin, and, if it's not straight 'A's, you go back to work," Carol warned me.

I assigned my secretary to get my transcripts and the catalogues and I looked for courses that met twice a week and didn't conflict with holidays. The course I selected would have run on Yom Kippur but that is a legal holiday as far as the school system in New York is concerned. It was Sukkot that I was worried about. In the end I settled on a course entitled "The French Revolution and its Aftermath." The course description said it would cover events preceding the revolution and would end with the exile of Napoleon and the restoration of the Monarchy.

I scanned the required text and I found a reference to Napoleon's relations with both the Jewish Community and the Land of Israel. I decided that my term paper would be in that area and my professor, who was Jewish, agreed to it. I had to scrounge to find a sports jacket for class and I made an attempt to dress casually. There were some 20 students in the class, fifteen of them female. About ten of the women were older history teachers who were taking courses to improve their credentials and salary. Certain school systems require teachers to continue their studies, others motivate them by salary incentives. The other five women were young graduate students. Three of the men were teachers and one was a businessman. I know all this because, at the first session, the professor asked each of us to give our names and say what we were doing. I said that I was Melvin Seidman, a buying executive at Buffalo Auto. The instructor, who had heard of the Seidman family, raised an eyebrow but didn't say anything.

He was a capable teacher who knew his subject well and presented his material in an interesting way. He told us that there would be some sort of essay examination at the end of the course but that the major work would be an original paper related to the course material. He suggested that we could get ideas from the bibliography at the end of each chapter in the text, and he handed out a reading list that no one seemed to take too seriously.

The people at work had some fun at the beginning but, after a while, they paid less attention to it. Carol would call me the professor on occasion and John Sinclair offered to write my term paper or, at least, to translate it into English. I thanked him but I didn't accept his offer.

I called Sandy just before Labor Day but I didn't even hint at what I was doing. She sounded a lot warmer than on my previous call and let me run up a big phone charge. For Rosh Hashana, I sent her mother chocolates and her I sent the flowers. Lili had told me to do it the other way around but I wasn't taking any notes during our meeting. I didn't lose anything by my mistake because I got a thank you call from both of them right after the holiday. That was the first time that I received a call from the Feldmans and I felt hopeful. By Thanksgiving time, I had completed a draft of my paper entitled "The Impact of Napoleon on Early 19th Century Jewry." It covered Napoleon's invasion of Palestine, his decrees of emancipation of Jews, his restrictions upon them and his attempt to organize some sort of Sanhedrin. That last part was easy for me because I knew something about the Sanhedrin from my studies at the yeshiva. I used the Jewish Encyclopedia, which my father had owned, for supplementary material. Most of the books on the subject were in French and I envied Sandy, who was conversant in so many languages.

The paper took form but it wasn't very polished. I resisted all offers of help because Sandy would have caught any outside writing at once. Instead, I struggled to put my ideas down in coherent form. On Wednesday afternoon, before Thanksgiving, I left work early and went over to the hotel for the convention. I had my NYHS card with me but I didn't go into the session until it was just about to get underway. I had joined the Society at the last possible moment because Sandy, as secretary, might have spotted the name. I waited in our office suite so I wouldn't run into her in the corridors. As I walked in, the chairman was introducing the Society officers seated on the dais. Sandy got a big hand as the chairman thanked her for her special efforts in preparing the convention. She looked unbelievably beautiful sitting up there. I sat in back and I didn't think she'd spot me because I was dressed in collegiate style. There were two papers scheduled to be delivered during the session. A professor from Albany was first and Sandy was up next. As soon as the chairman rose to introduce Sandy, I signalled the florist's helper waiting at the door and he brought in the flowers to the podium. Sandy smiled, thinking it was a presentation from the organization, and proceeded to thank whoever was responsible for it. I was amazed at the amount of work that went into her presentation. Facts, figures, quotations and even some graphics on a projector flowed in logical form. She didn't once refer to her notes and kept the audience awake with stories and anecdotes. She was a teacher par excellence. When she finished, the chairman asked for questions.

"Tell us your name and school before you ask your question," he requested.

When I stood up, Sandy recognized me and I could see that she was somewhat startled at my presence, as if to ask what I was doing there. I slowly introduced myself as Melvin Seidman, graduate student in the History Department of SUNY at Buffalo. Sandy blanched at the words, debating whether to expose me as a fraud. For some reason she held back. "I found the presentation of the last speaker to be comprehensive and very interesting but I feel that the data supporting her theory reflects smaller communities in the central part of the state which find themselves in proximity to large urban centers. Does the speaker feel that the theory will hold for more isolated communities in the Southern Tier?"

Sandy was stunned but too experienced to be flustered. She admitted that she hadn't studied any Southern Tier cities in depth but surveys including the Southern Tier tended to support her hypothesis. "Isolation from large cities may strengthen the cultural institutions in such communities," she said, "but not to a degree that would endanger the general theory. The question does show keen understanding of the hypothesis and is appropriate." That was Sandy regaining her composure and returning the compliment.

After a few more questions, the chairman closed the session and announced that the next session would commence at 8:00 P.M., after dinner. Sandy was furious when she got a hold of me.

"You devious son of a gun," she snarled. "Show me your membership card or I'll call the police. You have a lot of nerve sneaking in here and heckling me."

"Why, Sandy, I wouldn't do anything underhanded." I pulled out my membership card and showed it to her. Her signature was on the card as clear as day. The Society sends out the cards to the schools in advance. At each school there is a faculty person in charge of recruiting, whose duty it is to accept new members. When someone signs up, the stub is sent back to Sandy for processing. "As you can easily see I'm a bona fide member and I thought you made a marvelous presentation. By the way, the flowers are yours to keep."

"You sent them?"

"That I did. To my favorite lecturer."

"The flowers are nice. But why are you going to school and why history?

"It's a free country, Sandy. I felt an inner compulsion to broaden my intellectual horizons and understand what precipitated the French revolution."

"What course are you taking?"

"The French Revolution and its Aftermath. It's being taught by Professor Rechtman. How have you been, Sandy? You're looking great."

"I know the man and he's quite a scholar. I'm still confused and I don't know what to make of all this yet."

"I'll tell you what. Let me take you to dinner, and I will explain everything."

"I can't, Melvin."

"Why not? The next session isn't till 8:00 P.M."

"It's not only that. I know what kosher restaurants are like in small Jewish communities. I can't eat in any of those places."

"You won't have to."

"I won't go home with you."

"You won't have to."

"I won't let you eat a non-kosher meal for me."

"You won't have to."

"I can't go far from the convention. Something may come up before the evening session."

"You won't have to leave the hotel."

"You brought sandwiches?"

"Give me a break, Sandy. I may not know Sanskrit but I know how to take a woman to dinner."

"You have something up your sleeve, Melvin. I'm not sure I can trust you."

"How soon can you be ready for dinner?"

"Fifteen minutes."

"I'll wait for you right here."

She was skeptical and still confused, but no longer angry at being taken by surprise.

"OK, but no funny stuff."

"I promise on my last issue of the Journal of the American Historical Society, which I read from cover to cover."

Fifteen minutes later she came down relaxed and all smiles.

"What did you come up with?"

"You have to walk me to the third floor of the hotel."

"You expect me to go into a hotel room with you?"

"No, Sandy, they don't have guest rooms on the third floor. Buffalo Auto maintains a permanent office suite on the third floor where we meet clients and have business conferences. We can serve up to 40 guests in our rooms and there are people there now."

"Amazing," she said as she followed me up to the office area. The sign on the door did say Buffalo Auto and had the company logo. Besides the main room, we had a sitting area, a dining room and a good-sized kitchen.

I took Sandy into the sitting room and invited her to be seated on one of the easy chairs. I sat down on the adjacent one.

"Before we get to my history studies, let me explain this set up. It dates from the time that we expanded our business. We realized that we would need a place to meet clients and have company meetings. At that time, we hadn't yet built our office building. Dad wouldn't let us go to non-kosher places and we had a big problem with it. We decided to rent this suite from the hotel on a permanent basis. We remodeled it, furnished it and put in a first-class kosher kitchen. We hired a widow on a full time basis who was once a kosher caterer. She takes care of all the food service at our meetings. We give her 24 hours notice and she is always ready. There are some advantages to having it here rather than at the company office. We have privacy and we aren't disturbed by problems at work. Many of our clients stay at the hotel, so they don't have to travel out to the headquarters."

"What do you do for hand washing?"

"I go into the kitchen and make a blessing on some matzah."

"It's so much easier to keep kosher when you have money."

The waiter came in and asked us what drinks we would like. We ordered and resumed our conversation.

"Tell me the truth, Melvin. You didn't go to all the trouble of registering in a course just to make me feel that you're not a cultural disaster."

"No Sandy. You inspired me to do it but I am not pandering or trying to win brownie points. Remember at Lake Kinneret, when you told me why we were intellectually incompatible? You'd said that I don't read and can't write and that I am completely ignorant of the humanities and liberal arts. Your criticism was valid and I took it seriously. I realized that if I ever wanted to date a woman with a real head on her shoulders, I couldn't do so in the condition I was in. So I sat down and worked out a rehabilitation plan.

"You canceled your subscription to Business Week?"

"No, I didn't go that far yet, but I did buy season tickets to the Buffalo Symphony. I called a meeting of the Directors of Buffalo Auto, that's Carol, Jack and me, and I told them they would have to start attending their share of civic and social meetings."

"Good for you. Then you decided to go to school?"

"Yes, and to dress appropriately for it."

"Did you meet any nice coeds at school?"

"Just the ones in my class and the ones who use the library. A few of them asked me if I were married."

"They were delighted to hear that you weren't?"

"They must have been because they asked me to go out with them."

"Did you?"

"I'm a very serious student, Sandy. I really can't waste too much time chasing skirts."

"That's not a real answer."

"That's not a nice question either."

"The question is withdrawn."

The waiter arrived with the drinks and we continued the conversation.

"How did you find out about my speaking at the convention? Did you speak to Rivka Brill since you returned from Israel?"

"No. The rabbi was in America but he didn't come to Buffalo. He called to wish me a good year and didn't even mention you. I found out by reading the convention program on the History Department bulletin board and from Professor Rechtman, who told all the students to attend. My class is well represented at the convention and the professor himself was at your lecture."

The caterer came in to tell us that dinner was being served. She was always a quality caterer but this time she had really outdone herself. The tablesetting was elegant, with first class linen and china. I had told her that this was to be a VIP plus dinner and she got the message. The food was the best she had prepared in a long time, and she had gotten her most experienced waiter who knew how to serve wine as well as food. It was at the dinner that I brought up the subject of the paper. I told Sandy that the reason I wanted to see her was to discuss with her the term paper I had to prepare for the course.

"You know that I can't write your paper for you."

"I'm not asking you to. The paper is already written and John Sinclair didn't even see it. Aren't your journal articles sent out for peer review before you publish, and don't you then incorporate suggestions and criticisms from the reviewers? Better yet, I can assume that you are an expert on the subject and I can interview you."

"I'll buy that. What did you write on?"

I told her the topic and she said, "That's a very interesting subject. Did you read an article by Kobler, 'The Vision was There?'"

"I sure did. I had to get my copy from Albany and it was worth the trouble."

"The best reference is 'Napoleon et les Juifs' by Anchel but I don't think the work was translated."

I spent the next half-hour presenting my thoughts on the topic I had chosen. I was able to do so because, two weeks earlier, the professor had called on me in class to outline my paper to the students. He let about half of the students do that. The teachers were real good at it and class discussion followed. Some other students were tongue-tied and their presentations were brief. Mine lasted the full half-hour and drew a lot of interesting questions.

"That shows a lot of good work, Melvin. Did you express the ideas well on paper?"

"I did the best I can. I am going to leave a copy with you and I would be honored if you were to read it."

"I would be glad to."

For the rest of the dinner, Sandy spoke of the French Revolution and it was a dazzling display of knowledge. I found it hard to believe that someone so young had read so much and could express herself so well. I hung on every word and even asked a few questions to show that I understood. We enjoyed the desserts and Sandy's eyes were glowing from the wine.

"Do you know why King Achashverosh was willing to attend a second party with Esther?" I asked her.

"I imagine because he had a good time at the first one."

"Precisely. I have had such a good time today that I'd like to invite you for a Thanksgiving turkey dinner tomorrow afternoon. There are no sessions then at the convention."

"Will you offer me up to half your kingdom like the king did?"

"I hope that some day it will come to that."

"It'll kill my figure."

"You're so dynamic, you will shed the weight in a week."

"What time?"

"Any time after the morning sessions that suits you."

"The executives of the Society meet until two. I'll come here at 2:15 P.M."

"Great. I have one more request."

"No such thing as a free dinner. I might have known."

"This won't cost you a thing. I would like to treat you to a winter vacation in Miami for a few days during the Christmas holiday."

"I can't give you an answer on that now, Melvin."

"Why not?"

"I have to grade your paper first. I wouldn't go to a resort with anyone who is unable to earn at least a 'B' on a term paper."

"My destiny is in your hands, Professor. I hope you are a lenient marker."

"A fair one. Now I have a question for you, Melvin. I can't believe that you are as skillful in courting a woman as you seem to be tonight. I have this dreadful premonition that some of the best advisors that money can buy are guiding your amorous pursuits."

I didn't expect her to sense it but I guess she's very perceptive. Luckily, I was prepared for such an eventuality. "I must confess, I have the best advisor in the business."

"There, I knew it. You are a fraud. Who's helping you?"

"You remember that Rabbi Brill went to the airport to see me off. He asked me if there was anything he could do for me. So I asked him to put in a good word with the Lord on this matter and I'm sure he did so because God sent an angel to guide me."

"Gabriel, no doubt, to help you trumpet your cause."

"No, Raphael."

"Why Raphael?"

"Because he's the angel of healing who mends broken hearts."

The exchange struck her so funny that she started laughing hysterically for a few minutes and couldn't stop. When she finally did, she got up and said she had to go back to the convention. She kissed me on the cheek on the way out and thanked me for the dinner.

SANDRA

25

MEETING MELVIN IN BUFFALO WAS the shock of my life and the question he asked exposed a real oversight in my paper. I can't be mad at the question because if I am to be intellectually honest, I have to allow for people questioning a hypothesis. I was angry, though, because I thought he was bullying his way into the session in macho style. I guess I didn't realize that Melvin is a quiet guy who wouldn't do things in a devious way. When he produced a membership card with my signature, he really had me, and I calmed down. I still gave him a hard time but I did enjoy the dinner and drank enough to make me mellow. The kiss was impulsive and, I hoped, harmless.

After the evening session was over, I returned to my room. I had to talk to someone, so I called my mother, who was anxious to hear how my paper was received. When I told her that Melvin took me to dinner, she was ecstatic. She likes the Seidmans in general and Melvin in particular. She was even happier that I had a kosher meal and that I was going to have another one the next day.

"That's great news Sandy. Send my regards to Mrs. Seidman."

I then started to read Melvin's paper. The concept was worth an "A" and the organization maybe a "B+". The writing was poor, however, both stylistically and grammatically. It's amazing that some people can hold an MBA degree and still not write a proper English sentence. Based on contents and style, I could honestly give Melvin his "B+" and earn a four-day vacation in Miami. It's not the Bahamas and certainly not Europe, but that's the best that Melvin can do while he is tied to the need for kosher food and a shul to worship at each morning and evening. I decided not only to comment on the paper but to correct it as well. I made marks on almost every page and it took me a couple of hours. By the time I finished, I knew that Melvin would get an "A" if he accepted my suggestions.

On Thursday, the caterer did even better than before. She roasted a small turkey with delicious stuffing and served it with a lot of side dishes. Melvin carved the turkey and did it fairly well. We continued talking history until I returned his paper with the grade on it.

He was so happy with the grade that he could have cried.

"Listen, Melvin, I am willing to go to Miami, but we have to make special arrangements. There are no classy kosher hotels for me and I won't stay at the Caribbean. Book me at the Fountainbleu and book yourself at the Caribbean. I'll arrange for you to enjoy the facilities at the Fountainbleu and you arrange for me to eat at the Caribbean. You will also be able to have a minyan at your hotel."

"That's fine with me. I'll call my travel agent to rent the hotel rooms and a car. He'll mail you your tickets. Do you want to see Disney World? There's kosher food in Orlando."

"Not a bad idea. What will you do for a minyan?"

"If there is no shul in Orlando, I'll miss it. Remember that I am involved in trying to fulfill the Torah command to be fruitful and multiply, which takes precedence over prayer and kaddish.

Besides, my father never instructed me to say kaddish for him but he did command me to get married when he talked to me before his death."

"You mean that your intentions with regards to me are entirely honorable?"

"Absolutely."

"Drat," I said, and got him all red and flustered.

The vacation in Miami was delightful. That's when I really got to know Melvin well. Some people show everything they have on the surface while with others you have to probe very deeply. Melvin talked to me about his life and ambitions and ideals. I loosened up a little and didn't bite as much. When I wasn't intimidating him, he was a lot of fun. He had loads of funny stories to tell and a good sense of humor emerged.

Once more, as on the trip to Israel, my mother didn't let me take along any bikinis or two-piece bathing suits. She assumed that Melvin was too religious and too conservative to accept such extremes. I don't know whether she was correct in her estimation, but I saw no need to endanger the budding relationship with extraneous stress. I listened to her and made do with old-style one-piece suits. Even then I covered myself up except for the times I actually went into the water. As it was, Melvin got to see more of me than he should have, but he was a gentleman and didn't comment. That's what I like about Melvin. He was too astute to endanger his long-range goals for short term gratification.

Disney World was a little harder for Melvin. He was still too staid to really relax like a kid but he tried his best. We stayed overnight in Orlando and he didn't even suggest sharing a room. A real tzadik, like the Biblical Joseph.

When we got back home, we stayed in touch and he called me me three times a week. During one call he told that he'd gotten an 'A' on his paper and he'd registered for a course on the Roman Empire for the spring semester.

I asked him if the professor made any comments and he told me what the professor said.

"'Mr. Seidman, this is one of the best papers I've read in years. If I didn't hear you report on the topic so well in class, I would have suspected that someone assisted you with it.'"

"What did you answer to that?" I asked.

"I told him that it was my own work but that at the convention I'd discussed my paper with you. He asked me how I knew you and I said that your store buys our surplus when I make errors in buying. Then he looked at me a little strangely and asked if I were related to the Seidmans who owned Buffalo Auto. 'Sure,' I said, 'I'm one of the three Seidman children who own the firm.'"

"That must have thrown him for a loss. What did he say?"

"He said, 'Why is a multi-millionaire businessman taking a modern history course?' So I said that knowledge is not just the province of middle class academics. The rich are also entitled to it. Then, to make him feel better, I said, 'Now that I have earned my grade, I am free to present you with a Courtesy Card from Buffalo Auto. I really enjoyed the course.'"

"What's a Courtesy Card?"

"That's a card that bears a code like MSGWAL500 which stands for Melvin Seidman Good Will Account Limit $500 or whatever amount I choose. The store will give the person $500 worth of merchandise and charge it to my good will account."

"I helped you with the paper," I complained, "why didn't I get a card?"

"Any gift over $100 would be construed as an attempt to buy your love."

"That's a lame excuse. How much did it cost you to drag me down to Miami?"

"Shared social experiences are a legitimate expense in courtship. But you might consider material gifts as bribes."

"That's true, Melvin, but, given my social and financial status, you probably could raise the line separating casual gifts from bribes by a considerable amount."

"The card will be waiting at the Cortland store tomorrow."

I did check the store after teaching one afternoon and the card was waiting for me. It had the MSGWA prefix followed by GHTWSISWI. I couldn't figure out the code until Melvin explained that it stood for "Give her the whole store if she wants it."

In mid-February, Melvin called and told me with great sadness that he'd heard from Rabbi Brill that Rabbi Steiner's wife had passed away. He was thinking of flying out to offer his condolences but by the time he could arrange the trip it would be after the Shiva. Since he was planning to be there in June anyway, he decided not to go.

"Give him a call, Melvin, and I'll send him a letter."

Early in March, I invited Melvin to spend Shabbos with us at my mother's home. The courtship was getting more serious and I decided to push it along. I guess Rivka Brill's message and Melvin's persistence were doing their work.

A few weeks before Passover, Melvin was on the phone inviting me to spend the holiday with his family. I declined the invitation for technical and social reasons.

"What's the technical reason?" he asked.

"Our family spends Passover together. That's the worst time for my mother because my father's Yahrzeit is coming up and she gets terribly depressed. So the family gathers at the Seder each year and I show my brother how to conduct it."

"Consider this an invitation to your entire family to spend Passover with the Seidmans."

"That compounds the social problem."

"What is the social problem?"

"You know very well that if a woman and her family spend Passover with a man's family, people might think that something more than a casual relationship exists between the man and the woman."

"Why do you suddenly care what people think? It never bothered you before."

"It doesn't bother me when I know that what they think isn't true. This time there may be a grain of truth in it. What's more, you have a nasty habit of springing surprises on me."

"Don't worry. I won't spring anything totally unexpected on you."

My heart started beating rapidly and I was getting very agitated. I'd never been proposed to before. With Steven, I had to tell him that my father wouldn't let us continue living together unless we were married and that he threatened to disinherit me otherwise. Steven wasn't too happy when I told him that as much as I loved him, he wasn't worth the million dollars it would cost me to live with him in sin.

"What is not totally unexpected, Melvin?"

"Well, by pure chance I happened to run into Oliver Goldsmith this week."

"Goldsmith, the English poet?"

"No. Goldsmith of Buffalo Jewelers."

"Where did you run into him by chance?"

"In my office."

"You don't deal with Tiffany's any more?"

"Goldsmith is a very fine fellow and has worked with the family for many years."

"You placed an order?"

Now Melvin was being coy. "I wasn't sure of your size."

"They are adjustable, Melvin. I'm not committing myself to accept anything but, if you are curious as to my finger size, 6 3/4 is about right.

"The size is duly noted. Let me know if you are coming."

"When is the deadline?"

"Goldsmith needs at least a week and I need a few days to scrounge up the money."

"I'll bet."

Well, I was at the point of no return. If I went for Passover to Buffalo, I would be leaving Syracuse for good. I would also be getting married again. I drove over to my mother's place to talk things over with her.

"Melvin wants me and the whole family to spend Passover in Buffalo."

"That can mean only one thing, Sandy, and I am very happy for you."

"I'm not sure about it yet."

"No girl is ever sure, dear. I had my doubts about your father but it turned out very well. Melvin is a substantial man from a good family. He is religious and dedicated. Now you are a free bird but you can't fly around forever. You have to come down to earth. There is a lot to be said for a stable, secure marriage."

"I can say it in one word."

"What is that?"

"Boring."

"You are not being very smart, Sandy, with all your knowledge. You won't find a better man than Melvin, and Mrs. Seidman herself told me that Melvin is a fine boy. A man who respects his parents will also respect his wife. I'm not pressuring you but I would be very happy if you married Melvin."

That explains why on the eve of Passover our family drove to Buffalo for the holiday. My younger brother, Mom and I were in one car and my married brother, his wife and two kids, were in the other. There wasn't any point in the Feldman women offering to help because the caterer who works at the office suite was on the job and the regular maid and a helper were working the dining room.

Melvin was at the head of the table and the two families sat on either side of it.

My mother had the first seat on our side and I sat next to her. My younger brother came after me followed by my older brother and his wife. Mrs. Seidman was first on her side followed by Jack and Estelle and Carol and Joe. Their two housekeepers were there to look after the five children at the foot of the table.

Melvin conducted the Seder because he was the most knowledgeable. He had done so for the first time a year earlier, right after his father had passed away. That was a sorrowful occasion even though it was a holiday. This time, the spirit was much lighter.

After Melvin recited kiddish over the wine, the kids asked the Four Questions and Melvin performed the various rituals. It was taken for granted that I would steal the afikoman matzah. That was a Passover game with children. The kids steal the matzah and earn holiday gifts. All the grandchildren were bought off well in advance on this occasion and told not to go for it.

When Melvin left the room to wash his hands for the blessing on the matzahs, I lingered behind and lifted the afikoman from under the pillow and hid it quite well.

At the conclusion of the main course, Melvin asked for the matzah to be produced. "Who has the afikoman? Whoever stole it, please return it now."

Everyone greeted the announcement with a stony silence, which is part of the game.

"We can't continue the Seder without the afikoman," Melvin raged.

My little nephew, Danny, who was not properly briefed, piped up. "I saw Aunt Sandy swipe it."

Melvin pointed an accusing finger at me and said harshly, "So you're the thief. I might have known. What do I have to pay you to get it back."

To which I said, "I would normally say that it would take a lot of bread, but I can't say that on Passover."

"Ask him for a bike," Danny said.

"Not a bad idea, but let us start with four tires rather than two."

"That is a lot of lettuce, Romaine, of course. But I have no choice. You can have the tires and a used car to drive them home with." He produced a set of solid gold car keys. They looked like General Motors keys so I guessed I'd earned myself a Buick. But of course the gold keys were ornamental not functional, since Mel wouldn't handle real car keys on a holiday.

"Now, do I get the afikoman?"

"Not so fast. I'll need a garage for the car when I visit Buffalo."

Melvin quickly produced a key to his garage. The act was going great, but my mother was crying already.

"It won't work, Melvin. A single girl like me can't park her car in the garage of a single man. What will all the neighbors say, especially with a man who may someday be president of a shul?"

"We have a little problem here folks that will take a few minutes to work out. You will have to excuse Sandy and me to continue the negotiations privately."

We left the dining room and headed for the study. As I was leaving I saw Mrs. Seidman start to cry.

"You're a great actress, Sandy," Melvin said, as he slipped the ring on my finger and put his arms around me. "I love you and I want you to marry me."

"I love you Mel and I agree in principle to marry you subject to conditions to be worked out a later time."

"It has to be unconditional or I take the ring back."

I started to remove the ring and gave him a good scare.

"OK," he said. "Subject to minor conditions which, if they cannot be agreed upon, shall be submitted to binding arbitration by Rabbis Brill, Steiner and Goldberg."

"I agree." I pulled out a *sheitel*, a wig that married women are supposed to wear, and put it on my head to lighten things up for our return to the table.

"I'm the happiest man alive," Melvin said, in a rare show of emotion.

"No, you're not."

"Who is?"

"Oliver Goldsmith, the man who unloaded that rock on you. You sure made his Passover."

We returned to the dining room where everyone cheered as I flashed my hand for all to see. Everyone had to kiss the bride including all the brothers and kids and even the future brothers-in-law. I surrendered the afikoman and the Seder ran to a happy conclusion.

"When are you getting married?" Carol had to know.

I hadn't discussed the matter with Melvin but I had a feeling he wouldn't object. "The wedding ceremony will be at the Beit Meir Yeshiva in early June, and the reception will be at the Jerusalem Sheraton."

"Let me apply for Matron of Honor and I have a candidate for flower girl."

"You don't have a kosher gown in your whole wardrobe," Melvin said.

"I can wear a coat at the ceremony and take if off at the hotel," Carol replied.

I spent the next two days working out the marital conditions with Melvin and we came to terms without any problems. I agreed to observe the Sabbath, maintain a kosher home and let him assume the shul presidency in return for his quitting the Boards of the Boy Scouts and the Junior Chamber of Commerce. I won full freedom to pursue my academic career and stay far away from Buffalo Auto. He promised to continue his graduate studies until he completed at least thirty credits and to become more active in environmental and cultural causes. I consented to join the Sisterhood but not to assume any office. Mel held out for one book review a year. I finally consented, but without a vow.

On the first morning of the holiday, I went to shul with the family. Melvin was given the honor of *Maftir* and chanted the text quite well. The rabbi announced that he was being honored because of his engagement to Sandra Feldman. He added that I was an assistant professor of history at the State University in Cortland. The congregation shouted 'mazel tov' and sang a melody reserved for such occasions.

So far I hadn't told anyone that I had unofficial word that my request for a transfer to Buffalo had been approved, and that I would be raised to the rank of associate professor. I had learned not to make such announcements until I saw the offer on paper. My contact at Buffalo was Dr. Rechtman, who was the acting department head. I had applied when things started getting serious with Melvin, and I called him a couple of days before

Passover. When he asked me why I wanted to teach at Buffalo, I told him that I was hoping to get a chance to instruct one of the graduate students in the department, a brilliant fellow by the name of Melvin Seidman.

"He is a bright student and works quite hard, but I don't think that he is destined for an academic career. You aren't interested in him for other reasons, perhaps material ones?"

"Why," I asked in all innocence, "does he have any money?"

"Sandy," he said, sternly, "I know that his company sells your company a lot of stuff. Look, this is a permanent appointment and we are delighted to have you join our staff. I hope you are coming to Buffalo to advance your career, and not just to pursue a passing fancy."

"Unfortunately, it is no longer a passing fancy," I said. "Our engagement notice is appearing in the papers next week."

"Mazel tov," he said. "I guess the rich get richer all the time. Is this a merger or a marriage?"

"You didn't know that marriages are made in Heaven?"

"No. I thought that mine was made in the other place. Anyway, I'll get the paperwork done as soon as possible."

On the afternoon of the second day of the holiday, Melvin and I were sitting in the park. It was then that I told him about Rivka Brill's visit and the heroic effort she had made to bring me Rabbi Shayalevitch's message. I told him the gist of the rabbi's thoughts and I said, "I honestly believe that his words had a profound effect on me. It made me far more receptive to your efforts than I would have ordinarily been."

"If you are confessing, I might as well do so, too. Remember I told you that God sent me the angel, Raphael, to guide my actions? The angel actually appeared to me."

"In female form, no doubt?"

"Yes, but not in the form of Rivka Brill."

"It couldn't have been her. She almost died getting to Syracuse."

"You promise no recriminations against my angel or any change in our status if I tell you who she was?"

"It's too late for recriminations. I'm already in captivity."

"It seems that last August, Rivka and Lili Goldberg undertook a mission impossible. Rivka's assignment was to take care of you and Lili went to work on me. She outlined my campaign down to the flowers on the podium at the convention. That included registration at the State University, writing a history paper on my own and having you review it and coaching me with all the right answers."

I started to shout. "You mean I was done in by a low-down two-bit shadchan? I have never been so humiliated in my life. How could you stoop so low as to engage a shadchan? If it weren't too late, I'd walk out on you."

"Your two bit shadchan is the number one matchmaker in all of Jerusalem and has a graduate degree in psychology. Under no circumstances, however, did I seek her out or engage her services. She offered her advice freely, without charge, and I think her suggestions were brilliant."

Melvin then told me the entire episode and I had to admit that I had underestimated Lili. "Who do you think coordinated this mission impossible?"

Melvin spent some time in deep thought. "It wasn't Rabbi Brill or Rabbi Steiner, because they knew nothing about our situation and neither had any positive feelings about our match. It wasn't Rivka because she didn't have the required knowledge for it."

"That leaves Lili herself," I answered, "but I still don't think that she could have coordinated the whole thing or convinced Rivka to undertake the mission. Hey, wait a minute. I think I know the guilty party. Rabbi Shayalevitch was the one who sent Rivka out. Do you think he could have sent Lili, too?"

"He's supposed to be a profound scholar, but I don't know whether he could direct an espionage mission, especially one involving graduate schools."

It was then that Lovelace came to mind. "That's what you think. The man grew up in England and cites English metaphysical poetry. I'd bet dollars to donuts that he studied at Cambridge or Oxford."

"Soon you'll tell me that he worked for Her Majesty's Secret Service."

"I wouldn't be in the least surprised."

"If it really was Rabbi Shayalevitch, why would he want to do it?" Melvin asked.

"Rivka is one of his faithful devotees. She was very jealous of the attention that Rabbi Brill was lavishing on me and she asked her mentor for help. I think he felt that the only solution to the problem was to get me married, because Rabbi Brill would never pay attention to a married woman. Leave it to me Mel, I'll get to the bottom of it when we're in Israel."

"I should call Rabbi Steiner and tell him that we're engaged."

"I'm worried about that. He just got up from Shiva and he may want to sit down again."

"Why?"

"The custom is that when a son marries a non-Jew, the parents sit Shiva. He looks upon you as a son."

"I don't think he looks at you as a *shiksa*, just as a woman who is a little too outspoken and opinionated."

"It's worse than that."

"Why?"

"It's a case of too much learning, too little observance, and no deference to him at all."

"You should respect Torah sages, Sandy, it's a mitzvah."

"I respect him for his knowledge but not for his value system. It's a pity, because he did grow up in Vienna and his father was a great rabbi there. I feel that when he came to Jerusalem he developed the need to be more fanatic than everyone else."

"I'm studying the Roman Empire now."

"So what?"

"The first thing I learned is, 'When in Rome you do as the Romans do.'"

"Rabbis Brill and Goldberg and Shayalevitch are still tolerant even after being in Jerusalem for many years."

"They are American and British. They are very ethnocentric and tend to assimilate more gradually."

"Look at him. Six credits in graduate school and he is talking like a sociologist."

"Weren't you the one who wanted an educated man?" he said, with sadness in his voice.

I spend a lot of time apologizing for flippant remarks and I did so very humbly for this one. "I'm sorry, Melvin, I really appreciate the change that education has wrought in your ability to think and express yourself. I suppose the fact that Rabbi Steiner lived through the Holocaust may have caused his poor self-image and lack of confidence. He tries desperately to win peer approval and he worries constantly that other scholars will find fault in what he does."

"You must admit that your antics in Jerusalem exposed him to some ridicule and embarrassment."

"A public institution can't survive in obscurity."

We returned home and, when Melvin came back after the

evening services, our family packed and drove back to Syracuse. We left in three cars instead of the two we came with. I drove my new Buick sports car and it ran like a dream. Melvin thought I only had one car but I had two of my own and was the sole driver of the car my father left. If I told Melvin that I needed a special car for Shabbat, he'd dump me on the spot. So I figured I'd just have to get rid of the extra cars.

MELVIN

26

I CALLED RABBI STEINER AFTER Passover and phoned Sandy to report the results.

"Don't skip a thing Melvin, I'm dying to hear what he said."

"I called him up and I said, 'Rabbi Steiner, when I come to Israel, I would like you to be *Mesader Kedushin* and officiate at my wedding ceremony.' He replied, 'You are getting married, Melvin? Mazel tov. I am so happy to hear that. I hope you have chosen the daughter of a wise man.' There is something in the Code of Law which says that a man should seek to marry the daughter of a Torah scholar."

"I know that. What did you say to him?"

"I told him that the girl's father was deceased and he was reputed to be quite a scholar. In fact there is a library dedicated to his memory in one of the great yeshivas in Jerusalem. He caught on pretty quickly. 'Oh Vey,' he said, 'You are marrying Sarah Feldman?' 'Yes, Rabbi,' I said. 'She's the one, and I would be honored to receive your blessings.'"

"Did he bestow any on you?"

"In a way. He said, 'I don't have to bless you with smart children because you are smart and your bride is incredibly so. I don't have to bless you with beautiful children because you are handsome and your bride is a beautiful woman. The blessing you need is that you should remain truly observant and that your children should grow up to fear God because you are now observant and your bride's father was a God-fearing man.'"

"Two out of three isn't too bad, Melvin. Don't worry about the kids, though. I'll put the fear of God into them. Did he consent to preside at the wedding?"

"He is afraid that you will create problems for him."

"How so?"

"He thinks you will want to rewrite the marriage contract, change the order of the blessings, march around me in the wrong direction and ride up to the canopy on a donkey."

"Did you tell him that my first wedding was strictly according to the books?"

"I did. But he said that was because your father was alive and wouldn't tolerate any nonsense."

"What was his final word?"

"He said that if you promise to behave yourself, dress properly and avoid any publicity stunts, he will conduct it."

"Melvin, the choice of a clergyman is up to the groom. If you prefer to honor Rabbi Steiner, I'll toe the line."

"I do want to honor him and I think that's what my father would have wanted. You can have your fun at the reception."

"I will. Did you tell Rabbi Steiner anything else?"

"I asked him to inform Rabbis Brill and Goldberg of our forthcoming marriage and to thank them for their efforts in bringing us together."

The next night I called Rabbi Steiner to tell him that Sandy had agreed to all the conditions and would not interfere in any way with the traditional ceremony. She would also bring a note from the mikva. Rabbi Steiner said he'd informed Rabbis Brill and Goldberg of the events, and the two were in a complete state of shock. They claimed that they didn't even know we were seeing each other and both denied that they had in any way encouraged the match. "Why was I to thank them?" Rabbi Steiner asked me, "if they didn't do anything for you?"

I was treading on thin ice here because I realized that the two wives had undertaken their mission without their husbands' knowledge or consent and hadn't told them about it afterwards. The women might get into trouble if I let the cat out of the bag, so I backtracked and said, "I'm sorry, I didn't make myself too clear. I only meant to thank them for introducing us and arranging for Sandy to work on our affair."

"I understand," Rabbi Steiner said, "I thought you were saying that they helped get you together after you returned to America. When is your affair scheduled?"

"If God wills it, I plan to arrive in Israel on Wednesday, June 2. I would like to be called to the Torah at the yeshiva on Saturday and have the wedding on Tuesday. If the dedication dinner is scheduled for the following Sunday, we will require the recitation of the wedding week blessings at the dinner."

"That's fine with me. Rabbi Brill, however, is a little upset with the news. He was counting on Sarah to run the dedication ceremony but now she will be too busy to help before the wedding, and she is not supposed to work during the seven days of feasting following the wedding."

"I thought that when a man marries a divorcee he is required to stop working for only three days, even though he was single before the wedding."

"Did Sarah tell you that?"

"Yes, she did."

"Did she tell you where she saw that?"

"I believe she said it was the view of Maimonides."

"I might have known. The Rambam does in fact rule that way. Many of the later authorities, however, say that only because the wedding blessings for a single man must always extend seven days, even if he marries a divorcee, it is not proper for either party to work on days when wedding blessings are to be recited. Of course, in such a case, the woman may opt to forego the extra four days of rejoicing, but my practice is to advise her not to do so and, since the work involved has to be done at the yeshiva, I simply will not allow her to do it."

"I am sorry for Rabbi Brill but I am sure that God will help."

I related the conversation to Sandy and she said I did the right thing in not getting the wives in trouble. She added that when the men find out, there would be hell to pay. As far as not working for seven days, that was perfectly all right with her. "Remember that a virgin has to separate from her husband after the first night. Not being a virgin offers me the possibility of doing more enjoyable things during the first week than working on a yeshiva dinner, and please don't make any comments on what I just said."

Our family arrived in Israel Wednesday afternoon. The Feldmans had arrived on Sunday, so Sandy was able to send the bus to meet us at the airport and bring us to the Sheraton. She had completed most of the wedding arrangements at the hotel and gave me a full report.

On Thursday morning, Sandy took me to see Rabbi Shaya-levitch. He didn't live poorly, but was not rich, either. When we arrived, there were two or three women waiting outside his office to meet with him. We sat down and waited a full half-hour before he could see us.

The rabbi was a man of 70 with a trim, white beard and

dark eyes. He didn't look like a typical yeshiva rabbi but more like a merchant or executive. He spoke English with a beautiful British accent.

"Let me wish you 'mazel tov,'" he said to us, "I look forward to being at your wedding."

"We will be honored to have you attend and we will request you to recite some of the seven blessings."

"I will have to start practicing right away because I am only familiar with the two blessings that proceed the seven." He was telling us that he was more accustomed to receiving the highest honor, which was to be the official conductor of the ceremony. The officiating rabbi always chants the two primary blessings.

"We have already asked Rabbi Steiner to officiate."

"I know, I am only jesting. I will be glad to accept any honor that I am given. I don't know whether you intended to invite me to the reception but let me decline in advance." He was informing us that senior rabbis in Jerusalem do not attend affairs where the decorum and dress might be less than perfect.

At this point, Sandra took over and thanked Rabbi Shayalevitch for sending Rivka to see her with his message.

"As you can see," she said, "I took your words to heart and that accounts to a certain degree for the situation in which I find myself."

"Don't complain. I am sure that you could have done much worse."

"Tell me, Rabbi," she continued, "is it true that you grew up in England?"

"Yes, I did."

"And that you attended Cambridge?"

"Where did you hear that?"

"I can detect university education in the way you speak."

"If you must know, it was Oxford."

I couldn't believe that Sandy had the nerve to pose the next question and I was stunned when she did it.

"Did you work many years for Her Majesty's Intelligence Services?"

Rabbi Shayalevitch turned pale white. "Who told you anything like that?" he demanded. "Are you connected with the CIA or the Mossad?"

"My wife and I have never had anything to do with either organization," I said hastily. "I think she was just trying to flatter you."

Sandy gave me a dirty look and said, "Speak for yourself, Melvin. I have translated scores of documents for the CIA and other intelligence outfits. I know that the Special Services often recruit graduate students at Oxford and Cambridge to help them, and I imagined that Rabbi Shayalevitch might have done such work. I have no real information, just a hunch."

Rabbi Shayalevitch regained his composure. "I was not a field agent for the Services but, knowing Russian and Polish, I helped train a number of operatives and debriefed those who returned alive."

Sandy gave me an 'I told you so look,' and gave Rabbi Shayalevitch a broad smile. "In that case, Rabbi, I want to thank you for any additional assistance that you offered in the process of bringing Melvin and me together."

When we left, I told Sandy that I couldn't believe how much nerve she had to fish out the facts. She answered that the direct approach is the only way and the best way to gather sensitive information. "I feel a million times better knowing that I was seduced into marriage by an agent of Her Majesty's Secret Service rather than by a run-of-the-mill shadchan."

"Have you done anything for Rabbi Brill?" I asked her.

"I met with him briefly and advised him the best I could. There will be a dedication dinner and the rabbi prepared a brochure for fund-raising. The work, however, is not professional and I don't think he will be raising too much. There won't be any public meetings because Rabbi Steiner is not up to it. The audience won't be as large as at the last ceremony and we'll all fit into the dormitory dining room quite easily."

Our next stop was at the yeshiva, where we went to see Rabbi Steiner. I couldn't believe how bad he looked. I knew the passing of his wife had been a hard blow but I couldn't anticipate the distress and the agony that was reflected in his appearance. There was a mark of frailty in his walk and his voice sounded weak and trembling.

He ushered us into his office and both of us expressed condolences to him on his loss.

"I cannot let my personal grief stop the world from going on and I certainly don't want it to affect the happiness of others. I am delighted to be able to conduct your wedding and I want to thank you, Sarah, for agreeing to a proper ceremony without conditions."

"I have nothing against the traditional wedding service even though the blessings didn't come true in my first marriage. My parents were married in the same ritual and they did have a blessed life together."

"I take it that Menachem and you know all that has to be done prior to the wedding and that you will take care of it."

"How many days before the wedding should I stop seeing Melvin?" Sandy asked.

"You should have probably stopped seeing him already but, given the fact that you have both come from abroad and there are important arrangements to be made, it would be sufficient to stop seeing each other from tonight on."

On Saturday morning, I davened at the yeshiva and recited the reading from the Prophets. I also chanted the Musaf services. I had arranged with the yeshiva caterer for a deluxe kiddish and she prepared an abundance of food. Fasting before the wedding on Tuesday was hard because of the heat in Jerusalem, but I managed to do so. In late afternoon, the ceremony started. Rabbi Steiner recited the opening blessings and Rabbi Brill read the marriage contract. The closing blessings were split between Rabbis Goldberg, Gross and Shayalevitch. Rabbi Steiner also allowed Rabbi Goldberg to speak briefly in English for the benefit of the families.

There was a small reception for the guests before we went to the hotel. Sandy and I spent most of the time with the photographers and observing the post-ceremony rituals. We then drove to the Sheraton for the wedding reception and it was a good thing that the rabbis had the foresight to stay far away. I tried to tell Carol that she was in Jerusalem and not in Las Vegas but nothing could curb her exuberance.

Sandy wasn't wearing a full bridal gown but the dress she did wear was a tribute to an outstanding designer in Syracuse. I am convinced that between her hairdresser and dress designer, Sandy spends enough money to support several families in Israel for an entire year. It dawned on me that I would now be picking up the tab for these various expenses, but I figured that anyone I married would capitalize on my wealth.

Sandy observed our honeymoon very strictly and didn't call the yeshiva even once. Rabbi Brill didn't have the courage to disturb her during the days after the wedding. The only time he spoke to her was at the nightly wedding blessings at the yeshiva. We had them on Wednesday and Thursday at the yeshiva and the rest of the time at the Sheraton.

I didn't feel that the dedication ceremony was all that bad.

It did not meet Sandy's standards, but it was a far cry from the chaotic service that had marked the original yeshiva dedication. Rabbis Brill and Goldberg, assisted by their wives, had apparently profited from their experience at Sandy's earlier affairs and were able to muddle through. The appeal raised a significant sum. I don't know exactly how much, but I am sure that Sandy would have doubled or tripled the amount.

SANDRA

27

AFTER SAYING GOODBYE TO MELVIN, I returned to the Sheraton and stayed out of his way. Since he was going to be at the yeshiva on the Sabbath, I didn't have to worry about seeing him on the weekend. Sunday and Monday were spent making last-minute wedding arrangements and calling the members of both families to see whether they were actually coming in response to the invitations we sent out. I was happy to hear that most of the family would be on hand.

Rivka took me to the mikva on Monday and I picked up my papers at the Rabbinate, which allowed for the marriage to take place. The civil marriage would have to wait until we returned to Buffalo, but it was going to be a brief visit to City Hall and nothing more. On Tuesday I had a long session with the hairdresser and wondered why I was taking all the trouble when I would have to cover my hair anyway.

I had no complaints about the wedding and I had a very good time at the reception. There was no one happier than my mother, who now felt that I would be happily married and run a traditional home.

"My only regret," she told me at the wedding, "is that your father didn't live to share this happiness with me."

Melvin and I spent the next few days in our private suite at the Sheraton and got to know each other in the Biblical sense. We would have gone away but for the need to be at the yeshiva for the nightly wedding blessings.

The dedication ceremony at the yeshiva left much to be desired. There were no big crowds and no press coverage. The dinner brochure was replete with errors. Still, it was not a total disaster, and Rabbi Goldberg conducted the dinner with his usual skill. Rabbi Steiner was able to attend the dinner because he was no longer in official mourning but he was in very low spirits.

Our families returned to the United States and I stopped off in Syracuse for a few days. During that time, I arranged for the movers to ship my belongings to Buffalo. I didn't need much furniture because Melvin had a nice home of his own but I did have a library of thousands of books that the movers had to schlep. I also visited my older brother at the store and asked him to do me a few favors. One was to hide the three cars that I drove in Syracuse and keep the existence of the two cars that Melvin didn't know about a secret. The other was to put aside half of the yearly profit-sharing from the store in a secret account which would not be in my name but which could serve me as a rainy-day fund for any contingencies that might arise. I told Michael that the money should be invested in tax-free municipals to ease any problems with the IRS. As it was, I was bringing a lot of money into the marriage and I felt no qualms about hiding a quarter of a million dollars and three cars.

I said my goodbyes to all my colleagues on the faculty of the SUNY Division in Cortland. I also bid farewell to the store employees and the rabbi and other families at the synagogue. That done, I drove to Buffalo in my new Buick and arrived in time to help the movers unpack. The marriage got off to a good start and I spent my spare time preparing for the courses I would be teaching at SUNY in Buffalo.

In early August, I got a call from Melvin, who was at his office.

"We have a visitor, Sandy."

"That's nice. Who is it?"

"It's Rabbi Brill, and I hate to tell you what he looks like. He's a walking disaster and I have never seen a man so shattered in all my life."

"What happened? Rivka ran off with another man?"

"Please don't be flippant, Sandy. The man is really suffering and he doesn't know what to do. He appealed to me for advice but didn't tell me the problem because he wants you to hear it as well."

"I would rather not come to the office unless it is absolutely necessary. Send him over to the house and I'll break out some new dishes and the glatt kosher food that we got in New York." We had a full-time housekeeper who was well-trained in kosher cooking.

Melvin spoke to Rabbi Brill while I was still on the phone and arranged to bring him over at around four.

"I'm sure that he has a few books with him," I said. "If he wants to study, he can come here now."

"He won't stay alone with a married woman, Sandy. He'll have to wait until I can come home with him."

When Mel walked in with Rabbi Brill, I was even more shocked than Melvin was when he first saw him. For a minute, I thought that the rabbi was suffering from some serious illness. He looked nothing like the usually cheerful man that I knew in the past.

"Baruch," I said, "you look worse than Rabbi Steiner. Sit

down and tell us what happened. If there's anything we can do to help, we certainly will."

Rabbi Brill sat down on the easy chair facing the couch where Melvin and I were sitting.

"Before we start," I said, "I want to invite you to join us for dinner. I know that you wouldn't eat at my apartment in Syracuse but, in this home, I have put in a supply of glatt-kosher food and I will use a set of dishes that were immersed in a mikva before they were shipped. This service was never used before."

"That's very nice of you, Sarah. I'm not in the mood to eat too much but I certainly have no problem eating here."

"Your problems are related to the yeshiva," I ventured. "I have a fairly good idea of what happened, I just didn't know when the ax would fall. Tell us exactly what took place." Melvin looked at me in surprise.

"It was about a week after the dedication," Rabbi Brill said, "that I was asked to see Rabbi Steiner in his office. I had no reason to suspect that anything was amiss and I was working very hard at the time getting the yeshiva ready for the large influx of new students that we expected in September. Rabbi Steiner was quite distraught and spoke in a very weak voice. He spent a lot of time reflecting about the yeshiva and how it had developed over the years. He stressed the importance of my work in helping the yeshiva grow. He isn't usually lavish with praise, so I immediately began to suspect that something was wrong and became quite tense.

"'Baruch,' he said, 'you know of the severe loss that I have suffered. My health was already failing before my wife passed away and it has continued to deteriorate ever since. It is apparent that I no longer can continue as the head of the yeshiva and I am going into retirement.' That in itself didn't really surprise me. Since his wife died, Rabbi Steiner had done virtually nothing at the yeshiva but stare at the walls. I took care of the new dormitory construction and the expanded student recruitment. Rabbi Goldberg also joined in the work and rendered invaluable assistance.

"At first, I tried to persuade Rabbi Steiner not to retire. 'It's not customary for yeshiva heads to step down,' I said, 'even if they no longer can physically do the work. I stand ready to help the Dean in doing all that is necessary to run the yeshiva in his name.'

"Rabbi Steiner looked at me sadly and said, 'that would be the ideal way but, through personal weakness, I mishandled the situation and now I am paying the price. I should never have let you go to Buffalo and secure the funds for the new dormitory, or I should have refused to accept the donation. If I did accept the money, I should never have let you put up the building and bear the strain of it. Doing so has put a tremendous burden of guilt on me. If the yeshiva were small, I could have worked as long as possible and then let nature take its course. Or, I could have turned the yeshiva over to you or other interested parties for a reasonable amount, payable to my heirs over the years. My sons would have been content to stay where they were and use the payments to supplement their salaries. In that way, they would have had income from the yeshiva and escaped the burdens of running it.

"'All this has now changed. You, or any other rabbis who have the scholarly credentials, cannot raise sufficient sums to cover even the physical value of the property let alone the name and goodwill. What is more to the point, the yeshiva has now achieved such status that my sons would feel honored to take it over and give up their present positions to do so.' My spirit began to fail and the room became dark. For 14 years I had given my life to build the yeshiva in the hope that I would someday be the dean, and now Rabbi Steiner was preparing to tell me that he was about to name his sons to succeed him and leave me in the cold."

"Baruch," I said, "Such is the way of the world. A man has to be true to his own flesh and blood. There was talk of this in Jerusalem and I heard it but it was not for me to tell you because it would have destroyed the yeshiva, and I couldn't bring myself to destroy a Torah institution. For the very same reason, others were afraid to tell you. It's the old story. Everyone at the university knew that my first husband was running around but nobody had the heart to tell me. The wife is always the last to know. Anyway, what did Rabbi Steiner say next?"

"Rabbi Steiner told me that at the start of the new semester his oldest son, Yakob, would assume the title of Dean and become the kollel instructor. His next son, Reuben, would assume the title of mashgiach. I was on the verge of tears. Not only would I be denied my life's ambition but I was being demoted and my security was being endangered. 'Where does that leave me?' I asked."

"'You remember that I solemnly pledged that you would always have a position at the yeshiva. That pledge will be kept. I made both boys sign a paper confirming a permanent position for you, at least as an instructor.' The dean pulled out a copy of the document and handed it to me. He went on to say, 'You will have the highest class, Baruch, and as long as there are American students you will be their mashgiach, because my sons do not speak English.'"

I asked him about Rabbi Goldberg.

"Here Rabbi Steiner looked very sad. 'He is a fine man and he works very hard at the yeshiva, but I could not protect his position. You know, of course, that he never taught a regular class at our yeshiva. My sons want to give all the new positions to men who studied with them in the Israeli yeshivot. They do not think highly of American yeshivot and even less of the American Rabbinate. They do not feel that one who practiced as a rabbi in America could have learned enough Torah to teach a class in a Jerusalem yeshiva.'"

"I tried to reason with Rabbi Steiner. I told him I could cope with the situation if he appointed Yakob as dean and I lost the kollel. Yakob is a quiet, humble man, who is serious about his studies. He has the knowledge to teach at the kollel, although I am not sure of his ability to do so. What was impossible to accept was Reuben as a mashgiach. The man's scholarship is marginal and he has no humility at all. He is haughty and boastful and has a vile temper. The students would not relate to him and many would leave the school. It would be only a matter of time before we were in conflict."

"What did Rabbi Steiner say?" Melvin asked.

"He said that he was aware of Reuben's faults, but that I was painting a very harsh picture of the man. He felt that Reuben had matured in recent years and would be able to handle the position.

"'In any event' he said, 'I cannot favor the eldest son and ignore the next one completely. I do not have to worry about the children after Reuben because the next two are girls and the sons after them are still studying in the yeshivot.'

"I had a feeling that I wanted to run away from this betrayal but I had to ask him one last thing. 'The Dean has solved the teaching problem to some extent but who is going to manage the yeshiva? There is administration and fund-raising and recruiting. Neither of your sons has any experience in such work and, in all the years that you were struggling to keep the yeshiva going, they stood on the sidelines.' 'It is a serious problem,' he said 'but you will be here and, although you may be unhappy with the new arrangements, I am hoping that you will be of assistance to them in these areas. It will be in your interest, because if the yeshiva fails, even the position you have retained will be in danger.'

"'The Dean cannot expect me to turn the other cheek,' I replied. 'Even if I were so inclined, your sons would not let me work freely. They would insist on approving every decision and statement in advance and would make it impossible for me to conduct any school business.' Rabbi Steiner merely shrugged. 'You are a free man, Baruch, to do as you wish. If you undertake your annual collection this year, the yeshiva will pay your expenses.'

"Well, Mel and Sandy, that's my story. Rabbi Goldberg is out on the street and I've been demoted. I am not at all optimistic about my future at the yeshiva."

"I'm very sorry for you, Rabbi Brill, and for Rabbi Goldberg," Melvin said. "I hate to see such a miscarriage of justice at an institution that bears my father's name. While you were talking, I was trying to explore some possible courses of action."

"Like what?" Rabbi Brill asked.

"I could try to talk to Rabbi Steiner and exert some pressure on your behalf, but he will tell me that his hands are tied. The only leverage I have at this point is the annual mortgage payments that our foundation makes, but I can't even threaten to stop them. My father made me promise to continue making them until the mortgage is paid off, and the Steiners know about it."

"How about the government or the Ministry of Religious Affairs?" I asked Rabbi Brill. "Could they intervene?"

"I doubt it," he said. "In a case of gross mismanagement or corruption they could threaten to cut off subsidies. So far this hasn't come to pass. The Steiners could always hire some administrator to do the paperwork and keep the Ministry happy."

"Do you have any ideas of your own, Rabbi?" Melvin asked. "You've had seven weeks to think about it."

"Rivka suggested that perhaps I should look into the possibility of leaving Beit Meir and starting my own yeshiva."

My eyes lit up when I heard those words and my ears perked up.

"What did you tell her?" I asked.

"I told her that I thought it was a good idea. I would have no problem attracting students and I had enough administrative experience to undertake it. 'There is only one minor difficulty standing in the way,' I said. 'I don't have the million dollars necessary to buy a yeshiva building.'"

"Is that the only obstacle between you and a new yeshiva?"

"It is no trivial matter," Rabbi Brill said sadly.

Out of the corner of my eye I saw Melvin frown. I knew I had to proceed cautiously.

"The million you need isn't all cash, is it?" I asked.

"Only half a million has to be in cash. The rest can be in the form of a mortgage. But you know what Rabbi Shimon said in the Ethics, 'The good path in life is to see what will develop in the future and the bad path is to borrow and not repay.'"

"A lot of our customers at Buffalo Auto are on the low road," Melvin chimed in.

"How much do you think you can raise on your own from public and private sources?" I persisted.

"I would say a maximum of $100,000."

"So we're down to $400,000 in cash. Would you offer the name of the yeshiva to someone who raised that amount for you?"

"With some reservations," he answered. "The name would have to be a proper Hebrew one and I would require that any word preceding the name be taken from a verse in the Bible or prayer book."

"I'll tell you what, Baruch. Let's enjoy dinner and not talk about the problem confronting you. After dinner you can study from the Talmud while I talk to Mel and maybe we will work something out."

"You have a set of the Talmud in the house?"

"I have my own and my father's, Melvin has his own and his father's and Mel and I each have a Soncino translation."

"I shouldn't have asked," Rabbi Brill said with some embarrassment.

We enjoyed a wonderful glatt-kosher meal on the new china, although I had to keep a wary eye on our housekeeper to make sure that she made no mistakes. During dinner I asked Rabbi Brill how Rivka was doing in college.

"Very well. All 'A's, in fact, except for English Composition."

"If you didn't help her, Baruch, she would have gotten an 'A' in that subject, too."

"I meant well…" Baruch started to say before he caught himself. "I mean, I helped her a little with the English but, after 20 years in Israel, I guess I could use a refresher course myself. I am very proud of her and she is like a new woman. I keep telling her that some day she will write like Sandy Seidman. She also has kept her weight down. By the way, she confessed about her adventure in Syracuse and told me what Lili did as well."

"How did you get her to do that?"

"When Rabbi Steiner said that Mel wanted to thank Rabbi Goldberg and me for our help in making the match, I grew suspicious, because I didn't even know that you were seeing each other. Rabbi Goldberg didn't know about it either. When we left the office, Rabbi Goldberg said that the time had come to have a talk with our wives. 'I don't have to, Eliezer,' I said. 'My Rivka is not a matchmaker.' 'All the same,' he answered. 'Melvin said to thank you as well.'"

"Well, I confronted Rivka that night and asked if she had something to tell me. 'I never hold anything back from you,' she answered, and turned red. She must have thought of her little project at that moment. 'Rivka, even if you acted unwisely you shouldn't hesitate to reveal it.'

'You won't stop me from going to college if I confess?'

'Not unless you've fallen in love with one of your teachers.'

'I only love you,' she said. 'I got anxious when you started to pay so much attention to Sarah Feldman so I went to see Rabbi Shayalevitch for advice.'

'You are not going to put the onus on your mentor, are you, just as Eve blamed the serpent when she ate from the forbidden fruit in the Garden of Eden?'

'No, I'll take all the blame upon myself.'"

"Then she told me everything that had happened, including how she told Lili that you would be in Buffalo for Thanksgiving."

"I hope you didn't yell at her, Baruch. She meant well. Even I get nervous when I see some of the secretaries who work for Mel at Buffalo Auto."

"I didn't chide her except for risking her neck traveling alone to Syracuse without even having your address in hand."

"What happened to Lili?"

"Nothing. Rabbi Goldberg had a good laugh and suggested that Lili should work that hard for the paying clients. Maybe she would make more matches if she did."

"Don't tell Rabbi Goldberg," Mel said, "but Lili didn't lose anything for her efforts."

Mel has never told me about any payment that he made to Lili, but I am sure that he sent her a token of his appreciation.

After dinner I took Mel into the study for a serious bit of bargaining. That's the one thing I like about Mel's being a businessman. In academic negotiations, you can talk for hours and not reach a decision because the professors are so timid and indecisive. I grew up in a business family and Mel shares that experience. He always gets to the heart of the matter and reaches conclusions very quickly.

"Look, Sandy," he said, "I would like to help Rabbi Brill as much as you would, but you are talking about big money. Last year my family put half a million dollars into a dormitory for Beit Meir. I really can't ask for any more funds from the Foundation."

"Why not? There isn't enough money left?"

"Of course there is, but that is not the point. If I take a half million for another yeshiva, Jack will want a million for a home for wayward girls and Carol will want a million for a shelter for wayward cats. I got the money for the yeshiva because I said that Dad wanted it. If Rabbi Brill is to get any money, it can only come from our own pockets."

"You have deep pockets, Mel, don't you?"

"Not any more. You are forgetting that Max Glaser tied up all our money."

Mel was referring to the arrangement that Max Glaser had made so that we could pool our resources. I turned over my trust fund and other funds from the store profits amounting to about a million and a half. Mel turned over about three million of his accumulated funds. Glaser opened a joint investment account to be used for our children's higher education, or other big capital projects like a home, and he and one of us has to sign on the checks. Mel meets regular running expenses from his wages and I use my income for personal needs. Any profit-sharing from our respective business holdings goes into the investment fund. Neither of us has a claim on the other's business holdings in case those businesses are sold or go public.

Even though Mel's wages were substantial they couldn't cover major philanthropy. Somehow I suspected that a man as clever as Max Glaser would not leave Mel penniless. If I salted away a quarter million for a rainy day, I'm sure that Glaser put away much more than that for Mel in some petty cash fund. So I wasn't too worried about pressing him for some money.

"Listen, Mel," I said. "I want to have a yeshiva in my father's name just as you have one in your father's name."

"Sandy," he said, "I've heard of his and hers towels and I've even heard of his and hers Cadillacs but his and hers yeshivas, that's ridiculous."

"Life is funny sometimes," I said.

"Sandy, if you want a yeshiva in your father's name, you have to give more than half the money. I have to buy food and clothes, it says in the Ketubah marriage document, but nowhere does it say that I have to buy you a yeshiva."

"I should have known you're a tightwad, Melvin. You don't even know that every red-blooded American girl must have a few personal things like a car, a mink and a Talmudic seminary. I'll make you an offer you can't refuse. I will donate the first hundred dollars to give me a majority interest in the yeshiva. Thereafter, I will ask you to match whatever I can scrape together, dollar for dollar. If you agree to that, I will throw in free any three concessions you ask for in our marriage arrangements."

"Sandy, I am very happy in this marriage and you don't have to make any concessions to get me to match your charity."

"Don't be an idiot, Melvin, you will never get a chance like this again. If you were smart, you would take me up on my offer."

Mel thought for a minute and really threw me a curve.

"There were several things I wanted but was afraid to ask."

"Like what?"

"Well, you know Mrs. Fineberg from the shul? She asked me to talk to you about becoming Sisterhood president this Sukkot. I know how much you love Sisterhood work, so I was afraid that you would throw a book at me if I asked."

"That favor alone is worth a million dollars, but I always keep my word. Go easier on the next one."

"The second one entails less sacrifice. Estelle, my sister-in-law, never had a religious education and she feels very uneasy about it. She spoke to Carol and asked her to join in the project because she is afraid to do it alone. The two of them asked me if you would instruct them in Judaism once a week."

"That's another million dollars right there, but I accept. What's next?"

"The other is personal. I'm tired of having to sneak to read Carol's copies of Business Week and Forbes in the company dining room. I want you to resume my subscriptions and let me read them openly."

"That I can't do, Melvin. You'll endanger your studies and your new intellectual pursuits. You know how hard I worked to get you to read the Atlantic Monthly."

"You promised me three things. Otherwise no yeshiva."

"You took advantage of me."

"I'll tell you what. If my grades fall at suny, I'll let you cancel the magazines again."

"That's a fair deal. How much time do I have to raise my share of the money?"

"I'll give you half an hour. If it's more than $10,000, I'll have to talk to Max Glaser to make the arrangements and, Sandy, get that smirk off your face. A man has to have a few dollars to spend for odds and ends for which he shouldn't require his wife's permission."

I ran to the bedroom and got on the phone to my mother.

I told her the whole story and she felt terribly sorry for Rabbi Brill.

"How can I help you Sandy?"

"This yeshiva will be named after Dad, just as Beit Meir carries Meir Seidman's name. I would pay for it all by myself but my money is tied up in the marriage. I would like you to match me dollar for dollar."

"If it will make you happy, Sandy, I will be glad to do it. You made me happy by marrying such a nice man as Melvin. Someday, I hope to see some grandchildren from you."

"Give me a break, mom. You just finished three years of pushing me to get married. Now you've started a campaign for grandchildren. I have to get to know Melvin and I want to become a full professor before I worry about kids. Take your time."

"I'm not getting any younger, Sandy, but I won't bother you for a couple of years."

"Make it three."

"I'll think about it. How shall I make out the check?"

"Make it out to the Seidman Charitable Foundation."

"For how much?"

"$100,000."

"One hundred what? Did I year you right? How are you going to raise your $100,000?"

"Tell Michael that he should withdraw $50,000 from my rainy day fund and sell the three cars for another $50,000. Let him keep the proceeds and make out his own check to the Foundation. Send the two checks to me as soon as you can and I'll straighten out the tax problems later. Contributions to the Foundation are in themselves tax deductible, but we may want to claim them as direct gifts to the yeshiva at some point."

After the initial shock, my mother regained her composure. She would never have made such a big donation before I married Melvin, because she had hidden fears that she would be supporting me and a string of non-working husbands for the remainder of her lifetime. It wasn't only Melvin's money that reassured her but his serious attitude towards business and religion that gave her a feeling of security.

"All right. I will do it for you, Sandy. What will the school be called?"

"The Sefer Chaim Yeshiva, the Book of Life Yeshiva."

"Do I get another trip to Israel out of it? I miss the nice minister."

"This June."

I hung up and went speak to Melvin.

"That was quick," he said. "Is it more than ten?"

"I'm afraid so."

"Twenty?"

I kept quiet.

"Fifty?"

More silence.

"A hundred?

I shook my head negatively and raised two fingers.

"Two hundred grand! You are really going to make me pay for having you serve as Sisterhood president."

"Don't forget the Hebrew School teacher bit and the business magazines."

"I'll be paying about $500 an issue for the magazines. They can't be worth that much."

"It's very expensive to be a low brow," I said.

"You can get the money sent to the foundation this week?"

"Yes."

"Say, how much money did you stash away?"

"Much less than you have in that petty cash fund of yours, I assure you."

"Let me call Max Glaser."

Mel called the accountant and arranged for the Foundation to advance the $400,000 in two checks, one dated Sept 15, and the other, January 1 of next year. He promised to reimburse the foundation before the first date.

When it was all settled, we called in Rabbi Brill and told him the news.

"Rabbi Brill," I said, "'Mazel tov.' You are now dean of the Sefer Chaim Yeshiva in Jerusalem, which you will build, with God's help, during the coming year.

Rabbi Brill started to cry. "Thank God," he said, "you have redeemed me from sorrow. Blessed art thou, Oh Lord our God, King of the Universe, who is good and doeth good."

"Amen," I said. "There are a few conditions. Mel will explain them to you."

"Rabbi Brill," Mel said, "I am giving you two foundation checks adding up to $400,000, one dated Sept 15 and one dated Jan 1. When you leave here, hire a lawyer in New York City to incorporate the school and get tax deferment status from the IRS. Sandy is to be chairman of the board and Mrs. Herman Feldman a trustee."

"My mother has a lawyer who can do it for me," Rabbi Brill said. "What else?"

"Rabbi Goldberg is to receive a permanent appointment at the yeshiva as mashgiach or instructor. Try to get a 20-year mortgage and we will help you with the annual payments."

"That, I will do. I have one more problem. You saw what happened at the dormitory dedication when Sandy was too occupied to do it. I want to request you, Sandy, to help me with the dedication ceremony next June."

"Without a vow," Sandy said, "I will be there. After all, this is my yeshiva you're talking about. As chairman of the board I have certain requests to make."

"I'm ready to listen, Madame Chairperson."

"Baruch, keep your job at Beit Meir as long as possible and don't let the young Steiners upset you. Let Rabbi Goldberg work on the new school and maybe visit America to recruit students and raise funds. He can live off Lili's income for a year and whatever salary you can give him. Most important, don't tell anyone about your plans until the building is on the way up. Tell Yossi that whether he remodels an existing building or builds a new one I will personally check every last brick."

Rabbi Brill took leave from us ready to embark on his new life. Well, that brings us up to where the book started and it was a pleasure writing it. The story doesn't quite end here, though, so we have asked Rabbi Brill to read the book and write the final chapter. He graciously consented and wrote the concluding part. We received his section after the dedication in June and it is printed below.

RABBI BRILL

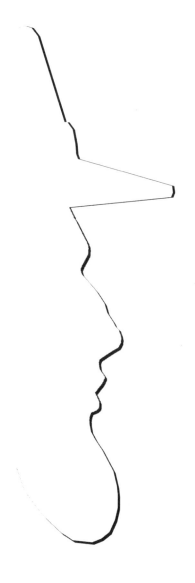

28

I RETURNED TO NEW YORK at once after my success in Buffalo and spent a day on the legal work for my new yeshiva. The money I needed was borrowed from my parents and my sister. Before I left to resume my collection route for Beit Meir, I contacted Rabbi Goldberg and told him not to take any other position until I met with him. He readily agreed to wait. The knowledge that I would have a brighter future in a short period of time made the collecting more bearable.

Back in Israel, I organized a planning group of Lili, Rivka, Rabbi Goldberg, Rabbi and Mrs. Gross and myself. Rabbi Gross was unhappy about losing his once weekly kollel lecture and the extra salary that went with it. He had no desire to work with the younger Steiners and told me that if I were to start a yeshiva he would be delighted to join the staff. I swore him to secrecy.

When I turned in my collections and went back to work at Beit Meir, Rabbi Steiner assumed that the worst was over. I told him that I would finish out the year and review my options thereafter. I would teach my class and advise the American students but would not do any administrative work.

I asked Rabbi Goldberg to help raise funds and guaranteed him a minimum salary. He told me not to worry. If he could instruct a class and serve half-time as the mashgiach in the new yeshiva, it would be well worth waiting a year rather than resuming elementary school teaching.

Next, I called Yossi and set up a meeting with him. He convinced me that it would be better to build from scratch rather than buy an apartment house and convert it. I would only save money if the existing building was in poor condition. In that case, the tenants would also be poor and not have anywhere to move. Evicting them would be difficult and might delay the project for years. To buy a number of apartments within a building, while the remaining tenants were still in residence, would only be asking for trouble. He suggested searching for a lot that was overlooked because it was hilly and required a lot of excavation. Most potential buyers were afraid of such situations because they overestimated the cost involved in clearing the lot. Many times there were architectural solutions to hillside construction that were available to public buildings but not to residential ones. I told him to get started right away and keep the matter quiet.

I gave up my office to Reuben Steiner. The dean turned his study over to Yakob. He still came to the school every day but only to sit quietly in a corner of the study hall and study Talmud. In January, I heard that the two Steiner brothers were planning a trip to America. My assumption was that they would do some recruiting and fund-raising. When they returned, I was curious as to the outcome of their visit, but no one told me anything about it.

I didn't find out the results until I got a long letter from Sarah. She began by requesting details of the new building and a copy of the plans. She was hoping to start work on the brochures and promotional material. I was glad to hear that she was thinking of our project and actually working on it. Then she went on to describe what had happened with the Steiner brothers and I quote from her letter.

"Last week we had a visit from Yakob and Reuben Steiner and I decided to give you a blow-by-blow account because you might hear garbled versions of it there.

"On a Wednesday, late in January, the two brothers came to Buffalo Auto at about three in the afternoon. Melvin was there but didn't recognize them until they identified themselves. They speak virtually no English. Mel understands classical Hebrew but could not understand their conversational Hebrew too well. He told them to wait and he called me to see if I could help out. I said that it would be all right if he brought them over.

"About an hour later, Mel brought them home, seated them in the living room and asked me to find out what they wanted. They explained that Beit Meir was beginning to experience some financial difficulty. The large enrollment kept them very busy and they couldn't spare enough time for fund-raising. What they needed was a fund-raiser in America and someone to underwrite his salary for the first year to the tune of $75,000. The brothers were asking Melvin to contribute the full amount.

"Melvin didn't have to think a long time. He signalled me to step out for a brief talk. He told me to tell them that the Foundation would continue to pay the mortgage on the yeshiva because that was his father's request. As long as the yeshiva retained the name Beit Meir it would get the money every January. As far as any additional support, there wouldn't be a red cent forthcoming. 'If they ask why, tell them we don't like what they did to Rabbis Brill and Goldberg.'

"I did as Melvin told me and sure enough they asked why we were being so inconsiderate. I stated the case as follows: 'Gentlemen, your father started the yeshiva fourteen years ago at a rather late stage in life. He worked terribly hard and struggled for years to keep the school open. He gave his life and health for it. All those years, you two sat on your hands and did nothing to help him. You enjoyed prestigious positions in the big yeshivot and it wasn't befitting your honor to be associated with a small and minor institution.

"Fortunately your father had a capable assistant in Rabbi Brill. He taught at the kollel, served as mashgiach, and was widely recognized. In the last few years, with the assistance of the Seidmans and Feldmans, the yeshiva doubled in size and became one of the better known institutions in Jerusalem. Rabbi Brill assumed even more administrative responsibility and he brought in Rabbi Goldberg, who has rendered priceless assistance to your father. Now that the yeshiva enjoys a much higher status, it befits you to come in and take over rather than follow your original intention of having your father sell the school to some other rabbi and let you live off the man's payments.'

"'To further your current intentions you demoted Rabbi Brill and humiliated him. Rabbi Goldberg you put out on the street altogether. Aren't you gentlemen aware that the purpose of a yeshiva is not only to teach Talmud but also to display moral and ethical behavior? Don't you understand that a dean and a mashgiach have to serve both as instructors and role models? The school may bear our name, but our family will not support a school where Torah ideals are only preached but not practiced.'

"Yakob Steiner listened to my scolding quietly, trying to prepare a response to the charges which, he knew, were in essence true. Reuben Steiner, in contrast, became enraged and livid. He was completely out of control when he turned to Melvin and began screaming at the top of his lungs: (I include the Hebrew words in case anyone doubts my translation.) 'Menachem Seidman, how can you stand there and let this audacious woman (*mechutzefet*) speak that way to the dean and mashgiach of your yeshiva? If your late father heard her speak so crudely, he would have thrown her out of the house. This immoral woman (*prutzah*) who showed her nakedness on the beaches of Europe....' He didn't get any further because by that time I was on my feet. I picked up the flower vase off the coffee table and raised it over my head with the full intent of crowning him. Unfortunately, Melvin was also on his feet and is pretty fast for a big man. He grabbed my arm in mid-swing and forced me to lower the vase. He then dragged me to the couch and made me sit down.

"In his pigeon Hebrew, the nearest he could come to telling them that they had worn out their welcome was, 'We don't want you in our house any more.' Yakob took Reuben, who had turned pale, and pulled him out of the living room. Melvin, ever the gentleman, called the housekeeper and asked her to drive the two men to the bus. 'We don't need your help,' Reuben shouted. He grabbed his coat and stormed out of the house dragging his brother with him. Melvin was going to go after them because they would have to walk a mile in below zero weather to the nearest bus, but I called him back. 'Let them go, Melvin, the walk will cool his temper off.'

"Other than that little incident, everything is quiet in Buffalo and we are very contented. My husband is really fulfilling the Torah command to make his wife happy during the first year of marriage."

I was upset by the letter, because some of the students had complained to me of Reuben's temper and strong language and I knew that Sandy was telling the truth. I didn't know whether it was my duty to inform Rabbi Steiner, so I didn't bring up the matter myself.

A week later, Rabbi Steiner told me that his son had advised him that he hadn't succeeded in Buffalo and that Sarah Seidman was abusive and impolite. "I can understand a family not wanting to make a donation," he said, "but why should they feel it necessary to abuse Torah scholars?"

I took out Sarah's letter and handed him the pages that told her version of the incident. "I think the Dean will find the information he is looking for in this document."

Rabbi Steiner read the letter and went into deep shock. "I know my son has a temper, but I can hardly believe that he was capable of saying such things."

The next day he spoke to me about it. "I called Yakob in and showed him the letter and asked him if the account were true. Yakob looked at me and said, 'Yes, father, she didn't misquote a single word.' I asked him why he hadn't told me about it and he said that he was too ashamed of his brother's behavior to tell me. After he left, I called in Reuben and spoke to him. 'You know, Reuben, the Proverbs teach us that a wise man loves admonition while a fool spurns it. It is especially the case when the admonition is true and well-deserved. But even if you weren't inclined to listen to the criticism, you should not have gotten angry. Sarah was merely following the command that requires every Jew to admonish his fellow Jew when he finds the latter guilty of wrongdoing. If you object to a woman chastising you, I want you to realize that she was only translating for her husband, who is certainly duty-bound to do so. The Talmud teaches us that the true character of a man can be determined by his spending habits, his drinking habits and his anger. You have revealed some very poor character by your behavior.'"

Slowly the dean continued to relate the story. "Reuben didn't offer any excuses and he apologized for his actions. I told him that since I was retired I was only a peripheral victim of his indiscretion. Sarah Seidman was the primary victim and the yeshiva's good name was the second injured party. 'Reuben,' I ordered, 'You are to drop whatever you are doing and sit down and write a long letter of apology to Melvin and Sarah Seidman. If you don't hand me the letter within two hours, I will follow the advice that Haman gave to King Achashverosh concerning Vashti, who was deposed and lost her queenship to someone more suitable than she.'"

I don't know whether Rabbi Steiner was still in a position to oust Reuben but I have a feeling he would have found a way. Needless to say, the letter was written and Rabbi Steiner mailed it personally. Reuben was chastened by the warning, and the complaints about his work have since diminished.

The next time I spoke to Rabbi Steiner was after Passover. "I gather you will not be returning to Beit Meir next year, Baruch." There was no point hiding it any longer. I didn't know how much he had heard, so I didn't tell him anything specific. "'Rabbis Goldberg and Gross and I will be starting a yeshiva of our own,' was all I said."

"You know how sorry I am that you are leaving, and I wish you the best of luck. I don't know why you are taking Rabbi Gross. He has no cause to leave and his departure will be an additional loss to Beit Meir."

"Well," I said, "he has, of course, been demoted. The important thing, though, is that now there is nowhere for him to advance at Beit Meir."

"What are you going to call your yeshiva?"

"The Sefer Chaim Yeshiva."

"After Chaim Feldman, I assume?"

"Yes."

"He was a fine man, Baruch, and I think that his daughter is on the road to repentance."

"She now has many mitzvahs to her credit, which may balance her past sins. I expect her to be here in June to help dedicate our new yeshiva and assist us in raising funds."

"She may not be coming, or may not be able to help if she does," the dean said.

I didn't know what he was driving at but I didn't press him. Since I had not shared any information with him, I couldn't expect him to do so with me. I had a letter in my pocket confirming Sarah's arrival and listing a whole set of instructions relating to the dedication, so I saw no reason for her not to help out.

It was on the first of June that I finally understood what Rabbi Steiner had meant. I had asked the Minister of Religious Affairs to get me permission to greet some guests as they disembarked from the airplane. A special dispensation is needed to welcome guests before they go through customs. He said he couldn't do it unless he himself were on hand when they came. When I told him that the Seidmans and Feldmans were coming, he agreed to join the welcoming party. Rivka, the Goldbergs and I drove to Ben Gurion with the minister. My heart fell when I saw Sandy come down the portable steps. Melvin was on her right side holding her firmly and another man was holding her just as firmly on her left. She looked at least eleven months pregnant and could barely move. After a long interval, she waddled up to the ropes holding back the welcomers.

"Hello Baruch," she said. "I'm sorry to report to work a little overweight but I will try my best to help out. This is Dr. Abramson, my obstetrician in Buffalo." She introduced the man at her left who had assisted her off the airliner. "El Al wouldn't let me on the plane unless we took him along." The minister congratulated Sandy and welcomed Mrs. Feldman, who extended her hand for him to kiss. He did the same for Melvin's mother.

I realized right away that Sandy wouldn't be doing much for me and that I would also have to worry about a *brit* – a circumcision ceremony – if the baby would be a boy. The Steiner brothers must have told their father that Sandy was pregnant at the time of their visit. I looked at Rabbi Goldberg and he shrugged. "That's life," he whispered to me.

There was a full week to the dedication, which was scheduled for the following Sunday night. Sandy did show up at my office in the new building, accompanied by the doctor, who wasn't leaving her out of his sight. Dr. Abramson said that she could work only about four hours a day with frequent rest periods. He wasn't making any predictions but he said that, based on his experience, she had less than a 50% chance of making it to the dedication. If she didn't give birth by the following Monday, he would probably have to induce labor. Sandy was booked at Shaarei Zedek, the nearest hospital to the yeshiva, and her doctor had made arrangements with the medical director to be in attendance.

While at work, Sandy concentrated on directing our crew in inviting people to attend. That was the highest priority. Next she lined up the speakers. The Minister of Religious Affairs said he could get the Minister of the Interior to show up. The Prime Minister would come if Sandy signed a statement that she would not pull any stunts on him. He still remembered her donkey escapade two years earlier. She faxed a signed statement but used the caveat 'without a vow.' When the Prime Minister's appearance was confirmed, she called the papers telling the reporters that she was back and that the Prime Minister was going to attend the dedication of Sefer Chaim Yeshiva despite his previous experience with her. One reporter, who had been at the cornerstone ceremony and remembered it well, ran the story with the extra information that when the Prime Minister was asked why he would attend after what happened at his last appearance, he pulled out Sandy's pledge and read it.

"Do you trust her, Mr. Prime Minister?" the reporter wanted to know.

"In politics, you trust no one. But maybe she has repented."

The article did generate some added interest and there was a good contingent of reporters on hand when the dinner got underway. I can't tell you how relieved I was Saturday night before the dinner when I called Melvin and found out that Sandy was still functioning. I was even more relieved when she showed up with her retinue on Sunday afternoon at the nearby hall we had rented for the occasion. The plan was to have the dinner first and hear the speakers. Sandy was then going to make the appeal. Following that, everyone would walk over to the yeshiva for the dedication rites.

As soon as the guests had been welcomed by Rabbi Goldberg, Sandy walked up to the emcee and whispered something in his ear. The rabbi looked surprised but accepted her request to be allowed to speak immediately. Sandy started speaking about the importance of Torah institutions in general and of Sefer Chaim in particular. A few minutes into the speech, she paused and held on to the lectern tightly in some apparent discomfort. She regained her composure and started telling everyone how important it was to subscribe to facilities described in the brochure. All of a sudden she was seized by intense pain. She was grimacing openly as she blurted out to the audience, "I'll have two minutes to the next one."

No one was going to give her the time she needed. Dr. Abramson, who was a little suspicious about the first pause, jumped up from his place as soon as the second pause began and started running to the rostrum. On his way, he yelled to me across the hall to call Magen Dovid Adom and get an ambulance immediately. Melvin was right behind the doctor and Carol was also moving. The two men got a hold of Sandy and pulled her away from the microphone. "Sign your pledges now," Sandy yelled to the audience as they sat her down on a chair. The cameramen and press photographers were busily recording the action.

The only one who remained calm was the Prime Minister. He told Dr. Abramson not to wait for the ambulance. He had a specially equipped car outside ready for emergencies and he told the Secret Service men to transport Sandy to Shaarei Zedek. Sandy was led out to the car and the doctor and Melvin joined her inside. Another car was made available for Mrs. Feldman, Mrs. Seidman, Carol and Rivka. Rivka had her Tehilim book out in a flash and was reciting the first Psalms as soon as the procession began to roll.

There was some misunderstanding along the way. The Secret Service signalled the local police that the Prime Minister's special car was on the way to Shaarei Zedek. The police understood this to mean that something had happened to the Prime Minister and that he was being rushed to the hospital. All city police cars, border police cars and security service vehicles that could move, sped to Herzel Boulevard and closed off all approaches to it. A sea of rotating blue lights dotted one end of the boulevard to the other. The hospital was alerted and every available doctor and nurse headed for the emergency room. The press and TV reporters who monitor the police frequencies stormed out to the hospital. By the time the Secret Service announced that it wasn't the Prime Minister on the way but only a member of his party, the special vehicle had arrived at the hospital. Sandy was put on a stretcher and wheeled into the emergency room. Even before she was transferred to the maternity ward, the baby was on its way.

Back at the dinner, Rabbi Goldberg restored order and introduced the Prime Minister. All the man could say was that this yeshiva dinner was a laborious affair. He insisted he would forgive

Sandy only if he were to be made the *sandek* – the godfather – at the forthcoming brit.

He was followed by the Ministers of the Interior and Religious Affairs, who announced grants for the new yeshiva. As soon as Ben Zur finished, the Prime Minister rose and asked for the floor. "I've just received word that it's a 3.3 kilo boy, and mother and baby are doing fine." There was a massive round of applause. "In honor of this birth, friends, please assist the birth of a new yeshiva and make generous pledges to help the institution grow." Despite the best intentions of Rabbi Goldberg and the Prime Minister, the people were too excited to concentrate on the donations. The total of the pledges fell about $60,000 short of the $150,000 that Sandy had promised to raise.

At the hospital, the TV cameras were standing by for a live broadcast from the maternity ward. The photographer wheeled the camera into Sandy's room and Sandy held up little Baby Seidman for the whole world to see.

I waited till noon the next day to visit Sandy. Only Melvin was left at the hospital because Sandy had chased the doting grandmothers out of her room. I met Melvin downstairs and asked if I could see Sandy. "Sure," he said, "but please come back here. We can have a bite in the cafeteria while I talk to you about the bris."

"How did you make out with the appeal after I was banished," Sandy wanted to know.

"Not as well as you did," I said, pointing to a collection of newspapers, all of which featured Sarah and her son on the first page.

"How much?" she insisted.

"$90,000."

"Not as bad as I feared. Look, I feel bad that I didn't keep my promise and that is twice in a row that I didn't come through. Can you hand me my pocketbook? I spoke to my brother Michael this morning, and he gave me his personal check for $10,000 and one from Daniel for $5000. I also made a small additional withdrawal from my rainy day fund. Please don't tell Melvin what I did or he'll have my head." She handed me the three checks and I told her it was beyond the call of duty. She didn't have to feel guilty about an act of God that did not let her fulfill her commitment, and I didn't want to take the money from her.

"I don't feel guilty, I just feel bad. You aren't allowed to reject charitable offerings. It was only when Moses collected enough charity for his tabernacle that he sent word for people to stop giving. Until that time, he accepted everything. Our yeshiva still needs a lot of money. By the way, Rabbi Steiner came to see me this morning."

"That was nice of him. What did he say?"

"He said it was a tremendous mitzvah that I did in helping you start your own yeshiva, and that you were truly qualified to be a dean. He is also happy that Rabbi Goldberg was given a class."

"Did he say anything about his sons?"

"He wanted to know why I let Melvin stop me before I administered justice to Reuben. 'Of all people,' he said, 'my son should have remembered that it is forbidden to remind a penitent person of her former sins.'"

"I told him that I was afraid of losing the baby so that I couldn't fight. I thanked him for the letter of apology that Reuben sent me."

"Are you really on the road back?" I asked her.

"At least my immodest days on the Riviera are behind me. Did you see my son? I think he looks a little like my father."

I went to the nursery to view the baby and then I went down to see Melvin. We had lunch at the cafeteria and I gave him a full description of the circumcision ceremony and the honors that had to be distributed.

"Rabbi," he asked, "is it really true that the mother gets the privilege of naming the first child? The baby resembles my late father. I would have liked to call him Meir."

"It certainly is the custom for Polish Jews, but I don't know about the Viennese. Why don't you call the baby Chaim Meir?"

"I was thinking about that," he said, "but second names are not always used. I don't know whether Sandy will have more boys but Carol forbade me to accept a second name."

"Why should it concern her?" I asked.

"Well, since Sandy came into the picture, Carol is no longer in the limelight. The only thing she could do to gain attention was to get pregnant. She says that she wants to be the first to name a child after dad, Meir or Meira as the case may be."

"That's reasonable, Menachem. What prompted Sandy to have a baby so soon? I was sure that she would want to wait for a while."

"That's what I thought. Apparently she was inspired on Rosh Hashana by the stories of Hannah and Rachel. On both days of the holiday, she recited the story of her namesake, Sarah. These historic figures yearned for children and prayed fervently for them. Here she was, a woman who could actually have children but wasn't doing so. She felt very guilty about it."

"What did she do?"

"She prayed for a son. After we broke the Yom Kippur fast, she told me that she had to visit a sick friend and took off. I didn't know where she was going but I understood she wasn't visiting friends. That night in bed her hair was wet and I realized that she had run to the mikva. Apparently she wanted her baby to be born in purity. In the morning, she told me that she had discarded a big package of pills that weren't exactly formulated to encourage procreation. She indicated that there was an excellent chance that I would be a father in the near future. I protested that family planning should be a mutual affair and that she should have discussed parenthood with me in advance. Do you know what she told me?"

"No."

"She said that only women have the right to plan babies. As a man, I was bound by the oath my soul took at Mount Sinai to accept the Torah. The very first commandment in the Torah, she reminded me, was 'Be fruitful and multiply.' Was she right, Rabbi?"

"Partially. It is true that women are not bound by the command to be fruitful and multiply while men are. That a man must have children is clear. That she has any right to delay your having children is not really true. What she probably meant was that if she were willing to have a child, you were no longer permitted to avoid your obligation and she didn't have to consult you."

"Of course I would have agreed if she'd asked me. I like children and I will be able to provide for them in the fullest measure. Oh yes, I wanted to ask you how bad the appeal was affected by Sandy's absence."

"I don't doubt that she would have raised the full amount had she been there. She promised me $150,000 and we raised only $90,000 at the dinner."

"The yeshiva has already cost me $200,000. But I feel bad that Sandy disappointed you even though it wasn't her fault. Please tell her that you found an anonymous donor to make up some of the shortfall but don't tell her it was me, because I am not supposed to have such private funds."

So saying, he took out a check of $30,000 made out to the Sefer Chaim Yeshiva from petty cash fund number 2. "That's where Max Glaser keeps my spending money."

I didn't even bother trying to turn it down because it would be of no use. The next day I got a call from Mrs. Feldman asking if she could see me at the yeshiva.

"I am the happiest woman alive," she said, when she arrived. "Sandy has produced a boy that looks just like her father and will carry his name. He is such a nice baby."

"This is my first chance to wish you 'mazel tov.'. You should have a lot of nachas."

"You know, Rabbi, God acts in strange ways. When I spoke to Sandy the first time about having a baby she said not to bother her for three years. When she got pregnant, I asked her what had happened. Do you know what she said?"

"No."

"She said 'I'm sorry mother, I guess I got a little careless.'"

"Mrs. Feldman," I said, "let me tell you something. Sandy is one girl in this world who never makes mistakes. Everything she does is meticulously planned and executed. I know for a fact that she wanted to have the baby and that she went to the mikva first to make sure that the baby would be born in purity. I think she is having a little fun at your expense."

"She shouldn't do such things, but I feel much better now that I know that she truly wanted to have a child. Listen, Rabbi, I have to tell you something else. You know I did my share in helping you build the yeshiva because one half of Sandy's contribution was my money. Still, I feel bad that Sandy didn't come through at the appeal and you fell short. I want to give you this check to help make up the difference. Please set aside a classroom for me in honor of my new grandson Chaim, and don't breathe a word of it to Sandy."

The classrooms in the new building were listed at $36,000, so I knew how much the check was for without looking at it. I thanked Mrs. Feldman profusely and realized that I had already passed well beyond the original fund-raising target.

However, I was far from finished with my collecting. That night I got a call from Jack Seidman saying that he and Estelle wanted to see me. It was Estelle who explained the purpose of the visit.

"Rabbi Brill, when Mel paid for part of Sandy's yeshiva, he imposed some conditions on her. One of them was that she had to teach Carol and me about the Jewish religion every week. Sandy does that and she is a wonderful teacher. I've learned more from her than from all the books I've read on the subject. I was not observant before but I want you to know that I became kosher this year."

"I am very happy to hear that."

"You may be happy, Rabbi," Jack said, "but her new observance meant four new sets of expensive china, a new stove, two sinks and a new kitchen."

"Are you bragging or complaining, Jack?"

"I guess I'm proud of her. My parents never ate at my home and Melvin didn't either. Now they do and it means a lot to me. At any rate, Estelle and I want to show our support for Sandy's yeshiva and make a small donation for its upkeep."

"You are not swearing me to secrecy on this gift are you?"

"Of course not. It's our pleasure." He handed me a check for $25,000, which I accepted with gratitude.

Mel had asked me to find a furnished apartment for him for a month until after the ritual of redemption of the first born would take place. I knew that one of the patrons of the yeshiva was planning to spend the summer in America and was leaving in a few days. I quickly arranged for a sublease. After Sandy was discharged, she moved into the apartment and Rivka spent a lot of time teaching her how to take care of the baby. The two grandmothers were too nervous to do the job.

It was at the apartment that Mrs. Seidman cornered Rivka and asked her to do a favor. She found it hard to get to the new yeshiva alone, so she wanted Rivka to give me an envelope.

"I am giving you this in honor of my daughter-in-law, Sandy, and my first grandson who, incidentally, looks very much like my late husband. I'm sorry Sandy couldn't finish her speech because I know how much your husband depended on her. I've donated two dormitory rooms at the yeshiva, one in honor of Sandy and one in honor of little Chaim. Don't tell Sandy about her room. A mother-in-law can't openly show any sentiment for her daughter-in-law, but I love her just the same." Rivka turned over the two checks for $18,000 each and I got a chance to thank Mrs. Seidman for them at the brit.

The brit took place Monday morning at the yeshiva. The Prime Minister held the baby on his lap until all the photographers had finished. He wasn't really serious about holding the baby during the circumcision. He knew that he didn't have the religious qualifications for serving as the sandek. He was, however, hoping for some publicity that would show him as a warm and congenial human being as opposed to a hard-boiled politician. "Maybe this time Sarah will let me get into the papers," he said wistfully. When the picture-taking was over, the *mohel* retrieved the baby in order to perform the circumcision, and gave him first to Carol and Joe, who were honored with carrying him into the ceremony. They handed the baby to Rabbi Shayalevitch, who served as godfather, the man who holds the baby on his lap during the actual circumcision.

Sandy had spoken to Dr. Abramson before the ceremony and told him, "Don't worry about the baby. We have the best mohel in Jerusalem and he knows his business. Keep your eye on Melvin, because he can't stand the sight of blood."

Melvin pronounced the blessing and did turn a little green when the mohel was doing his work. Rabbi Goldberg then held the baby while Rabbi Brill chanted the opening blessing on the wine.

Rabbi Steiner then came forward and recited the naming prayer. "Our God and God of our fathers, protect this child for his mother and father and let his name be called in Israel, Chaim, son of Menachem of the family Seidman.... May Chaim, the son of Menachem, become great. As he has been introduced into the covenant, so may he be introduced in future years to the study of Torah, the wedding canopy and a life of good deeds."

In speaking after the ceremony, I traced Chaim's glorious ancestry. Not every child in Israel has a choice of attending his father's yeshiva or his mother's yeshiva. "I am bidding for his attendance first and we are pleased to announce that Chaim Seidman has been awarded a full scholarship at the Sefer Chaim Yeshiva effective on his 18th birthday."

Carol came to talk to me after the ceremony and said, "Rabbi, I have something to tell you."

"You, too?" I asked.

"Yes, me. I know you didn't expect it from me. I don't hate Sarah but I am insanely jealous of her. I used to be the queen in the family and the resident expert on everything. Now nobody listens to me about anything. It's 'ask Sarah this' and 'ask Sarah that' and, with Melvin going to school and reading fancy books, I can't even tell him anything. Nevertheless, I appreciate her teaching Estelle and me and for all that she has done for Melvin. He's married a year and he still thinks he's on his honeymoon.

"I am making this contribution to Sandy's yeshiva, but

don't tell her about it. Now, I want a favor. I know you used your influence upstairs to help Melvin get the woman of his dreams. I want you to talk to the Almighty in my behalf, too. I know that He can't be bought for money, but there will be fifty extra big ones waiting for your yeshiva if the baby I am carrying turns out to be a boy. Sandy, the Rebbetzin, ruled that I am allowed to make a conditional vow because Jacob the Patriarch did the same thing."

"I will do my best, although yours might well be what we call a vow after the fact." The technicality did not prevent me from accepting her unconditional gift of $25,000."

One donation that I received was only for $1000. Joe gave me a check with an apology. "I am not one of the owners of Buffalo Auto. I only manage one of the stores and Carol keeps me on a tight leash. However, I guess every dollar helps."

You will never guess who made the next offering. It was Lili Goldberg, who is not known as a philanthropist. "Rabbi Brill," she said, "I want you to believe that I helped Melvin and Sarah get together out of the goodness of my heart and not for the sake of reward."

"I have my doubts, Lili, based on your past reputation. But, if you say so, I believe you."

"I hope you will. You know that I am obligated to tithe my income and I have always done so. It never hurt before because the fees were rather paltry. But the law is the law for better and worse," she said, as she handed me a check for $2500 with tears in her eyes.

The final donation? None other than Sandy's Sisterhood. Their letter read:

In honor of our outstanding president, who makes us work so hard, and in honor of her new born son, Chaim, we are donating $18 to the Sefer Chaim Yeshiva.

Yours truly,
Rebbetzin Ida Singer, Chaplain
Mrs. Tillie Fineberg, Honorary President
Mrs. Rose Goldstein, 1st Vice President
Mrs. Shirley Shapiro, 2nd Vice President
Mrs. Doris Lazar, Recording Secretary
Mrs. Henry Goldman, Corresponding Secretary
Mrs. Sally Glaser, Treasurer
Mrs. Bonnie Stein, Journal Chairman
Mrs. Sadie Milman, Hospitality Chairman
Mrs. Joan Adler, Good and Welfare
Mrs. Beverly Sneider, Program Chairman."

I hope that Sandy won't make me write each officer an individual thank you letter. At $5.00 each (our average cost for producing a letter), our net on the donation will be minus $37.00.

With the flood of family offerings, our yeshiva is bound to get off to a good start. I am beginning to suspect there was a guiding hand in the procession of donors, either God above or my blond angel from Syracuse or both, working together. I'll never know, but my sincerest thanks to whom it may concern.